Nightfall Berlin

JACK GRIMWOOD

MICHAEL JOSEPH
an imprint of
PENGUIN BOOKS

MICHAEL JOSEPH

UK | USA | Canada | Ireland | Australia
India | New Zealand | South Africa

Michael Joseph is part of the Penguin Random House group of companies
whose addresses can be found at global.penguinrandomhouse.com

Penguin
Random House
UK

First published 2018
001

Copyright © Jack Grimwood, 2018

The moral right of the author has been asserted

This is a work of fiction. Names, characters, places and incidents are either the product
of the author's imagination or are used fictitiously, and any resemblance to actual persons,
living or dead, or to actual events or locales is entirely coincidental.

Set in 13.5/16 pt Garamond MT Std
Typeset by Jouve (UK), Milton Keynes
Printed in Great Britain by Clays Ltd, St Ives plc

A CIP catalogue record for this book is available from the British Library

HARDBACK ISBN: 978–0–718–18157–4
OM PAPERBACK ISBN: 978–0–718–18158–1

www.greenpenguin.co.uk

Nightfall Berlin

Jack Grimwood, aka Jon Courtenay Grimwood, was born in Malta and christened in the upturned bell of a ship. He grew up in the Far East, Britain and Scandinavia. Apart from novels, he writes for national newspapers, including *The Times, Telegraph, Independent* and the *Guardian*. He is a two-time winner of the BSFA Award for Best Novel with *Felaheen* and *End of the World Blues*. His literary novel, *The Last Banquet*, as Jonathan Grimwood, was shortlisted for Le Prix Montesquieu 2015. His work is published in fifteen languages. He is married to journalist and novelist Sam Baker. *Nightfall Berlin* is his second novel as Jack Grimwood.

jackgrimwood.com
jonathangrimwood.com
j-cg.co.uk
@joncg

For Charlie
May you always have your lock picks
and a spare padlock.

'There are some things which should
be done which it would not do for
superiors to order done . . .'

– Abraham Lincoln

I

April 1972

It began as a Swallows and Amazons sort of day.

The lake was calm and the wind warm. It was too early in the year for that many tourists and most of those walking the hills or along the lakeshore were second-home owners. The locals were busy running pubs and village shops or working on the hill farms that characterized this part of the Lake District. The old man heading for the lake, with his grandchildren straggling like ducks behind him, was staying in a grey stone house overlooking the shore.

It was to be a wet summer. So wet it would spawn headlines that screamed *flood,* and showed photographs of holidaymakers huddling on beaches under umbrellas. No one knew that yet. So far the weather was mild, the papers taken up with inflation and, for the man walking down to the dinghy, it was a year like any other.

He was in the autumn of his life.

Famous, successful, quietly rich and widely respected.

He'd had a good war, gone into politics for lack of anything more interesting, and had taken his place in the Lords when his father died. He now sat in opposition to Callaghan's government, but was known to be moderate.

An old-school Tory in the proper sense of that word. *Much loved* was the phrase mostly used about him.

'Me,' said a small boy following.

'No,' another said, more loudly. 'My turn.'

He turned back, remembering to frown, and the five children came to an abrupt halt. They had orders to behave. Mummy had been firm about that. If Grandpa let them sail with him, they were to behave. It was only the third day of the Easter holidays and they didn't want to upset him, did they?

The man up on the hill with the binoculars watched them stop and wondered at the neatness of their world.

They could have wandered out of a children's book or one of those Sunday afternoon BBC serials. He'd had four days to set this up and had been in place before the family arrived. When the old man pointed at himself and then at the smaller boat, before pointing at the rest of them and indicating the larger one, the man in the hills crossed himself.

The youngest of Lord Brannon's grandchildren looked about five, his oldest no more than fourteen. He could remember being that age but not that innocent.

Down on the lake's edge the children were laughing and shrieking at the coldness of the water as they struggled to push the larger of the boats into the lake. And the old man grinned, and tried not to show how hard he found the work, as he came alongside to help.

Knee-deep, and apparently not feeling the cold, he pushed them off and shouted orders that had the girl scrabbling for the rudder, while one of the boys raised a sail that caught the wind and – with the help of a brutal yank on the tiller – swung them towards the middle of the lake.

The boat leant, the girl kept her line true and a spreading wake showed that the dinghy was picking up speed. The old man smiled to see them go.

Then he pushed his own, much smaller, dinghy into deeper water.

He stopped for a second to watch his grandchildren disappearing into the distance. On the terrace above, a woman came out of the house, saw the dinghy heading towards the middle of the lake and called to her husband, who came through the French windows, looked at the vanishing boat, shrugged and laughed.

Up on the hill, the man turned his field glasses back to his lordship, whose dinghy was now making for a tiny island with a single –

'What are you doing?' said a voice behind him.

The girl was young, ten, maybe eleven, and had her bottom lip stuck out as if he'd surprised her in the middle of a sulk; rather than her surprising him. He glanced towards the dinghies. They were still within reach.

'Birdwatching.'

She looked contemptuous.

'Don't you like birds?'

She looked ready to say she hated them. Then honesty got the better of her. 'Some of them. My great-aunt has a parakeet. It's old and manky and it swears. She hates it.'

'Why keep it then?'

'It was Great-Uncle Robert's. That means she can't get rid of it.' The girl looked at the man with the binoculars and shrugged as if to say she didn't expect that to make sense to him either. 'Can I borrow those?'

'I'm using them.'

Sucking her teeth, she said, 'They left me behind for being naughty. That's why I'm not out there.'

'They're your family?'

She nodded slowly, took a step backwards, then another, and he wondered if his voice had been strange. He could still reach her if she made a run for it. Break her neck before she had time to ruin everything.

'I never had a family,' he said.

She stopped backing away, torn between trying to look sympathetic and obvious envy at his being family-free. It was a lie, of course. But it did the trick. The moment had gone and everything was reset.

'I'd better go,' she said.

He nodded.

Distance was critical to what came next. The man in the hills had spent the last three days establishing the family's routine. He already knew that Lord Brannon sailed alone if possible, used the smaller dinghy from choice and shared it reluctantly. In London, he might have a bodyguard who checked under his car each morning, but his bodyguard wasn't here, and even if he had been, he might not have thought to check under the dinghy's simple seat.

The sky was blue, the sun was bright, and the breeze was warm.

All things the papers would mention when they came to write tomorrow's headlines. Opening his rucksack, the man in the hills found the little black box he'd been promised would work. He turned a switch that he'd been told to turn, lifted a protective cover and pushed a button.

Out on the water a fireball blossomed.

The explosion was so loud that crows rose from trees right along the lake's edge. Fragments of the dinghy cartwheeled into the air and for a split second there was a red mist, instantly swallowed in a fireball, pieces of dinghy falling in flat splashes. The old man was gone; ripped apart so savagely his coffin needed bricks to make up the weight.

2

On a far hillside, a man who'd been watching the scene unfold flipped open his notebook and put a line through *Great Eagle.* That was the last of the rare birds. There were half a dozen crossed out before, and a dozen lesser species to be sighted over the page. Someone else could collect those.

3

1986, US Naval Base, Guantánamo, Cuba

The boy looked at the sign with its skull and crossbones and large red letters announcing 'Danger! Mines', then at the rusting razor wire. He was eight, almost. Old enough to do this.

One roll of the wire had come away.

If he turned sideways he could squeeze between it and its post without doing more than scratch his wrist. Sucking at the blood, he turned his attention to the mine-field in front of him. It looked bigger now he was standing on its edge.

Stepping forward, he froze as dirt sunk beneath his feet, unfreezing when he realized he'd crushed an ants' nest. He chose his next step more carefully, welcoming the feel of solid earth. Mines were round and made from metal. They contained explosives. Their top plates gave when you trod on them. That was what tripped the deto-nator. Detonators made them blow up.

He knew these things.

Solid earth was good. Solid earth was safe.

In the distance a thick wall of prickly pears marked the border between where he stood and a different world.

The sun was hot and his mouth dry.

Very carefully, the boy looked at the dust around his

7

feet, noticing rough grass and dead patches of thistle. The sun was so hot that the earth had split and a riverbed was now dry pebbles, with an iridescent lizard basking on a rock in the middle. It flicked its tail and vanished when he went to take a look.

The boy bit his lip.

He knew he shouldn't be here.

Yesterday he'd seen big signs that said anybody crossing the minefield would be shot. Taking another step, the boy looked for a step after that, lifted his foot and changed his mind at the last second.

His shoe caught something and he shut his eyes.

One, two, three, four, five, six, seven . . .

He could stop counting now. Scraping the dirt with his shoe, he found the rusting rim of what looked like a Coke can. Painted green. He'd expected the mines to be round like a plate. Maybe some were, and others looked like this.

'Come on,' he told himself.

At this speed he'd be here tomorrow.

The wall of cactus in the distance looked no closer; and, even if he ran, the field would take ages to cross. He stared at the dirt in front of him, then at the scrub in front of that. He noticed dead patches, spider cracks in the earth, sickly clumps of grass.

When he started again it was at a trot.

'Charlie . . .'

The boy froze at the sound of his name.

When he turned it was reluctantly. A US Army jeep had screeched to a halt by the sign and soldiers were tumbling out, clutching rifles. One of them screamed at him not to move. Another screamed at his father, who began pushing between razor wire and post, ignoring the blood that began to flow from his hip.

'Charlie,' he shouted.

The small boy looked from the prickly pears in the distance to his father, who was trying to work out where to put his feet. Charlie's father stared at the ground, swallowed and began walking.

'Stop,' Charlie shouted.

His father froze, his foot a few inches above what he had to realize was a mine.

'To the left,' Charlie shouted. 'My left.'

His father hesitated.

'Your right.'

Daddy put his foot down and his relief was visible. Behind him the soldiers had stopped shouting and a second jeep had parked behind the first. Mummy sat in the front. He hoped she wouldn't be cross with him in public. She probably would. She often was.

'Stay there,' Charlie told his father.

'Slowly,' his father shouted.

Charlie kept walking at the same pace.

He could have reached the prickly pears too. He knew that now.

Once you worked out where to put your feet, it was easy. Maybe not at all times of the year, but now when the sun was high and the afternoon so hot he could feel sweat running down his back. Although that might be the thought of being in trouble. He wasn't always good at knowing when he was in trouble.

'Look for cracks that go both ways,' Charlie said.

Daddy stared at him.

'And sickly grass. That's how you know where mines are. The rest of it's fine, although anthills feel a bit . . .' He searched for the word, failing to find it. 'Not safe,' he said finally. 'Everything else is good.'

'Step where I step,' he added.

Before Daddy could open his mouth to object, Charlie edged around him and took slow slides so his father could see where to put his feet.

It was further to the wire than he expected, which meant he'd done better than he imagined. By the time they reached it, American soldiers in thick gloves were lifting razor wire aside to let them though.

'Those must be hot.'

The soldier looked at Charlie, nodded.

Major Tom Fox dropped to a crouch in front of his eight-year-old son. He knew the American soldiers were listening. That whatever Charlie said would get back to the base commander.

'Why did you ignore the sign?'

'I wanted a prickly pear.'

Tom Fox looked at the small boy, who looked at the ground, his bottom lip folded in where he chewed it. Blonde, blue-eyed and fair-skinned, Charlie took after his mother in looks. Tom wasn't sure who he took after in temperament. He waited for Charlie to say more and realized that was it.

'You wanted a prickly pear?'

The boy turned and pointed into the distance. 'See,' he said. 'Over there. There's a whole wall of them.'

'There's a prickly pear by our bungalow.'

'It says, "Do not pick". There's a sign.'

'There's a sign there,' Tom said. 'It says "Danger! Mines".'

'But it doesn't say you can't go in and it doesn't say don't pick the prickly pears. It doesn't. Does it?'

Wrapping his arm around his son's shoulder, Tom steered him back to Caro, who watched Charlie approach with something resembling resignation. As he did so, a slightly pudgy American in dark glasses and a Hawaiian shirt clambered from the second jeep and asked if he could talk to the English boy.

Tom nodded.

Dropping to a crouch, the man asked Charlie how he'd known where to put his feet and listened carefully as Charlie explained about cracks in the dirt, weak grass and dead patches. 'Could you get to the other side?'

Charlie's mother opened her mouth to object.

'I'm not saying he should,' the man said. 'In fact, he very definitely shouldn't. I want to know if he could if he had to.'

'Of course,' Charlie said.

'Interesting. You and I should talk sometime.' The man held out his hand. 'I'm Felix,' he said. 'Felix Propotsky.'

'Charlie,' the small boy said. 'Charlie Fox.'

'I know,' Felix said. 'I've worked with your father.'

Charlie and his father had finished a burger each, eaten a portion of fries between them and shared a chocolate shake thick enough to be liquid concrete, and cold enough to make their teeth hurt. Then they transferred to Baskin-Robbins for an ice cream, and were sitting under a red umbrella outside when Felix pulled up in a jeep, jumped out, and nodded at an empty chair. He took Tom's silence as permission and sat opposite Charlie.

'Eat up,' he said. 'It'll melt.'

'Too late,' said Charlie. 'It's melted already.'

Felix peered into the cardboard cup, reached for Charlie's plastic spoon and stirred a couple of colours together.

'You finished with this?'

Charlie nodded.

When Felix had finished spooning melted ice cream into his mouth, he dug into his trouser pockets and pulled out a padlock with one side cut away, and a little leather case that zipped up the side.

'A present,' he said.

Taking the lock, Charlie examined it carefully, angling the cut-away bit into the sun to examine a row of spring-loaded pins that kept its clasp shut. When he unzipped the leather case Tom had a feeling his son had already worked out what he'd find. Although he probably didn't expect to find so many.

'Overkill,' Felix said. 'I usually use these.' He pulled out a pick that turned up at one end, a rake with four sharp bumps like a little mountain range, and what looked like a pair of bent tweezers. 'That's a torsion bar,' he said.

He lined them up in front of Charlie.

Before he could say anything else, Charlie put the strangely angled end of the tweezers into the key shot, turned it to put pressure on the lock's cylinder, and began raking at the pins with the pick that had four bumps.

'Slowly,' Felix said. 'And put the rake in first, then the torsion bar. Look at how those pins are arranged. You can't work the first pin if you put the rake in second.'

Swapping them round, Charlie raked the pick slowly back and smiled as the pins aligned inside, the cylinder turned and the lock sprung open with a satisfying click. 'That's all I need,' Tom said.

'Keep them,' Felix said.

Charlie looked shocked. 'Really?'

'Empty your head when you do it. Preferably think about something else entirely. Even better, think about nothing.'

As Tom watched, his son shut the padlock, reached for the odd-looking tweezers and upturned pick, turned the cylinder until the pins pushed against the shafts that held them, and very carefully began to move one up and down. He looked happier than Tom had seen him in a long while.

4

'Ready?' Felix shouted.

Charlie tried to keep his skis together and the rope in place and nodded, although he wasn't ready, not really.

'You have to say *ready*.'

The boy stared at Felix's speedboat just off the rocky beach.

'You have to say *ready*,' Felix said. 'And when you're really ready, you have to say *hit it*. That tells me it's time to open the throttle. The acceleration will pull you upright. The secret is to –'

'Keep your legs straight,' Charlie called.

Felix laughed. 'Right,' he said. 'Let's try it again.'

The boy angled his skis, until just the tips jutted above the waves rolling in from the Caribbean, and felt Felix nudge the boat forward to take up the slack. Charlie knew his mother and father were watching, even though they had promised they wouldn't.

'Ready?' Felix shouted.

'Ready,' Charlie shouted back, meaning it this time.

He looked at the shiny black outboard engine, and decided it was one of the coolest things he'd seen. One of the most powerful too, if Felix could be believed, and he probably could. Felix was a bit like Charlie.

Charlie didn't know how to lie either.

'Okay,' he shouted, which wasn't in the script. 'Hit it.'

And hit it Felix did.

The huge outboard chewed water fast enough to push Felix back in his seat and jerk Charlie upright as the boat rocketed out into the bay, substantially faster than the signs on shore allowed. 'Relax,' Felix shouted.

Charlie tried really hard.

He hit a wave, almost lost his skis and found himself still standing, his arms stretched in front of him, fingers gripping the handle and the rope taut right the way to the speedboat beyond. He tried to remember the diagrams Felix had drawn on the back of an old envelope.

Leaning back countered a boat's forward thrust.

Gravity wanted you to sink. The speed of the boat prevented that.

Downward thrust could be countered by upward thrust. If those were in balance you were fine for going in a straight line. If you crossed the wake then centripetal force came into play. Charlie liked the sound of that and decided it was probably time he had a go. Keep the rope taut, Felix had said.

That was the key to everything.

'Tom . . .'

Tom looked up from his *Washington Post* to where his son jumped the wake like a professional, running out as wide as the rope would allow, cutting a wave of spray before racing back through the middle to do it all over again on the far side.

'We're not meant to be watching,' he said.

His wife smiled. 'He doesn't care if we're watching.'

'We promised we wouldn't.'

'That was when he wasn't sure he could do it.'

'If you're sure?' Tom said.

Caro looked at her husband more fondly than she had for a while, and raised her rum and coke in a salute. The little paper umbrella it arrived with was resting on the side. 'Believe me,' she said. 'He wants us to watch.'

So Tom did. He watched his son jump the wake time and again, until the boy looked rock solid in the turns, and his perfectly executed fountains of spray had others on the beach looking up.

'What now?' Caro asked.

Instead of sweeping out to the far side, Charlie had stopped in the middle, arms out and rope taut. He stayed like this until Felix looked back to see what was happening. Dropping one hand, Charlie tapped his leg.

Felix pumped one fist in the air.

As the boat ran in a circle back to the beach, Charlie suddenly shot out to the far side, swept back across his own wake and, as if aiming for Caro and Tom, kicked off one ski that surfed in towards them.

And that was when he lost his balance.

'Christ,' Tom said. He was up and headed for the water, then waist-deep and already striding out, heart tight, when Charlie surfaced. It took Tom a moment to realize his son was laughing.

He'd lost his other ski and his trunks were dangerously low; something he realized with a start, dragging them up and glaring in case anybody had noticed. 'I'll get it right next time,' he shouted.

'Who taught you?' Tom shouted back.

'Felix. It's physics. Easy really.'

Then he trekked off towards his missing ski, which had beached in front of an American service family having a picnic on the largest blanket Tom had seen. A dark-skinned girl Charlie's age looked up. She wore an Alice band and a swimsuit fluorescent enough to be seen from space. Whatever she said, Charlie dropped to a crouch, joining her on the blanket when she shuffled up to make space for him.

'Don't worry,' Caro said. 'They'll send him back when they get bored. Do you want the other half?'

Tom's rum and coke was blood-warm and attracting wasps. Its slice of lemon had wilted along the edge. He shook his head.

'I'll get you a beer.'

'A coke is fine.'

'I'll get you both.' Her hand rested briefly on his shoulder, and Tom leant his head into it, realizing that Charlie was watching from the blanket.

The boy's eyes were huge and his face serious.

'He's scared,' Caro said.

'Of me?' Tom tried not to sound shocked.

'For you. For me. That it will all go wrong again. They hear things at that age. You know. They see things . . .'

Tom wanted to ask what things.

What things did Charlie see in the months before their teenage daughter put her Mini into a tree? . . . What did he hear in the months his parents twisted their marriage to the edge of destruction? The accident. That was how Tom was teaching himself to think of it.

Becca's accident.

She'd put her little Mini into a tree.

At 80 mph, on a clear night, on a straight, dry road. She'd been pregnant. Her boyfriend hadn't been the father. Those were the things Tom wasn't meant to think. Those were facts he was teaching himself to wall away.

What exactly did Charlie overhear?

He'd ask Caro, but she was already at a shack run by a Cuban who'd had the job before Castro took over. That's how it worked. None of the Cubans working on the base could be replaced. All those who'd had jobs got to keep them.

'I know,' Caro said, on her return, 'that we should let the past go. But I'm going to say something. Not for your sake. For mine. I want it off my chest.'

She scowled as he glanced at her.

'Behave for a second.'

Her swimsuit was Italian and flattered her figure, which was good enough not to need flattering. She'd always been well dressed.

Being independently wealthy helped.

'What are you thinking?'

'About your money.'

'I thought that didn't worry you.'

'It doesn't,' Tom said. 'I was just thinking you've always looked . . .' He hesitated. 'Like you. Yourself.'

'While you, it turns out, have been half a dozen different people in the last ten years. And I haven't known about any of them. Was it hard? Being undercover?'

Of course it was hard, he wanted to say.

If he never went back to Northern Ireland that would be fine.

Military Intelligence, via the priesthood. It wasn't an

obvious career path. He was good at it, though, being undercover, inhabiting other people's lives. It was coming back to his own that had given him problems.

Reaching for his beer, Tom smiled as Charlie looked round and waved to see him watching. He was digging a trench with the girl with the Alice band and laughing as waves swept over his toes.

'Look. He's made a friend.'

'Tom . . .' Caro said.

He knew it wasn't going to be good.

'In Moscow you told me you'd been sleeping with other women. I knew. A woman always does. We're better at that than men. How many?'

'A handful,' said Tom, watching the horizon.

'A handful five or six? Or a handful fifteen, twenty?'

'Does it matter?'

'How many?' Caro demanded.

And before he could answer, she added. 'I loved you, you know. Right from the beginning. It wasn't a game for me. I didn't set out to ruin your life. I was young, very young. But I still wouldn't have –'

'You didn't ruin my life.'

'Yes, I did. You'd probably be teaching History at Ampleforth, collecting T. S. Eliot first editions and going for walks over hills. You'd wear tatty coats, and the boys would be slightly afraid of you and secretly fond. You'd have been ordained –'

'And ended up drunk or defrocked, losing my faith and intoning empty words to a congregation of passing tramps who smelt of piss and only came for the heating. Anyway,' said Tom, 'I *was* ordained.'

'In the Church of England. Your being a major's my fault too.'

'*Caro* . . . What's going on?'

Her face was paler than he remembered, her cheeks hollow. 'I'm sorry,' she said. 'I'm just having a bad time of it.'

'Seven,' Tom said. 'I think seven.'

'Think seven lovers. Might have been eight or nine?'

'Think seven. Might have been six.'

'Did any of them matter?'

'One, maybe. She was kind.'

'Oh God,' Caro said. 'I'm sorry. I'm really sorry.'

'Caro. This is —'

'Unlike me? Heavy tears expected. Gusts of emotion. Possible outbreaks of guilt later. That was a Caro weather warning.'

Knocking back her drink, she held up her glass and the Cuban in the shack raised his hand to say he understood.

'I'll take Charlie for a walk. If you want a rest later.'

'You don't want to have a rest with me?'

Their son was laughing with his new friend, both of them sticky with dried salt from their doomed efforts to build a wall big enough to hold back the Caribbean. He'd made a friend and Charlie never made friends.

'Does he look like he's going to rest?' Tom asked.

Caro took the question seriously. 'He'll either keep going all afternoon or fall over suddenly, get tearful and want quiet time to himself.'

'Maybe I should take them both for a hamburger.'

'Are you going for sainthood?'

'No,' Tom said. 'Just trying to make amends.'

'No need. But if you're serious about taking Charlie off my hands . . .'

She stood up, let her hand brush Tom's shoulder and hesitated.

'I haven't said what I was going to say. I'm having an affair. Long term and nobody you know. The stupid thing is that under other circumstances you'd really like him. I'll finish it the moment we get home . . .'

5

Hotel Splendide, Grand Bahamas

'You okay?' Caro asked.

'I'm fine,' Tom replied.

Her face tightened and Charlie put down his lock and picks and stared miserably at his flying fish. Without thinking, he pushed his plate away.

'Too much sun,' Tom said. 'Sorry.'

'Really?' Caro said. 'You have a headache?'

Dipping for her bag, she extracted a packet of Anadin, popped two through the foil and pushed them across, sliding Tom's water glass towards him.

He swallowed them dutifully.

'Sorry,' Tom said. He was looking at Charlie.

His son shrugged, remembered his manners and said he hated headaches too. He hoped Daddy would get better soon. The boy had been miserable since they landed in the Grand Bahamas that morning. He was missing the girl he'd met at the American base in Guantánamo. Tom's joke about almost eight being too early to have his heart broken hadn't helped.

'You could always write to Anna,' he suggested.

Charlie looked up from his plate. 'I don't have her address.'

'I'll get it for you.'

'Really? You promise?'

'You find a postcard in the hotel shop, Mummy will buy it and a stamp, and I'll have Anna's address for you by tomorrow.'

Charlie attacked his flying fish.

'I'm going for a walk in a while,' Tom said. 'Anyone want to come?'

'Not me,' said Caro. 'I need to wash my hair.'

As outrageous a lie as Tom had heard. He doubted she'd ever washed her own hair, except perhaps at university or boarding school.

'You go,' Caro told Charlie.

The night was hot and the beach deserted. Palm trees overhung the sand on one side, and the sea lapped the shoreline a few paces to the other. Tom and Charlie walked along a strip of fading light while stars came out overhead and yachts glittered out on the water.

'What do you want to talk about?' Charlie asked.

'*Charlie . . .*'

The boy shrugged, but lightly, and stepped in closer so their footsteps left a tight trail. 'It's all right,' he said. 'I already know what.'

'Mummy and me?'

'The minefield.'

Tom stopped, putting his hand to Charlie's shoulder, as if checking the boy was really there. He was so small and his shoulders slight. His seriousness was too serious. Too serious for his age.

'It wasn't that clever,' Tom said.

Charlie stepped away, instantly hurt.

'I knew what I was doing,' he said tightly. 'Felix said it

23

was very clever. He said you had to be like me and him to work it out.'

'Work what out?'

'Where to put your feet. Weeds dislike growing on mines and grass looks weaker. The sun makes bigger cracks where earth covers metal. He said working that out was clever.'

'You really knew?' Tom said.

'I told you.'

'What if you were wrong?'

'Then I wouldn't be here. I used to think I wouldn't mind that. After Becca died. When you and Mummy . . . Now.' Charlie wiped his eyes and Tom pretended not to notice.

They walked, because that was why they were there. In silence mostly, because their conversation was done and neither of them were the kind of people who chatted. The yachts still twinkled on the horizon and stars glittered high and bright. The lilt of a steel drum began behind the palm trees, its notes liquid and unearthly.

Charlie sat, when Tom suggested they sit.

'Look,' the boy said suddenly. He bent to retrieve the skull of a bird from the foot of some twisting mangrove roots. Tom stopped him.

'I'll do it,' Tom said.

For a second the bleached bone felt hot.

'Can I?' Charlie asked. He stroked the skull as gently as if the bird was still alive. 'How do you think it got there?'

'Probably fell from here.' Very carefully, Tom put the skull back into a triangle formed by three roots that crossed in front of a sandstone boulder. The skull looked right there. It belonged.

24

'Ribbons,' Charlie said.

Tom looked at the rags tied to the roots, and at the blackish smears on the rock face behind, some faded, some fresh.

'Paint,' Charlie said. 'Why would people do that?'

'I think it's an altar.'

'There isn't a cross.'

'A different kind of altar.'

The boy's eyes widened. 'Black magic?'

'Charlie. Who's been telling you about that?'

'We do spooky stories at school. Ghosts, demons, were-wolves.'

'This isn't that,' Tom said firmly.

Where he diverged from other padres was in his willingness to believe there might be lesser gods; hundreds, perhaps thousands. He'd met a few. At least, he believed he had. Some good; some substantially less so.

'Look,' Tom said. 'I've been away too much and it made Mummy unhappy. I got cross because she was unhappy.'

'And she got cross with you?'

'We're trying to make it better.'

The boy leant in, Tom's arm went round his shoulder and they sat together in as much silence as the crickets, the lapping waves and the steel drum allowed. Out on the horizon a liner moved like a drifting star. Tom was on the point of suggesting they go back when Charlie said, 'Do you think Mummy would let me go to another school?'

'You don't like St George's?'

'It's a very good school,' Charlie said carefully. 'It's just not a very nice one. And I'm not very happy there. I'd like to go somewhere else, if I'm allowed.'

'I'll talk to her,' Tom said.

'Promise?'

'Anything else?'

'Life's a minefield, Felix said. People like us pick their way through.'

Tom hugged his son tight. 'It's my job to worry,' he said. 'It's practically compulsory.'

Caro was in the foyer, her hair exactly as it had been before they left, and whatever she'd been preparing to say about how late they were went unsaid when she realized Tom and Charlie were holding hands.

6

Breakfast at the Hotel Splendide was served under an awning on a patio overlooking the beach as tiny birds hopped between tables to pick at crumbs. 'So beautiful,' said Caro, finishing her coffee. 'What do you think this place used to be?'

'A slave plantation,' Tom said.

Charlie put down the postcard he was writing.

'Is that a guess?' Caro asked her husband.

'No. There's a sanitized history in the men's loo complete with old photographs. Faithful black servants born the children of slaves, etc. Men working cane presses, stripped to the waist. Women cutting sugar cane, ditto . . .'

'Anna's black,' Charlie said.

'Your friend from the beach? Half black,' Caro corrected.

'She says she's black,' Charlie said firmly.

Tom smiled despite himself. 'She can be what she wants.'

'Can I be anything I want?' Charlie asked.

'Yes,' Tom said, before Caro could disagree.

'Yes?' she said.

'He can be anything he wants.'

Caro smiled. 'Within reason.'

'I'm not sure reason has anything to do with it.'

'Maybe not,' she said, but her voice was kind, and she went back to her novel and was quickly lost in its hero's search to discover which of fifty parrots had been the one to sit on Flaubert's writing desk.

'Is your book good?' Charlie asked.

She answered without looking up. 'It's interesting.'

Charlie raised his eyebrows and returned to his lock, which he could now open without looking. In fact, that seemed to make it easier. Dipping into his pocket, Tom produced a shiny brass padlock and Charlie grinned.

'Where did you get that?'

'I asked the hotel to buy it for me. There's no window in the side though.'

'I don't need one,' Charlie promised.

Charlie took the lock, turned it over in his hands and, absent-mindedly, and entirely without knowing he was doing it, began humming the song they'd heard sung to the steel drums.

The poor cook got the fits,
Throw away all of my grits,
Captain's pig done eat up all of my corn.
Let me go home, I want to go home,
I feel so break-up, I want to go home.

He reached for his pick with the ragged end, changed his mind and selected a simpler one. Noticing his father's surprise, Charlie said, 'Rakes are practically cheating. Like bump keys. Felix said so.'

'Bump keys?'

'They work. But that's mostly luck.'

'Luck is good.'

'Skill is better,' Charlie said firmly.

*

Out beyond the rocks, a catamaran was decanting sun-cooked tourists into a rubber dinghy, and conveying them ashore. Tom could think of nothing worse.

'Major Fox?'

He looked up to see the hotel manager.

'Is everything all right?'

'This arrived for you, sir, from London.'

The man held a copy of that day's *Times*.

A Foreign Office comp slip with Tom's name and rank was stapled to the top. Looking up to thank the man, Tom discovered he'd gone.

Bomb attack in Beirut.

State of emergency in South Africa.

Interim report on the *Challenger* disaster, complete with pictures of the shuttle exploding. City of London to be deregulated . . .

Caro looked up from her Julian Barnes to find Tom scowling.

'What's wrong?' she asked.

'This came for me.'

'I didn't know you could order *The Times*.'

'You can't,' Tom replied.

Nine in the morning Grand Bahamas meant 2 p.m. in London.

Eight-hour flight time, an hour to get it delivered, perhaps an hour to get it biked out to Heathrow in the first place. Someone had acquired an early edition of the paper, put it on a plane at 0400, and arranged for its arrival to coincide with Tom's breakfast.

'Daddy,' Charlie said.

The manager was back.

'My apologies, there's a Lord Eddington on the phone.'

Caro instinctively pushed back her chair and the man looked embarrassed. 'He asked to speak to your husband.'

'You're sure?' Caro said. 'He's my father.'

'Quite sure, Madame. He definitely asked for Major Fox . . .'

7

The hotel telephone was at one end of the reception desk.

Three young women behind the desk looked at Tom as he headed towards them and hastily looked away. At a frown from the manager they hurried off to find other things to do while Tom took the call.

'Fox,' Tom said, picking up the receiver.

'Tom? It's Charles Eddington.'

'Everything all right at home?'

'All fine,' Caro's father assured him. 'How's the holiday?'

'Good, I think. Charlie's learnt to waterski and Caro's reading her way through a suitcase full of novels.'

'And you?' Lord Eddington asked.

'I'm enjoying being with them.'

'Is that true?'

Tom had to stop himself taking offence.

At various times Caro's father had been Minister for Education, Minister of Defence and Home Secretary. These days, he sat in the Lords and was a member of Margaret Thatcher's Cabinet. Six months before, he'd put divorce papers for Tom in the diplomatic post. And Caro's mother had despatched her daughter to Moscow, with orders to make him sign them.

She'd arrived as Tom was heading out. He'd arranged

to swap incriminating photographs with a renegade Soviet general in return for the British ambassador's kidnapped daughter. Tom barely escaped with his life.

He said, 'Can I ask you something?'

'You can ask.' Caro's father kept his voice neutral.

'What did you have against me?'

'*Tom* . . . Dear God. You turned up at my house with my teenage daughter on the back of your bloody motorbike. You were training for the Catholic bloody priesthood, and I walk into the dining room to find my daughter wrapped round you like ivy.'

'She meant you to find us.'

'I know that.'

'I didn't,' Tom said.

'No. I don't imagine you did.'

'And she wasn't a teenager,' Tom said. 'She'd turned twenty.'

'Only just, and already pregnant. Which none of us knew, thank God. I'd probably have shot you.'

'That's it?'

'That isn't enough?'

Tom hesitated. 'I've always felt there was more.'

'Look, I had someone positive vet you. Actually, a bit deeper than that. I had to know if you were after Caro's money. You weren't. I realized that quickly enough. But, you know, at the beginning I wondered . . .'

'Caro thinks I should resign my commission.'

'*She what?*'

'I think she sees me as the chaplain of some public school, leading the cadet force and turning out to cheer the boys on from the side.'

'Sounds hideous.'

Tom had to agree.

'Look,' Eddington said, 'if you're really enjoying your-self then I'm sorry. I thought I might be doing everyone a favour by giving you a chance to cut things short. How-ever, needs must, I'm afraid. The MOD have agreed to let my department borrow you.'

Tom felt his guts tighten.

'You did get today's *Times*, didn't you?'

'That was you?' Tom said. 'It's just arrived.'

'Bugger. I thought it would be there hours ago. Read the letters page?'

'Not yet,' Tom said.

'Do, please . . . I'm about to go into Joint Intelligence. Call me back in an hour.' The line clicked as, on the other side of the Atlantic, Caro's father killed the connection.

'Your father sends his love,' Tom told Caro. 'And to you,' he said, looking at Charlie. 'I said you'd learnt to waterski. He was impressed.'

'Did you tell him about the locks?'

'No, but I have to call him back so I'll tell him then.'

Caro looked up.

'I'm sure it's nothing important,' Tom said.

A hijack in Karachi. Prince Andrew and Fergie on holiday, again. The USSR had named its team for the disarmament talks. Sir James Anderson, an ex-Labour minister, had died in a cottage fire . . . Tom skimmed the news as he headed for the letters page, which was its usual mix of the erudite, the deluded and the obscure. He didn't have to read far.

Sir Cecil Blackburn wishes to return.

Sirs, I realize that an announcement of my wish to return will be greeted with disbelief, and that the first instinct of Sir Geoffrey Howe, as Her Majesty's foreign minister, will be to decide that my friends in East Berlin would never allow me to return to the country from which I felt myself exiled so many years ago.

I can assure Sir Geoffrey that this is untrue.

I write this with the GDR's blessing, and their guarantee that once London has granted permission, Berlin will make immediate arrangements for my safe passage to England. The world is changing. Let none of us be in any doubt of that. The East Germans do this in a spirit of glasnost and perestroika.

[Openness, rebuilding – ed]

To my own country, the country that made me a Cambridge provost, honoured me as a professor of Classics, and knighted me for my work as an art historian, I am a turncoat. 'What's done cannot be undone.' Lady Macbeth could no more wash Duncan's murder from her fingers, or Patroclus deny Hector's death, than I can deny that charge. I wish to return all the same.

I accept that I will be put on trial. That I will, despite my age, in all probability be sentenced to prison. I accept without equivocation the authority of the English courts to pass sentence. My only wish is to return to my family, stand trial for treason and die in my own country when the time comes.

Yours faithfully
Professor Sir Cecil Blackburn Bt

'Oh shit,' Tom said.
'Tom . . .'
Charlie was grinning and Caro looking cross.

Instead of apologizing, Tom pushed the paper across, and ruffled Charlie's hair, which would usually have elicited a furious shrug, but this time only merited an eye roll. Tom watched Caro re-read a phrase, mouthing it aloud.

'Patroclus didn't kill Hector,' she said. 'Hector killed Patroclus. Achilles slaughtered him for it, tied his battered corpse to the back of his chariot and dragged it round the walls of Troy.'

'Who's Achilles?' Charlie asked.

'Greek,' Tom said. 'Blood-thirsty, good with a sword.'

Having considered asking more, Charlie asked instead if he could have a milkshake. Caro told him to order it at the bar, remember to say *please* and *thank you*, and watched him go with relief. 'That's why Daddy called?' she said, the moment Charlie was inside. 'Because of a letter in *The Times* from someone who doesn't even know his Greek history?'

'Seems to be.'

'What does Daddy want?'

'I'll find out in half an hour.'

'Don't let him bully you. He'll take advantage of the fact we're getting on.'

'I thought you liked him.'

'He's my father. I love him to pieces. He's still a nightmare.'

Tom looked at his wife in surprise. Pushing back his chair, he let his hand brush her shoulder. 'I'm getting another coffee. Want one?'

'I'm fine. Here's Charlie . . .'

The boy was on his way back with a sweating glass in

35

which two fat straws jutted from mud-coloured sludge. He smiled when he saw his father looking.

'Mummy's going to take you to the pool while I telephone Grandpa. Then I'll take you waterskiing and Mummy will read her book. Okay?'

Charlie nodded happily.

Caro's father answered first ring.

'Tom. Is that you?'

'Yep,' Tom said. 'It's me.'

'You've read Blackburn's bloody letter then? The Blessed Margaret is furious. She thinks it's a trick.' Caro's father sighed. 'Unfortunately, these days she thinks everything's a trick. That idiot husband of hers doesn't help.'

'Is he ill?' Tom asked. 'Is he coming home to die?'

'First thing the Foreign Secretary asked. There's no mention of illness in his bloody letter. And, believe me, there would be. He wouldn't miss a trick like that. Dying old man, filled with regret, wants only to be allowed to breathe his last in the land of his birth. He'd have led on it and added some bloody quote from Dante to give it a veneer of cultural respectability. Insufferable man.'

'You know him?'

'He taught me Classics at college. Hell of a shock to discover he was one of theirs. Least political man I've ever met. Wouldn't have had him pegged as a communist. Far too fond of the good life.'

'Why's he coming back?'

'That's the point, Tom. We don't know.'

'And that worries you?'

'Of course it bloody worries us.'

'What made him defect?'

'Something to do with a *Sunday Times* investigative team digging up dirt. This must have been early seventies. He got out just ahead of a police raid. A small boat from Deal to the French coast is the rumour. A lift in a lorry to Brussels. I bet he loved that. A train to Hamburg. It's said he went round the top, landed at Archangel and reached Berlin from the east via Moscow.'

'Sounds a little complicated.'

'*Lex parsimoniae*. Occam's Razor and all that. Far simpler to put the bloody man on a Baltic steamer to Rostock and transfer there. Nothing to stop the Russkies interviewing him in Berlin . . .'

Caro's father was talking too much. The kind of too much that said he didn't want to give Tom time to think or get a word in edgeways. So Tom let Eddington talk and waited for the words to run out before asking his question.

'What do you want?'

A tight silence followed. 'I'd have thought that was obvious,' Caro's father said finally. 'We want you to go and get him.'

'Who's we . . . ?'

'Me,' Eddington said heavily. 'The Foreign Secretary, the PM. You'll need to interview Blackburn. Ensure this is what it seems. That the bloody man really does want to return. He's doing this of his own will. If he is . . . Well, bring him back. But make bloody sure he understands he'll face trial.'

'Why me?'

Eddington hesitated. 'You know how these things work, Tom. The Soviets are the real power in East Berlin.

37

After that recent business in Moscow you have friends in the Politburo. That might be useful.'

If everything goes tits up?

'That's it?' Tom said.

'Not entirely. Blackburn asked for you.'

'How does he even know I exist?' Tom said.

'I don't know,' Eddington replied. 'Why don't you ask him when you get there?'

8

A week before Sir Cecil's letter appeared, Sir Cecil had stopped in front of the squat black weight of Berlin's Domkirche, looked up at the cathedral's over-heavy façade and knelt to tie his shoe. Then, securely laced, he headed for the Grande, a hard-currency hotel for foreigners. One of the few places it was occasionally possible to find an English newspaper.

The hard-currency hotels reminded him of *Casablanca*.

Areas of ambiguity filled with prostitutes, spies, under-cover police, fantasists and passing commercial travellers. Sir Cecil proclaimed himself endlessly shocked not to find Rick's Bar in the basement.

In summer he had coffee. Almost drinkable.

In winter he ordered hot chocolate, properly made in front of him from cocoa powder, sugar and cinnamon. Invariably he ate a pastry.

Today he waited for a dour-looking Scot to finish a copy of the *Telegraph* he shouldn't have brought across the border. Having spent more time than Sir Cecil could stand looking at share prices, the man turned to the sports section, as if anybody cared about that stuff.

The moment he abandoned his seat, Sir Cecil went to claim the paper he'd abandoned. Taking it back to his sofa, Sir Cecil turned to the crossword and pulled out his red Parker 51, reading the first clue carefully.

Crossword filled in, he skimmed an advertisement for a

Wedgwood plate celebrating the marriage of Prince Andrew to Sarah Ferguson. It was almost as ugly as the happy couple. He was discarding the paper when a little man sidled over. 'Don't suppose you've finished with that?'

Having claimed the copy, the man returned to his seat, ordered another coffee and skimmed the crossword. Sir Cecil had answered every question correctly except for 9 down, 13 letters.

In place of an answer he'd written the name of a Conservative grandee killed in a terrorist outrage more than ten years ago. The little man tried to remember the details and couldn't. There'd been something about grandchildren. A connection to Intelligence that had seen newspapers point fingers at the IRA. There'd been a service in Westminster Abbey, if he remembered rightly. One of the Royals attended. Charles, probably.

He had time for things like that.

It was three days before Sir Cecil returned to the hotel.

On the first day he bought a small pot plant outside a shop where Rosa-Luxemburg-Strasse met the square, then stopped for a second to look at the People's Theatre, damaged in the war like everything else, people included. No one appeared to be keeping an eye on him.

Evgeny, whose job that was, was off with his girlfriend.

Sir Cecil could remember when the city had been in ruins. He'd come up here with other officers, in the first few months after the end of the war, when everyone could still pass freely. You had to have been there to understand the joy of it. The sheer relief of finding yourself alive and on the winning side.

Everything they wanted was there for the taking.

On the second day, Sir Cecil stood at a corner on Unter den Linden, holding a copy of *Neues Deutschland*, which had a review of a film based on a play he'd written to order shortly after defecting.

It was on the third day that he returned to the hotel, ordered himself coffee and claimed a copy of R. K. Narayan's *Under the Banyan Tree* that a woman discarded as he approached the tables.

'If you've finished with that?'

He looked up to see the same little man.

'Certainly,' Sir Cecil said. 'The last story's particularly interesting. About a village storyteller who takes a lifelong vow of silence.'

A few minutes later, the little man slipped a note into his pocket. Later still, he encrypted it, wrote it out on rice paper and secreted it in his Omega, which had been fitted with a thinner movement to allow for this. It wasn't until that afternoon that things began to go wrong for him.

Having passed through Checkpoint Charlie, the little man retrieved his hire car from where he'd parked it and headed for Tempelhof to catch his flight for London. At first he thought the lorry that drew alongside on the Bundesstrasse 96 simply wanted to overtake. When it stayed alongside, he speeded up.

This was a mistake.

The lorry swung hard over and ran the Englishman off the road. It was another day before a detective with the West Berlin police paused to wonder why a dead commercial traveller with a plane to catch hadn't been wearing a watch.

9

'Bloody, bloody man . . .'

'I'm sorry,' Tom said.

'I don't know what you're apologizing for,' Caro said. 'He's *my* father. What did he tell you to tell me?' She smiled, and Tom smiled back; although there was enough flint in Caro's gaze to let him know she expected an answer.

'That he was sorry.'

'What else?' Caro asked. 'In order.'

'That just because I have to fly out tomorrow doesn't mean you can't stay. If you insist on cutting the holiday short, however, you should fly first class. Charlie would like that and your father will pick up the tab.'

'That's it?'

Taking a deep breath, Tom blew it out.

'I'm to tell you your father wouldn't take no for an answer. That Sir Cecil asked for me by name. The PM approves. If all else fails, I'm to say it's my duty. You're his daughter. You won't argue with that.'

'Fucker –'

'Caro!'

'*It's your duty* . . .' She wrapped her arms round his neck, seeking comfort rather than anything else. 'Don't tell Charlie until tomorrow, okay? Let him have the rest of the day.'

'You think he's going to be upset?'

'He'll be devastated,' Caro said. 'We're meant to be here for another week. It's the first holiday we've had together since . . .'

She didn't need to say it.

Becca died.

Caro sat in the shade of palm trees on a recliner, eyes hidden by huge dark glasses and the brim of her straw hat pulled low. A new novel lay unopened beside her.

'Book no good?'

'My head hurts,' Caro said. 'I think it's the light.'

'Want me to pull your chair further into the shade?'

She stood up dutifully and Tom moved it half a dozen paces, glancing up to check that he hadn't positioned her directly under a coconut palm. 'Go inside if it gets worse,' he said. 'I can field Charlie.'

'I want to stay.'

'Caro . . .'

'You're going tomorrow,' she said miserably. 'That makes this our last afternoon. I want Charlie to remember it being good. I want to be here.'

'I'm sorry,' Tom said.

'For what?'

He crouched beside her. 'Everything.'

She reached for his hand and gripped it tight as they both watched Charlie jump the wake, hurtle out to one side and happily kick off a ski, remaining upright as he cut back across the waves and headed for the other side.

'Is that the first time he's done that?' Caro asked.

'I think so,' said Tom.

'He's good.'

'It's all mathematics, apparently.'

'I'll tell him at breakfast. I'm going to take Daddy up on his offer, you know. We'll be flying first, and if Charlie wants some overpriced gizmo in duty-free he can pay for that too. Bloody man.' She sat back and reached for her Coke. 'Do you think he was telling the truth about Sir Cecil asking for you by name?'

'That's the bit that makes no sense.'

'You've never met him?'

'Not that I can remember.'

'And your orders are to bring him back?'

'Could be worse,' Tom said, watching his son send a fan of spray into the air as he reached the end of his rope and turned in again. 'They could be to kill him. Except, I imagine, even we draw the line at trying to kill one of our own under the noses of the East Germans.'

'*Tom . . .*'

'That was a joke.'

'Was it?' Caro asked.

10

Above Tom's head bats flittered like bits of torn sky, while around him palm leaves whispered dry secrets as he crossed the hotel courtyard. The night was hot, despite being the wrong side of midnight, and Tom had needed air and not wanted to wake Charlie by using the balcony.

A fountain in the middle splashed softly enough not to upset goldfish circling a huge bowl below. Sitting on its edge for a second, Tom dipped his fingers into the water and flicked them dry. He was saying goodbye to a place to which he'd probably never return. The thought saddened him.

Having found the right set of stairs up to his room, he expected to find the lights out and Caro asleep. Her bed was empty and the bathroom door ajar. He was just beginning to worry when he realized the balcony door was not quite shut.

She sat in a rattan chair, her knees up and arms hugging her legs. She appeared to have been watching Charlie sleep. When he crouched in front of her, he realized she was crying. 'You're back,' she said.

'Sorry I was gone so long.'

She took his hands and looked at them in the glow of an uplight in the garden below. She turned them over, examining the shadows that fell across them and finally gave them back, releasing his fingers.

45

'You killed someone,' she said.

'Caro . . .'

'I saw it in a dream.' She hugged herself. 'You were standing there with a gun . . .' Her face looked haunted when she raised her eyes to fix her gaze on him. 'That's what you do, isn't it? Kill?'

Kneeling, Tom took her hands and found them frozen. How could her fingers be cold on a night this hot? He put his fingers to her forehead and realized her skin was slick with sweat.

'Will you be all right to fly home?'

'What choice do I have? I told Charlie, you know.' She glanced towards the sleeping child. 'He woke and wanted to know where you'd gone. So I said you must have gone for a walk by yourself. And then he asked me why you'd want a walk and somehow I ended up telling him about tomorrow.'

'How did he take it?'

'He hates you. He hates me. He hates school. He knew it wasn't going to be a proper holiday. Not really. The only person who ever loved him was Becca, and she's dead . . .' Caro sounded lost. 'How can anyone be that unhappy at eight? I don't want him to be unhappy. Becca was bad enough.'

He held her tight and felt the heat from her body.

Reaching for her hand, he helped her from the chair. He put his hands under her arms, feeling them clamp down when she staggered slightly.

'I'm not drunk,' she said.

'I didn't think you were.' The hotel had a doctor and Tom wondered if Caro would forgive him for calling him. Probably not, knowing her.

'I'm scared,' she said later.

46

They were in bed and Tom half asleep. He pulled himself back from the comfort of darkness. 'Scared of what?'

'I don't know.'

Her voice sounded like that of a child.

Tom wanted slammed doors and shouting. He wanted thrown toys, tipped-over orange juice and broken plates. He wanted the things Becca didn't do. He wanted signs that were impossible to miss.

Listen to what they're not saying.

That was what a friend of Caro's said after Becca was gone; when it was too late to do any good and close to cruelty even to be talking that way . . . When they're slamming doors, bursting into tears, shouting at you, listen to what they're not saying. The worst of it was that Charlie decided to be brave.

Tom blamed himself. He'd taken the boy out along the beach in the early hours, leaving Caro to sleep fitfully. They'd walked to the little shrine and stopped to look at the bird skull. 'I can't take it home,' Charlie said. 'Can I?'

Tom shook his head. 'Afraid not.'

'It might be bad luck?'

Tom remembered the flicker of heat when he first touched the skull, the slight taste of electricity and darkness. 'This is where it belongs,' he said. 'I think this is where it wants to stay.'

Charlie nodded to say that made sense.

'Mummy said. About you having to go to Germany. She said . . . Grandpa asked you?' There was enough doubt in Charlie's voice for Tom to smile. 'She said it was important,' Charlie added. 'That it had to be you.'

'That's what Grandpa told me.'

'I wish he hadn't.'

'I wish he hadn't too.' Tom turned to look at the sea and noticed that the tide was out and a rock shelf exposed. A post he hadn't seen before peeked from the water. 'You want to walk out?'

'We'll get wet.'

'Doesn't matter.'

When they got back to the suite, Caro was awake and stuffing dirty laundry into a suitcase. 'You're wet,' she said.

'My idea,' said Tom.

'Of course it was. There's toast,' she said. 'And buns.'

Buns in Caro-speak translated as anything resembling cake.

'Have you eaten?' Tom asked her.

'I'm not hungry.'

He'd have said something but for Charlie being there.

'I'll eat on the plane,' Caro promised. 'You go ahead.'

Charlie packed his own things into a small blue rucksack and went to get his flannel and toothbrush from the bathroom.

'It might be best if we said our goodbyes here,' she said.

'I was going to see you off and wait for my plane.'

'Please don't.' Caro shook her head.

'Are you going to be all right?'

'I'll have to be.' She shrugged. 'There are days I hate my father. You're okay. You're allowed to hate yours. As mine will tell you, he's only ever wanted the best for me. Doesn't mean there aren't days I'd slaughter him.'

'Today being one?'

She smiled past Tom at Charlie, who'd fetched his things

as instructed, and also taken one of the hotel towels with a gold crown in the corner.

Tom said, 'I'll tell them we've taken it at check-out.'

They said their goodbyes on the steps of the hotel and Tom kissed Caro on the cheek and then hugged her, gripped Charlie's shoulder and then hugged him too. The little boy made it to the car before crying.

I I

The Pan Am stewardess smiled sympathetically at the late-comer in the lightweight suit, noticed his Omega, because she'd been trained to notice such things, and showed him where to stow his briefcase.

His seat was the best on the plane. In the first row, to the left of the aisle, and in splendid isolation, having no other seat beside it.

The door at the front finally closed, the steps were wheeled back, and the plane began to taxi. A moment later the pilot came on the intercom to say they'd be making an immediate takeoff, and not to worry about the delay because backwinds meant they'd make up time. Five minutes after that, the Bahamas were a patchwork of browns and greens set in a spread of impossible blue.

Before the seat belt sign was even off, the stewardess had abandoned her post to crouch beside Tom. 'I was asked to give you this, sir.'

It was an HMSO envelope, with one of those double tags that were wound with string. Someone had decided string was not enough and had dripped sealing wax over the top, stamping the lion and unicorn into it.

There was a file inside, inside which was a second envelope. Tom supposed he should be grateful this wasn't sealed with wax as well. Taking it out, he stopped at the sight of his father-in-law's writing on the front.

A single word.

Patroclus.

'Sir.' The stewardess was back. 'Can I get you . . . ?'

'I'll eat later.'

Lady Macbeth could no more wash Duncan's murder from her fingers, or Patroclus deny Hector's death . . . Caro had thought Sir Cecil's muddling of Patroclus for Achilles in his letter to *The Times* was ignorance. But it wasn't, Tom was almost certain. It was intentional.

A code of some sort, perhaps a challenge.

Slitting the envelope, Tom extracted three reports typed on official flimsy. The earliest report was dated 1966, the next 1979, the last the previous year. A list of committee members was given for each.

Eight people on the first, twelve on the second, fifteen on the third.

Tom was reminded of a CIA memo issued to assets inside inconvenient committees. *Refer all matters to the full committee. . . . Attempt to make these as large as possible, never less than five people. Bring up irrelevant information as frequently as possible. Haggle over precise wordings of communications, minutes, conclusions, and resolutions . . .*

Caro's father was the only common point in the three lists. He'd been the assistant on the first, a member of the committee on the second and had chaired the third. *You have until you land to read these. They'll be collected in Frankfurt, at customs. Read the reports first, look at the photograph later . . .*

What photograph? Tom wondered.

Each of the files followed the same format.

A statement that the committee had been asked by the

PM to look into rumours that sexual corruption existed within the British establishment, bound by the code of *omertà* and drawn from members of the Church, the Universities, the Commons, the Lords and Intelligence . . . In the first report they were referred to as pederasts, in the second perverts, in the third paedophiles.

The reports spoke of men interviewed – discreetly, quietly – in their clubs, in the corner of the members' bar in the Commons, in Patisserie Valerie, Maison Bertaux, the Colony Club, and Bar Italia in Soho, in their flats at Dolphin Square . . . The enquiries revealed what was expected. Those interviewed had led blameless and reputable (or disreputable, but still blameless) lives.

On instinct, he flicked to the end of the first report.

Many of the supposed victims were already known to the police, in some cases to the police and Intelligence. As were the half a dozen of those interviewed under caution. Despite the frequency of the rumours, and the unsavoury way of life of a few of those interviewed, there was no evidence children were involved.

The second report was almost identical. It spoke – at least the bits drawn from Met reports – of perverts and queers. And though it acknowledged the existence of nonces, and admitted that every station knew of one, it stressed that these were outsiders, loners, freaks. There was no suggestion they held positions of power in Parliament, Intelligence, the military or the BBC.

The conclusion to the 1979 report noted that the Home Office had recommended lowering the age of homosexual consent from twenty-one to eighteen. It reminded those reading that most of what qualified as criminality in the report would no longer qualify if that change was ever made.

The third and final report was fatter.

One paragraph, spliced between two others on children's homes in Northern Ireland, was redacted, black ink blocking the entire paragraph. Tom knew the first home mentioned as a place of ferocious cruelty. He wondered if the report was redacted before Eddington got it or if Caro's father had ordered it done. Either way, it made him suspicious.

This time, there were names he recognized. Sir Henry Petty, the actor, had been questioned under caution. The officer interviewing had dismissed the enquiry as ridiculous. That was the opinion of Sir Henry too.

The report's conclusion was firm.

Individual incidents were not evidence of conspiracy.

This time round, a note reminded those reviewing the file that homosexuality and paedophilia were not to be regarded as interchangeable. They were not. Most of the cases mentioned, while morally questionable, would not count as criminal if the heterosexual age of consent were applied.

Having cracked and signalled that he'd like a glass of Chablis, Tom sat and thought about the report's conclusion for a while. He decided that it was a very measured, very fair and very civilized answer to another question entirely.

Then he took the hand-addressed envelope Caro's father had told him to open last and shook out a single photograph.

It landed face up.

A naked boy not much older than Charlie glared at him.

He was crouched in a corner, his fingers hooked into claws and his teeth bared. It hadn't done much good. And he'd learnt soon enough there were some things you couldn't fight. Not if you wanted to stay alive.

Tom was looking at himself.

12

On his way through Frankfurt airport Tom vomited memories into a bin and made it as far as the men's lavatory before vomiting again, wiping his mouth on the back of his hand and swilling water round his mouth before spitting the last of it down a sink. His skin in the mirror had a poisonous sheen.

Charlie's voice was in his head. The lyrics they'd heard sung to the steel drums outside a shack on the beach in the Bahamas.

> *Let me go home, I want to go home,*
> *I feel so break-up, I want to go home.*

It wasn't simply that Tom was the wrong man for the job. He couldn't do this. Not now. Eddington had to understand that. Tom would find a telephone the moment he got through customs to tell Caro's father so.

'I thought you'd be first off . . .'

'I was,' Tom said.

The Englishman looked puzzled.

They were in an interview room and Tom had just been pulled out of the customs queue. Random search was the reason given. About as subtle as he expected. An official from the *Zollkriminalinstitut* had led him into a room and left him there. The Englishman had arrived a few seconds later, giving Tom a firm handshake and his card.

'I know,' he said. 'I know . . .'

Spook pretending to be someone else produces a card to prove he's the person he's pretending to be. It was clumsy ten years earlier. Probably clumsy ten years before that. It didn't matter what his name was. Tom doubted they'd see each other again. 'You all right?' the man asked. 'You look . . . slightly ill.'

'Bumpier flight than I expected. You're from Bonn, the embassy?'

'The Frankfurt consulate.'

Tom doubted that. 'An interesting post?'

'Very,' the man said. Entirely unironically.

Dipping into his briefcase, Tom extracted the file he'd been given on takeoff. 'I'd ask you to send his lordship my regards and thank him for ruining my holiday, but I plan to tell him myself in a moment. He'll still need this, though.'

'It contains a photograph in an envelope?'

'There is no photograph.'

The man stared at Tom, momentarily thrown. He was thickset, muscled. Useful in a scrap probably. All the same, someone who followed orders rather than gave them. 'I was told –'

'I tore it and the envelope into a hundred pieces, pissed on them and flushed them somewhere over the mid-Atlantic.'

'You're really planning to call him?'

'Just as soon as I reach the Arrivals hall.'

'Then I should probably give you this.'

Tom's name was on the front in Caro's father's hand-writing. He ripped the envelope open knowing he wasn't going to like what he found.

Tom,

Three investigations have found no evidence that the Patroclus
Circle exists, never mind acts as a clearing house for organized
filth. An ex-commissioner of the Met has told me to my face not to
believe the rumours. Sir Cecil says otherwise. The bloody man's
writing his memoirs. Obviously enough, he says they'll reveal all.
He also claims to have a list of everybody implicated.

You're to extract him.

We need you to keep up the pretence that this is an exemplary
example of cooperation between old foes. At no point must East
Berlin know that our interest is anything above humanitarian.
But we need him, his memoirs and any list he might have. One
final point. That photograph.

I assume you flushed somewhere over the Atlantic.

If you didn't, feel free to burn it. You have my word the negative
was destroyed a very long time ago. You asked what I had against
you. And I said that when you first appeared with Caro, on the
back of that damn bike of yours, I asked a friend to run due
diligence. That photograph was the last thing to turn up.

You were what? Ten, eleven?

No one is responsible for his, or her, childhood, Tom. It's taken
me longer to realize that than it should. I've never mentioned the
photograph to my daughter. I will never mention it to my daughter.
Whether or not you do is your choice. I will say this, though.
Your son is almost eight. I don't know what was happening to you
when you were eight. But do you really want a world where men
like the one who took that photograph go free?

'Bastard,' Tom said. 'Bastard. Bastard. Bastard.'
Pulling a lighter from his pocket, he put it on the table,

folded pleats into his father-in-law's letter and lit the top edge, sitting back to watch the flame sink in an unsteady line towards the table's Formica top.

'You've changed your mind?'

The man opposite put up his hands.

'I'm just the messenger,' he said. 'Shoot someone else.'

Putting a first-class train ticket from Frankfurt to Brunswick on the table, the man placed a travel warrant beside it. The warrant was for the *Berliner*, the British military train that ran through East Germany to West Berlin.

'They told me I was flying.'

'This way you can meet your handler.'

Tom looked at him. No one had said anything about a handler.

'I thought I was acting alone,' Tom said.

'Oh, you are. Entirely alone. Sir Cecil requested you.' The man looked thoughtful. 'Don't suppose you know why? I'm meant to ask that.'

'No idea,' said Tom.

'I rather thought that was what you'd say. Now remember, our line is you're a friend of a friend of Sir Cecil's. No official standing. You're simply there to give an old man moral support.'

'Do the East Germans believe that?'

'I doubt it.' He handed Tom an envelope labelled 'Deutschmarks', then produced another, far thicker one, labelled 'GDR Marks'. 'Don't get caught taking in Noddy money. You're meant to buy it at the border. And you'll need this . . .' He put a wad of US dollars on the table. 'There are clothes shops near Frankfurt station. Buy yourself something less tropical. They'll roll their eyes when you offer dollars but they'll take them.'

'The rest is for bribes?'

'Be careful though. The last man didn't make it back.'

Tom looked at him. 'The last man?'

'They didn't mention him? Had a car crash. Could be coincidence.'

Tom wondered if Cecil had also asked for him by name.

13

The showers at Brunswick station were hot enough to scald and even that didn't make Tom feel clean. So he rewashed his hair using liquid soap from a swivelling bottle on the cubicle wall, wrapped himself in the towel he'd been given, and headed for the white-tiled changing rooms to dry himself and dress. His face in the mirror was tanned.

That was about all he could say for it.

He had no trouble meeting other people's eyes but there were days when he found it hard to meet his own. The tan made him think of the West Indies, which made him think of Charlie, which made him curse his father-in-law all the more. Splashing water on to his face, Tom towelled it dry, dressed quickly and headed for the concourse of Braunschweig Hauptbahnhof.

Three p.m. 1500 hours in army-speak.

The *Berliner* left for the second part of its round trip at 4 p.m. An hour's time difference between here and the UK . . . A bank of phone boxes stood almost opposite. If he called now, Caro should be home.

'How was the flight?' he asked.

'The stewardesses were kind to Charlie. The captain asked if he'd like to see the flight deck. That helped. Where are you now?'

'Brunswick station.'

'I thought you were flying,' Caro said.

'So did I. Apparently not. I'm taking the military train.'

'Bloody Daddy. That's probably his idea too. That's where I've been, you know. They're keeping Charlie for a few days. He'll enjoy that. He likes being at the Hall. Don't forget his stamps, will you?'

What stamps? Tom almost asked.

'A postcard of Checkpoint Charlie, remember? With as many Bundespost Berlin stamps as you can fit on it. Some of those marzipan sweets too.'

'The ones with Mozart on the front?'

'That's them. Have a good trip, if possible.'

'You're going to have a quiet afternoon?'

'I'm on my way out.'

'Where?'

Caro hesitated. He wished she hadn't.

'Things to do,' she said. 'I should go.'

'So should I,' Tom said. 'I'm meant to be meeting someone before I board. He's going to brief me, supposedly. I imagine he just wants a look.'

'Better go then.'

'Better had,' Tom agreed.

Tom took his unhappiness out into Brunswick's Berliner Platz. Of course, what else was it going to be called? Head down, he kept walking. Wondering what would happen if he missed the train.

If he headed off and never came back.

A poster for *Rambo 2*, with a half-naked Sylvester Stallone clutching an RPG-7, stared down from a tattered hoarding. The bar under it echoed with Nena's '99 Luftballons'.

Three streets, twenty minutes and a dozen snatches of the same song later, Tom was wondering if West German bars played anything else.

They did. In a café two shops later, a boy was singing along to 'Heroes'.

A kid sat in the doorway beyond, knees drawn up to her chest, her gaze fixed blankly on her feet. The couple ahead of Tom walked straight past her. She had the sheen of a user, her hair was oily and her skin shiny. He could smell it the moment he stopped, the stink of someone with nowhere to wash.

The girl looked up, wondering what he wanted and how much it was worth.

Looking around him, Tom confirmed what he already suspected. No one was watching. He wasn't being followed and, for the rest of the world, being with her had rendered him invisible. Splitting the bundle of Deutschmarks he'd been given, one third/two thirds, he held out the smaller bundle and watched her eyes widen. Seconds later her face closed down.

She shook her head.

'I don't want anything,' he said.

If he'd had time he might have seen if he could find out where she came from, put her in a taxi home and hope that, in some way, home wasn't worse than being on the streets. But he didn't have the time.

He left her staring after him as he walked away.

Cars crowded the street, and neon signs lit shop windows, despite it being a long way from dark. A traffic policeman wore his hair in a ponytail. A rack of cheap leather jackets attracted Tom's attention outside a jeans shop.

'How much?' he asked.

The boy from the shop looked at the unpriced jacket and named a figure that had Tom putting the garment back. The leather was cheap, the lining synthetic, the stitching crude. Caro would have hated it.

They settled on £35, give or take.

Stuffing his old jacket, shirt and tie into a Levi carrier bag, Tom examined the T-shirt he'd also bought, dragged on the leather jacket and checked his reflection in the shop doorway. He looked more like the man he remembered. As he headed for the station, he felt happier.

He had a job to do.

Dm Militärzug
Helmstedt-
Marienborn-
Berlin Stadtb

15.54
Abfahrt
Gleis 2 West

It took Tom a while to find the right departures board but his train was waiting at Platform 2 when he got there. Blue and cream carriages had carefully painted Union Flags beside their doors. *Royal Corps of Transport* was picked out in gold lettering along the sides. It all looked so English he laughed.

Squaddies on leave from NATO bases in West Germany were heading to West Berlin for a long weekend of drinking and brothels. There were NCOs and their families. An officer with his wife, and two small children who trotted at their heels like gundogs. The second-class coaches were already crammed, one of the first-class carriages was nearly full, and a thickset man blocked the entrance to the final first-class carriage. Tom was approaching it when the train warrant officer peeled off from talking to a lieutenant.

'That's officers only.'

Maybe it was Tom's cheap leather jacket that tightened the WO's face. Or the fact his face was unshaven. Perhaps he simply looked jetlagged.

'Your pass,' the warrant officer demanded.

Tom felt in his pockets, realized it was in the pocket of the jacket he'd bundled into the Levi jeans bag, and crouched to retrieve it. As he did so, he looked up and caught the gaze of the thickset man by the door. The man was laughing.

'Making an entrance?' he asked.

'Apparently,' Tom replied.

The man put himself between Tom and the WO. 'Long time no see.'

Tom looked at him.

'It's been . . .'

Not long enough, Tom thought.

Henderson, who in Tom's experience liked to be called 'H', gave the warrant officer his brightest smile. 'He's the reason we have a fourth carriage.' Turning to Tom, he added, 'I'm glad you decided to join us, I thought I was going to have to hold the bloody train. Come on.' He pushed between a family, slowing to take advantage of the view as he edged past a teenage girl in a thin top. 'A man has to find his amusement somewhere,' he said.

'If you say so,' Tom replied.

Henderson stopped on the steps, turned and grinned.

'You po-faced bastard. I thought you meant that for a moment.' He entered first and Tom followed, finding himself in a carriage old-fashioned enough to belong in a Poirot film. Its dining table was already laid. This was higher than Tom expected, as were the chairs. A bottle of white wine chilled in a silver bucket. A bottle of good claret stood open and airing. A port decanter rested on the side.

'We don't touch that until Potsdam,' Henderson said.

Tom raised his eyebrows.

'Potsdam port. It's a tradition. There's a loco change at Potsdam, from theirs back to ours. That's when we'll start drinking. Glass for glass until we reach West Berlin. Now, I should tell you, I've been running the *what ifs*.'

'The what?'

'What's the worst that happens if we leave Sir Cecil there? What's the worst that happens if we don't? The obvious questions . . .'

Tom realized that Henderson didn't know that Sir Cecil was wanted back at any price. That thought worried him. The options being Henderson didn't have the full facts . . . Or, if he did, he didn't trust Tom enough to share them.

Either way, not good.

A low thud as the engine started was followed by a lurch as the couplings engaged. Braunschweig Hauptbahnhof began slipping away behind them. 'Next stop,' Henderson said, 'Helmstedt. Where we'll get an Eastie Beastie.'

'An East German loco?'

'You've got it.' He smirked. 'A veritable Trabant among trains. Stinking of exhaust and over-heated oil. We'll be keeping the windows shut.' Glancing between the ice bucket and the already-opened bottle of Margaux, he said, 'White or red?'

'White,' Tom said. 'Less likely to make my jetlag worse.'

Henderson's gaze sharpened. 'I rather thought you'd travelled out from London. No one said anything about having to fly you in.'

'West Indies.'

'Dear God, what have we got going on there?'

'I was on holiday.'

'Really? I didn't have you pegged as the holiday-taking type.'

'Sometimes I surprise myself.' Taking a swig of wine, Tom felt a headache hit. Not from the alcohol but because it was too damn cold. Besides, he had a low tolerance for being patronized.

'How's your German?' Henderson asked.

'My Russian's substantially better.'

'That's good,' said Henderson. 'Their side of the Wall, speaking Russian means you're important. Not liked, but important. They're still the power behind the throne whatever the East Germans like to pretend.'

And I have friends in Moscow.

Caro's father had made it clear he expected Tom to trade on that if necessary.

'You've been briefed?' Henderson asked.

'On Sir Cecil? A little.'

'He was in Germany after the war. Nothing special in that. Half the British Army was there.'

'I know,' Tom said. 'I've met some of them.'

Pouring himself a glass of red, Henderson downed it and reached for the bottle. Outside, their engine was being swapped for an East German model. The track beyond Helmstedt turned out to be flanked by barbed wire, watchtowers and minefields. 'Not that the Ossi are afraid of their people escaping,' Henderson said sourly.

'*Ossi* is what they call themselves?'

'*Ostdeutsche*, East Germans, Easties. It's what we and the West Germans call them . . . Here we go,' he added. Ten minutes later the edges of a town appeared and the train slowed as it approached Marienborn. 'You might want to watch this.'

The warrant officer Tom had seen earlier, the lieutenant he'd been talking to and another soldier clambered down and marched – parade-ground perfect – up the platform towards a waiting officer, who stood ramrod straight.

'He's Soviet,' Tom said.

Henderson nodded. 'Ossis inspect civilian trains. The Sovs this one. That was the original 1945 agreement and the Sovs are damn well sticking to it. Worked well enough for forty years. Probably work for the next forty too . . . And here we go . . .'

All four men vanished through a station door.

'Who was our third man?' Tom asked.

'Translator. He relays any questions to both sides. You noticed he carried a NAAFI carrier bag?' Henderson grinned. 'Thought you might . . .'

It had been hard to miss.

'Porn,' said Henderson. 'Nescafé. Tights for their wives. Spark plugs for their bloody Trabant cars. Helps keep things smooth.'

'What do we get in return?'

'Vodka so bad you wouldn't use it to light a barbecue.

Right, here we go again. Next point of interest, Magdeburg. Famous for its twin-spired cathedral, political prison and agitprop murals. It's also where we start supper. Great juicy steaks to upset the Ossi commuters. It's all theatre. Them, us. This whole bloody train.'

'Dear God,' Tom muttered.

Outside the window, a work party came into view. A couple of the group were men, the rest women, stripped to their waists, in bras and khaki trousers, heads down and backs running with sweat as they swung their pickaxes. The afternoon was hot, the embankment sun-baked and the *Berliner* might as well have been invisible for all the notice they took of it.

'Politicals,' Henderson said. 'With orders not to look at us. Doesn't mean we can't look at them.' He was staring at the youngest, her grey bra so sodden with sweat that it might as well have been invisible.

Tom sighed. 'Let's go back to Sir Cecil. What's he like?'

'You know that certain kind of Englishman who hides his razor-sharp intelligence behind being a bit of a buffoon?' Henderson said.

'That's Sir Cecil?'

'He'd like to think so. Opinions differ.'

'What was the man doing in Berlin after the war?'

'Cyphers.'

'Any problems?'

'What exactly are you asking?'

'I was wondering if we had anything on him.'

'You mean, if the East Germans had anything on him.' Tom knew what he meant.

'He had Third Reich Intelligence files put on microfilm

and flown back to London for decryption and archiving. Thousands of the bastards, tens of thousands. Brilliant idea. He made bonfires of the originals.'

Henderson turned back from the window.

'Any idea why they picked you for this?' he asked.

'None whatsoever,' Tom said.

'I asked what your clearance was. London told me I didn't have sufficient clearance to know.' He shrugged. 'Their idea of a joke, apparently. They did send your file though. Most of last year was missing.'

Tom realized that Henderson was waiting for him to explain. This was absurd, obviously. If he'd been allowed to explain it wouldn't have been missing. What would he have said anyway? *I helped thwart a coup against Gorbachev? Met a beggar who turned out to be Maya Milova, the missing wife of a Politburo grandee?*

Not simply a grandee, but Marshal Milov himself, the power behind Gorbachev's throne. 'Passing swiftly on,' Tom said.

Henderson's sigh was theatrical.

'As you know,' he said, slightly tightly, 'East Berlin and Moscow are having a bit of a scrap.' Seeing Tom frown, he said, 'I put this in your briefing.'

'Which never reached me.'

Henderson scowled. 'Think of it as Soviet mid-life crisis meets East German adolescent rebellion.' His gaze, when he turned to Tom, was focused in a way it hadn't been before. 'Moscow's Germans don't want to be Moscow's Germans any more. Don't want to be our Germans either. More's the pity.'

He paused to pour himself more wine.

'For them, Gorbachev's flirtation with democracy is as pitiful as discovering your father is bonking his secretary. Their great hope is that the USSR returns to the marital bed. Personally, I doubt it. The GDR has 180,000 unofficial collaborators, *inoffizelle Mitarbeiter*, reporting to the Stasi. The Stasi has 90,000 staff of its own. At its height, the Gestapo only had 40,000 to handle a population four times as big. These days the Ossi are more Soviet than the Soviets.' Leaning forward, Henderson drained his glass. 'I'm still trying to work out why they'd let Sir Cecil go.'

14

Pushing away his hotel breakfast, Tom picked up a *Herald Tribune* and skimmed its first page. He didn't like that any better.

A British Cabinet minister dead in a car crash on the M1. Fallout from the explosion of the Chernobyl reactor in the Ukraine had drifted as far north as Scandinavia and was poisoning the moss. There was a suggestion that reindeer herds would have to be slaughtered.

'Bad business.'

Tom recognized Henderson's voice, and if that wasn't enough, there was the way he stood, legs slightly apart, as if balancing on deck. The words and his way of standing took Tom back to the Tair Bull, a pub in the shadow of Pen y Fan. Tom had been doing a combat refresher course at Sennybridge when he was told there was someone he needed to meet.

They'd discussed Belfast.

Henderson had used exactly the same words then. He'd been right, it was a bad business, and shortly after Tom arrived it was to get much worse.

'May I?' Henderson indicated a chair.

'Of course.' Tom moved his plate of sliced meat, tomatoes and cheese. It was mostly uneaten. He reached for his coffee instead.

'They'll do you a fry-up,' Henderson said.

Without waiting for Tom's agreement, he clicked his fingers for a waiter and fired off a rapid order, then indicated Tom's coffee and said he'd have one too. The waiter brought a cafetière. Five minutes after that he brought Tom a huge plate of bacon and eggs and a side order of toast.

Henderson grinned as Tom cleared the plate. 'That bad, eh?'

Tom looked up.

'I mean. As morning-afters go . . .'

As mornings went it wasn't even close. Tom kept that thought to himself.

'Right,' Henderson said, when the plate was clean. 'Sir Cecil wants sight of you.' He laughed. 'Think he's worried we might be sending an assassin.'

'If we were going to do that we'd have done it years ago.'

'Might be best not to say that out loud. Frederika's meeting us at Café Adler opposite the checkpoint. She'll have your transit papers.'

'Who's Frederika?'

'Seriously, no one briefed you?'

'I was on holiday in the Bahamas when Lord Eddington called me. Theoretically, I'm still on holiday . . .'

'And his lordship is really your father-in-law?' Henderson's gaze was cool, almost appraising. 'How much did you tell him about Belfast?'

'What do you think?'

'I think we go and see Sir Cecil.'

Sitting in the back of a blue government-issue Jaguar, indistinguishable from the official-issue one he'd used in

Moscow, Tom did his best not to feel sick as he boned up on Frederika Schmitt, East German gymnast and close personal friend of Sir Cecil Blackburn, a man old enough to be her grandfather.

She'd been identified as Olympic material at the age of six by the Deutscher Sportausschuss, the state committee for sport, and moved to a special school. In 1965, her parents had been relocated from Dresden to Berlin, her father promoted, and her family given a four-room apartment with its own kitchen. Frederika joined SCD, the Berlin flagship of Sport Club Dynamo, the training ground for most of the GDR's Olympic champions.

She was eight.

Having won intercity competitions in 1967, 1968 and 1969, she took gold two years later at the GDR's national games. A year after that, she took silver at the Munich Olympics. By then she was fifteen. The medal earned her the Patriotic Order of Merit, Second Class. In 1975 she took gold at the European Championships in Norway. A year later she made the Olympic team for a second time, taking bronze in Montreal. By the time of the 1980 Moscow Olympics she was training others. Most of the Soviet bloc boycotted the Los Angeles Olympics in retaliation for Reagan's boycott of the Moscow Olympics four years earlier. While Ecaterina Szabo was taking gold for Romania in America, Frederika was training younger gymnasts for the Soviet-run alternative. She was sent home before the games started. Injury during training.

Twenty-seven in 1984. So, twenty-nine now.

'When was this taken?'

Tom held a mugshot, more or less. A dark-haired girl in a

sweatshirt staring at the camera. She wore clip earrings and a gold Snoopy on a chain. Glancing across to check it wasn't from the games, Henderson said, 'Last year? Maybe this . . .'

'She looks about twelve.'

'Tom . . .'

'Fifteen then.'

'More like twenty. Drugs probably slowed her puberty. You saw the bit saying she's addicted to painkillers? Most GDR athletes are. I'm told her coach got her pregnant a few months before Munich, then had the team doctor abort her baby. The extra oxygen in her blood was what gave her an edge.'

'Christ,' Tom said. 'That's grim.'

'We also believe that their Institute of Sports Medicine has developed performance-enhancers. We need to stand that up.' Henderson shrugged at Tom's surprise. 'Inevitably they'll find a military application. That makes them of legitimate Intelligence interest.'

'How does she fit into Sir Cecil's life?'

'Are you always this prissy? How the fuck do you think she fits? She's his gatekeeper, cum mistress. They're shacked up in squalid splendour on the top floor of an apartment block in the Nicholas quarter. He doesn't let anyone in to clean. She doesn't do any cleaning herself. He plays with his cameras or works on his memoirs. She opens factories and teaches hopefuls for the next Olympics. You can ask her yourself. Café Adler's over there.'

'Does she come with him?'

'To England? Absolutely not.'

'Do you think she knows that?'

'Best not to make waves,' Henderson said.

'It won't be his family he returns to, anyway. It'll be prison.'

'Do you really believe that?' Henderson looked amused. 'An old man, a distinguished old man, misled, misguided, repenting of his naivety . . . If his lawyer is half decent he'll argue Sir Cecil's time in East Berlin should count as sentence served. That would go down well with the judge and the press.'

'Have you met him?'

'I saw him lecture in Cambridge once. He's a bit of an oddball. You know, unworldly. I could see how he might have been led astray.'

'I thought he was meant to be brilliant?'

'He certainly believes so.'

15

Café Adler occupied the ground floor of one of those grand yellow-stone European buildings that look like someone's idea of how a very exclusive department store should look. Jewels, first floor. Silk dresses, second. Furs, third . . . The side windows had sharp pediments; the corner windows had pillars; the roof overhung as if someone was trying to put cornicing on the sky.

Caro would know what the style was called.

'Welcome back, sir.'

Henderson shook the man's hand and nodded towards a table near a window that was being cleared by a waitress in black uniform.

'You wouldn't like . . . ?'

The man indicated a pavement table with its view of Checkpoint Charlie, which looked like nothing so much as a Brighton beach café, with a red and white barrier and slowly flapping flags. A green 2CV, a blue VW Beetle and a yellow campervan were queuing to enter East Berlin.

'Let's leave that for the tourists.'

Henderson led the way inside, settled himself facing the door and indicated that Tom should sit beside him.

'The GDR changed the rules, you know. Births, marriages, deaths and family illnesses used to be the only reason that they let East Berliners visit the West. Now anyone can go if they leave collateral.'

'Collateral?'

'Husband, wife, child.'

Passing Tom a menu he obviously knew by heart, Henderson skimmed both sides and ordered what he probably always ordered. A cappuccino and a slice of chocolate cake. With a shrug, Tom did the same.

'Before you leave for good you have to try the schnitzel. I suggested, given they're directly opposite the checkpoint, they put up posters reading *Schnitzel to Die For*. They didn't think it funny.' He shrugged, thanked the girl delivering his coffee and sat back. 'So, how did you and Caro Eddington meet?'

Beneath Henderson's question was another.

How did someone like Lady Caroline Eddington – Roedean, King's College, daughter of an earl – meet someone who'd spent half his childhood at something little better than a reform school?

Tom might pass these days, if he needed to, but Henderson had read the file. He knew where Tom came from. Civilians merely saw the version Caro created. There were other versions that not even Caro knew about, not really. One of them used to trawl Belfast's backstreets with a cosh in his pocket, a gun in his belt and a list of those so dirty even hell would think twice about taking them. That version was no more. He'd been retired. At least Tom hoped he had.

Looking up, he found Henderson waiting for an answer.

'Do you remember that big 1960s Vietnam rally?' Tom said. 'The one in front of the US embassy that turned nasty? Some lunatic from the Flying Squad was trying to open a girl's head with a truncheon. So I hit him, grabbed the girl and ran. The girl turned out to be Caro. Things sort of went from there . . .'

'I bet Lord Eddington loved that.'

'She'd told him she was visiting the British Museum.'

Henderson laughed and clicked his fingers for a waitress who smiled and nodded. Tom wondered if he was the only one to notice her scowl as she turned away. Henderson didn't. He'd gone back to his cake by then.

Tom saw Frederika before Henderson did.

She crossed with a group of off-duty US soldiers and returning tourists. She walked alone, head down, her eyes shielded behind dark glasses, her hair hidden under a silk scarf. She looked tiny. There was an elegance to her that had the soldiers staring. Her chin went up and she stood a little taller when she noticed.

Even at a distance it was obvious she limped.

Tom pushed back his chair.

'Let her come to us,' Henderson said.

She was ushered through with no fuss, a US sergeant turning to watch her walk away. Once through, she seemed to breathe more easily, stopping for a second to stare at a huge poster for Calvin Klein Obsession, before squaring her shoulders. She headed for Café Adler and Tom stood to greet her. But it was Henderson she shook hands with first.

'You know each other?' Tom asked.

'We've met,' Henderson said. 'This is Major Fox. The man I told you about.'

'He's going to take us to London?'

Henderson's smile was silky smooth. 'Let me order you a coffee.'

'Hot chocolate,' Frederika said. 'And *Sachertorte*. Real *Sachertorte*, not that fake stuff.' She kept glancing at those who trickled in to fill the other tables. After a while, Tom realized she was waiting to be recognized.

'I saw you take a medal in Montreal,' he said.

She looked up, eyes suddenly alight. 'You were there?'

'No,' Tom said. 'I only saw it on television. It was on the news.'

'They showed it on your news?'

Becca had liked floor routines. The preciseness of the movements and tight self-control probably attracted her. They'd certainly played their part in the rest of her life. 'Yes. I watched it with my daughter.'

Frederika smiled.

She ate her chocolate cake, scraped the plate as clean as she could manage with her fork and excused herself, walking towards the *Toilette*.

'You cynical bastard,' Henderson said.

'It was true.'

'Of course it was. Every word of it.'

She came back wiping her mouth and stopped to pour herself a glass of water from an ice-filled jug used by waiters.

'We should go,' she said.

Henderson reached for his briefcase.

'Not you,' she said. There was a ghost of spite in her voice. 'I only have papers for the major.'

'This isn't what we agreed.'

She shrugged.

'Half an hour to cross,' Henderson said tightly. 'Half an hour to get to Nikolaiviertel, the Nicholas quarter. A couple of hours for you and Sir Cecil to get to know each other. An hour to get back. Technically, they shouldn't search you in either direction. But they're capable of asking if you mind and being difficult if you do. So, let's allow an hour and a half for your return. I'll meet you here at fifteen hundred.'

'No,' Frederika said. 'That's not right.'

She unfolded a form that gave Tom permission to enter East Berlin and return forty-eight hours later. It stated that he had two nights' accommodation booked through Interhotel. He would be staying at the Palasthotel on Karl-Liebknecht-Strasse . . .

'*Frederika.*'

'Sir Cecil insists.'

Henderson looked furious.

'The GDR will pay,' Frederika said, as if that was the problem. To Tom, she said, 'The Palasthotel is where we put important foreigners.'

'Six hundred beds,' Henderson sneered, 'A thousand rooms. A two-thousand-seat conference room. Meeting rooms. Bars, restaurants, its own cinema. A swimming pool, a gymnasium and hot and cold running Stasi . . .'

Frederika glared at him. 'It does not.'

'They even have their own entrance,' Henderson told Tom. 'Their own offices. It's said the clerks who listen in take up an entire floor. So, if a pretty girl in the bar offers you a good time, remember that she's more interested in your secrets than your shekels or sexual technique.'

'I don't have secrets,' Tom said.

'Everyone has secrets,' Henderson said flatly. He reached for the Interhotel form and turned it so he could see it better. 'A suite,' he said. 'That probably means you get video cameras as well as microphones.'

He pushed back his chair. 'If you'll excuse me.'

Heading for the bar, he demanded something of the girl behind it and the manager appeared a few seconds later. He and Henderson did that little handshake where money changes hands and Henderson headed for the kitchens. Frederika grinned sourly, put on a croaky little voice and said. 'Mr H. Phone home . . .'

Tom stared at her.

'You've never seen *ET*?'

'I think my wife took . . .' Tom hesitated '. . . someone.'

It was the first time he hadn't named Becca. It felt like a betrayal, but he didn't want questions about her. He didn't want to have to explain to this stranger that she was no longer alive, that, yes, he was getting over it.

'Are you all right?' Frederika asked.

'I'm fine,' Tom said. 'Why?'

'You look sad . . .'

'And you look in pain.'

Her eyes widened and she nodded. Dipping into her pocket, she flipped open a pill box and extracted a pill. She reached for her water, hesitated, and extracted a second, swallowing both.

'What are they?' Tom asked.

Frederika shrugged. 'Does it matter?'

'I was shot. I found getting off opiates hard.'

'I fell,' Frederika said. 'I'll be on these for life.'

The flatness of her voice said she liked discussing her accident even less than Tom liked talking about Becca. So they sat in silence, while those who'd simply come for coffee and cake paid their bills, vacated their tables and left to do whatever they needed to do. They were replaced by locals arriving for lunch.

'He'll be back soon,' Frederika said.

'You don't like him?'

'I have my reasons.'

'Want to tell me what they are?'

'Some other time.' Frederika nodded to where Henderson watched from a doorway. He looked grim as he headed for their table. So grim, Tom imagined he'd lost whatever argument he'd been having.

'We'll be making a complaint,' he said.

'About what?' Frederika asked. 'About the GDR putting your man up in a five-star hotel, picking up the bill, paying for his meals and having official guides take him round Berlin, if that's what he wants? This is a big decision. Sir Cecil needs time to consider things carefully.'

'You offered us full cooperation,' Henderson said crossly.

'You have our full cooperation,' Frederika said. She pointed at the reservation for the Palasthotel. 'How could we possibly cooperate more?'

'You realize she's Stasi?'

'I'm not,' Frederika said sharply.

Tom pushed back his chair. 'You mentioned Sir Cecil needing time to consider things carefully. Is he getting cold feet?'

'About England? Absolutely not.' Pushing back her own chair, Frederika smiled. A slightly strange smile. 'He knows he's going to be tried. He's looking forward to it. He's taken to calling it *The Show*.'

16

'You shouldn't be here,' Charlie said.

'Nor should you.'

'Mummy and Grandpa sent me. After you know what . . . I don't think they knew what else to do.'

'I'm sorry,' Becca said.

Charlie shrugged. 'What's it like?'

'What's what like?'

'Being dead.'

'Boring. I'm not sure I'm properly dead yet.'

'They buried you.' Charlie scowled at the memory. 'Mummy wouldn't let me go. She said the funeral would upset me.'

'What did Dad say?'

'Daddy didn't say anything. He was being odd . . . He's getting better,' Charlie added quickly. 'Mummy likes him now.'

'That's a start. You should be asleep.'

'I'm not tired. Do you want to come for a walk with me?'

'Better not. It's time I went.'

'Why?' Charlie asked crossly.

'Because you're crying.'

'That's not you.'

'Yes, it is,' Becca said. 'It always is. I'm sorry.'

She raised her hand slightly, a half-goodbye. The way she used to when friends were round and she had to be too cool to say goodbye to her little brother but didn't really just want to walk away. She looked exactly how he remembered. That was good. The first time she visited, before she turned round, he hadn't known what to expect. He'd been afraid she might look broken.

17

'You are now leaving the American Sector . . .'

The sign was so famous that you could buy postcards of it in the newsagent behind Café Adler.

Between the end of the Second World War and 1961, 3.5 million people left East Germany. That was 20 per cent of their population; the majority of them professionals. Barbed wire along the internal border helped slow the flow. But in the eighteen months before the Wall went up, nearly half a million East Germans left, many crossing from East to West in Berlin.

The Wall put an end to that.

'Look at that man,' Frederika said scornfully.

A clean-cut American soldier marched smartly to a hut. A bigger guardhouse beyond, with a concrete watchtower, was where East Germany began. Vanishing inside, the sergeant reappeared seconds later, his message delivered. His eyes flicked to Frederika, missed Tom altogether and he was gone, climbing into a jeep to drive away. Frederika sucked her teeth.

'You dislike Americans?'

'Also the British and the French. How would you feel if we occupied New York and London and Paris?'

'You did occupy Paris.'

'I wasn't even born then,' she said sharply.

A taxi, half a dozen Beetles, a VW campervan and a

lonely looking Trabant waited to enter East Berlin; the road in the opposite direction being now almost empty. Pedestrians waited to cross no man's land.

'Declare any currency,' Frederika said.

Tom glanced across.

'And you must change fifty Deutschmarks. You have fifty Deutschmarks, don't you?' She waited for Tom to nod. 'Good. Also, no books, no newspapers, no religious pamphlets . . .'

Reaching into her jacket, she unfolded a letter purposefully. It was signed with a huge squiggle and stamped in red with the GDR emblem of a hammer and compass enclosed in a fat circle of rye.

'You have your passport?'

'Yes,' Tom said.

'And it looks like you?'

'A bit younger, a bit thinner.'

'If it doesn't look like you they'll turn you back.'

'It does,' Tom reassured her.

It took less than a minute for Tom to be waved through by a US sergeant. Frederika took longer, with the sergeant sending for an officer who studied her papers, studied her, made a quick telephone call and sent her through. By then Tom had been summoned by an East German guard, who'd grown nervous about Tom loitering between the West and East and letting others go ahead.

The man looked at Tom's passport carefully. Russia, Cuba, Bahamas, United States . . . He was reaching for a phone when Frederika appeared and he hesitated, returning her smile without even realizing.

'He's with me,' Frederika said.

At least that's what Tom thought she said.

Her German was too fast and too guttural for Tom to get more than a sense of it. And, by then, Frederika had moved on, producing her stamped piece of paper, which the man took almost reverently. He glanced at Tom, looked at Frederika and called for his officer. But only so his officer could read the letter.

'What was that about?' Tom asked, when they were through.

'We're not allowed to pass through that checkpoint. Our rule not yours. That order made an exception and granted me passage. It says we're travelling together on state business and you're a friend of the GDR.'

'Who signed it?'

She smiled. 'Erich Honecker.'

The East German premier himself had signed an order allowing Frederika to take Tom through a checkpoint forbidden to East Berliners? It could be a diplomatic nicety. A display of glasnost, the new openness. Then again, it might indicate that they wanted Cecil Blackburn out of their country. And Tom was *sans papiers*, without diplomatic status. He wondered if he should be worried.

More worried . . .

18

The cottage the young man needed was first on the left, and only a cottage in the sense that a six-bedroom Victorian house in Wiltshire, with three acres, stables and a derelict tennis court, was a cottage if it said so on the gate. Its drive was brick, the turning circle recently swept. A lawn to one side had rusting croquet hoops. A mallet was abandoned to dampening grass.

The young man rapped twice.

'Who is it?'

'Delivery,' he said.

'I didn't hear a van.'

'It's parked in the road.'

There was the click of a key and the clang of bolts. When the door finally opened it was still secured with a brass chain. The old man peering through adjusted his bifocals to get a better look. He was wearing cords, a twill shirt and a knitted tie. The young man could hear Radio 4 in the background, the government's Chief Scientific Advisor talking soothingly about Chernobyl.

'Let me turn that down,' the old man said.

When he got back, his visitor held up a bottle of whisky. The label made it look ordinary but from the way the old man stared it obviously wasn't.

'This is for you,' the young man said. 'And I'm to give you these.' He held up a large box of chocolates.

The old man looked puzzled.

Undoing the chain, he took the Talisker and put it on a table inside the door. Then he reached for the Milk Tray. Somewhere between reaching for it and feeling its weight, his face changed. Opening the box, he looked at the small silver revolver inside.

'Do I know you?' he asked.

'I don't think so,' the young man said.

'Did they tell you why I've been sent this?'

His visitor hesitated. The man who sent him had said nothing about how he should answer if asked that or any other question. He'd simply told him to put the bottle and chocolates into the colonel's hands.

'Yes,' he said.

'You'd better come in then.'

An elephant foot umbrella stand stood in the hall. An inlaid brass tray on a carved table held the keys for a Rover. An oil painting next to an ornate gilt mirror showed an attack on an Arab town. Armoured vehicles had gathered before the walls. Helicopters hung like birds over the distant hills.

'Helen liked it,' the old man said.

'Helen?'

'Didn't they tell you about my wife?'

'No, sir. I'm afraid not.'

The man looked at him sharply. 'Not just a delivery boy, then?'

'I'm not here to do the job. If that's your question.'

'But you would, if ordered?'

'Of course. You sold out men who trusted you to the communists. People died because of you. Good people. You're a traitor.'

'Ah. Is that what I am?'

Picking up the bottle, the old man walked into his dining room without waiting to see if his visitor would follow. He was taking two Waterford tumblers from an oak corner cabinet when the young man came in.

'I won't, sir.'

'You will. But don't worry. I'll wash up your glass, dry it and put it away before I do the decent thing . . .' He hesitated. 'There was a lot of it about, you know.'

'I'm sorry, sir?'

'This treachery of mine. Is that what they're going to say? I was a traitor? A man who killed himself when faced with arrest?'

'No, sir. I believe they'll announce you've been battling ill health.'

'Unsound mind?'

'Temporarily disturbed.'

'How simple you make it sound.'

Disappearing into another room, the old man returned with a photograph of a very young, very beautiful teenage girl in ATS uniform. 'Spring 1940,' he said. 'We hadn't even met then. We had an arrangement, you know. Later. Lots of war marriages didn't last. Ours did.'

'It's a beautiful photograph, sir.'

'She didn't know, you know. She didn't know any of it. We were more private about stuff in those days. I don't want anyone thinking she knew.'

'I don't imagine they do, sir.'

'Am I allowed to ask who sent you?'

'Best not.'

'I thought they'd forgotten me, you know. Either that, or

decided I wasn't important enough.' Picking up the little revolver, he looked at the Milk Tray box. 'A bit insulting, don't you think? It's hardly Charbonnel et Walker.'

His visitor wasn't sure if he was joking.

Flipping out the cylinder, the old man extracted a round. 'French-made, extinct calibre, old-issue ammunition. Exactly the kind of weapon an old fool like me might have kept as a memento.' He put the bullet on the dining-room table, flipped the cylinder, and looked for a maker's mark.

'Pre-war,' he said. He smiled. 'This is the point you should go.'

The young man looked at him.

'Don't worry. I'll lock the door behind you.' Picking up the photograph of his wife when young, the old man peered at it and shrugged. 'Tell your people there'll be no note. No plea for understanding. No request for forgiveness.'

Ushering his visitor into the hall, he nodded politely before shutting the door firmly behind him.

The report in *The Times* was brief and respectful.

Colonel James Foley, ex-REME, later Foreign Office, had killed himself while suffering depression following the death of his beloved wife. He'd been found by his gardener, who, unable to raise him, had walked round to a window and realized what had happened. There was no suggestion of foul play. Indeed, the front door had been so securely bolted the constabulary had to gain entry through a window at the back.

The coroner made much of a bullet left on the table, suggesting that Colonel Foley, being uncertain of his actions, had perhaps spun the cylinder to see if God would spare him the fate he wished on himself.

A Colonel FitzSymonds, described in court as a family friend, confirmed that this would be entirely consistent with what he knew of the man's temperament and faith. The verdict given was suicide while of unsound mind.

Lacking family, his son having died in the service of his country, the colonel was cremated and his ashes interred beside the body of his wife.

19

From the bridge, Nikolaiviertel – with its pretty little houses lining the riverfront – looked old and quaint. An unlikely survivor in a city mostly destroyed by bombs. A closer look by Tom revealed half-built steel frames in the shapes of houses, and lorries delivering pre-fabricated façades. Forty years after they were destroyed, East Berlin was putting its medieval buildings back.

After a fashion.

Workmen laid cobbles on to sand in front of taverns that looked hundreds of years old but were not yet finished. A photographer, in black roll neck and leather jacket, was getting in everyone's way.

A poster showed the area as it had been before Allied bombers reduced it to ruins. Another showed how it would look by the year's end. The smiling, strolling couples, with their laughing children and fashionable clothes, bore no resemblance to anybody Tom had seen so far.

East Berliners smiled, true enough. Like everyone else, they smiled at each other, at their children and dogs, and sometimes at nothing at all. And they certainly strolled . . . There was little of West Berlin's heads-down frenzy, and it seemed to Tom that this half of the city moved at an altogether slower pace. It was just that none of the cars he'd seen were this big and shiny. None of the people that well dressed. East Berlin had a drab conformity that reminded him of growing up in the 1950s.

Frederika gestured. 'Our brand-new historical district.'

'You disapprove?'

She shrugged. 'You have Disneyland,' she said. 'We have this.'

Tom was expecting her to walk with him to the door. Instead, she gave him Sir Cecil's address and told him, 'You can't miss it.'

'You're going somewhere?'

'I have to meet a friend.'

Tom watched her go, and when she turned back at the corner, it was to give him a wave that said she knew he'd understand. In her hand was the packet of fresh coffee she'd bought before leaving West Berlin.

What Tom sensed as he walked towards Nikolaiviertel was not the buildings being put up, but those missing. The squares and scruffy parks he'd passed through to reach here existed because constructing them was easier than replacing the buildings that once kept the edges of the gaps apart.

The city felt stunned and stunted.

This half of it anyway.

The other half felt desperate in its glitter; dancing to keep the darkness at bay. Tom wondered what would happen if the two halves ever joined. If the city would regain its soul, history and composure. Or if the rips in its psyche were too savage and its ghosts too unforgiving.

20

Sir Cecil's minder met Tom outside one of the few buildings in Nikolaiviertel to have survived the bombing. He
nodded to Tom's shadow, a pimply young man who was half-
heartedly lighting a cigarette against railings overlooking
the water's edge. The boy had been waiting beyond Checkpoint Charlie, cigarette butts littering the pavement at his
feet. His street skills were so bad Tom assumed he'd been
chosen to make sure the Englishman knew he was being
followed.

'I'll get rid of him in a moment,' the minder said.

'You knew I was on my way?' Tom asked.

'Frederika just telephoned.'

He saw Tom's expression and his lips twisted.

'Yes,' he said. 'We have call boxes . . .'

Whatever he said to Tom's shadow was effective because
the young man shrugged, flipped up the collar of his jacket
and sauntered away, obviously happy to have the afternoon to himself. Returning, the man said, 'So, what do
you think of this beautiful city?'

For a second, Tom was tempted by the truth.

Soberly dressed men in cheap suits. Drab women in
badly fitting dresses. Small boys in sandals with pudding-
bowl haircuts. Teenagers doing their best to look different.
It was the England of his childhood.

The man pushed out his hand. 'I'm Evgeny.'

'From Leningrad?'

The man's eyes widened. 'You speak Russian?'

'Enough to recognize your accent. Certainly enough to get by. And much better than I speak German. Although that's not hard.'

'Better than I speak English then.'

'You need it with Sir Cecil?'

'His Russian is non-existent. His German . . .' Evgeny wobbled his hand. 'His hearing is bad. His temper worse. We'd better go up. He's waiting. Although who knows exactly for what . . .'

Evgeny didn't seem the most contented of employees.

'Ex-army?' Tom asked. 'Paratroops?'

The man nodded slowly.

'What happened?'

'Shit happened.'

Since he was fit, had both his eyes, all his limbs and didn't limp, the shit had to be the other kind. 'Know the feeling,' Tom said.

Heavy glass doors led through to a high-ceilinged entrance hall with alternating black and white tiles and a staircase that spoke of old money. Each landing had a tall window overlooking the river, heavy gilt mirrors, paintings of forests and obligatory busts of Marx. This was where important people lived. It made Tom wonder about Sir Cecil's neighbours. Mostly, it made him wonder why they didn't object to the music blasting from the top flat. Shostakovich, from the sound of it. 'Let me turn that down,' Evgeny said.

Sir Cecil stood at the head of the stairs, smiling benignly.

His hand was already out to envelop Tom's. First one soft hand, then another, as he did that double shake meant to indicate friendship or power. He was older than his pictures, in a lightweight tweed jacket, cotton shirt and needle-cords.

'I'm Cecil Blackburn,' he said. Although he must have been aware that Tom didn't need to be told. Peering over Tom's shoulder, he said, 'Frederika . . .'

'Had to run an errand,' Evgeny said.

Sir Cecil sighed.

Tom was led into a room that looked as if it belonged to an Oxbridge college. There was a Persian rug, frayed at both ends and threadbare in one corner. A leather sofa had a Turkish throw across the back. A Moroccan poof had camel stitching and hide so waxed it was black. Empty packing cases lined one wall. An old-fashioned typewriter stood on a table, with a sheet of paper ostentatiously left in the roller. A fat typescript sat beside it.

'My memoirs,' Sir Cecil said.

'You've finished them?' Tom asked.

'All except the appendices.'

Tom looked beyond the typewriter and froze.

'Isn't she striking?' Sir Cecil said.

It wasn't the oval miniature of a heavily jawed woman that had stopped Tom in his tracks. It was the toy car by its side. He'd had one of those once. Despite himself, he bent to take a closer look.

'Jaguar 2.4,' Sir Cecil said.

'Original?'

'Of course,' Sir Cecil said. 'I collect them. I was going to give you this later.' He pulled a tiny Trabant from his pocket. It had a cream body and doors that opened, jewelled headlights and slightly tinted windows.

'Thank you,' Tom said.

He pushed the model car deep into his pocket.

'A souvenir from East Berlin. It's not Corgi, of course. I have more toy cars in the study, if you're interested.'

'There'll be time for that later.' Frederika stood in the doorway. She looked altogether more relaxed than earlier.

'You managed to get my coffee?'

'Not this trip.' She smiled brightly. 'But I definitely will next time. I'm off to have a shower. Why don't you two discuss our move to London while Evgeny makes you some tea?'

That was the last anyone saw of her for an hour. And when she did reappear, it was to say she'd been asked to take a class. So could Evgeny drive her to the gymnasium and wait? She'd be back in time for supper.

21

The route to the restaurant where Sir Cecil wanted to eat took them past the Soviet embassy, which turned out to be the bastard child of a Babylonian ziggurat and one of Stalin's famous wedding cakes. A building so solid it squatted like a sullen toad. Tom couldn't deny it was imposing, though. It reminded him of the Masonic Temple in central London; although he doubted that his father-in-law would thank him for observing the likeness.

'And now for the Gate.'

'My love. He doesn't want the full tour.'

'Of course he does.' Sir Cecil pulled an envelope triumphantly from his pocket. 'I've acquired permission.'

Frederika looked across, and Tom noticed Evgeny's shoulders stiffen. The Russian was in the front, his eyes more on what was happening in the back of the car than on any danger from outside.

'A short stop,' Sir Cecil said. 'Then supper.'

The driver had obviously known all along where they were going because he pulled up at a stone guardhouse.

'I'll just have a quick word,' Sir Cecil said.

A green-uniformed sergeant stamped out. His hand was on his rifle but the fact it was an official car gave him pause. He listened to what Sir Cecil said, listened again because he obviously hadn't understood it the first time, and disappeared.

The officer he returned with was the one who had barriers moved so they could reach the ruined grandeur of the Brandenburg Gate.

Beyond the Gate stood the Wall, constructed from concrete slabs and topped with rusting metal. Behind them, tank traps cut off Unter den Linden, the impressively grand boulevard they'd driven down.

'The Gate looks lonely,' Frederika said.

Tom had to agree with her.

'Seen enough?' Sir Cecil asked.

Six guards, a watchtower, the Gate's shabby greatness and the Wall itself, sweeping out in a half-circle so as not to cramp the triumphal arch that had been cramped by barriers anyway. Tom nodded.

'Good,' Sir Cecil said. 'Then let's eat.'

The restaurant was on the corner with Friedrichstrasse, opposite the site of a half-built hotel intended to be several times larger than London's Savoy. A vast hoarding showed an artist's impression. The East German flag flew proudly from the hotel's huge roof, smart black limousines were drawn up in a line, uniformed commissionaires ushered fur-clad guests inside.

'For foreigners,' Frederika said. 'Hard currency only. It will have its own gymnasium, an Olympic-sized swimming pool, a beauty salon . . .'

'And Stasi,' Sir Cecil said. 'Lots of Stasi.'

'You haven't left yet,' Frederika said.

'Ah yes,' said Sir Cecil. 'Of course. They're my friends. Aren't they, Evgeny? You'll be sure to tell them that, won't you? And I really do need to talk to Tom about this suggestion that I return.'

Suggestion?

Sir Cecil saw Tom watching him and smiled blandly.

Inside the restaurant, a party of middle-aged men looked up and one waved. Frederika smiled and waved back. Her limp was less obvious, and Tom realized she was working hard not to let it show. A glass of Rotkäppchen Sekt appeared the moment Sir Cecil sat, and disappeared just as quickly. Sliding from the shadows, a waiter refilled his glass. 'They know me,' Sir Cecil said.

Tom wondered if he meant the waiters or the other diners. Given the obvious size of the man's ego, quite possibly he meant both.

'You know why we came here?'

Sir Cecil was addressing Tom, obviously enough.

'It's not bugged. You know why? Because we're all good party members. Senior ones at that. God forbid anything we say goes on record.' He reached for the menu and Frederika caught Tom's gaze, shrugged and reached for a menu in turn, skimming it with the carelessness of someone who knew it by heart.

'You're a party member?'

'Long term,' Sir Cecil said.

'They back-dated his membership,' Frederika said sourly. 'To when he said he first became a communist.' She looked at Sir Cecil. 'Wasn't that what you told me? He told me a lot of things, you know. In the early days.'

Sir Cecil scowled at her.

Evgeny poured Frederika the water she asked for, his fingers just brushing hers as he steadied her glass. It could be accidental. Then again . . . A bottle of Riesling and a bottle of Bulgarian red arrived shortly after.

They didn't help Sir Cecil's mood either.

He sat sullen and silent, only speaking to vent his out-rage about whatever imagined insult or privation came to mind. Tom wondered if he'd noticed Evgeny's fingers brush Frederika's hand, because whatever had upset Black-burn it wasn't the things he was talking about. At one point he was almost shaking with fury. A moment later he looked close to tears.

'You know the waiting list for a Trabant?' he asked sud-denly. 'Thirteen years. For a two-stroke you wouldn't use to power a lawnmower.'

'They gave you a Trabant?'

'Of course they didn't give me a bloody Trabant. They gave me an EMW.' Sir Cecil saw Tom's puzzlement and sighed. 'East German version of a pre-war roadster. Beautiful machine. Should be. They stole BMW's assem-bly line.'

Silence returned for as long as it took Sir Cecil to finish his Swabian stew, which he did with angry mouthfuls he appeared not to taste and which sometimes fell from his fork, landing back on the plate.

That done, he launched into a dissertation on the Hohen-zollern family, Berlin's rise under Frederick the Great, its glory years as Bismarck's capital, how it defined the newly created German empire. He stopped with the abdication of the Kaiser, which was either unusually delicate of him or the end of his historical interest. Tom suspected the latter.

The Kaiser's abdication coincided with the arrival of a tray of Königsberger marzipan; and that Sir Cecil *did* taste, closing his eyes to savour each mouthful and looking disappointed to find the dish finally empty. The waiter asked if they wanted coffee and Sir Cecil rejected the offer without asking the others first. Then he pushed back his chair, and hesitated . . .

Here it comes, Tom thought.

Everything about the meal had been strained.

'What?' Frederika asked.

'I've changed my mind,' Sir Cecil said. He sat back in his chair, looking old and suddenly obstinate. The way he folded his arms suggested he never intended to move again.

'You want coffee after all?'

'No, you little fool. About London. I'm not going. I'm staying here.'

22

Writing out the phone number, Tom pushed the form across the wooden counter in the Palasthotel's reception and watched the receptionist pick up a telephone to get clearance to place the call. A few seconds later the telephone rang and he watched her glance at him and wondered what the Stasi officer on the other end said.

There couldn't have been many guests who asked her to place a call to a member of the British government. The call would be recorded. There was nothing strange in that. Tom imagined that all calls in and out of the Palasthotel were recorded. The same went for all East German hotels.

'I'm sorry for waking you,' Tom said.

'Everything all right?'

'I'm calling from the Palasthotel.'

Silence greeted his statement. If the conversation wasn't being recorded at Eddington's end before this, it was now.

'You're in a room?'

'In a bank of phone boxes next to reception.'

'I see . . . How are things going?'

'This evening was a little less fun than I expected.'

Tom could almost hear his father-in-law wonder how to frame the next question.

'Anything in particular?' he asked finally.

'I've never really liked cold feet.'

'Cold feet?'

'Frozen.'

'Oh God . . .'

'I wouldn't make any arrangements for a welcome-home party,' Tom said, 'because, as things stand, you'll be missing guests.'

'Christ, Tom . . .'

'Not everyone wants to come.'

'I don't have to tell you who has an interest in this.'

The Prime Minister. Yes, he'd said. The Prime Minister, the Foreign Secretary and the Intelligence services. Tom's father-in-law too, for reasons he hadn't really made clear. Unless pleasing the PM was enough.

It was for half her Cabinet.

Tom hadn't forgotten how his job had expanded from accompanying Sir Cecil to bringing him back at all costs. He needed to know how that actually translated.

'We could cancel the party games,' Eddington said suddenly. 'If that's the problem. Perhaps even have presents.'

'No tears before bedtime?'

Eddington hesitated. 'Bloody man. Do his friends know about this?'

He thought about what he'd just asked and answered his own question. 'Of course they do. And if they don't, they will soon . . .'

Two days after the meal at Casper's on Unter den Linden, a butterfly fluttered against the glass of a window in Nikolaiviertel, increasingly frantic to find its way blocked to the world outside. Stunned, it dropped to the window-sill and rested there, wings quivering. Then it rose and skittered up the glass, brought short once again by the top of the window. This time it crawled over the lip and found itself free, in the brightness of a Berlin afternoon, where a stiff river breeze cooled Nikolaiviertel, and teenagers crossed the bridge towards Spandauer Strasse, having just been released from school.

The house into which it had ventured and from which it had just escaped was older than most; much older than the replicas around it. It had survived fires, riots and floods, and all that before the First War came, never mind the Second. A war so terrible few other buildings survived unscathed.

The butterfly knew nothing of this.

It was three days from dying, and already in the embers of its life, having hatched from a chrysalis three weeks earlier. Caught on the breeze, it let itself be swept westwards, past the Komische Oper and over Potsdamer Platz and the wasteland both sides of the Wall. It landed in Tiergarten, West Berlin's famous park, and settled on the wrist of a child, who froze in delight and was quieter and stiller in those few seconds than she'd been all day.

And then, refreshed, it took off again and headed for the bright blaze of a flower. On the small girl's wrist it left pollen, soot and infinitesimal traces of the human blood on which it had been feeding all those miles and minutes before.

24

There were a number of things that Frau Eisen didn't like about the English woman she'd been ordered to meet at Schönefeld airport, and deliver to Comrade Sir Cecil Blackburn's house in Nikolaiviertel, so she could accompany her father home to London. Her clothes were a disgrace for a start.

No woman her age should go without a bra.

Obviously, the human body was a marvellous thing, and skinny-dipping, naturist beaches and naked camps were an integral part of East German life, for young people comfortable with that kind of thing. But a teenager who went out dressed like this would be in trouble.

That a grown woman . . .

The stern-faced Stasi officer sniffed. Amelia Blackburn might not be wearing a bra. She was, however, wearing patchouli, black lipstick, torn jeans and a T-shirt with a tiger on it. Her army boots had flowers painted on them, which Frau Eisen regarded as the final insult. Nonetheless, from the moment she met Amelia's flight at noon until now, as they walked between workmen laying cobbles on the riverfront at Nikolaiviertel, she'd performed her task with quiet efficiency.

Dr Amelia Blackburn had hated her on sight.

When the German woman put her finger to Sir Cecil's doorbell, Amelia said, 'I'll go up by myself. There's bound to be a café where you can wait.'

Frau Eisen shook her head.

'We go up together.'

Amelia Blackburn scowled.

She barely remembered her father, having been thirteen when he left, and already at boarding school. She was twenty-eight now and not sure why anyone, especially her mother, would want him back. She'd been in Kiev, taking a year out from Imperial, studying wolves, when Chernobyl imploded. She should be there now, recording the effects of the fallout, not letting herself be blackmailed into going to Berlin to play happy families.

Hold his hand when you get off the plane.

When she'd asked her mother if she was serious, Amelia had been reminded that appearances mattered. They did. Amelia was willing to admit that. They just didn't matter in the way her mother imagined. Ten years of studying and teaching Zoology had taught her that.

'I'll go up by myself,' Amelia said firmly.

Before Frau Eisen could answer, the door opened and a leather-jacketed man blinked to see them. Thrusting his hand into his pocket, he pushed rudely between them, put his head down and strode towards a bronze statue of St George killing the dragon, which workers were repairing.

Frau Eisen stared angrily after him.

'Which floor?' Amelia asked her.

The Stasi woman consulted a red file.

The first two floors seemed entirely normal. On the third, a woman came to the door when she heard steps, decided they weren't who she expected and went back inside. On the fourth, an old man at the bottom of the stairs to the fifth simply stepped back without a word.

'I saw nothing,' he said.

Frau Eisen hesitated. 'Wait here,' she told Amelia.

'No way.' Pushing past her, Amelia hurried up the last flight of stairs and stopped abruptly at the feral stink. She'd been around animals most of her adult life. She recognized the smell of death, both natural and violent. This smelt of predators and predated. Of blood, flesh and voided bowels.

The door to her father's flat had been crowbarred open. A man lay just inside. He was young, shaven-headed and thickset.

'Don't touch,' Frau Eisen ordered.

Amelia ignored that too.

There was blood on the back of his skull, a dressing-gown cord tight around his neck. His face was purple and his tongue protruded. A puddle of urine spread around him. Amelia wondered how quickly he'd died. His broken fingernails said not quickly enough. She checked for a pulse anyway.

'Dead,' she pronounced, stepping over him.

In the sitting room, embers glowed in the hearth despite that afternoon's heat. The ghost image of burnt pages still visible in their ash.

'*Scheisse*,' Frau Eisen said. Grabbing a poker, she hooked at the ash, cursing as the ghost pages disintegrated, black butterflies rising in a flock.

It was the body in the study that stopped Amelia in her tracks.

She didn't scream or burst into tears. She simply put up a hand to try to catch the vomit that splattered through her fingers. Shock, she told herself. 'You shouldn't be here,' Frau Eisen told her.

Amelia couldn't help herself.

The crowbar used to break the front door's lock had been used on her father's head. In case that wasn't enough, its hooked end was buried in his chest. He'd been hit there more than once to judge from the pulp where his ribs should be. Blood was blackening the carpet beneath him.

His room was in ruins.

A Chinese vase had been smashed. A leather armchair was savagely torn where someone had sunk the crowbar into its arm and ripped it free. Did that mean her father had been sitting, Amelia wondered. A collection of toy cars littered the floor like wrecks in a junkyard. Framed pictures of Premier Honecker and her father lay smashed to splinters, torn paper and shards of glass.

Frau Eisen reached for the study telephone and hesitated.

Shrugging, she pulled a handkerchief from her pocket, wrapped it around her hand, and lifted the receiver, dialling through to her office. It was the Stasi rather than the local Volkspolizei she called. Amelia's German was good enough to understand that. Frau Eisen was talking to her boss from the sound of it.

'No point, sir,' Frau Eisen said.

Someone on the other end spoke firmly.

'Of course, sir. I should have thought of that.' Putting down the phone, she turned to Amelia. 'I am to tell you that your father has had a heart attack.'

'He's what!' Amelia stared at her.

'He has had a heart attack. An ambulance will be here soon to take him to hospital. We will put a notice to that effect in the papers.'

'He's been murdered.'

'It would be best if we agreed he's ill.'

'Best for whom?'

'For everyone,' Frau Eisen said firmly.

Amelia shut her eyes and opened them again.

Her father looked old and fragile, his cheeks sunken, his hands as liver-spotted as his face. His nose had spider veins and his eyes were cloudy. He stank of old age as well as death. She wondered what he'd hoped to gain by uprooting everybody's life at this age.

Somehow, she'd expected him to be younger.

If she'd thought of him at all, it was as the age he'd been when he defected. Still handsome, his hair still thick and swept back, his face strong and without jowls. That was how he looked in the photograph the papers used. It was how he'd look in the photograph they'd use when they came to write . . .

'We must go,' Frau Eisen said.

'I'll just . . .'

Frau Eisen shook her head. 'This a crime scene.'

For a heart attack, Amelia wanted to say. She controlled herself.

25

Antoine le Clerc was on the ninth day of a six-day package holiday, which was three days longer than he could afford. And it wasn't really a holiday anyway. Travelling as a tourist had been easier than admitting he was a photojournalist and trying to wrangle a work visa. He'd thought that extending his stay would be cheap, East Berlin being communist and all, but the rate of exchange was murderous, and he lacked the nerve to use the black market, even though he'd smuggled in $100 for that very purpose.

In his rucksack he carried a worthy-looking paperback on *Plattenbau*, the East German system of constructing apartments from concrete slabs. The cameras in his bag were not those for photographing buildings, however.

His 35mm Leica, with its red dot painted out, was his go-anywhere/pass-unnoticed item of choice. He had a Nikon SLR too, although he'd had to leave his fuck-off telephoto at home. He'd fitted it with an innocuous 35–105mm Nikkor, stacked up on thirty-six-exp fine-grain, and trusted to good light, God and his developer. The camera he wore in public was a 35mm Praktica.

Nothing should be read into that. He'd bought it secondhand because it was East German and he hoped it would give him a talking point if stopped by the Volkspolizei. So far he'd been lucky.

His fear was that this wouldn't last.

Four days ago his Stasi shadow didn't turn up until lunchtime.

The day after that, after Antoine bought himself a Lenin badge and a biography in English of Premier Honecker, and spent the entire afternoon in a café, religiously reading the biography, this shadow hadn't bothered to show up at all. Antoine imagined he was at home, filling out fake reports that read *took photographs, took photographs, took photographs, boring, boring, boring* . . .

So now Antoine was eleven floors up, in a poky little *Plattenbau* flat overlooking Nikolaiviertel. The flat had been assigned to the grandmother of the receptionist from his hotel. The bed behind him was a ruin of stained sheets, the sink stacked with dirty crockery, the grandmother with her brother in the country, and the girl dressed and safely back at the hotel for her afternoon shift.

When three women, the last of them a famously reclusive East German gymnast he'd only just seen rush in, exited Sir Cecil's apartment beside stretcher-bearers, Antoine realized his luck had changed. The man on the stretcher wore an oxygen mask and had a surgical cap tied under his chin.

The little party stopped at the rear doors of an ambulance, and Antoine made himself slow the shots down. The gymnast's face was in ruins. Mascara streaking her cheeks and her mouth twisted in despair.

Syndication rights.

He could buy himself a new car with what that shot would earn.

Antoine had come to Berlin to get pap shots of Sir Cecil. His best hope had been to capture the traitor with his daughter, preferably leaving for the airport.

Now . . .

Taking a final shot as the ambulance pulled away, with a police car in front and another behind, Antoine wound back his film, flipped open the camera and removed the canister, loading new film from habit.

Looking up, he saw a second stretcher.

There were no paramedics this time, no police, no flashing lights and no oxygen mask. Simply an arm dangling over the side, and a sheet drawn up to indicate he was dead. No ambulance, either. Two men stashed him in a baker's van. By then, Antoine had fired off all thirty-six frames and was reloading. All he needed now was to get himself out of East bloody Berlin.

Buy himself a car? He'd be able to afford a house.

Antoine didn't simply have the shots this time. He had the story, and a big one.

26

The first thing that Tom did on returning from Sir Cecil's was order himself a bottle of Riesling. He made sure the receptionist understood he wanted it well chilled. And then, his wine having been delivered to his room at the Palasthotel, he removed the bottle from its bucket and pushed his fist into the ice.

After dealing with his burnt hand, he washed down four paracetamol, demolished three handfuls of peanuts, and sat back to think through what he'd just found. Sir Cecil and Evgeny dead and no sign of Frederika.

He'd looked, fearing that he'd find her murdered too.

But the flat was a ruin, Frederika nowhere to be found, and Sir Cecil's memoir in flames in the fireplace. He'd no sooner finished looking for her than the buzzer announced visitors at the main door. The two women he'd seen on his way out, mostly likely.

Sir Cecil's being threatened. We need to meet – Frederika.

That was the note that had drawn Tom there. Had she fled? Had she been taken? He doubted she'd been killed. At least, not there. And if she had, it was cleanly and her body had been removed.

That's what a professional might have done.

Neither Sir Cecil's nor Evgeny's murder had looked professional though. Tom wondered whether either of the women at the door had got a good look at him. With luck they hadn't and he'd taken care, both coming and going, to check that he wasn't being followed. As much as anyone, even someone with his background, could be entirely certain of that in a place like East Berlin.

Pouring himself a glass of the Riesling, Tom began to examine the scrap he'd dragged from the fireplace in Sir Cecil's flat. The half-page was singed and blackened, its words single-spaced and typed on a manual. There was no smudging on the rear to suggest the person typing used carbon paper.

Appendix 13: The Importance of being Lady Windermere by Messrs Blackburn & Wakefield. It appeared to be a cast list.

Uncle Max – Freddie Brannon
Violet – James Foley
Aunt Agatha – Robby Croft
Philodendron – Cecil Blackburn
Flo – Anthony Willes-Wakefield
Little Peter – Henry Petty

Tom recognized Sir Cecil's name, obviously. Willes-Wakefield, he'd been a society doctor who disappeared, no one knew where. Henry Petty's *Hamlet* at the National was famous. As for Lord Brannon, anyone over a certain age remembered the outrage that greeted his murder. Photographs of his grandchildren walking behind his coffin had been everywhere. As had a shot of splinters of dinghy floating on the lake.

It should have been obvious they'd know each other. Men of that background invariably did. If this was the standard of the rest of his memoirs they hardly seemed worth burning. Never mind killing their author with a crowbar.

Blinded – saw something he shouldn't. Tongue cut out – said something he shouldn't. Ears removed – heard something he shouldn't. Hands off – took something he shouldn't. Bollocks gone – that one was obvious. Staving in someone's chest with a crowbar didn't suggest a message.

It suggested panic or fury.

Perhaps both.

And there was Evgeny. Soviet ex-Para. Built like a brick shithouse and too young to have run to fat. Tom could have taken him, maybe. He wouldn't have looked forward to it though. There were only two ways to get a ligature round someone like Evgeny's neck: have unusual speed and skills, or have him trust you. So . . . one of Evgeny's own? KGB? Possibly Stasi?

Tom tried to remember more about the two women entering Sir Cecil's building. One definitely wore Stasi uniform, the other had flowery boots. If he could remember that much, chances were they'd remember something about him.

That thought didn't make Tom feel any better.

Who gained from Sir Cecil's death? Who lost? That was the question he needed to answer. Did the GDR gain in not losing a famous defector? Did they lose in not ridding themselves cleanly of someone they might want off their hands? They'd been at pains to say they respected Sir Cecil's decision. That could be a bluff, of course. How about the Brits? Did London want to save itself the embarrassment of putting him on trial?

Much simpler to refuse to let him return.

And Eddington, Tom's father-in-law, had seemed entirely genuine in his desire that Tom should change Sir Cecil's mind about not leaving. He'd need to call Eddington later. That would be a fun conversation. Assuming Tom could find a way to word it to give Eddington the bad news without making it obvious to the Stasi that Tom already knew.

Could Sir Cecil's family have been behind it?

Revenge for his desertion, distaste at the thought of his return, greed in not wanting to share any wealth he'd left behind? All possible, but who would they have found to kill him for them? Far easier to express disgust and simply disown the man. If not Sir Cecil's family, how about his friends?

Three police investigations into Patroclus might be hard to fix, but not impossible. A lot could turn on the strictures put on the enquiries. What if Patroclus still existed? Well-connected, far-reaching, spider-like . . .

Sir Cecil had been careful to mention the name in his letter to *The Times*. What if Sir Cecil's old friends weren't keen to see him return?

It took reception several minutes to connect him.

'How are the party preparations going?' Eddington asked. 'Any closer to arranging transport for our guest?'

For a second, Tom almost told the truth, but it was an open line and telling Eddington what he knew would be telling the Stasi that he knew it too. He wasn't here in any official capacity. It felt too big a risk to take.

'I'm working on it.'

'I knew we could rely on you. Anything I can do?'

'Do you know if all the guests want everyone to come?'

Tom listened to the silence as Eddington tried to unpick that. 'You mean,' Caro's father said, 'might some not like the latest invitation?'

'Slightly stronger than that.'

'Ah. Might some of them object to there being a party at all?'

'Yes,' Tom said. 'That's it exactly.'

'It's possible,' Eddington said. 'Shall I ask around?'

'Keep it discreet,' Tom said. He took a deep breath, wondering how close he dared come to the truth. 'Look,' he said. 'It's possible they may get their wish. The party may need . . .'

'Postponing?'

'Cancelling even.'

'Dear gods, Tom . . .'

'I'm going to call Caro now.'

'She's out.'

Tom wanted to ask how Eddington knew that.

'What time's she back?' he asked.

Caro's father hesitated. He knew that Tom had noted the slight hesitation because his answer was altogether too abrupt. 'No idea, I'm afraid.'

When Tom returned from taking a shower, his bedside telephone was ringing. 'Caro?' he said.

'This is Henderson. Where have *you* been?'

'Having a shower.'

'You've seen the news?'

'What news?'

'Sir Cecil's had a heart attack.'

'*A what?*'

'It's just been reported on GDR TV. His daughter flew in to bring him home and found him on the floor. Apparently, she's in hospital, sedated. So they're saying.'

Fuck, Tom thought. *Flowery boots.*

'His daughter?'

'I know. When did you last see him?'

It was a day for lying. 'The night he told me he'd changed his mind. I've been trying to fix a meeting ever since. With Frederika saying tomorrow, tomorrow, tomorrow . . .'

'We've asked the GDR for an update.'

'I should get back to West Berlin.'

'Good idea,' Henderson said. 'No . . . Wait.'

Tom could hear the words, *Yes, I'm sure*, down the line. 'We've just heard Amelia Blackburn's been released. They've put her in a car back to the Palasthotel. Perhaps it's worth your trying to have a word with her.'

And if she recognizes me?

'Look,' Tom said. 'Her father's just,' he caught himself, 'had a heart attack. I doubt she'll be hanging round the bar.'

'I'd be in the bar if I'd found my father like that.'

And so would I, Tom thought, *celebrating probably.*

'Go see,' Henderson said. 'Find out if he told her anything about his memoirs.'

Tom thought of the pile of ash in the fireplace. 'All right,' he said. 'I'll go down now.' He said it more to get Henderson off the phone than from any belief Amelia Blackburn might show up.

'Let me know if you discover anything.'

'Will do,' Tom said.

'It can wait until tomorrow.'

In other words, don't for God's sake say anything over the phone with a tape spinning and a Stasi clerk standing by to translate it, type it up and pass it on to her boss the moment the call's done. Which was exactly what would happen with the conversation they'd just had. Henderson had mentioned Blackburn's memoirs. Tom wondered if that was intentional and decided it must be. He spent the rest of his way downstairs wondering why.

27

The moment Tom settled into a banquette in a darkened corner of the Palasthotel's main bar, a pretty blonde girl slid herself on to the red velvet bench beside him. She was wearing an evening dress cut to show her breasts and a smile so knowing it looked practised. Her English was good though.

'Aren't you going to buy me a drink?'

Tom put his hand on her knee, slid it a few inches higher and felt her freeze. Her smile relaxed itself a few moments later. She leant in close and let her dress fall away. Her nipples were sharp and he could see to her navel.

'You see those two over there?' Tom said.

She looked towards the table he indicated.

'They're Australian. They were talking last night about how easy it is to make a profit out of you lot because you don't really know how the market works. They're signing a big contract soon. Apparently the price you quoted them is ridiculously cheap. They'd have been willing to pay fifty per cent more.'

The young woman looked at him.

Tom shrugged apologetically. He felt sorry for her and that didn't make him like himself any better. Either she was a prostitute, and that was a hard way to earn a living, or she was Stasi, and he wasn't sure that wasn't worse. Especially if her orders involved following the deception through to the end.

'Australians are richer too,' Tom added.

Just in case she really was a working girl.

After she'd gone, he ordered himself a Glenfiddich and a small jug of tap water, tipping a splash of it into his whisky glass as he watched her settle beside the two Australians. One of the men suggested they swap places. After which she sat between them.

Stasi, Tom decided.

She was trying much harder than she had with him.

That was good. Very good. It meant the Stasi hadn't nailed him as the man coming out of Sir Cecil's flat when Sir Cecil's daughter was waiting to go in. If they had . . . it wouldn't be a girl in a bar they sent across. It would be police, armed and unforgiving. And he'd be heading for a court where the verdict had probably been decided in advance. Tom tried to remember if East Germany had the death penalty. He had a nasty feeling they probably did.

28

'I think you should see this, sir.'

Henderson's assistant put the copy of *France Soir* on his desk.

A huge photograph on the front page showed Amelia Blackburn, face stricken and eyes haunted. A stern-faced Stasi woman stood opposite. Underneath were smaller photographs. Two of stretchers. The man with the oxygen mask must be Sir Cecil. The other undoubtedly his minder.

Henderson chewed his lip. Some heart attack.

'Go,' he told her.

His assistant went.

An ambulance stood in the shadow of a huge bronze of St George killing the dragon, and in the shadow of St George's horse, his hands pushed into his pockets, stood Tom Fox. 'Oh fuck,' Henderson said.

He peered at the shapes on the stretchers. The oxygen mask over Sir Cecil's face was obviously supposed to make people believe he was alive. Maybe he was alive? Henderson's moment of hope faded as he re-examined the minder's stretcher. Blackburn carried out following a heart attack, while simultaneously and entirely coincidentally, his minder's dead body disappears into a baker's van?

'Sir . . .' His assistant was in the doorway.

'What?' Henderson's face darkened.

'Apparently, *France Soir* have a photograph of Amelia

Blackburn face to face with Tom Fox, whom they've identified. They're running it tomorrow. Our ambassador in East Berlin has just been asked for a quote. He's also been asked to present himself to the GDR's Ministry of Foreign Affairs.'

Henderson put his head in his hands.

'He's told *France Soir* he knows nothing about this at all. He's told the East Germans that the man in the photograph looks East German to him. Off the record, he wants to know if you knew.'

'Knew what?' Henderson demanded.

'That Major Fox was here to kill Sir Cecil, I imagine.'

29

Dr Hall was old when he arrived at the school in the autumn of 1958, desiccated like a dried insect and slightly stooped as if trying to hide his height. He was the only master who ever wore a gown. He was told, the boys overheard, that gowns were no longer necessary and Irongate Hall was, in any case, not really that kind of school. It was state-funded, dedicated to providing education to children of difficult families. The kind of children who ended up here because nowhere else would take them. And he'd nodded, and smiled to show he understood, and turned up next morning for Latin in his gown just the same.

The day he died he took Classics for a double lesson in the morning, umpired a rugger game for the under-elevens from the touchline, and stripped the carburettor on his new, very red and very shiny Austin-Healey Sprite, a sports car so small that no boy knew how Dr Hall fitted inside.

After that, he played the organ at evensong. A wheezing bellows of a machine that gasped and thudded its way through 'The Day Thou Gavest Lord Has Ended' ... A short while after, he retired to his room at the foot of the bell tower that had been a classroom in its day and had a heavy oak door scarred from decades of long-gone boys throwing knives.

Inside, he made himself tea, read a little Catullus, and

retired to a hot bath in the tiny bathroom next door, where he opened his wrists, having carefully placed the chrome parts of the Gillette safety razor on a shelf above his basin.

He left Albinoni's *Adagio* playing on a Bush record-player, although by the time he was found next morning the LP had long since played out and simply turned, the crackle of the needle sounding like static.

One thing went unmentioned in the list given to the police of things Dr Hall had done that day in the hours leading up to his unexpected suicide. Between playing the organ for evensong and retiring for a bath he had made tea for two. The boy who drank the second cup, and left without saying goodbye, was eleven, already regarded as a troublemaker.

The headmaster, a New Zealander who'd left his home country for reasons never disclosed to the board of trustees, had called the boy to his study and asked him if he had anything to say.

'About what, sir?'

'Why Dr Hall sent for you?'

The eleven-year-old had looked at the headmaster and said nothing. The headmaster was aware that the police had announced their intention to speak to the boys. Something the boy had overheard or deduced for himself.

It was rare for lambs to escape the fold.

Rare, but not impossible.

Looking into the dark eyes of the boy in front of him, who stood in the awkward wastelands between childhood and adolescence, the headmaster knew he'd misjudged his charge. It was the boy's question that decided him.

'When exactly are the police coming back, sir?'

It was a dangerous moment. The boy was not aware then how dangerous. But he knew he was taking a risk and that not showing fear was his key to surviving.

The headmaster stood slowly, pushing back his chair and edging himself round the desk, stopping to half sit on the desk, his face pushed very close to Tom's. His bottom lip had thinned to a tight line and his eyes were murderous.

The boy kept very still.

He breathed through his mouth to spare himself the stink of the man's breath, and didn't flinch. He didn't blink either.

He didn't dare.

The two of them stared at each other, and then the headmaster sat back, his eyes lost their blackness and he waved the boy from his room.

Both left with their questions unanswered. The day the police came back to interview Dr Hall's class, the boy and three others were on a route march over the Downs with their Geography teacher. They camped under a beech tree by a river, ate beechnuts from the ground, smoked a Capstan each, which the master pretended not to notice, and returned next morning with sore feet, mosquito bites and woodsmoke in their hair.

The headmaster left at the end of that term and was replaced by the Geography teacher. The reason for Dr Hall's suicide was never explained. The letter that the boy swore to Dr Hall he'd written to the police, and posted in the village rather than having it inspected first and posted by his house tutor, was neither answered nor acted upon. It had never been written. Tom Fox told the school padre this under the seal of confession.

30

The two Volkspolizei guarding the door of Sir Cecil's apartment block stopped mid-conversation as a leather-jacketed man strode towards them, his contemptuous glance already dismissing them. He was hard-faced and his hair looked recently cropped. His cheeks were hollow, and dark circles suggested he hadn't slept in days. He wore black leather gloves, his jacket was battered and he stank of cheap vodka and even cheaper cigarettes.

He barked a demand in Russian and when they didn't move quickly enough strode up the steps and rattled the handle.

'KGB,' he said.

One of them hurried forward.

He slammed the door behind him, grateful, it seemed, to be rid of the sight of fools, and stamped up the wide stair-case. A woman, still in her nightdress, looked out from a flat on the first floor, opened her mouth to ask a question, changed her mind and went inside. Tom was glad. He hoped she hadn't got a good look at him.

He'd woken to his name on a radio in the next room.

Someone listening to Radio Free Berlin or whatever this year's West German propaganda programme was called. Paranoia had taken him to the window and shown him police gathering in a car park below. Dressing faster than he'd have thought possible, he'd chosen his most anonymous clothes, and let himself out through a service door at the back, carrying a bin for disguise.

The question was what he should do next.

He couldn't simply turn up at the British embassy on Unter den Linden. That would be a disaster. This wasn't Moscow. This time round he was *sans papiers*, without credentials, certainly without the kind that might persuade an ambassador to spirit him out of the country rather than just hand him over.

If Tom had been our man in East Berlin, he'd have been on to the Politburo denying responsibility. *God, no, nothing to do with us.*

That was the truth of it too.

And Tom could go that route. *God, no, nothing to do with me. I just happened to stumble over the bodies. Frederika sent me a message saying we needed to talk. She didn't say when, so I thought I'd drop by to see if she was there . . .*

He could really see that working.

Would Caro's father believe he'd done it?

Worse still, would Caro? Tom wanted to call her to say that it wasn't him. All that would do, though, was to help the Stasi pinpoint his location. As things stood, he couldn't get a message to London, had little chance of the Stasi assuming he was innocent, and had no diplomatic status and so no immunity.

Plus. He was the wrong side of the Wall.

What really frustrated Tom was that Sir Cecil's murder made no sense. The East Germans didn't need to kill the man to prevent him leaving. They could simply refuse permission. And why would London kill like that? Far easier to arrange a heart attack as he was flying home.

As for Moscow? *See* Berlin . . .

It was the fact that the murder made no sense that dragged Tom back to the crime scene. That and the chance Cecil Blackburn might have hidden a copy of his memoir. Coming back here was a risk. A dangerous one.

He'd need to work fast.

Tom wished he'd had time to search properly earlier.

Reaching the top of the stairs, he found Sir Cecil's door fastened with a Kriminalpolizei seal, reached for his lock knife and hesitated. *Get in, search the damn place, get out again.* Not giving himself a chance to decide this was a bad idea, Tom cut the seal.

Chalk circles marked blood-splatter on the walls. The Persian rug was gone, squares had been cut from brocade curtains, and fingerprint powder bloomed like spores across Sir Cecil's desk. The fireplace was clean though. Tom wondered why. He'd taken the last page not entirely burnt and there seemed little chance forensics could do much with the ashes.

Standing in the middle of the study, he shut his eyes and tried to reconstruct what he'd found but not had time to examine. Evgeny just inside the door; eyes scarlet where blood vessels had burst, the cord around his throat so tight it dug into flesh. Sir Cecil on his study floor; left temple crushed, the clawed hook of a crowbar in his heart. No lividity, though.

Tom stopped to think about that.

Blood pooled in the lower edges of a body thirty minutes after the heart stopped beating. So Tom's visit had to be inside that time frame. The two men had been killed no more than half an hour before he came looking for Frederika.

Tom checked the flat door, finding the frame crushed where a crowbar had been pushed in below the lock. How could the people below have heard nothing? How could those inside . . . ?

Sir Cecil's record-player had been hissing noisily, its needle endlessly jumping a final groove. Could Beethoven have covered the break-in? God knows, the music had been loud enough the first time Tom came.

Taking a closer look, he wondered if the bruising to the frame was deep enough. What if it had been damaged later to throw the police off the scent? Maybe no murderer had smashed his way in. The reason Evgeny didn't fire through the door was that the killer was already inside.

Far from trying to keep him out, perhaps Evgeny had been the one to invite him in? Tom filed that thought for later.

He searched Sir Cecil's desk first, but it had been emptied, and anything deemed not to matter – which included HB pencils and a bottle of Quink – loaded on to a wooden tray by someone who liked neat parallel lines. A collection of Corgi toys had been tossed into a cardboard box at the side.

Someone else had done that.

The effect was too chaotic for the pencil arranger. Two crime scene technicians working together but with different approaches perhaps. Tom removed each drawer in turn, examining its back and underside. Nothing had been taped to the wood. Dragging the heavy desk away from the wall, he found nothing taped to the back either. The preciseness of the dents in the rug said the police hadn't bothered to move the desk. That was good for Tom.

If they hadn't bothered to do that they might have been too slack to check other places properly too. They'd taken down two oil paintings, however, revealing patches of slightly less faded paint. Looking for a safe probably.

A mahogany sideboard revealed bottles of Scotch, their shoulders dusted with fingerprint powder. Those searching hadn't realized the trove they'd found. How did Sir Cecil, in disgrace and effectively in exile, paid by his new masters in a soft currency, come by whisky this good?

Friends back home seemed the obvious answer. Rich ones.

Tom checked the top of a dresser, moving tankards and finding dead spiders, desiccated flies and an old George V halfpenny, dark with age. It was propping up a pewter tankard that was engraved on one side.

Cecil Blackburn. Captain, 1st XI. Summer 1924.

Tom pocketed the coin and was about to put the tankard back when he saw a photograph, face out and so dark that it blended against the pewter.

A boy holding a cricket bat, standing beside a man Tom vaguely recognized. The man wore an old-fashioned frock coat and celluloid collar. On the back of the photograph, in elegant script, was written: *Quid datur a divis felici optatius hora?*

What is there given by the gods more desirable than a happy hour?

Tom had enough Latin to recognize it as Catullus, a Roman poet best known for versifying the death of his mistress's pet bird, when he wasn't writing limericks later judged too pornographic to translate.

A grown man quoting Catullus at an eleven-year-old?

Going to the window, Tom scanned the river walk below. The longer he remained here the greater the risk. He'd given himself ten minutes and was already over that. Knowing he should be gone, he stripped books from the shelves, flipping them open to see if they were hollow or hid anything between their pages.

Halfway along the second shelf a small buff-coloured notebook fell from a paperback guide to forest walks. It was filled with names written in tiny crabbed writing. *HMSO* was printed on the front.

Her Majesty's Stationery Office.

Blackburn claims to have a list of everybody implicated.

Lord Eddington's words came back to him.

Tom had just started skimming the names when steps pounded up the stairs and the flat door crashed open. A police officer he hadn't seen before stood in the doorway. He was holding a Tokarev and panting from the climb.

'What are you doing here?' Tom demanded.

The Volkspolizei officer looked suddenly uncertain.

'This is a crime scene,' Tom said, his Russian heavy. 'Who said you could come in? Who authorized this?'

Luckily, the newcomer's Russian was bad. His main concern not getting himself into trouble and, having sheepishly holstered his sidearm, he happily passed the buck up the line, giving Tom his boss's name and rank.

'Don't touch anything,' Tom warned him.

The young officer shook his head.

'Wait . . . *Why* did your captain send you?'

'One of the men on the door said you were here and he sent me along in case you needed help.' *To see who you were,* he meant.

Tom sighed. 'I'll talk to them on my way out. Shut the door when you go. Have it resealed.' Pocketing the notebook, he headed downstairs without looking back.

31

Hide in plain sight.

Tom had Belfast to thank for his experience doing that. It was a good rule; not infallible but, in his opinion, often safer than going to ground. All the same, he couldn't shake the feeling that he was being watched. And if he was being watched, why didn't the East Germans make their move?

Two teenage girls sat smoking cigarettes beside the fountain in front of the Palasthotel. One wore a red jacket, black jeans and red shoes, the other a sweatshirt and patterned skirt that reached her ankles.

Sitting himself on the far side, Tom unfolded a *Neues Deutschland* and lit a papirosa; then hoping his newly cropped hair and cheap East German shades would be enough to help him blend in, he began watching the hotel door.

Frederika or Amelia Blackburn?

He'd had a quick tussle with himself as to which he should try to talk to first. Amelia won. She might not be the only person who'd know if Sir Cecil had made a copy of his memoirs, she might not even know herself, but she was probably the only person who'd tell him if she did.

She also needed to know that Tom hadn't killed her father.

In front of Tom, bolted to a plinth, three bronze girls

and a boy sat back-to-back, realistic enough to have been cast from life. One of the teenagers opposite saw Tom admiring the figures and sneered.

A group of men at a table out front were holding some kind of business meeting. They had their jackets off, shirt sleeves unbuttoned and folded up. All of them smoked and one was talking while the others nodded.

None of them seemed interested in Tom.

When Tom looked back the girl was watching.

Because he'd noticed her? She scowled and pointedly looked away. Seventeen probably, maybe eighteen. About the same age as the nude statues. About the same age as . . . Tom took a deep breath.

You have to stop doing this.

Other families got over children dying. Pulling Sir Cecil's notebook from his pocket, he folded it back so no one would see *HMSO* on its cover.

Reinickendorf-Tegelerforst 1945–46.

The names listed were mostly English, possibly American, a few French, fewer still Russian. Only in the early days of the Occupation could forces have mixed like this. Tom recognized people from the cast list he'd found.

Cecil Blackburn, James Foley, Robby Croft, Anthony Willes-Wakefield, Henry Petty . . . All five had been in *The Importance of being Lady Windermere.* Someone had ticked their names in pencil. In ink, in the original hand, beside each was an α.

Other names had beta, β. A few γ, gamma.

Tom realized in shock that Sir Edward Masterton, Her Majesty's ambassador to the Soviet Union, and the father of the kidnapped girl he'd helped rescue in Moscow, was there. He was down as Eddie Masterton though. The alpha beside his name was crossed out and replaced with beta. The Russian on the line below had his name crossed out entirely.

Caro's father was there. Lieutenant Charles Eddington. He had a gamma. The real shock came a page after that.

Milov . . . He'd been a colonel back then.

A tank commander and a genuine Soviet hero. These days he was a Marshal of the Soviet Union, a member of the Politburo, and *éminence grise* behind Gorbachev's throne. Tom had made friends with the man, if that was the right term, after Edward Masterton's daughter went missing.

Tom owed Milov his life. And Milov owed Tom for the fact that a coup against Gorbachev by the Soviet old guard had been thwarted.

Milov had been with the Red Army that took Berlin. Edward Masterton had arrived shortly afterwards, as had Cecil Blackburn and Caro's father. Tom would put good money on the list being drawn from people stationed here. The other thing Tom noticed was that the notebook had staples where it had once been stitched. He counted the pages and there were still sixty-four, as claimed in tiny type on the back. So, if pages *had* been removed they'd been returned later.

Shutting it, Tom pushed the booklet into his pocket, glanced round to check he wasn't under observation and went back to watching the hotel, while wondering if the Greek letters beside the names might be as significant as the names themselves.

One of the girls was looking at him again. It could be nothing. The fact a woman who'd glared at him for discarding a papirosa butt was also looking could be nothing too. The men at the table had stopped talking. One of them pushed back his chair.

Tom felt hairs rise on the back of his neck.

Stubbing out his cigarette, he folded his newspaper, tucked it under his arm and clambered to his feet, heading for a path at the side of the hotel. No one shouted, none of the couples coming towards him suddenly unclasped hands to become police officers. No shots came from behind.

He hurried all the same.

32

Tom sat in silence in a barber's on Karl-Liebknecht-Strasse, feeling clippers scrape his skull. Outside, two kids kissed at a tram stop, looking pretty much like kids everywhere. He found it hard not to envy their youth, innocence and blind ignorance of what life could be like. They were gone by the time the barber finished repairing the mess Tom had made cropping his own hair that morning.

Tom looked more like a squaddie than ever.

A sergeant maybe. A soldier on leave.

As long as he didn't look like himself that was fine. The Stasi would be out hunting. He didn't have enough knowledge to judge how hermetically sealed East Berlin was, how much news bled in from the West. But, unless the East Germans had decided to try to keep Sir Cecil's death under wraps, he had to face the fact they might have shown his mugshot on TV already. He half expected to turn a corner and come face to face with his Wanted poster.

He followed three punks down some river steps. Their hair was dyed black and their jeans were ripped at the knees. He wondered how much trouble they attracted. Whether their families were powerful enough to let them get away with dressing like that in a city like this. Overtaking, he took fresh steps back to street level, stopping at the top to light another papirosa, while he glanced around him.

No one watching. At least, not obviously.

He had to hope that he'd slipped safely into anonymity. Just another Berliner in a cheap leather jacket, carrying that day's *Neues Deutschland*, chain-smoking his way through a packet of foul cigarettes. It was essential that he blended in and remained under the radar while he came up with a plan.

Keep moving, keep thinking, be aware of everyone around you.

When an old boy with a Trabant engine in a wheelbarrow caught Tom's eye, he followed the man down Spandauer Strasse, until he cut under train tracks to reach open ground. Tom stopped, shocked at how quickly the city changed. Open space stretched either side of a narrow road, where an old bombsite had been scraped free of rubble, sown with grass and planted with sickly linden trees.

Battered Trabants were parked in a line, the nearest with its bonnet open. There was a space where the 600cc two-stroke would go. In the distance, a tram rolled along a mostly empty street, and beyond it, squeezed into a gap between apartment blocks, stood a café with two metal tables and five chairs at the front.

It reminded Tom that he was hungry.

Soup of the day. Beef with onions. A Hungarian stew. Rabbit with mushrooms. Three kinds of omelette. The menu was impressive. The third time Tom was told that unfortunately his choice was off, he asked what the woman did have.

She pointed to the sausages.

'What else?'

She pointed to the sausages again.

Tom laughed, ordered the sausages, asked for a Pilsner and complimented her on her Russian, only realizing his mistake when her face clouded. She'd have been tiny when Hitler came to power, just into her teens when Berlin fell. A bad place for a teenage girl. The *frontoviki*'s revenge for what the Wehrmacht had done in the USSR was so brutal that it even shocked its own officers.

'You don't look Russian,' she said.

'Who knows what that looks like?' Tom said. 'Tall, short, squat, thin, dark, fair . . .' He smiled at her. 'And that's just my own family.'

She laughed and lifted a mesh cover, impaling a bread roll on a chrome spike, with a slightly obscene twist of her wrist, before scooping a sausage from simmering water and squirting bright yellow mustard inside the roll. She slid the sausage after it and put Tom's lunch in front of him.

'Another beer?' she asked.

Looking at his bottle, Tom realized it was empty.

'Want one yourself?'

Her smile said she wondered what he was after. There were a couple of answers to that. Neither of them what she imagined, probably. First off, he needed somewhere to sit, and this was good. He had a clear view all the way to the railway arches. Second . . . he'd get to that. Maybe.

A thickset teenager was loading empty beer bottles into a crate with agonizing slowness. 'Your son?'

'Grandson. My son died.'

'I'm sorry . . .'

She shrugged, as if to say it wasn't that big a deal, although the way that she turned away told him it was.

'Do you know,' he asked, 'someone who does rooms?'

The woman looked troubled. For a moment, he thought she was going to ignore his question but she glanced at the boy filling crates, then at her unsold sausages as if they were part of the question.

'You mean without having papers?'

'There's this girl . . .'

Much of the tension left her face.

In Moscow earlier that year, Tom had found that fixing a hotel room was next to impossible. All hotels needed to be booked in advance. Proof of ID was required and the desk recorded your details. Richer teenagers and married lovers used couchettes on a river boat, the only beds in the city that could be bought without trouble. East Berlin was undoubtedly the same . . .

'Ah,' she said. 'Men . . .' She glanced at iron steps probably leading to a flat above. 'No,' she said to herself. 'Carl would hate that.'

'He's sweeping up?'

She scowled to say Tom shouldn't listen in on her thoughts but nodded all the same. 'He doesn't like change.'

'You were going to let me use his room?'

'I have a better idea.' She nodded to the back of the bar and a sign reading *Toilette*. 'Down the stairs, straight on. See what you think.'

He pushed back his chair . . .

'This girl,' the woman asked. 'She's pretty?'

'Yes,' Tom said. 'I think so.'

The woman chuckled.

The room on offer had been built as the cellar. These days it doubled as a boiler room, with a badly rendered end wall hung with a pickaxe, a garden fork and a reel of plastic hose. Shelves below were stacked with enough bottles of industrial alcohol to start a small revolution.

'It's ideal,' he told the woman.

She tried not to look surprised and Tom shrugged.

'What time will you come back?' she asked.

'I'll need it for a week.'

The woman blinked. 'I was thinking an evening. Perhaps overnight.'

'I'm going to need it for longer.' He pulled out a roll of GDR banknotes and hesitated . . . 'I have Western currency if you'd rather. In my job it's important.'

'Your job?'

'Deutschmarks or US dollars?'

Her sour smile said she knew he was dodging her question. 'I'll take both,' she told him.

'Dollars can get you into trouble.'

'I'm already in trouble. I'll be in trouble until I die. My husband wasn't good at keeping his mouth shut.'

And yet you run this? Tom thought.

An old and not very popular bar but a bar all the same.

Since the state allocated jobs, someone somewhere still had her back.

'He was a party member?' Tom asked.

'In the war.'

That took balls. A communist during the Third Reich. Tens of thousands of politicals had died in the camps. Many had been worked to death or simply put against a wall and shot. A few had been publicly beheaded. Even the suspicion of sympathizing with communists had seen entire families slaughtered in the dog-days of the war.

145

Maybe, in letting her keep the bar, the state felt its debt had been repaid. 'I'll need a key,' Tom said.

He peeled off five $20 notes, watching her eyes widen.

On top of that he added enough GDR marks to buy her silence all over again, or compromise her totally, depending on how you looked at it. He nodded towards the back, making clear which door he needed a key to.

'There's an alley beyond?'

'A yard. You'll need the key for that too.'

33

It was her cropped hair, dark glasses and painted boots that gave Amelia Blackburn away. Tom was back on the Spreepromenade, when he glanced across the narrow river to see her scowling up at the Berliner Dom.

The GDR had finally started repairing it in the 1970s, on the understanding that repairs to the cathedral should include removing as many crosses as possible. Tom doubted that bit was mentioned in her guidebook. Or the fact that as the scaffolding went up at the front, workmen at the rear took down the Kaiser's chapel with dynamite.

Stepping aside, Tom let a couple pass, keeping his gaze on Amelia, while simultaneously checking that the couple kept walking and didn't immediately stop to admire the view. This being what they'd do if they were there to keep an eye on him. Paranoia was dangerous. It also kept you alive.

And that was what made it addictive. Because paranoia's logic said that the more paranoid you were, the more likely you were to stay alive. Tom had seen for himself that this didn't hold true. Being careful, now. That was different.

Even that could get you killed, though.

Having said something to her minder, Amelia headed for a women's lavatory and vanished into its tiled underworld. Realizing her minder was engrossed in a guidebook, Tom quickly crossed the short bridge and followed. He needed to talk to her. He really needed to talk to her.

The lavatory was large, clean, white and apparently empty.

There was no hatchet-faced *Toilettenfrau* collecting coins and handing out a regulation two sheets of stiff paper. For that he was grateful. One cubicle was shut and he waited, relieved when the cistern finally flushed. Amelia Blackburn blinked to see him. Tom waited for some flare of recognition and when she still stared, he pushed out his hand, which she ignored.

'I'm sorry,' he said in English. 'About your father.'

'You couldn't wait outside?'

'I'm not a hack.'

'Then what are you doing in here?'

'I needed to get to you away from your minder.'

'You're from the bloody embassy? You've ignored two messages so far.'

Had they now? Tom considered that.

'Why didn't you simply visit them?'

The woman's face darkened. 'I'm here as a guest of the East German government. An indication of their willingness to let my father return home. They've been keeping me busy while he's recovering.'

'He's dead,' Tom said. 'You know that.'

He watched her eyes widen. And realized that if she was still pretending her father had had a heart attack, then the news of Sir Cecil's murder hadn't been released and that meant his own mugshot hadn't yet been on TV.

That was something.

'How do you know?'

'You called the embassy from your hotel?'

'Where else would I call them from?' Amelia demanded.

'And they answered in English?'

'Obviously.'

'Good English?'

'Perfect.' He watched her face cloud. For the first time Dr Blackburn looked uncertain. 'Almost too perfect.' She reassessed Tom's question. 'Oh shit. They wouldn't, would they?'

'This is East Berlin,' said Tom. 'Of course they would. I'm told the Stasi have offices at the hotel. That the twenty-five largest guest rooms . . .'

There were sounds from the stairs.

Amelia looked outraged as Tom suddenly pushed her towards the stall she'd just vacated. He raised his finger to his lips and for a second he thought she'd punch him. She looked more than capable. Then he heard her name called and she was the one to bolt the door behind them.

'Dr Blackburn . . .'

Pushing Tom into the far corner, Amelia Blackburn sat herself. Anyone glancing carelessly under the door would have thought her busy.

'Are you all right?' Frau Eisen asked.

'A stomach upset,' Dr Blackburn replied. 'If you could wait upstairs.'

'No problem. I can wait here.'

'It would embarrass me,' Dr Blackburn said.

A heavy sigh came beyond the door. 'There's nothing embarrassing about bodily functions. They are part of the natural order . . .'

'All the same,' Amelia said.

'If I must . . .' They heard heavy steps and Amelia stood, flushed the lavatory, and opened the door carefully, peering through. When she turned back, it was to say, 'How long had you been following me?'

'I haven't been.'

'I saw you across the river a minute ago. I recognized the jacket. It's too hot for leather.'

'This is Berlin,' Tom said. 'They probably wear leather to the beach. I have been hoping to see you, though.'

'This is about my father?'

'Yes. I'm really sorry . . .'

'I barely knew him,' Dr Blackburn said flatly. 'I was only just in my teens when he left and he was rarely home before – Christ,' she said suddenly.

Her face twisted and for a second she was frozen with terror.

Then she backed out of the cubicle, and bumped into the missing *Toilettenfrau*'s table with its saucer of change as she turned for the stairs. Without thinking, Tom dipped for a coin that fell to the tiles.

A gesture so banal it apparently reassured her.

'I didn't kill your father,' he promised.

'I saw you leaving . . .'

'If I had it wouldn't have been like that.'

He could see her thinking that through. She stepped back another pace, but it was to take a better look. 'You're not embassy, are you?'

Tom shook his head.

'Why run if it wasn't you?'

'I had a message to meet . . .' Tom hesitated '. . . his mistress. He was dead and she wasn't there. I'm the man who was meant to take your father home. Would you have believed me? We need to talk . . .'

'About what?'

'Who might want him dead.'

'He abandoned his family. His country. Now he's abandoning those who took him in. Take your pick.'

'Did you want him dead?'

Her voice was flinty. 'For much of my childhood I thought he was. That's what my mother told me. *Daddy's dead.*'

'When did you learn the truth?'

'Fifth form. At breakfast. They brought round the papers and there was my father standing next to the East German premier. Bloody man . . .'

Tom wasn't sure which of them she meant.

'There's a café in Hackescher Markt,' he said. 'Under the bridge and past the parked cars. Meet me there later if you can.'

'And how do you suggest I escape Frau Eisen?'

'Tell her you have gut rot and need an early night?'

'You'll be there?'

'If I'm not, say you're waiting for Tomac. The old woman will be expecting you.'

Dr Blackburn looked surprised.

'I needed a room and told her I was having an affair. She thinks I'm Russian. She'll think you're the person I was talking about.'

'And who were you really talking about?'

'Nobody. I needed a room. I lied.'

34

Darkness was settling when Amelia Blackburn appeared under the railway arches near Hackescher Markt, hesitated for a second and then began heading for the café. She stopped only once, removing a trainer, and pretending to shake a stone from it as she turned to check no one was following.

Tom was impressed.

There were couples walking. The old man he'd seen with the wheelbarrow was now sponging a dusty Trabant in the half-dark. A traffic policeman, by the bridge, was talking to two men who stood by a truck with its bonnet up. One was shaking his head, the other smoking.

The sound of a football match on TV came from flats behind the café. Someone groaned and, seconds later, half a dozen people cheered, their cheers echoed from other open windows. Amelia resumed walking.

She was doing her best to look confident.

Her clothes were well chosen. Nothing too outrageous, nothing obviously Western. She'd solved the problem of her cropped hair by wearing a scarf, which made her look slightly dowdy. Tom imagined that was the effect she was after.

He stood as she approached, gripped her shoulders and kissed her warmly on both cheeks, hugging her tight for a second. He felt her tense, and then hug him back when she realized they were being watched.

'A beer?' Tom suggested.

'Do they have wine?'

'Beer's probably safer.'

He ordered himself another Pilsner and one for her.

The old woman nodded, looked at Dr Blackburn and then came closer to take a better look, nodding approvingly. Amelia Blackburn blushed and the old woman chuckled, tossing a comment to Tom as she walked away.

'What did she say?'

'That I shouldn't let your husband find out.'

'She really thinks you're Russian?'

'She speaks Russian the way half the Berliners in West Berlin speak English. Well enough to make sense. Not well enough to tell if I'm a native speaker.'

The old woman gave Amelia a clean glass and settled herself behind the counter to watch them. She had only two other customers. Young men in mechanics' overalls who wandered in, nodded to the television on a crate in the corner and, receiving permission, turned it on and began fiddling with the aerial until the football match appeared through a blizzard of snow.

'Why's she staring at us?'

Tom glanced over and the old woman smirked.

Amelia saw her nod to Tom and jerk her head towards the rear door.

'She's found me a camp bed that looks as if it hasn't been used in thirty years. She's waiting to see how long it takes me to get you there. We could always go down? It would be safer for talking.'

'In a moment,' Amelia said.

'You said you were here at the GDR's invitation?'

'A gesture of friendship. They paid for my flight and hotel . . .'

'And they seemed happy enough for your father to leave?'

She sipped at her beer. 'Yes,' she said finally. 'They seemed entirely relaxed at the prospect of him going. Almost keen . . .'

Almost keen?

Across the bar, the mechanics were jeering a commentary they could barely hear and gesticulating at footballers they could hardly see. Groans from the flats behind the bar said whatever had happened on the pitch was bad. Seconds later, cheers indicated that balance had been restored.

'In what sense *keen*?' Tom asked.

Amelia seemed distracted by the match. 'I don't know, Major Fox,' she said. 'It was just a feeling. I'm only here because my mother practically ordered it.'

Reaching for her glass, she took a heavy swallow. She stared at the road and Tom wondered what she was looking for. When one of the mechanics scraped back his chair, she flinched. The whistle went, the mechanics stopped watching their flickering screen, and Tom realized that Amelia was looking at police officers and so were they. Three figures had appeared under the arches, their advance suddenly blocked by a rumbling tram.

Major Fox. She'd called him Major Fox.

When had he told her his name?

As one of the mechanics shifted, reaching inside his jacket, Amelia pushed back her chair, obviously trying to move out of the way.

'I'll be back,' Tom told her.

He called for another two beers, despite Amelia's being almost untouched, and headed for the loos, apparently changing his mind at the last minute to return to the counter. 'Tell them I said I was KGB,' he told the old woman. 'Say I spoke only Russian and showed you a KGB card. It looked real to you.'

The old woman opened her mouth and shut it again.

He could feel her gaze as he made for the door, walked straight past the steps down to the gents beyond and let himself out into the yard, then into the alley beyond, locking the gate behind him.

He was fifty paces away and walking fast when the shouting started.

As someone began kicking the yard door, Tom lifted his head, took his hands out of his pockets and sprinted for the end of the alley, almost running head first into a group of crop-haired football fans. At least half of them wore leather jackets. More than half were drunk. Sliding his way into the group, Tom grinned at one and clapped another on the back.

'Dynamo?' the man asked.

'Dynamo,' Tom agreed enthusiastically.

The man passed him a half-empty bottle of brandy and Tom took a noisy gulp. 'We won,' shouted a fat man dressed in the maroon and gold of Berliner FC Dynamo. The others took up the chant and the crowd moved off to find a bar to celebrate their victory, gathering other fans on the way.

Tom went with them, head down and screened by jubilant East Berliners who drowned out the other shouting and swept him away, on a wave of excitement, from the sirens beginning to wail.

35

The crack of a pistol shot in a backstreet . . . The scream of a seagull . . . Another of a fox rutting that sounded like . . . Tom's dreams went, promiscuous and skittering, to a married woman in Belfast who bit his hand when he tried to muffle cries as she bucked beneath him. Remembering her summoned a smoke-wreathed Provo pub. From there, to burning leaves in those early years of taking Charlie down to Caro's parents. And, before that, a trash fire behind the block where Tom's dad ran the stores. The clash of army boots on sticky tarmac, the smell of road and parade ground one and the same. He'd been born dead, in a hospital on the edge of a British base in Cyprus. A midwife resuscitated him.

More than once, his dad regretted that.

Tom was his memories. Sometimes they were all he was. It was unfashionable to believe in evil: more than that, it was actively frowned on. The problem was Tom had seen evil, tasted it and could identify its stench in the air and its stink on human skin. He knew, at least in his dreams he did, that each time he touched evil it left him tarnished. Rolling over, he scratched a fleabite in his sleep.

'Here,' said a fat man, holding out a blue and yellow box.

The boy didn't want to take it but a sudden tightness in the fat man's eyes warned him he should.

'Here,' the man repeated.

The boy's throat was tight enough to strangle him.

Inside, he was screaming. Outside, outside it was important that nothing showed. He tried to keep his face a mask. Bland, polite, attentive. The kind of face the man's eyes could pass over without finding anything to object to. But the man put out his other hand, took the boy's chin and turned it to the light.

'I slipped,' the boy said.

He said it too hurriedly. His next words were slower, blander, stripped of emotion. 'Running in a corridor. It was stupid of me.'

The man sighed.

'Boys will be boys,' he said.

The boy knew the rules. Move slowly. No noise. Speak when spoken to. No answering back. Above all, never stare a grown-up in the eyes.

The rules were simple. Easy to understand and easy to obey, once you understood the price of disobedience. That thought was enough to knot his stomach, to pull it tight to his spine. He'd learnt to sense the slightest shifts of mood. To know exactly where grown-ups were standing.

Who was angry; who wanted to be angry. Who was simply bored. He should have kept better control of himself.

He needed to be polite.

'Thank you,' he said, taking the little box.

'Open it, then.'

He already knew what was inside.

What was always inside boxes handed to the select few after the guests had gone, daylight was due and it was time to be returned to school.

Corgi, said the box. Jaguar 2.4.

He opened the end flap, being careful not to tear the cardboard, slid the little diecast Corgi toy on to his hand and made himself smile.

'It's beautiful.'

The man smiled back. 'My pleasure.'

36

Most of the riders gathered in the pub car park were dressed in *ratcatcher* – tweed coats and tan breeches – as befitted a local foxhunt in the cubbing season. The cubs were near full size, if not yet sexually active, and still lived in their family groups. The hounds were mostly young too. Although there were a few experienced pairs to stiffen the pack.

This was a midweek hunt, nothing fancy and certainly not worth getting dressed up for, even if it had been the right part of the season for that sort of thing. There were three old hands, a couple of local teenagers, including a new girl from the village. For the most part, though, it was what you'd expect. Local farmers and the local vet, the landlord of the posher pub, a retired brigadier with nothing better to do, and an incomer from London who'd bought the Hall . . .

He was an appalling rider, but a generous contributor to hunt funds. This helped Robby Croft, the master of the hunt, overlook the newness of his clothes, his lumpen children and the vulgarity of his oversized car. People like this had become necessary if hunting was to survive.

'Sir . . .'

A young man Robby didn't recognize had drawn alongside. He was well turned out in a Harry Hall jacket, had a good seat and seemed polite enough.

The master smiled.

'I just wanted to present my compliments.'

Robby looked at the young man, little more than a boy really, and wondered if he should know who he was.

'My Great-Uncle Max asked me to present his compliments.'

'Max . . . ?'

The young man nodded and the master smiled, leaning across to shake hands. 'How is the old rogue?'

'Old, and roguish.'

Both men laughed; and then the hunt moved off, slowly through the village, and carefully over the crossroads, where drivers who didn't understand horses sometimes went too fast. They turned up the side of St Peter's and under a yew tree, through the lych gate and out into Farmer Clark's fields.

The young man rode well, stayed in his saddle and didn't falter at the jumps. Invariably, he went over rather than round. The master liked that in a man. Robby was aware, as they drew ahead of the others, that he was riding a little too fast, approaching his jumps a little too harshly.

And at some point, and Robby wasn't quite sure when, the boy had stopped trying to keep up with the master and the master had begun trying to keep up with the boy. The rest of the hunt was half a field behind now, with the whippers-in and the hounds slightly off to one side. He should slow, they both should. But it was a long time since Robby had ridden like this. It made him feel young.

The gate they galloped for was a high one.

Edging his horse slightly forward, the master jerked his chin to indicate he had precedence, and the boy nodded, falling back slightly. Exactly as it should be. Using his heels, the master nudged his horse, felt it adjust its stride and head for the gate. At the last moment, Robby realized the boy had drawn alongside and intended to jump too. Yanking on his reins, the master felt his animal shy and felt himself thrown. It was a bad fall.

The boy just about made it over, landing in brambles that slashed his face and left his hands and wrists bleeding. He was trying to stand when the hunt rode up. 'Stay still,' a middle-aged woman ordered.

When he ignored her, she dismounted.

'You could be concussed,' she said. 'You might have internal injuries. You might have fractures.' Seeing his look, she added, 'I'm a doctor.' Glancing at the gate, she said, 'What happened?'

'I don't know. I really don't.' The boy sounded bemused. 'I had the jump. The master indicated that I had the jump.'

'You're lucky to be alive.'

The boy nodded. 'He's . . . ?'

'Oh yes,' she said. 'As a dodo.'

37

Tom woke under a bridge in half-darkness, his temples hammered by a hangover louder than any cathedral bells. He knew on waking that he needed to hide the notebook. The reasons caught up with him a second later. He'd be a fool to try to cross the Wall carrying it. The last thing London needed was for him to be captured and deliver it straight into East German hands. If he could have called Caro's father, he would. If he could have got a message to Henderson . . .

Neither of those was possible.

His best hope, perhaps his only hope, was to get home and tell Century House where it was hidden. Someone less compromised could retrieve it. He had no idea what the Greek letters meant; if alpha was better than beta or gamma. He simply knew Sir Cecil was dead and his memoirs probably burnt. *He claims to have a complete list of everybody implicated.*

This was it. Tom was sure of that.

Flicking it open, Tom skimmed the list, looking for the names he'd recognized earlier. A Cabinet minister. A war hero. An entertainer, newly knighted for his charity work, and known to be a personal friend of the PM. All marked alpha. Sir Cecil was the same. Tom flicked forward, trying to remember where in the notebook he'd seen Lord Brannon's name. Alpha again.

Since he couldn't cross the Wall as Tom Fox, he'd have to cross it as someone else. Someone who wasn't being hunted. Throwing off his jacket, Tom rolled from the ledge on which he lay, descended to the water's edge and stripped off the maroon and gold Dynamo shirt he'd obviously swapped for his own. He scooped cold water on to his aching head and splashed it under his arms, hoping that the vomit he needed to wash from his shoes was someone else's.

It probably was. His mouth tasted dry but not foul.

Tom refused to acknowledge the things in the tunnel with him. He refused to let them out from the walls. Having pissed and shat, he wiped himself Arabic fashion and rinsed his fingers in the river, kicked litter over his dirt, and emptied his pockets, looking for what would effectively be a dead-letter drop for whoever came to collect the notebook.

The ledge where he slept was too obvious. An indentation just inside the tunnel too shallow. There was a cast-iron bridge though, rising in an arch and dropping to the opposite bank. It was old and black, studded with bolts holding its girders together. Tom chose a join between struts, as awkwardly placed as possible. His fingers came away sticky with grease and grime.

Around him he felt the darkness settle.

Until finally it became simply the start of daylight; and he became a man in a strange city suffering the after-effects of an unsettling dream. It had been close, though. Had it got any worse he'd have been kneeling by the river's edge, vomiting. The monsters would have crawled from the walls.

38

The sun rose inexorably, glittering on the river's surface and burning away the shadows under his bridge until Tom had no choice but to face the light. So he abandoned the place he'd slept and began walking. A man walking purposefully looks like he belongs. Belonging is the first step to being invisible.

The Dynamo football shirt helped.

You're a Berliner, Tom told himself. *This is your city. This is where you belong.*

A traffic policeman looked at him and Tom made himself nod. A second later, the man nodded back and Tom kept walking, his pace steady. He was hungry and thirsty and imagined he looked hung-over. He just hoped he didn't look too much like a fugitive who'd slept rough under a bridge.

It was a poster that stopped him.

Not the propaganda one, showing bright-faced schoolchildren holding hands as they strode into the future. An advertisement for *Giselle.* The prima ballerina looked enough like Frederika to remind Tom that that's where he should have been going. She'd sent the note that brought him to the flat. He needed to know who'd been threatening Sir Cecil — more importantly, why. She might also know if he'd made a copy of his memoirs.

It was the hope of finding a copy that decided Tom.

He'd have to risk seeing her.

A map outside Alexanderplatz station helped him identify the gym where Frederika taught. It showed train, tram and bus routes in East Berlin. A smaller map showed Greater Berlin, and, beyond that, East German countryside. West Berlin was simply blank. A featureless, unannotated white space that ate half the city.

Stepping back, Tom bumped into a teenager.

When the boy swore, Tom swore back, his Russian raw and brutal. The boy's stammered apology confirmed his suspicions. The Soviets might have returned this part of the city to its inhabitants but they'd never left in spirit.

The gym was red-brick, with faces carved above each window and tendrils of ivy carved down their sides. The plaque over its front door read *1905*.

A weedy path led down one side and Tom took it.

The morning was already hot enough for a sliding door into the gym to be open, and Tom stopped to watch. A troop of bare-chested boys vaulted a horse, using a springboard for takeoff. Each waited his turn, made the same vault and ran back to rejoin the queue. They went round twice before Tom stopped watching.

An open door beyond revealed a stairwell and he hesitated.

Fire exit, read a sign. *Keep shut.*

A door off the stairwell led to a changing room where a boy sat vestless on a bench nursing his sprained wrist. It was only when the child stood that Tom realized the shorts were a skirt and she wasn't a boy at all.

'Frau Frederika Schmitt?' he asked.

The girl pointed her finger at the ceiling.

39

Returning to the path, Tom found a fire escape leading to open doors above. The steps were black, painted with something that was failing to kill the rust that kept breaking through. The music coming through the doors sounded like seventies disco. Actually, it sounded like a bad imitation of seventies disco.

The track ended, and there was sudden silence.

When it started again, Tom heard grunts, thuds and the sound of a girl flipping herself across a thin mat. She finished her routine just as Tom reached the top of the steps. He watched her steady herself, arms thrown out and torso pushed forward, her feet trying to hold their place.

Momentum carried her a half-step forward.

She looked so mortified that Frederika limped over and wrapped an arm briefly around her shoulders, before putting the child's arms back where they'd been, bending her spine so her torso came forward, and tapping the girl's stomach to lessen the curve. 'Again,' she ordered.

The girl launched herself across the floor, her feet barely touching the boards as she somersaulted and twisted and backflipped to the opposite corner. This time she landed perfectly and stood quivering.

Frederika nodded.

Another girl clapped and Frederika scowled, turned to

reprimand the girl and saw Tom backlit in the doorway. He thought for a second that she hadn't recognized him. Until her scream said she had.

Pure fury. It echoed off all four walls.

Her students froze, open mouthed.

'*Run*,' she told them. '*Fetch help.*'

They began to edge towards the door and Frederika moved to stand defiantly between them and Tom. 'You don't touch them,' she said.

'I didn't kill Sir Cecil.'

'*Liar . . .*'

He only just blocked the fingers clawing for his face. Grabbing her wrists, Tom narrowly avoided a knee to his groin and finally wrestled Frederika to a standstill. She spat at him. Her glare so fierce he had no doubt she'd kill him if she could.

'Who was threatening him?'

'You were. It must have been you . . .'

'Frederika. I didn't do anything.'

'A Frenchman photographed you leaving. He worked for *France Soir*. The police showed me the paper. It's obvious that it was you.'

She was shaking with fury, one of her students just standing there, when the door was thrown open and her other student and a security guard rushed in.

'Shoot him,' Frederika ordered.

The man fumbled at his holster.

Gripping Frederika's wrists tight, Tom backed towards the fire escape and ducked down when the man tried to take aim. He only let go at the door, twisting his way down the iron steps and sprinting for the corner.

166

No shots followed.

In a yard behind the gym, he stopped, ready to take the guard if he came down the steps after him, but no one did. Someone had spray-painted a naked girl facing a naked boy on the gym's back wall. Silhouettes faded as they blended to brick. No, not painted. Bleached out of the dirt . . .

Tom listened for footsteps and heard sirens instead.

Move, he told himself.

A metal fence edged the yard and he ran at it, levering himself up and over, dropping to a crouch in a ruined playground. A young woman holding a small boy stared at him. Her hair was unwashed, her oversized jeans were cinched with a belt and rolled at the bottom. She wore a string vest with nothing beneath. A hand-rolled cigarette hung from her mouth.

She examined Tom impassively.

And that's where the encounter might have ended had Tom not heard the sirens stop, as police cars screeched to a halt on the road in front of the gym. Reaching into his jacket, he found his wallet and extracted five $10 bills, fanning them out like cards and stepping back when she reached for them.

'*Komm mit uns*,' she said. She gestured that Tom should follow.

They slipped through a door into a hallway where every window had been boarded up, the first dozen steps of the communal stairs had been ripped out and wires hung like snakes from the walls where they'd been disconnected and cut in two. The doors were missing too.

'*Kommen Sie.*'

Tom followed her through a doorway. He'd been hoping it led to a street but he found himself in a stairwell bolted to the back of the building, with concrete steps leading both up and down. As he waited to see which she would take, she pointed up, then edged around him and let herself out through a fire door, heading for a police car that was cutting under an arch to park on communal grass.

How much should he trust her? Not at all seemed sensible.

All the same, Tom waited at a broken window to see how things would unfold. He could go further up, he could go back down, and he could try to lose himself in the main building.

He kept those in mind as he watched her approach the car.

She turned away long enough to scoop up the boy, raise her singlet and let him clamp himself to her nipple. And that's how she remained, with the boy at her hip, as the Volkspolizei climbed from their vehicle. One of them asked something and she shrugged, adjusting her breast and the boy.

The policeman asked the boy.

He shook his head without bothering to disengage.

The policeman smiled and Tom couldn't see, from where he watched at the edge of his broken window, if the woman returned it.

'You up there?' she asked, when she got back.

Tom headed down and hit ground level just as a bearded man came up from the cellars clutching electrical wire, insulating tape and a pair of bolt cutters. He shot a question at the woman, whose reply was too fast for Tom to understand.

'Do you understand Russian?' Tom asked.

The man's eyes narrowed.

'Or English,' he added hastily.

'Both,' the man said. 'I used to be a lecturer. She understands English better than she speaks it. No Russian though.'

'How did she learn English?'

'How does anyone here learn English?' Pulling a transistor from his pocket, the man twisted a knob and Bruce Springsteen's 'Born in the USA' blasted out until the woman reached across, took the little radio from him and turned it off.

'We get Radio West Berlin,' she said.

'When it's not being jammed,' the man added.

Maybe Radio West Berlin was a real station. Maybe she simply meant they got radio from across the Wall.

'She says you have money.'

Tom took the five $10 notes he'd shown the woman and handed them across. She looked at them thoughtfully and then gave them to the man, who folded them in two and pushed them into the back pocket of his jeans.

'I'm Helga,' she said. 'He's Franz. We're *Instandbesetzer*.'

'Squatters,' Franz said, seeing Tom's face. 'For us, it's political.'

'I left Mylo out there,' she said. 'Let me get him.'

In the canyon made by the flats, the boy was singing to himself, his song unnaturally amplified, sounding both close and distant. Tom and Franz watched Helga pick up the boy, who nuzzled her vest until she pushed his head away. He was grinning. 'How old?' Tom asked.

'It makes her happy,' said Franz, answering the question

Tom had really been asking. 'Three now. Four in a month or two. She'll probably stop then.' He shrugged. 'Then again, maybe not.'

At the top of the steps, a doorway draped with brocade led through to a floor where every internal wall had been removed, and the ceiling ripped out. A huge skylight had been cut crudely into the roof above. He was in a studio, Tom realized. A black canvas the size of a missing wall had knife slashes from ceiling to floor. Holes had been stabbed through it and threaded with ribbon that looked like stitches to a wound.

'Why do the police want you?' Franz asked.

'They think I killed someone.'

Franz stopped, turning to stare.

'I didn't,' Tom insisted.

'You would say that.'

'Yes,' Tom said. 'I would. This time it's true.'

'This time? No.' The man shook his head. 'I don't want to know.'

40

President Reagan was wrangling with Congress over his Star Wars initiative; the World Court had decreed that the US shouldn't have mined Nicaraguan waters. The Soviets were trying to contain fallout from Chernobyl. The Norwegians were scared that the fallout would contaminate their reindeer . . .

'What are you listening for?' Helga asked Tom.

It was Franz who answered. 'News of the man he killed, obviously.'

'Didn't kill,' a grey-haired woman corrected. 'That's right, isn't it?' She was talking to Tom. 'That's what you're listening for?'

Tom didn't deny it.

From the markets, the West German newsreader went to sport . . .

They were artists, poets, writers, dissidents, the grey-haired woman told him. *Instandbesetzer.* They didn't exist. They were ghosts squatting in the cracks of Marx's machine. She was pleased with that phrase. So pleased she pulled out a notebook to write it down.

Cecil Blackburn, James Foley, Tony Willes-Wakefield . . .

Tom recited the cast list from *The Importance of being Lady Windermere* in his head, wondering if it was coincidence they'd all been marked alpha. It didn't feel like coincidence.

There was a pattern. He just had to recognize it.

The grey-haired woman was still talking when Tom returned his attention to her. Apparently, squatting took pressure off the waiting lists for decent housing. The housing for heroes they'd all been promised. The *Instandbesetzer* occupied buildings no one else wanted. They kept them functioning. Sometimes they even repaired them. In return, the state pretended they didn't exist.

'How do you live?' Tom asked.

'We steal,' she said flatly. 'Also, we sell.'

'You sell what you steal?'

'Mostly.'

'The police leave you alone?' Tom asked.

'We're tolerated. Look, they say, we have bohemians too.'

Tom glanced round the room and the woman read his mind.

'Helga has real talent . . . Her friend?' She nodded to the huge canvas with tears and stab wounds. 'His work has a certain crude simplicity. Also his father heads up a regional committee of the Socialist Unity Party.'

'That helps?'

'Of course it helps. An apparatchik with a delinquent for a son? That gives the party leverage. They don't even have to threaten.'

'You speak like an insider.'

'I taught at the Humboldt, Berlin's oldest university. Marx studied there. Also, Max Planck, Heinrich Heine, Otto von Bismarck. Although we don't talk about him much these days, imperial chancellors being out of favour. You should go. The library is amazing. You'll find books not allowed anywhere else.'

'Why aren't you still there?' Tom asked.

'My husband was shot trying to cross the Wall.'

'And you were disgraced?'

'Oh no. I told them he was a filthy traitor and I'd have turned him in if I'd guessed for one second what he intended. We'd never loved each other. He was a brute, and an ignorant one. They were surprisingly forgiving.'

'So why did you leave the university?'

'I had a breakdown. It was the lying, you see.'

She held out her hand and Mylo toddled over with what was left of a joint, which she sucked so hard cardboard flared; she coughed, then spat ruefully.

'Last month,' she said, 'they brought an American here.' She gestured at the squat. 'So he could go home and say the GDR has bohemians too. He was writing on youth culture. Punks in Moscow, heavy metal in Vilnius, nerds in Belgrade ... You know Yugoslavia broadcasts software? First you build your computer, then you turn on your radio and tape software. Load up the cassette and your computer will play. There's a game where you repeatedly fly a plane over a city until you've bombed it flat. He couldn't understand why I didn't like that idea.'

She looked sober for a moment.

'I was eight when the Red Army arrived. Forty years later there are still bits of this city we haven't rebuilt. I told him I didn't think that game would be popular here. He told me it was just a game ...'

'Did he interview you?'

'Mostly he took photographs.'

Tom glanced towards Helga.

'Oh yes, feeding Mylo obviously. Franz barefoot and playing a trumpet with his shirt hanging out. Mylo got to ride a trike through puddles of paint in the playground, doing skid turns on a huge piece of canvas and laughing.'

'And they agreed?'

'Have you ever been locked up?'

Despite himself Tom shivered. Hearing steps on the stairs. Knowing that hiding made no difference. Not inside a cupboard. Not under a bed.

'Yes,' he said.

He could see she knew he had too.

'Now,' she said. 'Tell me about this murder you didn't commit.'

41

Tom arrived at the Bösebrücke crossing on Barnholmer Strasse at a time an East Berliner might arrive if he'd got up early to face an unpleasant day. The kind of day that saw a man briefly reunite with West German cousins to bury his grandfather; an old man he'd not seen since the Wall went up twenty-four years before. Checkpoint Charlie was for foreigners only. Diplomats, tourists, serving personnel from the Western military. And, of course, Frederika, but she had special dispensation.

This man, the man Tom was, probably didn't even know what *dispensation* meant.

An iron bridge rose above the railway tracks that marked the border in this part of the city. You entered the waiting area for the bridge under the flat gaze of Grenztruppen, border guards chosen for their absolute loyalty. These were volunteers, not conscripts, the dark green of their uniforms marking them out from the NVA, the regular forces.

A brick hut stood at the entrance. Huts beyond held guard quarters, search areas, dogs. Concrete barriers were positioned to prevent cars from trying to break through. Mesh fences helped corral people and stopped them going places they shouldn't go. Guards on top of a concrete tower watched to make sure.

To get from the waiting area to the bridge you had to be inspected, approved, possibly searched and still make it through a final barrier. Road traffic had a clearly marked route, with a special lane for VIPs. Everyone else used a walkway along the edge of the bridge.

There was less theatre than at Checkpoint Charlie and there were fewer signs. For all the Grenztruppen were armed, this crossing ran with a skeleton staff on both sides. It was functional, with no need to impress.

'Warm,' a woman said.

She was talking to him, Tom realized.

'It's going to be a long one,' she added.

The queue stretched ahead of them, self-servingly neat. No one wanted to be shouted at, nor sent to the back by boys in green uniform who'd done this so often that they might have been herding cattle.

'Family business?' she asked.

Tom nodded, not trusting his accent enough to reply.

Maybe she decided he was the silent type, maybe it didn't matter and she just needed someone to talk to and he was it. She was older, if not by much, with wide shoulders, a waist thicker than it had been once, and her hair hidden beneath a brightly coloured scarf. Her clothes were functional.

She talked for the next ten minutes and Tom took his cues from her face and nodded and smiled and frowned as he did his best to pretend that he understood more than every other word.

'Cigarette?' he offered.

She took one, let him light it from a box of matches that exhorted them both to exercise regularly and get plenty of fresh air, and lapsed into silence as the queue shuffled forward another few feet. When she looked as if she might strike up conversation again, Tom offered her a second cigarette, and let his fingers brush her hand as he offered her a light. She blushed and looked away.

His friends in the squat had done well. The suit they'd found him was shabby, slightly too large in a way that suggested he'd shrunk recently. It was the kind of suit that lived in the back of a closet or was folded and wrapped in plastic if no cupboard was available. Exactly the kind of suit a man not used to wearing suits might drag out for the funeral of a grandfather he'd not seen since 1961.

The only flamboyant touch was a Lenin badge on his lapel.

It was small, circular and cheap, its enamel some kind of resin set over red paint. The grey-haired woman had been pleased by its tackiness. Loyal, and insignificant, she explained. The ideal East German combination.

Its owner wouldn't be needing his suit, his travel papers or his badge. A hundred dollars had convinced him to spend the next three days drunk with grief. So drunk he couldn't be expected to notice he'd been burgled. There was no crime in East Berlin, but what there was was committed by gypsies or delinquents. One of these had obviously found him passed out on his floor and stolen what little he owned.

Who knew what they'd taken?

Poor Johan wasn't even sure why he'd applied for travel papers for a day and a night. He hated the West and his family there weren't much better. He'd told lots of people he was going. That must be how the thieves discovered he had a pass. Of course, when it came to it, he couldn't bring himself to go. He hadn't seen his grandfather in twenty years. He had no idea who'd gone in his place.

That was Johan's story and he'd be sticking to it.

42

'Papers.' The East German border guard held out his hand.

Handing over the pass that gave its owner thirty-six hours in West Berlin, Tom shuffled his feet and stared at the dirt as the guard checked its stamp and glanced at the photograph on Tom's borrowed ID.

He barked at Tom to remove his cap, which Tom did, straightening up so the guard could see his face. Unshaven, red-eyed. He looked like someone whose grandfather had recently died.

The guard pointed at Tom's case and he opened it meekly. Inside were tatty pyjamas. A washed white shirt still slightly grubby at the collar. A black tie faded to charcoal. And a washing bag with a drawstring holding a toothbrush, toothpaste, a safety razor and shaving soap.

That was it. The rest of the cardboard case was empty.

The guard ran his hand under the clothes, checking for anything hidden, and felt along the inside edges, despite it being bare cardboard and having no lining. A vague wave dismissed him and Tom shut his case, clicked its locks and turned to join the queue of those about to enter West Berlin.

The chatty woman was behind him. She sounded nervous now, the guard having to ask her something twice.

'Keep up . . .'

Tom nodded his apologies.

He refused to let himself look at the far end of the bridge. *Think nothing*, he told himself. He tried to let his shoulders relax and felt sweat bead in his cropped hair and begin to trickle down his ribs. It was all right though. A man like him would be nervous. He'd have spent a lifetime obeying orders and trying to avoid being noticed. The grey-haired woman's words were in Tom's head: *obedient and insignificant*. The guards would expect a man like him to look worried. And he'd be hung-over. His face was bound to have an unhealthy sheen. All the same, Tom felt his chest tighten and his stomach pull against his spine.

The queue shuffled forward and he shuffled with it: keeping inside painted lines, trying not to catch the interest of a pair of Grenztruppen with sub-machine guns. Beyond the two men, on the other side of the bridge, were their West German equivalents. Occasionally one of the two Grenztruppen would turn to stare at them. Mostly though, they watched those approaching.

Tom let his shoulders droop.

He was almost at the final gate with only a handful of others ahead.

Nobody was looking at him. No one had followed him here. He was almost sure of that. He'd slipped from the ruined flats near Hackescher Markt when it was still dark, stamping up to Alex station like a man on his way to work, cut through the huge station and out the other side. No one had followed.

He'd stake his life on it.

He *was* staking his life on it.

Behind him, the woman's voice was suddenly raised

and the two guards doing the final inspections looked up, like hunting dogs sensing prey. One of them stood on tiptoes as he tried to see better, as incongruous as a booted ballerina.

Breathe, Tom told himself. *Act normally.*

The guard held up his hand, stopping the line dead.

People at the back pushed on, not knowing what was happening. A shout came from behind as someone began elbowing through the crowd. As Tom turned, the woman he'd been talking to pushed him aside and ran for the gate, barged through and began to climb the steps to the walkway.

The sound of a shot brought the bridge to a standstill.

Tom watched her stumble, trip and fall. For a second there was ringing silence. Then the shouting began.

Rushing forward, the guard who hadn't shot her gripped the screaming woman's ankles and began bumping her back down the steps, only stopping when a West German guard ran forward, racketing the slide on his Browning Hi Power to slot a round into the breech. The two men glared at each other.

Then the East German shrugged.

'Your choice,' he said.

A GDR border guard appeared with a Praktica camera, and began photographing the woman to prove that she was still on East German soil. The crowd watching was as silent as a theatre audience. The West German guard who'd run forward glanced back.

He looked less certain of the situation.

'You can't have her,' the East German said. 'Although why would you want her? Still, if we must, we can wait here until she bleeds out . . .'

'You'll get her help?'

'If you haven't made us too late.'

The guard indicated that his colleague should haul the shuddering woman to her feet. He did so and dragged her away without bothering to look at the West German guard again. For a second, there was nobody ahead of Tom.

Nobody to stop him crossing.

Before Tom could take a step, however, a hand came down on his shoulder, and as he turned, he felt something jab his ribs and found himself looking into the eyes of a thin man, wearing a suit, wire-framed spectacles and a long black coat.

He had the long, elegant fingers of a pianist. One of them was curled round a trigger. Nothing in his gaze suggested that he'd hesitate to fire.

'Major Fox,' he said. 'If you'd like to come with me . . .'

43

'Your confession, Mr Fox.'

The Stasi colonel with the thin face opened a file, turned it the right way around for Tom to read and put it on the table in front of him. He added a pen, positioning it on the space at the top of the first page, exactly parallel to the first line.

'I haven't made a confession.'

'We took the liberty of preparing it in advance.'

The man's English was excellent and his shoes polished. He wore a gold Ruhla, with a sweep second hand, and a pin of the Patriotic Order of Merit.

Tom kept his hands to his sides and made no attempt to reach for the pen or read the neatly typed words in front of him. The thin man nodded as if to say this was exactly what he expected.

'Take your time.'

The door shut behind him with a click.

My name is Thomas Fox and I confess to the murders of Sir Cecil Blackburn and Lieutenant Evgeny Zhebenev . . .

Lieutenant, not ex-lieutenant.

If Evgeny was still serving, what was he doing miles from home guarding an Englishman? Punishment, for the shit that he talked about? Reward for surviving whatever it was? Or was he simply a man doing his job?

Whatever that was . . .

Tom went back to watching a bluebottle climb a window-pane, never quite making it over the lip. After a while he forgot about that too and simply waited. Tom was good at waiting. Problem was, in his experience long periods of waiting tended to end with short bursts of extreme violence. Sometimes his, mostly not.

The colonel came back an hour later, picked up the confession, checked it hadn't been signed and put it down again. His smile said he wasn't remotely surprised. Sitting opposite Tom, he examined him as if from a distance. His gaze was hard, clinical. He could have been looking under the bonnet of a car, wondering what was worn, how long before a major piece needed replacing. There was nothing personal in it.

'You've read your confession?'

'The first line . . .'

'You don't like it?'

'It's absurd.'

The man's smile was thin. 'Too crude. Too clumsy. I said you wouldn't sign it.' He ripped the confession in two and extracted a second from his briefcase, positioning the pen as before. 'You might like this one better.'

Leaning forward, Tom shut the file.

'Colonel Schneider,' the man said, introducing himself.

When Tom opened his mouth, the man held up his hand. 'It's all right,' he said. 'We know who you are.'

'You know I can't sign a confession.'

'But you must . . . What if we promised to deport you if you sign? Although we wouldn't mean that and you wouldn't believe it. Why would you? You're not a stupid

183

man, Mr Fox. You know we can never release you. How could we? You're a spy and a murderer.'

Tom opened his mouth again . . .

'Yes, I know. You disagree.'

Colonel Schneider sighed and for a moment Tom thought he was going to say more. Instead he stared out of the window, watching something Tom couldn't see from where he was sitting. Street life, to judge from what he said next.

'You think people here are unhappy. You're wrong. We give them jobs, housing, education, medicine, holidays, pensions . . . Most are happy enough. Why wouldn't they be? They have friends, families, lovers, favourite cafés and films, favourite campsites, chalets and hotels, memories that matter.'

'I didn't kill Sir Cecil.'

'You were photographed coming out of the building shortly after the murder. We know it was shortly afterwards because bodies retain their core temperatures and the pathologist was able to give us an estimate.'

'But you don't know when the photograph was taken.'

'Shadows, Major Fox. I'm sure you realize that we can pinpoint the time a photograph was taken from its shadow. Besides, you were seen leaving. Frau Doktor Blackburn has identified you from a photograph. As for your second visit . . . Well, one of my men found you inside. That was you, wasn't it? He said you pushed something into your pocket. Would you like to tell me what?'

'He was wrong. I took nothing.'

'Ah well, we can get back to that later. I assume you're working with Henderson? Perhaps even for him . . . ?'

'Henderson?'

'You think for a second we weren't watching that café when Frederika met you? Of course we identified the other man. A good operator, by all accounts. Thorough. Efficient. Did he tell you about his time in the Niger delta? No? The locals were causing problems for European oil workers. Henderson didn't have the resources to burn their village to the ground so he rounded them up at gunpoint and made them do it for him. One has to admire pragmatists.'

He glanced pointedly at the confession.

'You're saying Henderson would sign?'

The colonel smiled grimly. 'A man of that calibre? I doubt he'd have let himself be caught. Rewrite it, if you don't like the style. Say the British sent you and we'll go easy. Better still, confess and claim asylum. You'll find us sympathetic. We all knew London were never going to let Sir Cecil go home.'

'Why not?'

Pushing back his chair, Colonel Schneider picked up his briefcase and headed for the door, which someone began unlocking before he'd reached it. *'There are some things,'* he said, *'which should be done that it would not do for superiors to order done* . . . Abraham Lincoln said that.'

Tom looked puzzled.

'Feel free to take your time.'

44

'Go away.'

Sir Henry's shout echoed down the corridor of the West End theatre. The young woman raised her hand to knock again, decided not to bother and pushed her way into his dressing room instead.

'I said . . .' The old man looked puzzled. 'Who are you?'

'Hello, Sir Henry –'

'What are you doing here?'

'I wanted a quick word.'

'I'll have you fired,' he told her. 'No one comes in here before a performance. No one. I need –'

'Time,' the young woman said. 'To focus. Time to inhabit your part. I know, you mention it endlessly in interviews. You have a tendency to repeat yourself. Has anyone told you that?'

She wasn't an assistant stage manager or any of those people. He's realized that. They'd learnt to be polite. 'How did you get in?' he demanded.

'The stage door.'

'I don't talk to journalists.'

'Of course not. You have people to do that for you.'

She walked across to his dressing table and opened the case containing his pair of ivory-backed hairbrushes. A present from Olivier. He'd even had Sir Henry's initials monogrammed in red on the back. Instead of taking a brush she lifted the velvet bed on which the brushes nestled, revealing a syringe and a handful of glass ampoules beneath.

A single drop still hung from the needle.

'I do understand,' she said, 'why you need those last few minutes alone.'

Taking an ampoule, she broke its glass neck and slid the needle of the syringe into the morphine below. When the syringe was half full and the ampoule empty, she broke another and repeated the process, placing the fully loaded syringe in front of him.

'There you go,' she said.

He made no move to touch it. Instead he stood up, walked to the door and opened it. 'I don't talk to journalists and I don't pay blackmailers.'

'Do you get many?' she asked, sounding interested.

'Get out,' Sir Henry said.

'You don't mean that,' she said.

He opened his mouth to shout for help and then shut it again.

'That's better,' she said. 'I have to ask. Were you expecting me?'

He was. It showed in his expression. Somewhere in the back of his mind he'd known something like this was coming.

'What tipped you off?' she asked. 'The fire at the cottage in Wiltshire? Colonel Foley's tragic suicide . . . ?'

Sir Henry hesitated. 'Robby Croft's fall. Report said he'd

given that boy right of way. Robby never gave anyone right of way.'

'No, I don't imagine he did.' Taking a Kleenex from its box on Sir Henry's dressing table, the young woman removed her fingerprints from the syringe and put it back in front of him.

Sir Henry shook his head.

'Why drag this out?' she asked.

'You can't make me.'

'Of course I can.'

He looked at her.

'And I will,' she said, 'if necessary. But let's look at this. You're a national treasure. A knight of the theatre. You've performed with the Royal Shakespeare Company and had a part on *Coronation Street*. Your charity work is legendary. You also have granddaughters aged twelve and fourteen. Such an impressionable age. Do you want them to remember you for this?' She gestured at the posters on his dressing room wall. 'Or for headlines, sensational revelations, the fact their grandfather died in jail?'

'They'll say I killed myself.'

'If you don't, they'll say far worse.'

He knew that was true. She could see it in his face.

'Only it won't come to trial,' she told him. 'Put baldly, you have a choice. Do this now. Or I can come back after the performance with two men to hold you down. Can you do it? Go out on stage knowing that awaits?'

'My audience –'

'Will be shocked and saddened, and later, after we've told the papers how brave you were in the face of a cancer that you'd kept secret, and for which morphine brought relief, they'll understand. They'll be impressed.'

She nudged the syringe towards him and this time he nodded, his fingers trembling as he undid his cuff. Her face was impassive as she watched the tearful old man position the needle and slide it into his vein.

45

The interrogation room in the Volkspolizei station was spartan: a wooden table with two chairs on one side, and a single chair, Tom's chair, on the other. The walls were white, a bulb hung in a metal lampshade overhead. A mirror on one wall might be two-way or there to improve what little light there was.

Scraping back his chair, Tom walked to the mirror.

His reflection floated on its surface rather than behind. Two way, then. Squinting, he tried to see shadows but the room behind was too dark for show-through. He thought it had to be about midday.

The pen he was meant to use to sign his confession was a Heiko, with a gold-plated nib and swirling blue Bakelite barrel. Not quite the Mont Blanc that Caro gave him one Christmas but better than the pen Charlie used at school. Maybe Colonel Schneider was right. What you grew up with was what you knew. Jobs, housing, education, medicine, holidays, pensions . . . It didn't sound that bad a life, didn't sound that different. In many ways it sounded better than bits of his own.

After a while, Tom did what he'd told himself he wouldn't – opened the rewritten confession and began to read. He had no intention of signing it, but might as well know what he was refusing to sign.

He'd expected this confession to be as stilted as the

first. It was surprisingly reasonable, however. He confessed to having been sent by London to kill Sir Cecil but insisted that he was simply obeying orders. He bore no personal animosity towards Sir Cecil or the GDR. He was a soldier. He did what he was told. London would deny this but that was the point. Her Majesty's government needed deniability. Everyone knew they'd never let Sir Cecil go home . . .

That 'Her Majesty' was a nice touch.

Tom was rereading the line about obeying orders, when the door was thrown open and a Soviet general stamped in, flanked by two KGB sergeants. Without hesitating, the man closed the gap, lifted Tom by his throat and sucker-punched him under the ribs.

Soviets?

Breath left Tom's lungs and he jackknifed forward.

The next strike would have ruptured his throat if Tom hadn't twisted sideways in time. It still knocked him from his chair. A boot stamped for his head, scraping his face and catching his ear. He fought to stay conscious and failed. When the room returned Colonel Schneider was back; although he might as well not be, for all the attention the Soviet general paid him.

'I'm told you speak Russian,' the Russian said. He swung a kick and Tom rolled out of its way, clambering unsteadily to his feet.

'*Da, nemnogo.*'

'More than a little, I'm told.'

Tom shook his head.

'You're a spy . . .'

'I'm an army officer.'

191

'Not here you're not. Here you're a spy and a murderer.'

'You're Moscow's *rezident*?'

'See. How would you even know about KGB Heads of Station if you weren't a spy? You killed them both.' The Soviet's simmering fury indicated that this was personal in some way. Perhaps he'd known Sir Cecil. Maybe Evgeny had been a source of his. Something dark was driving that anger.

Colonel Schneider stepped forward and the rezident ignored him.

'With respect, Comrade General. This is not the way to handle it.'

'You think your way is better?' The rezident gestured contemptuously at the confession and the pen that rolled from the table to the floor. 'You think for a second he's going to confess unless he's forced to?'

Walking behind Tom, the rezident stepped in so close that Tom could feel the heat from his body. He waited for a blow to knock him sideways but the man simply stood there. Out of sight and silent.

Colonel Schneider seemed to be holding his breath.

And then, sighing, the rezident walked to the other side of the table, took a chair, put his elbows on the table and stared at Tom.

'Do yourself a favour,' he said. 'Sign.'

'Your friend told me to take my time.'

Reaching into his jacket for his ID, the rezident flipped it open and turned it so Tom could see the photograph and read the name below.

General Gregori Rafikov.

The KGB shield occupied the top-left corner. The insignia of the Soviet Union filled the top right. The photograph had been taken years before.

'I'm Russian,' General Rafikov said, 'he's East German. It would be stretching a point to call us friends.'

'We're comrades,' Colonel Schneider said.

The general smiled thinly.

'As you surmised,' he told Tom, 'I run HQ Karlshorst. You should know that under a long-standing protocol, KGB agents in Berlin have full authority. That is, we have exactly the same authority as we have in Moscow.'

Colonel Schneider's face tightened.

'You're being held by the Kriminalpolizei,' Rafikov said. 'I've suggested that their First Deputy Minister pass you to the Stasi. I don't actually understand the delay. Anyone but a fool can see this is a state-sanctioned assassination.'

He glanced at Colonel Schneider.

'Apparently, senior people in the GDR disagree. Still, that's not your concern.' Checking his watch, he said, 'Lunchtime. How convenient. If Colonel Schneider would like to give me a few minutes to myself...'

For a second Tom thought the colonel would refuse.

Instead he turned on his heel and marched from the room, shoulders stiff with anger, his junior officers trailing behind. The door shut with something that wasn't quite a slam. At a nod, one of the rezident's men bent Tom double and cuffed his hands below his knees, cold metal biting into his wrists. Then he lifted Tom into his chair and stepped away.

Putting on a single black glove, General Rafikov pulled a spring-loaded cosh from his pocket and put it on the table. The cosh was small, the leather so old it was cracked and black. The spring curved slightly to one side.

'You may go,' he told his men.

46

General Rafikov watched flat-eyed as his men departed, waiting until he heard an outside door close. Then he turned, and Tom barely had time to twist away before the cosh grazed his cheek, numbing half his skull.

The second blow caught his shoulder.

Pain lancing down his arm to freeze his wrist.

An abrupt punch knocked Tom from his chair and he tensed his guts half a second ahead of a kick that would have ruptured his liver if he hadn't. He managed to roll himself out of the way of a stamp aimed at his groin.

'You understand I'm going easy?'

Rafikov looked at him, and stamped again. Sneering when Tom jerked away to crouch behind a chair. Gregori Rafikov had the look of a cat deciding whether to drag out the killing of a mouse. 'Maybe I should take you back to Moscow.'

'That would be good,' Tom muttered.

General Rafikov's gaze sharpened.

'I have friends in Moscow.'

'Your embassy won't help. They won't even know.'

'Not at the embassy,' Tom said. 'Russians . . .'

'You're saying you're a double agent? You're one of ours?'

The general swung his cosh against his own hand, look-ing thoughtful. He seemed to be judging Tom's words and its weight at the same time. Perhaps he was simply wondering how thick Tom's skull was.

'Well?' he demanded.

'God forbid.'

'God's dead. Didn't anyone tell you?'

Tom spat, seeing blood-flecked saliva. When he checked his lip with his tongue it felt fatter than he'd imagined. He could feel sweat under his arms and smell fear on himself. He wondered if the general could smell it too.

Reaching for his pistol, General Rafikov jacked its slide and curled his finger around its trigger. 'Get up,' he ordered.

Tom crawled to his feet.

'Sit down.'

As before, the man came to stand behind Tom. This time he kept his distance, until Tom felt the Makarov touch his skull. 'Don't worry,' Rafikov said. 'You won't feel a thing.'

'I'm not sure that's true.'

'We did tests. Rounds travel faster than brain tissue tears. *Snapback* destroys a zone ten times a bullet's diameter. By then, no thought process.'

'I didn't kill Sir Cecil.'

'Of course you did. Evgeny too.'

'Believe me. I'm not going to confess.'

Rafikov's pistol slashed into the side of Tom's head and the room blazed red. Warmth seeped from his skull and filled his mouth. As salt as the sea. Tom shut his eyes to stop himself vomiting. When he opened them again the general was waiting. 'Evgeny was my nephew,' Rafikov said. 'Did they tell you that?'

Evgeny's uncle was the rezident? Tom needed time to work out the implications. There would be implications. 'I'm sorry,' he said without thinking.

The room flipped as the general slashed his pistol into Tom's temple, setting fresh blood flowing. He regained consciousness back in his chair, and watched the general circle the table like a wolf testing the edges of its cage.

'You were seen leaving.'

'Leaving,' Tom said.

'You ran.'

'You'd have stayed? What do you think would have happened if I'd telephoned Kripo to say I'd wandered past Sir Cecil's and found him dead?'

'You could have called your embassy.'

'I'm here as a private individual.'

'A private individual would have called his embassy.'

General Rafikov was probably right about that.

'It was my duty to get home,' Tom insisted, doubting that the general would believe him. 'At the checkpoint, what gave me away?'

The general shrugged. 'Who knows? I've seen your arrest photographs. You look convincingly miserable, downtrodden, hung-over and cheap.'

'You don't like East Germans?'

'They are our glorious allies. Efficient, loyal, trustworthy.'

'God, you really don't like them, do you?'

Unexpectedly, General Rafikov sucked his teeth. 'Nothing gave you away,' he said flatly. 'You were . . . How to put this?'

Sold out?

'If I was my counterparts, I'd be asking why didn't they

197

give you up before?' His face hardened. 'Now. Tell me why you killed Sir Cecil and Evgeny.'

Tom hesitated. 'How good was your nephew?'

'Very good. I trained him myself.'

Arrogant . . . As arrogant as any Roman governor in some provincial backwater. Tom saw Rafikov wonder what was behind the question.

'You'd expect him to be better than me?'

'He was younger, fitter, better trained. Of course I'd expect him to be better than you. He was *spetsnaz*. They make your special forces look like children.'

'Then why aren't I dead?'

'Because you shot him through the head the moment he opened the door. You shot him, and then you shot Sir Cecil.'

'Neither of them was shot,' Tom said flatly. 'Sir Cecil had his skull cracked and his chest caved in with a crow-bar. Your nephew was garrotted.'

Rafikov shook his head.

'I saw the bodies,' Tom insisted.

'He was shot,' Rafikov said, 'from close range. They both were. Through the heart and head. It's in the reports. How do you call it? Double-tapping. A typically English way to kill.'

'General . . .'

The man held up his hand. 'There was clear evidence of powder burn on Evgeny's forehead, on the doorjamb and the edge of the door. Proof my nephew was shot through the gap. I've read the report.'

'Did you see his body?'

'The lid was screwed down. His skull was destroyed.'

'His skull was mostly fine. His throat wasn't.'

The two men looked at each other and Tom watched the general glance at his cosh and then at his pistol, both now neatly laid on the table.

'You've been lied to,' Tom said.

Rafikov scowled.

'Were you told who gave me up?'

'Artists,' the general said, distractedly. 'Squatters. Nobodies.'

'Of their own accord?'

'What does it matter? Art is immortal. Thankfully, artists are not.'

'It matters to me.'

'Being a romantic is not good in an assassin. Assassins should have no illusions. No preconceptions . . .'

'I'm not an assassin,' Tom said.

Abruptly, the rezident flipped his chair round and straddled it. Pulling out a packet of Arkika Special, he put the cigarettes beside his pistol and dug into his pocket for a lighter. Gold from the look of it, with an enamel cartouche of Lenin on its side. Rafikov saw Tom looking.

'After Stalin's death,' he said, 'the cult of personality was demolished. That's what we were told. Except, of course, it never works like that. Our dead tyrant was swapped for a dead saint. Your terms, not mine. And the paintings and posters and statues of The Great Leader came down and those of Lenin went back up. Have you read Frazer's *Golden Bough*?'

'Yes,' Tom said, sounding surprised. The health of a kingdom mirrored the health of its king. The belief underwrote dozens of fairy tales.

'I studied Anthropology,' the rezident said tightly. 'Don't

think we're fools. The KGB takes the best. Why wouldn't we? We get first pick.'

He tapped his packet of cigarettes.

'Want one?'

Lighting two cigarettes, the rezident stuck one between Tom's broken lips and stood back to admire the effect. He seemed pleased with it, because he smiled to himself, and drew deep on his own.

'The last cigarette of the condemned man.'

Tom spat it out. It tasted foul anyway.

'Never get too complacent,' General Rafikov said, stubbing out his own. He sat back with a grunt. 'Now,' he said. 'The truth. Evgeny?'

'Hit on the back of the head. Then strangled with a dressing-gown cord.'

'Whose?'

'Sir Cecil's, I would imagine.'

General Rafikov considered that.

Tom felt that the man was starting to believe that he might be telling the truth. What puzzled Tom was why the GDR would lie about how Evgeny and Sir Cecil died, and to a KGB rezident. There was something else. Tom had been seen pocketing something on his second visit to the flat, yet the general didn't even seem to know that there'd been a second visit. Whatever Colonel Schneider's game, Tom needed it to stay that way.

'These friends in Moscow?' General Rafikov asked.

Tom felt relief surge through him and did his best to hide it. Rafikov could find out the details for himself. What Tom told him he'd double-check anyway. He might as well hear it first hand from the lion's mouth.

'I was there a few months ago.'

The Russian smiled thinly. 'Of course you were. Holiday?'

'My bosses were hiding me from a Select Committee. A government enquiry,' Tom added. 'One too stupid not to ask difficult questions. So they sent me to Moscow for a few months to look at religion.'

'If faith can move mountains.'

'Exactly . . .' Tom was impressed.

It had worked well enough in Afghanistan, where the CIA were now arming US-trained mujahideen with US-made missiles to bring down Red Army gunships.

'Quiet visit, was it?' General Rafikov asked.

Tom thought again of Maya, the beggar woman who'd turned out to be an ex-Stalingrad sniper, and of her husband, one of the most powerful men in the Politburo, who'd believed her dead. With their help, he'd tracked Sir Edward Masterton's kidnapped daughter to a deserted Soviet slaughterhouse and helped kill her kidnappers.

'Moscow? Very quiet,' Tom replied.

47

'Humphrey-Baker, Sherwen, Wong, Michaelides, Bennett, Fox . . .' Mr James walked the length of the junior table at St George's Prep School, handing out that morning's post. He turned back, handed a fat envelope to Onyilo, which had obviously got out of sequence.

'Right,' he said. 'Remember to take the envelopes with you.'

They would. If one boy left rubbish then the whole table got into trouble. And everyone knew who the trouble-maker was, because his name was on the envelope for a master to read out. Leaving rubbish behind was anti-social. Anti-social was about the worst thing you could be at school. If it didn't get you into trouble with the masters it did with other boys afterwards.

Charlie Fox was teaching himself not to be anti-social.

He kept a list in his pocket of things that were frowned on and tried not to do any of them. He picked up his dirty clothes and put them in the basket. He didn't open or shut windows without asking if others minded. He especially didn't do more than slash in the downstairs loo next to Latin class. If he wanted to do more he headed for the changing rooms. Using the little loo near Latin for any-thing more was the height of anti-social.

The others had envelopes. He had a package. A

package wasn't what he wanted. What he wanted was a letter from Mummy. She hadn't written for two weeks and
she always wrote. Her letters arrived on Friday.

'It's not your birthday, is it?' Mr James said.

'No,' Charlie said hurriedly. 'That's November.'

'He's lying, sir.' Michaelides obviously.

'I'm not.' Charlie's voice was fierce. 'It's on my passport.'

'It's on my passport,' Michaelides mimicked. He had
believed it was November though, and some of the wild
joy at the thought of being able to give Fox the bumps for
his birthday had gone from the bigger boy's face.

'Beautifully wrapped,' Mr James said.

He was the kind of master who'd notice such things. He
was thin and slightly boyish-looking, with a stammer and
a way of absent-mindedly swiping a lock of hair out of his
eyes when it fell forward. Willo didn't like him. Willo
taught Geography and Gymnastics. His real name was
Smith but Willo was a play on words. Willo the Wiff,
because he smelt.

So far none of the masters had worked that out.

'Aren't you going to open it then?'

It wasn't his birthday and there was no *sent by* address on
the brown paper under the neatly tied string. Charlie
thought you had to have a *sent by* address by law. Mummy
said you did. Also, the knot was so neat he wasn't sure how
he was meant to untie it.

'Slip the string over the end,' Mr James suggested.

'It won't fit . . .' Charlie replied, remembering in time to
add *sir* to the end of it.

'You know that, do you?' Mr James said.

203

Charlie nodded and the master smiled.

'Here,' he said. Dipping into his pocket, he passed a pearl-handled penknife to Charlie, who cut the string in a single go. The blade was sharp. He should have known Mr James would have a penknife with a sharp blade.

'Thank you, sir.'

'My pleasure.' He hovered at Charlie's shoulder while Charlie slid his finger under a tiny tab of Sellotape put there to keep the paper fastened.

James Bond. 007. Aston Martin DB5.

A drawing on the box showed someone bad being ejected through the roof while machine guns spat fire from beneath the front lights and an armour-plated shield at the back stopped baddies shooting the driver.

Opening one end of the box carefully, Charlie slid the car on to the table and looked at it for a moment, before picking it up and finding the buttons that worked the guns, and bullet shield and ejector seat. The little man in the ejector seat flipped halfway across the table and Mr James laughed.

'May I?' he said.

Charlie handed the car across.

'Thought so,' Mr James said. 'It's an original. That means it's from the 1965 run. Looks new too. You're very lucky.'

He handed the Corgi toy back to Charlie and looked at the brown paper that now stood neatly folded on the table with the string curled, equally neatly, beside it. He seemed to be looking for a note of some sort.

'Who sent it, Fox?'

The boy looked worried. 'No idea, sir.'

The question nagged at Charlie for the rest of the day

and he was still picking at it when lights out came and the others settled into their snoring, farting, sleeping selves. Charlie wasn't sure that he liked people. Well, he liked some individually. Not many, admittedly. Together they were too animal-like. After an hour of listening to people sleep, he climbed from his bed, found his lock picks and his practice padlock and went to the little loo by the Latin room, shutting and locking the door before turning on the lights.

It would take him ten or fifteen minutes of picking at his locks to calm down. He didn't want anyone disturbing him before that was done.

He left the James Bond car by the side of his bed.

48

Tom was left alone in the interrogation room for so long that a cockroach that dragged itself into daylight through a rip in the skirting board returned in darkness. Lights came on in the corridor outside and showed under the ill-fitted door. Tom wondered why the door fitted so badly and decided it was so that those in line to be interrogated could hear what was happening inside.

The really dirty work was probably done in the cellars, though.

In Tom's experience, the really dirty work was always done in the cellars.

Cellars were dark and soundproofed, and there was something very final about being surrounded by earth. A reminder of the grave.

His bladder was full and his stomach empty.

He was barefoot, his hands cuffed under his knees, still wearing the cheap and shiny suit in which he'd tried to cross the border. And he was beginning to wonder what was keeping the rezident.

Break it down.

You could survive most things if you broke them down.

Well, most things that didn't actually kill you. And a brutal ache in your shoulders, fingers frozen from the cuffs and a desperate desire to piss yourself were hardly going to kill you. The cockroach didn't reappear, but daylight did. The darkness endlessly diluted, like ink into which someone kept adding water.

It was when daylight hardened, and Tom realized he'd been in solitary for almost a day, that he began to wonder if he'd simply been forgotten or was being watched on camera; if General Rafikov had better things to do or was simply letting him sweat. That was before he even began to wonder why Colonel Schneider hadn't returned.

Sometime around noon General Rafikov did.

Slamming the door in the face of whoever had been following him, he stamped across to the desk, sat himself in a chair and pulled out a packet of cigarettes. This time round he didn't offer Tom one.

'I'm back from Moscow. They've never heard of you.'

Tom stared at him in shock.

'When I first called, it was suggested . . .' He looked disgusted '. . . that I fly home and present myself on the third floor. You know who was in that room when I walked in? The Chairman of the KGB, the heads of the First and Second Directorates, and Gorbachev's shadow, Marshal Milov himself.' Stabbing out his cigarette, General Rafikov lit another and took a hard look at Tom.

Tom's squalid state seemed to sooth him.

'The field marshal wanted to know why I was wasting the Politburo's time. Why I was involving HQ Karlshorst in minor GDR business. He said, if he were me, he'd concentrate on important matters. And perhaps suggest to Berlin that if you were innocent they let you go. And, if guilty, that they have you shot . . .'

'That's impossible.'

Before Tom could say more the door opened and Colonel Schneider strode in, followed by three Stasi underlings. 'You demanded twenty-four hours,' he said. 'It's up. You've been to Moscow, I hear.'

'Can I ask who told you that?'

'You were seen getting on a Moscow flight.' Colonel Schneider's voice was little short of contemptuous. Tom wondered what had changed and decided Schneider knew the general had been rebuffed. The question was why? Why would a Soviet grandee like Milov lie about knowing Tom?

Tom was picking at that thought when General Rafikov went on the attack. Although he began slowly enough. 'I should point out that our Englishman here insists he didn't kill his countryman.'

'Of course he does,' Colonel Schneider replied. 'That's exactly what you'd expect him to say.'

'But you have evidence of his involvement?'

'He was seen leaving the crime scene.'

'Leaving it,' General Rafikov said. 'Not committing the crime. Can you even prove he went into the flat?'

'We found fingerprints,' Colonel Schneider said crossly.

'On the crowbar?'

'What crowbar?' It was said too fast.

'The one used to crush Sir Cecil's chest.'

'Sir Cecil was shot in the head and heart. It's the English method.'

'This crowbar that doesn't exist. Do you still have it?'

Colonel Schneider's glare was murderous. It was fixed on Tom though. He stepped towards Tom's chair, blinking when General Rafikov moved to put himself in the way.

'I'd like to inspect the Englishman's body,' Rafikov said. 'Have someone tell Central Morgue that I'll be visiting.'

'It's gone, Comrade General.'

'The English took it?' General Rafikov sounded shocked.

'His daughter refused custody. She told us he was our responsibility. She suggested we deal with the corpse quickly and quietly.'

'So. No hero's funeral?'

'He was cremated yesterday.'

'And Evgeny?' General Rafikov said quietly.

'His body was returned to Moscow, Comrade General.'

'When?' Rafikov's voice was so sharp that Colonel Schneider flushed. The German might be elegantly dressed, and important in his own world, but the general had the physical authority and wore his superior rank with ease. Besides, he was KGB, and for all that Gorbachev's policy of glasnost meant the relationship between the USSR and East Germany was more strained than it had been in decades, that still counted for something.

'When? This morning, I believe. By train.'

Before the general could say more, Colonel Schneider nodded at his nearest underling and nodded dismissively towards Tom. 'Have that unshackled. Take it for processing.'

49

The stink in the back of the police van was as familiar as static. It had a gritty, dusty, burnt quality. The smell of old vans, powerboats on summer lakes, motorcycles waiting at traffic lights, and something else . . . Tom fought a memory that hung greasy beneath the surface of his childhood and shied as it rose towards the air. Pushing it down, he held it under until it stilled. When he released it, it hung for a second, bitter and hungry, before sliding into the depths.

Oxygen starvation, Tom told himself.

He was alone in the back of a Barkas B1000. From the front, the Barkas was enough like a VW Campervan to be disconcerting. If VW produced a special-issue underpowered model, with a tiny windowless cell fixed to the back.

Fumes from an exhaust that was either cracked, drilled through or otherwise intentionally altered leaked from a grille in the floor, which was the only source of ventilation for the van's rear.

With his escort up front on a bench beside the driver, Tom had the cell to himself. It had no bench, so he sat on the corrugated floor, his wrist handcuffed to a crossbar behind him. The sun was high, his metal cell already hot, and the steady leaking of the exhaust through the grille only made things worse.

Marshal Milov, the old bastard, had talked about

dushegubka and Tom wondered if he was meant to arrive at all. The fascists, as the marshal invariably called the Nazis, had trucks designed to asphyxiate their victims using exhaust fumes. Maybe this van was more for garbage than deliveries.

Every time the driver braked, Tom slid across the floor, until his wrist brought him up short. Every acceleration slid him into the bar behind. He knew left and right turns from the way his body twisted. They'd left the city almost immediately, heading east, as far as he could tell on a road that required less stopping and turning the longer they were on it.

Tom tried not to be worried.

It was fifty miles from Berlin to the Polish border.

If they took him across, would they take him on? It was less than 400 miles to Russia itself. It might have been quicker to fly him, and simpler to send him by train, but this was discreet, and his chances of getting a message to the world beyond were non-existent. Tom had just decided that this was what was happening when the van turned hard north and kept going.

And kept going, and kept . . .

He woke to find the side door open and his escort and the driver growling at each other. Having prodded him with a rifle butt, his escort said something dismissive to the driver, who shrugged. When Tom begged to be let out to piss, they slammed the door in his face. So he shrugged in turn, pissed himself and watched the acrid puddle find its own way to the grille.

He wondered what the British had been told, what they knew. Was London making a fuss? He imagined that

Caro's father was. He was a man with power. But how much weight would he carry against *Realpolitik*?

There was another round of Strategic Arms Talks coming up. Everyone approved, at least in public, of glasnost and perestroika, this great thaw between East and West, but no one yet quite believed it would happen. If the British government went into battle on Tom's behalf, the Soviet Bloc might decide it proved he'd been sent to kill Sir Cecil.

Those days were meant to be over.

Hunger, car sickness, and the carbon monoxide trickling through the grille reduced Tom's thoughts to their simplest forms. How long before they let him out? Would he ever get out? The friendship of a Soviet field marshal had been his trump card. When he'd told General Rafikov to talk to Milov, Tom had been convinced he could survive this. He liked the odds much less now.

When the van lurched to a sudden halt, he kept going and the yank on his wrist almost dislocated his shoulder as he spun into the side of the van. It hurt. Of course it bloody hurt. His right eye was filling with blood when his escort yanked back the side door, swearing at the carbon monoxide.

He gave Tom's cell a second or two for the air to clear.

Then he crawled in, undid Tom's cuff and dragged him out, dropping him to the tarmac. When Tom struggled to stand, he realized the man knew what he didn't. Tom's legs weren't ready to support him.

'All yours,' he said.

Fresh hands dragged Tom upright. They bundled him through a door, with the kind of glass that sandwiched mesh in its middle, into a changing room where they stripped him, spun him in a circle and cavity searched him, before dragging him to a white-tiled shower room, where they tossed him against a wall and used a fire hose to blast him into a little ball in the corner.

It was entirely casual.

In some ways he needn't be there at all. In some ways he wasn't. He had no idea if they knew he was English, no idea if they knew his name or what he was meant to have done. The prison uniform they gave him was coarse, badly patched and filthy. It saved him the trouble of catching lice by having the lice there already. No one fed him, no one took his name or read him the rules. He was simply pushed into a room containing three double bunks, pointed towards one of them and told to shut up, not make any noise and not cause problems. He'd be processed in the morning.

Sometime after midnight they came back.

There'd been a change of plan. He was to be shot.

50

Blinding lights picked Tom out.

They pinned him to the water's edge, where the surf-tossed grit and gravel of a beach shifted below his heels. At his back was the Baltic; a flat black sea that stretched out for ever. There were no ships to light the darkness. No cities or towns to either side. Only the shuffle of gravel, the scraping of the soldiers' boots and the glare from the searchlights.

He wondered if he was meant to turn and swim for it. What his chances might be of escaping into the darkness before machine-gun bullets began ripping into his back and neck. He stood naked, and unashamedly frightened, in front of six hard-eyed boys, his hands cuffed behind him.

With their thumbs on pressure points in his shoulders, the boys had steered him out of the camp, down to the stony beach to leave him in the waves. Tom wished the lights would go off. The boys were quite close enough to kill him with a simple sweep of their AK-47s. Burn out the magazines and he'd be no more. They didn't need lights to pick him out.

Forgive us our trespasses as we forgive those who trespass against us.

The only bit of the Lord's Prayer that really mattered to him, and the bit that worried him the most. Too much of what he'd done was unforgivable. The truth of that filled his eyes with tears and he thought of Charlie trapped in that damn school the boy hated, Caro wondering what had happened to him. And Becca . . .

He wanted to believe he'd see her again.

Lead us not into temptation.

Tom hadn't done very well with that one either. Perhaps better than people thought, though. But not good.

For thine is the kingdom, the power and the glory.

Those words had always moved him. Even now, long after he had begun to worry about what, if anything, they actually meant.

For ever and ever.

Naked as the day he was born, blinded by the light, Tom shivered in the cold wind scraping the shingle, and watched the boys holding Kalashnikovs, their fingers already on the triggers.

They'd arrived that night in the total darkness, kicked open the cell door Tom had thought locked, barked at the men in the other bunks to stay the fuck where they were, not move, not look, not speak, unless they wanted a kicking.

At the same time, they'd dragged Tom on to the concrete, kicking and stamping. One man went for his groin and caught his thigh, trapping flesh between heel and floor. The flash of pain left Tom gasping. Before he could act, before instinct could even curl him into a tight ball, he was dragged upright and thrown into a wall, then slammed straight back into it when he bounced off. And, as he tottered, wondering why they were avoiding his face, he felt his arms yanked behind him and cuffs locked on his wrists.

Dragging him from his cell and along a dark passage

towards a heavy door, they bundled him downstairs. Tom hoped they lied. That they were taking him to an interrogation room. Perhaps to the cellars. But he found himself outside, frogmarched through the silent camp. Razor-wired gates were dragged back to let his party through.

The gap between the gate and the Baltic was narrow. The dirt hard and the grass coarse and sharp-bladed. A wind, which blew across what looked like half a lagoon, tasted salt and sharp and primitive. If there were stars, they were beyond the brightness of the searchlights.

Without being ordered to, the boys dragged him to shore, pushed him to his knees and one of them yanked back the charging handle on a Kalashnikov, stepped back and put the muzzle to Tom's skull.

Instinctively, Tom shut his eyes.

The boy didn't fire, he simply stood there grinning and waiting for Tom to open them again. At his nod, the others dragged Tom to his feet and began stripping him with a lazy efficiency that was more chilling than the breeze.

As Tom watched, they stepped back, looked at him with vague interest and turned to watch a young officer, who was buttoning his jacket as he approached. A sergeant walked at his side. The sergeant was scowling.

'Couldn't this have waited?' the lieutenant muttered.

The boy who'd pretended to shoot Tom shook his head. 'Has to be tonight, Comrade Lieutenant. Don't ask me why. Orders.'

The comrade lieutenant grunted.

'I suppose I'd better check if he wants to confess.'

This is happening, Tom told himself. He looked at the

shingle under his feet, wondering why it wasn't heightened, why he wasn't seeing it in a way he'd never seen things before. Only, all he really wanted was to piss and be allowed to go back to sleep. The second of those wasn't going to be a problem much longer and he felt suddenly ashamed that pissing himself was probably the first thing he'd do in death.

'Do you speak Russian?' Tom asked.

Behind the lieutenant, the boy in charge of the troop looked suddenly alarmed. The alarm was there, and then it wasn't as he met Tom's eyes, shrugged and prepared to carry out his orders anyway.

'I do,' the sergeant said. Tom had thought he might. His hair was grey and his eyes lined. He looked the right age to have grown up under Soviet occupation.

'Ask the lieutenant if confessing would make a difference.'

The sergeant did, his mouth twisting sourly as he relayed the reply. 'Only to your conscience, apparently.'

Tom snorted. He was proud of that.

'Then I'm glad it was only a technical question. Tell him I didn't do it. I have no intention of confessing to a murder I didn't commit.'

'You're Russian?'

'I have friends in Moscow. Friends in high places.'

The sergeant shrugged. 'Not high enough.'

'They come no higher,' Tom said with feeling. He didn't know why the commissar had betrayed him, and he didn't expect his words to save him this time, any more than they'd managed to save him last time, but he wanted them said.

'You really didn't kill this man?'

'I really didn't kill him.'

'That's a shame.'

When one of the boys stepped forward with a hood, Tom shook his head. It was the sergeant who told the boy to step back. At his order, the boys set their AK-47s to single fire.

'Ready . . .'

Tom made himself meet their gaze.

'Aim . . .'

He couldn't see them against the brightness of the light.

But he made himself lift his chin and stare as steadily as he could at their silhouettes. He imagined he saw the boys' trigger fingers whiten as they took up the pressure. And then the lieutenant raised his hand, the lights from the towers snapped off and the Kalashnikovs opened up as he let it fall.

Pain blossomed across Tom's chest, the few rounds that missed whistling into watery darkness behind. The force of the rounds threw Tom back and he stumbled, trying to find his balance before falling to his knees. The waves were gentle, the pebbles on the edge of the water gleaming in unexpected moonlight as his face went down to meet them.

51

'In the beginning there was darkness . . .'

The words came out of that darkness and Tom's body was on fire. It burnt in a band across his chest and even breathing hurt.

He shouldn't be breathing.

He tried to move. He tried to raise one wrist, expecting it to be fastened to the trolley on which he lay, but it lifted away. He tried to turn his head towards where the voice had been.

'Well . . . I suppose we'd better have the light.'

Fluorescent tubes flickered into life and Tom realized that he was lying on a steel trolley in a morgue. The man standing by a throw switch that belonged in an old Frankenstein film was wearing a green apron, holding a scalpel and smiling.

He was also speaking English.

Touching the scalpel to Tom's shoulder, he ran it down to Tom's breastbone, tutting when Tom winced. 'Barely a scratch,' he said, lifting the scalpel to the opposite shoulder. He made another equally shallow incision and then ran the blade down towards Tom's groin. Stepping back, he pretended to open Tom up, as he would do if performing a real autopsy.

He mimed pulling out Tom's lungs, cutting them free and dropping them into buckets. In a moment of absurdity,

Tom almost asked if he shouldn't weigh them first but this didn't look like the sort of morgue where technicians bothered to weigh body parts.

After the lungs came his stomach, liver and viscera. All lifted invisibly, cut free in mime only and dropped into buckets and trays. The man looked into the empty trays and sucked his teeth, stopping to make a note on a pad with a stub of pencil. When he was done, he stepped back and lit a cigarette.

'Well,' said the man. 'That was impressively baroque.'

He put down the cigarette, picked up a round of ammunition and tossed it on to Tom's naked stomach, then watched Tom grab it before it could roll to the floor. Tom regretted everything about that movement.

'See what I mean?'

'Dummies?'

'You tell me . . .'

The round was squat, lacking the right length. Tom squinted, trying to make sense of it through his pain.

7.62 × 39mm. Standard Eastern Bloc issue.

Except the case . . . Not crimped, so not a blank. More . . . He tried to remember the batten rounds issued in Ulster. They'd replaced rubber bullets, being judged less lethal, lower muzzle velocity too. The rounded projectile here was softer, almost waxy.

'Up you get.'

Tom gasped. 'Give me a second.' He sounded back from the dead.

'Come on,' the man said. 'You can do it.'

Very carefully, Tom slipped one leg over the edge and stopped to catch his breath. Should he swing the other leg over or see if this one would reach the tiles? He doubted if he could stand. The man must know that.

'Take these,' the man said.

'Painkillers?'

'Opiates. The Huns think you're dead.'

'*Huns?*'

'Well, certainly the boys who shot you.'

Stepping forward, the little man gripped Tom under the arms and turned him so he sat on the edge of the trolley. He gripped Tom's hips and pulled them towards the trolley's edge, catching Tom when his feet wouldn't hold him.

'Perhaps not yet.'

He sat Tom back and bent to take a closer look at the bruising across his chest and stomach. He sucked his teeth.

'Bloody awful shots.'

Tom tried to look for himself.

'Keep still for a second or you'll make yourself sick.'

'You're a doctor?'

'Once upon a time. Now . . .' The man looked round his morgue. 'Now I work down here. And help a little upstairs. If they want a surgeon there's one about fifty miles away. Mostly they ask me. Less paperwork.'

'You're a prisoner?'

The words came more easily and Tom risked checking his bruises. Glancing down didn't make him sick but the extent of the bruising did. A cold lurch that translated as *Oh fuck*.

'Nothing broken,' the man said.

'Really?'

'Well, maybe a few ribs. Nothing serious.'

'Where am I?'

'In an autopsy room having been cut open.'

Tom looked at him.

'Oh, don't worry. No one will come in. And I was the one to collect you. I'm always the one to collect the dead. Doesn't matter who they are or how they died. It's a bit of a tradition.'

The man had another go at helping Tom to his feet and this time Tom was able to stand, although he swayed a little and the lights made him feel sick. Stepping away, the little man used one hand to hold Tom steady.

'How's that?'

'I hurt.'

'You're alive. Concentrate on that.'

Walking around Tom he looked at the bruises, raising his eyebrows occasionally. Once he stopped to touch the scar on Tom's shoulder. 'New,' he said. It wasn't a question. 'Small calibre,' he said of the one in Tom's thigh.

He was bald, with wire-rim glasses. And, although it was clear to Tom that he was English, his words were so obviously inflected in the wrong places that it had to be years since he'd spoken his own language.

He had all the presence of Dr Crippin blinking in the dock. A man whose murderousness had been matched only by his apparent meekness. You had to be resilient to survive in a place like this, though. To be foreign and become trusted took unusual skill. Even for someone medically trained.

Grunting, the man reached for his pad.

He looked Tom over one final time and sucked his teeth.

'You drink, don't you? I thought so.' Dragging the

yellowing pad towards him, he flipped it open, and scrawled *Alcoholic? Ex alcoholic?* across a page. 'You have the look,' he said. 'Something about the eyes. And it shows in the skin around your cheekbones . . . It always shows.'

He stared at Tom and began to make notes on the ready-inked outline of a human body. That done, he sketched in the scars that he could see from the front: knife, bullet, bullet . . . The wound in Tom's shoulder stopped him.

'Crossbow,' Tom said.

The man snorted as if it was a joke.

He touched the arrow's exit, tapped the damage left by a small-calibre bullet that almost ended Tom's life on an Ulster hillside and hesitated at a whip scar that curled across Tom's lower back and on to his buttocks.

'That is old,' he said.

'Very.' Tom kept his response simple.

'Right. You died of heart failure. I found evidence of pulmonary valve stenosis. Congenital. That means you've had it since birth. And your liver . . .' He looked sombre. 'Cirrhosis. Your kidneys were almost as bad. Your spleen. Well, you'd probably have been fine if your liver wasn't buggered. As it is . . .' He finished scrawling and signed and dated the page. 'I'm surprised I haven't seen you earlier.'

'They think they shot me.'

'They did shoot you. But I can hardly write that down, can I? Random foreigner, shot. Heart attack, heart attack, heart attack . . . You'd be surprised how many of those we've had recently.'

'What happens now?'

'Oh. We cremate you. Obviously, that's a bit of a loaded

subject for most of the older Germans but it's efficient, cheap and growing in popularity with the young. The bishops don't like it for different reasons. But it's His Holiness Karl Marx who holds sway round here.'

Loaded subject?

'Do you know who invented the first proper crematorium? Sir Charles William Siemens. Sounds English, doesn't it? He wasn't. His nephew, Carl-Friedrich, perfected it. German efficiency.'

'You have one here?'

'Of course.'

'Don't tell me,' Tom said.

The little man nodded. 'I started it earlier. And yes, that's my job too. So I guess I'd better do it. Reckon you can get yourself down there?'

He led Tom to green-tiled stairs that Tom negotiated by gripping a rail and moving crabwise, gasping at every step. At the bottom, the man pushed open the door to a double-height room and winced at the heat. A steel door that should have been in a bank vault opened when he tugged a lever.

'Christ,' Tom said.

'It does get a bit hot in here. Still, in you go . . .'

The man mimed pushing a body along steel rollers into the furnace and yanked the lever that shut the door. Flames roared on the far side of thick glass in a little window in the grey door's middle.

'Job done. Let's have a drink to mourn your passing.'

52

Back in the autopsy room, the man took a bottle of surgical alcohol from a medical fridge, filled two small beakers
about a third full, topped them up with chilled water and
put one of them in front of Tom, raising the other in salute.

'Your health.'

Tom raised his own glass. The rawness of it made him
cough.

'Tony Wakefield.' He looked at Tom archly. 'Although
my friends used to call me Flo. That was back then, obviously. When Berlin was more interesting than it probably
is these days. And I wasn't. Not even close.'

'Wasn't what?'

'A Flo.' Wakefield sipped at his glass, winced at its taste
and knocked it back in one. For a second, with his head
tipped back and his eyes staring at something long gone
he looked like someone else.

'This,' he said, 'is where you're meant to tell me who
you are.'

But Tom's thoughts were gnawing at the man's name.
He knew it, and through the shock of being shot, and the
fierceness of the pain, he remembered where.

'*The Importance of being Lady Windermere.*'

Wakefield's mouth fell open.

'You wrote that with Cecil Blackburn.'

Blackburn's name seemed to rattle him. His face

hardened and his voice became waspish. 'I didn't write that with dear Cecil. I wrote the bloody thing full stop. Cecil just added his name to it. As he was wont to do to everything. Loathsome man.' Reaching for the bottle of surgical alcohol, Wakefield poured himself a healthy slug and drank it down in one.

'He's dead,' Tom said.

Wakefield sat back, his face so pale that Tom wondered if he was about to pass out. The doctor's gaze flicked to the door as if expecting someone to burst in. Without even realizing, he reached again for the bottle. Tom pushed it closer.

'You're sure?'

'I found his corpse.'

'As in, didn't kill him yourself?'

'No,' said Tom. 'I definitely didn't kill him myself.'

'Pity. I'd like to shake the hand of the man who did. You know, you still haven't told me your name, why you're here and who sent you.'

'You were expecting me?'

'Yes. I was told yesterday I'd be getting a body. I was to take good care of it. I've been here more than twenty years. And I'm still alive against all odds. Sometimes the odds change. One side or the other was going to send someone eventually.'

'I'm not here to kill you.'

'You probably are.' Wakefield poured a glass for Tom and another for himself. 'You just don't know it yet. Drink up. Alcohol will help numb the bruising. And I suppose I'd better let you dress.'

Tom looked at him.

'Are you sure you wouldn't like to introduce yourself?

Your name is our security, that's something we used to say. I could trade you the clothes?'

'You should probably just give me them.'

'You're probably right.' Wakefield smiled. 'Death comes in so many guises. Some less kempt than others. Let me get you today's disguise.'

There were two parcels wrapped in brown paper and tied with string. One was lumpy and the other smooth, with rounded edges. It could have contained folded blankets. About the right size for that too. Wakefield cut the strings with a scalpel and pushed both parcels across.

'Go on then,' he said.

Ripping off brown paper, Tom stopped. He took the khaki jacket by the shoulders and shook it out, noting the cornflower-blue collar tabs. Shoulder bars proclaimed the owner a lieutenant colonel in the KGB. Extracting a shirt, tie and trousers Tom shook those out too, hanging them over the edge of the desk.

The second parcel contained an officer's cap with a cornflower-blue band and blue piping. Gold braid crossed the band below a hammer and sickle inside a sunburst. The hammer and sickle were red enamel. The sunburst gold.

KGB issue, officers. Standard daily.

'See,' Wakefield said. 'Many guises.'

Tom took a look at himself in an ancient mirror above a sink in the corner of the autopsy room. He looked no stranger in this than in his usual uniform.

One side or the other was going to send someone eventually.

He was on the shores of the Baltic, no longer certain he was even in East Germany. He'd arrived not knowing why he'd been sent here rather than somewhere else. As certain, as much as he was of anything, that finding himself here was a chaotic mix of incompetence, happenstance and bad luck.

Now he wasn't sure.

What were the odds of him ending up in the same camp as one of Sir Cecil's old colleagues? Someone whose name was on the cast list?

'Bastard,' Tom said.

Wakefield blinked.

'Not you. Milov. The Soviet field marshal. *He says he's never heard of you. He wasn't sure why I was bothering him.* General Rafikov too. They're both bastards. Milov's the reason I'm here. He had Rafikov set this whole thing up.'

Reaching for his beaker, Tom drained it down.

'You look like you needed that.'

'More's the pity.'

'Full blown?' Wakefield asked.

'Recovering. Maybe recovering. I'd got so used to the stuff that half the time I couldn't work out if I was drunk or not. What about you?'

'Oh, I'm always drunk.'

Wakefield reached for the flask and refilled his beaker. He was careful not to refill Tom's, simply moved the bottle within reach so Tom could fill his own if he wanted. It was a surprisingly gracious touch.

The morgue was still as squalid as Wakefield's prison uniform. The man himself was clean though, his hair almost neat. Pushing back his chair, Wakefield went to a steel cupboard and dug among boxes of yellowing bandages for a pack of tarot cards. Shaking free the cards, he cut the pack.

'How am I doing?' he asked.

'No idea,' Tom replied.

'Pity.' Wakefield scooped the cards up, closed his eyes and shuffled, then cut again and put one card on the table. 'Helps me think,' he said.

The card showed a naked man and woman climbing from separate coffins with a child kneeling in a smaller coffin between them. In the sky above, an angel circled by stars spread flaming wings.

'How fitting,' Wakefield said.

He pushed the card towards Tom who turned it round and found *Judgement* written in gothic script along the bottom.

'Yours or mine?' Tom asked.

'Both, I'd say . . .'

'I'm surprised they let you keep the cards.'

'You don't believe?'

'Not in Tarot.'

'What do you believe in?'

'The power and the glory.'

'How romantic. Did they beat that into you at school?' Wakefield shrugged. 'I can recognize lash marks when I see them.'

'Those weren't school,' Tom said.

Wakefield became very still. 'Are you sure you didn't kill Cecil?' he said.

53

Wakefield cut the tarot cards as he waited for Tom to answer.

'Sir Cecil was going home,' Tom told him.

'He must have been mad.'

'All the same . . . I was sent to collect him.'

'And our friend got there first?'

'Which friend?'

'This one.' Turning the pack face up, Wakefield revealed a skeleton wielding a scythe, which he tapped lightly. 'Tell me,' he said. 'What do you know about Patroclus?'

'Hector killed him. And Achilles killed Hector.'

'Not the man. The club.' Wakefield sounded tired. 'I always wondered what he'd do with it . . .'

'Who?' Tom said. 'With what?'

'Rafikov. With my confession.'

'What did he do with it?'

'Sent you. Apparently. It was meant to be a simple camping holiday, you know. With a friend of Cecil's. Beautiful mountains, clean rivers, little clearings in the forest where we could sunbathe naked. He turned out to be KGB.'

'You never suspected?'

'He was so very beautiful.'

That had to translate as *no*, or perhaps *didn't care*.

'Tell me about Patroclus,' Tom said.

Reaching for the cards, the little man began shuffling them with an ease that looked almost lazy but saw the cards align perfectly and so loosely that the sides could be tapped into place. Shuffling the cards one final time, he passed the pack to Tom and told him to turn up the bottom card.

It was the skeleton again.

Then he told Tom to cut the pack near the middle.

A young man in ankle boots holding a flower and looking at the sky was about to step off a cliff while a dog gambolled at his heels.

'How appropriate,' Wakefield said.

He put *Death* and *The Fool* side by side and face up.

'You know the first well. The second less so.'

'They're both me?'

'Obviously.'

Scooping up the cards, Wakefield shuffled again and passed the pack to Tom, telling him to cut near the top. A naked girl knelt beside a pond holding a water jug in either hand. A huge star, circled by other stars, shone in the sky above her shoulder. He looked at the card and then back at Tom.

'Who did you lose?'

Tom felt his voice tighten. 'My daughter.'

Wakefield cut the pack and laid out three cards, aligning them exactly and tapping the corner of each as he gathered his thoughts. 'You think her death is your fault. It isn't . . .'

'I don't think it's my fault.'

'You do. Now, Patroclus was a bit of a movable feast. It wasn't a real club. Well, it was, but not the kind you're thinking. It was over an Italian restaurant in Old Compton Street. The floor was given over to three rooms of Kashmiri throws and battered chairs, Moroccan mirrors, Zulu masks. This was the sixties. You can imagine the sort of thing. The restaurant downstairs . . .'

Wakefield shrugged.

'Reassuringly ordinary; round tables with paper cloths, metal chairs, blown-up photographs of Mount Etna and the waterfront at Palermo framed in painted plywood arches. Ad people ate there, tourists occasionally, the Tin Pan Alley crowd, couples having affairs. Nice bottle of Valpolicella, a couple of pizzas, a shared gelato and on your way to bed somewhere.

'There was a little door at the back with a sign saying *More Tables Upstairs*. No one was shown up who wasn't known.'

'Whose club was it?'

'Eddie, an ex-copper, owned the building. At least he did on paper. So either the bribes were good or he was fronting for Cecil. Mind you, Old Compton Street, slap bang in the middle of Soho. All those brothels, strip clubs and clip joints. Maybe he really did own it. Not a nice man, our Eddie.'

Wakefield put his hand on Tom's wrist. The gesture was almost fatherly. Assuming you had the kind of father where it wasn't safest to duck every time his hand moved. 'Did he know what was going on upstairs?' Tom asked.

'It wasn't,' Wakefield said. 'Not in the way you imagine. That went on elsewhere. In reform schools, mental asylums, orphanages. Anywhere that held children nobody really cared about. That's what I mean about it being a bit of a movable feast. There was a place near London. One in North Wales. Another in Northern Ireland . . .'

Tom tried not to react.

'Ah,' Wakefield said. 'They worked like hell to keep the last of those out of the news but they started late . . . And there was that boy.'

'He talked to the police?'

'He died,' Wakefield said flatly. 'It was getting to be a habit.' He caught himself. 'Not exactly a habit but it wasn't the first time. Cecil gave everyone up, you know. When the authorities found out. And then the clean-up began.'

Wakefield looked haunted. 'Some of us bought our lives,' he said. 'Most weren't offered that choice.'

'What was the price?'

'Total obedience. I got a call saying Cecil was lonely. Missing home, they said. Why didn't I take a holiday in Berlin? They told me to play up the "old friends" act. See what I could find out about his defection. Cecil suggested a camping holiday. Just us and a couple of local boys. A week later I'm here. He came to see me, you know. Cecil. All shocked at the misunderstanding. He wanted to help . . .'

'What did he want in return?'

'Are you sure you didn't know him? He wanted something of mine. A tiny notebook I'd kept for sentimental value.'

'Really . . . Did you give it to him?'

'It was at my mother's. In London.'

'And British Intelligence hadn't asked for this?'

'Oh, they didn't know. It was a list of names from just after the war, no one important. A handful of sketches of a friend. Honestly hadn't occurred to me.'

Tom stared at him. 'You told Sir Cecil who had it?'

'Like a fool . . . I never saw him again. Luckily, I still had my uses.'

'Where did you and Sir Cecil first meet?'

'Berlin,' Wakefield said. 'It was where everyone met. You have no idea of what it was like to be in Berlin in those days.'

'The horror?'

Wakefield almost sneered. 'The power,' he said. *To thine own self be true.* The self can be pretty vile if let off the leash. And whatever we did, it couldn't be worse than what the people we replaced had done. There was always that.'

'Berlin changed you?'

'The ruins turned us all into rats.'

It sounded like something he'd heard said or had said himself and was simply repeating. Tom tried to imagine the trajectory of the little man's life. The points through which he'd had to pass to get from the ruins of post-war Berlin to a camp on the Baltic, via children's homes in the United Kingdom and a club in Soho that sounded to be more of a clearing house.

'*You have your uses.* What uses?'

Tom must have sounded sharper than he intended because Wakefield reddened and opened his mouth to say something cutting, took a look at the uniform Tom was now wearing and shut it again.

Institutionalized.

'No notebooks,' he said. 'Not these days. I don't ask or know the names, occupations or crimes of those I treat. The guards bring me men who are broken. I patch them up or put them out of their misery. Every now and then, the guards bring me their wives or daughters and I do what's required and another baby who isn't needed escapes being born . . .'

'Back to the club,' Tom demanded.

'Upstairs was a meeting place for the like-minded. A place where telephone numbers could be given, addresses swapped.'

'Of those who went?'

Wakefield sighed. 'Of places those who went might want to go. As for the club . . . There were waiters, waitresses. All over the age of consent. Well, the waitresses were. As the boys were the same age they should have been. Sir Cecil was very careful not to have problems brought in.'

'It wasn't enough?'

'The vice squad got greedy and put up their price. When Sir Cecil went over their heads, Vice raided it anyway. MI5 were furious. So I was told. I think it actually cost a chief inspector his job. He died in a car crash the following year so chances are it cost him more than that. All those names delivered to the plod on a plate. There was talk of Cecil setting up a new club and then he vanished. The next anyone knows, he was suddenly a lifelong communist and had defected. He took the last secret with him.'

Tom stared at Wakefield.

'I have no idea if he ever gave it up.'

'You didn't . . .'

'Oh. I never knew it.'

The man pulled the pad towards him, reached for his pencil and proved himself a liar. As he began writing, he said. 'There was a laundry list, Cecil said. Of those who needed to die. It was divided up between cleaners who never met. One target didn't make it on to the list.'

Turning the pad, he showed Tom the name he'd written. And Tom reached for Wakefield's drink and downed it without thought.

Lord Brannon.

The Queen's cousin.

'We're talking about the name you never knew?'

'Yes,' Wakefield said. 'We're talking about the name I never knew.'

'It died with Sir Cecil?'

'I would imagine so.' Reaching for a box of matches, Wakefield folded the note into a neat little fan and set it alight; his eyes following the flames greedily. 'According to Cecil,' he said, 'permission to clean was sought and granted, with one stipulation. It could be an accident, it could be a terrorist outrage, it could be an inexplicable murder by a –'

'Lone lunatic.' Tom finished the sentence for him. 'What it must never ever be was traceable to those who sanctioned it?'

'Exactly.'

'Pity you don't know it then.'

Wakefield shrugged. 'Perhaps.'

54

Seventy-six hours later Tom found himself back in East Berlin, dressed in full KGB uniform. He'd been delivered there by a Soviet sergeant, who'd arrived at the camp, saluted smartly and said absolutely nothing for the entire return trip. Since Tom was dosed with painkillers, and his bruises prevented him getting comfortable, he was grateful.

The NCO had been told the colonel was not the talkative type.

So now Tom sat in an office in KGB Karlshorst, reading an obituary for Sir Henry Petty in a three-day-old *Daily Telegraph* he'd found beside a telephone on the desk. The telephone didn't work or he'd have tried to call Caro, taped conversation or not.

The actor had been found dead in his dressing room five minutes before a performance. The obit talked of the greatest of his Shakespearean performances, his eccentric family, his famous irascibility, the fact his interest in charity work sprung from helping orphans in post-war Berlin.

Sir Henry had been in the little notebook, and on the cast list for *The Importance of being Lady Windermere*. As had Colonel James Foley, lately dead by his own hand, and lately of Berlin.

What were the chances of two suicides on that list in the same year? Tom needed to find out if any of their friends had died recently. More than this, Eddington needed to know about Sir Cecil's claim that Lord Brannon, the Queen's cousin, had been murdered by British Intelligence. Except that even knowing that put Tom in danger. He trusted Eddington, more or less. But he couldn't say the same for the high brass at Century House. And it went without saying that he had to keep that information out of the hands of the Soviets.

Tom sat back in his chair and stared at the ceiling.

He knew he should be working out his next move and turning Rafikov's unexpected, and obviously dangerous, patronage to his advantage but more than anything Tom wanted to talk to Caro.

I'm alive. He needed her to know that. He wanted Caro to be the first person he called. What would Rafikov say if asked to get a message through?

What would he demand in return?

HQ Karlshorst was south of Tierpark, with its huge zoo, rambling park, formal garden and famous palace. The KGB compound itself was less of a campus and more of a small town. And as for Tom's office . . .

It looked down upon a tank on a plinth. The Museum of Unconditional Surrender of Fascist Germany in the Great Patriotic War was contained within the compound, Karlshorst being the place where Marshal Zhukov ratified Nazi Germany's surrender.

Putting his feet on the desk, Tom leant back and stared at the ceiling. Like cracked ceilings everywhere, the cracks could be made to look like anything you wanted. In this case they looked uncannily like a map.

Of where, Tom wasn't sure.

*

The delivery of a new colonel to the KGB compound at Karlshorst had drawn stares; but that could have been the brand-new Volga that delivered him to the door, or the way General Rafikov came down the steps, gripped the newcomer warmly by the elbow and steered him away from the others.

'The Stasi are furious,' he muttered.

'About what?' Tom asked.

'Your death. I'm not sure Colonel Schneider believes it though. He has men watching the crossings and endlessly picking up litter outside your embassy on Unter den Linden. Best if you don't contact them or try to cross until things settle a little. A few days at most.'

'General –'

'Trust me,' Rafikov said.

He caught Tom's expression and burst into laughter.

The sound of it was loud enough to make those in the hallway turn, smile and get on with their own lives. 'Your face,' Rafikov said. 'Find your office, read the paper, then take a walk. The zoo's nice at this time of year.'

'The zoo?'

'A four-hundred-acre oasis in the middle of a city. I've always liked the flamingos. Oh, and before I forget, Marshal Milov sends his regards.'

He left Tom staring after him.

55

East Germans moved out of his way as the KGB colonel
strode towards them. A few of the younger men made
themselves meet Tom's eyes, then glanced aside. Women
blushed or simply pretended not to notice his gaze.
Maybe it was the KGB collar tabs that made everybody
nervous.

Soviet officers couldn't be that rare.

Hide in plain sight.

A bunch of Nationale Volksarmee conscripts stepped
back to let him through. A traffic officer came to attention
without noticing. A grey-haired Kripo major clicked his
heels. A move so unexpected Tom wondered if it contained some coded insult. If others noticed him Tom
didn't notice them.

At the zoo he walked to the head of the queue and no
one complained as he paid his pfennigs, pushed his way
through the turnstile and stopped inside to look at the gift
shop. A young mother, swollen with milk and busy feeding, saw him stare and Tom dipped his head in apology.

Instead of being cross, she smiled.

He missed Charlie. Caro, too.

A huge map showed where animals could be found.

Notices reminded visitors that the elephant house was
being rebuilt, the flamingos had a new lake, now with an
island in the middle, and that the huge wolf run about to

open on the park's northern edge was part of a breeding plan for reintroducing the Russian forest wolf (*Canis lupus lupus*).

Tom watched the woman with the baby for a while, and wondered how much he was simply filling time, and how much of the sadness that the sight of her brought was guilt for not being there when Becca was young.

Caro had fed both Becca and Charlie, and had a hard time of it. She'd insisted, against her mother's advice, against her friends' warnings it would damage her figure, quite possibly against her own wishes. But she did it for Becca, in that bloody-minded way of hers, because it was the right thing, and for Charlie because she'd done it for Becca.

'You have children at home, sir?'

The woman was in front of him, her blouse re-buttoned and the baby slung over her shoulder to burp on a blanket resting over her blouse. Her Russian was halting and she blushed at having asked the question.

Tom nodded and she sucked her teeth sympathetically.

'It must be hard,' she said. 'Missing them.'

She walked away and stopped by the map, laughing ruefully when the baby hiccuped milk on to her shoulder. Tom watched her go and then struck off in the other direction, the path splitting to offer him a choice of petting zoo or the new lake for flamingos. Remembering Rafikov's words, he chose the lake.

Those around him had an understanding that Tom simply wasn't there. They stepped aside as if without noticing. He chose a table in front of a kiosk at the water's edge, and the woman sitting opposite casually decided she'd had enough of her coffee, stood up and headed for the lake without looking back. Tom stared after her, saw the man beyond, and had to stop himself from swearing.

It was impossible. But it was also true.

Harry FitzSymonds, Tom's old boss, the man who brought him into the business, was leaning against a fence, watching the flamingos. He was dressed in a blue blazer and fawn trousers, with a panama hat pulled low. In Eastbourne he'd have been invisible. In Tierpark he was unmissable.

As Tom watched, Fitz raised his hat to the woman, swept fingers through his greying hair and scowled at the heat. He had the patrician look of a retired brigadier or a successful confidence trickster. Shooting his cuff, he checked his Rolex. He had it on a NATO strap, for God's sake.

Although, Tom thought, *why not?*

No one looking could imagine he was local. And he was entirely too well turned out for a tourist. Tom looked for Fitz's shadow and identified a pimply youth, who shuffled nervously, looked at Tom and glanced away.

'What's your name?' Tom demanded.

The boy looked round in pretend surprise, bit his lip and mumbled something that ended in *sir*.

'Take a walk,' Tom said.

The boy glanced towards Fitz.

'He'll still be here when you get back. And, if not, I'll return him to here when we're done.' Tom had no idea how much of his Russian the boy understood but it didn't matter because, as far as the boy was concerned, Tom was a KGB colonel, with all the authority that gave.

The boy would write something in his report.

And if anyone bothered to read it, they might pass it up the line, so someone could have a word with Karlshorst about the need for Berlin to be kept in the loop. And that might spark someone in the KGB compound to ask questions.

Then again, maybe not . . .

Intelligence services believed the more information the better. Tom knew, because he'd seen whole departments drown in it, that this was rubbish. If you wanted to paralyse an enemy's Intelligence you fed it so much data it didn't know where to start. Too much time went into filing for anyone to analyse what was really there. The old man staring at the flamingos had taught him that.

56

'Who are you meant to be meeting?' Tom asked in Russian.

FitzSymonds almost jumped, but his pride in his trade-craft was too great to allow him to do that. Instead he stared ahead. His knuckles where he gripped the fence were white. 'Christ,' he said. 'Is it really you?'

'Yeah,' Tom said. 'It's me.'

'We were told you were dead.'

'You were told wrong.'

'They've rebuilt the flamingo lake.'

Tom glanced at it. 'You've been here before?'

'In the late seventies. Based out of 32–34.' He used short-hand for the British embassy on Unter den Linden. He'd have been in the cellars, Tom imagined. In the comms room. Most of the really interesting work was done there.

'That's when I met Rafikov. Can't say I was expecting to get a call from him. London was in two minds about letting me come.'

'You were here officially?'

'I'm official now too. Embassy-based.'

He stared at the shallows, where pink flamingos stood in warm water up to their knees. The water shimmered in the sun and reflected the blueness of the sky and the occasional white cloud. The afternoon looked and felt idyllic. FitzSymonds's smile was sour. 'That uniform suits you rather better than it should.'

'Sir. What are you doing here?'

'Coming out of retirement to clean up your mess. You were photographed coming out of that building where they butchered Cecil Blackburn. I mean . . . Christ, Tom. Did I teach you nothing?'

Tom felt his face redden.

He was one of Fitz's boys. Fitz's boys didn't let things like that happen.

'How do you rate your chances?' Fitz asked.

'Of what, sir?'

'Getting out of this alive,' Fitz said flatly. 'Rafikov claimed I'd be meeting a Soviet attaché who could confirm your death. Because that's what London currently thinks, you know. That you're dead. A heart attack in some godforsaken Baltic slave camp. I was the man who told Blackburn to ask for you. Told him you were a good man. You'd keep him safe.'

'You said you were here in the seventies.'

'Didn't say I hadn't been back since. This is a fuck-up, Tom. Even for you.'

'Fitz. That's not fair.'

FitzSymonds fed Tom's words back at him and they stung.

'We should walk,' Tom said.

'Don't want to make it easy for them,' Fitz agreed.

'Although where'd they position a parabolic mic?'

'No mic could filter out that lot.' Fitz nodded to a group of Young Pioneers in shorts or short dresses, with white shirts, and red scarfs tied neatly round their necks. For all their neatness they were noisy. And for all there were flamingos, the children walked right past them.

245

Birds doing nothing were birds doing nothing. There were more interesting animals ahead. Three rhinos for a start. Tom and Fitz fell into step behind the group and let their chatter wash over them.

'Never expected to have you to blame for me being dragged away from my roses. First I'm told you're on the run in East Berlin. Then I'm told the GDR have you and want to swap. Suddenly that's off and you're dead. Really sorry and all that.'

'Surprising honesty.'

'Made me wonder what they were hiding. And now here you are, popping up like Hamlet's father to scare the children. Who knows you're poncing round the city dressed like this? Because I'm pretty sure the Stasi don't. So, my next question has to be, has Rafikov turned you?'

'Of course not.'

'And you wouldn't tell me if he had. Make no mistake about it, Tom. Rafikov's a nasty piece of work. I'm surprised he hasn't got you locked up. That would fit better with his style. Make us waste years wondering if you're alive.'

'Like Tony Wakefield?'

Fitz blinked. Tom saw it. When the old man spoke, his tone was entirely too casual. 'You ran into Flo Wakefield?'

'Very briefly.'

'And where was that?'

'The camp near the Baltic.'

'Were you still in East Germany?'

Tom thought about the journey and had to admit he didn't know if they'd crossed a border or not. He'd seen no border post on his return. But the landscape had been flat and wild and the roads narrow and largely deserted.

Up ahead, the Young Pioneers had stopped to stare at rhinos standing desolately in the middle of a dusty field. It wasn't much of a swap for the savannah, but it was better than a cage. Shutting one eye, Fitz tipped his head slightly sideways and pretended to aim. His bullet noise sounded authentically silenced. Not something a big-game rifle might produce.

'You used to hunt?' Tom asked.

'Back in the days when it wasn't reprehensible. I was based in Mombasa for a while. Suppose I should ask: get much of a chance to talk to Tony?'

Tom hesitated. 'Not really,' he said.

'Pity. And Rafikov extracted you, I imagine?'

'Ahead of a Stasi colonel called Schneider ordering me killed. If Rafikov can be believed.'

'Which he can't. He's probably running some sort of double bluff designed to keep you unsettled. I still wouldn't have thought he'd let you run free. I'd have expected something altogether nastier.'

'Nastier, sir?'

'You know, dripping stone cell, unearthly screams from your neighbours, wild dogs howling outside your window, waves clashing against a cliff . . .'

'You're thinking of Château d'If.'

'Probably. Love that book. It's one of the great texts on how to knit yourself a legend and go undercover. Dumas père . . . Man was an absolute genius. Did you know that your nickname was Dantès for a while?'

'No, sir. I didn't.'

Edmond Dantès. Alias the Count of Monte Cristo.

A local boy trapped in a lie, who escaped captivity and

became a pretend aristocrat to take his revenge on the world. Yes, that made sense. Fitz would have had fun coming up with that moniker. Tom sometimes wondered if the whole world was simply something between a quiz and a crossword for the old man.

'Tell me,' Fitz said, 'how you became involved with Rafikov.'

Tom stared at the rhino Fitz had pretended to shoot and used the time to put his thoughts in order. Every time he thought he had it, he had to go back a little to something that had happened before. In the end he began with the *Berliner*, the military train he'd boarded at Brunswick. Fitz was interested in Sir Cecil's flat and what Tom made of the crime scene.

Tom had known he would be.

'The first time, I'd literally just arrived. I got up to their floor and someone started leaning on the bell before I'd done much more than notice the door had been smashed open.'

Looked as if it had been smashed open, Tom reminded himself.

He talked Fitz through the position of the bodies, the efficiency with which Evgeny had been garrotted, the sheer brutality of Sir Cecil's death. He mentioned the lack of lividity, Sir Cecil's broken ribs, the way the crooked end of the crowbar had been left buried in his chest.

FitzSymonds looked shocked.

'It was pretty grim,' Tom admitted.

'Find anything of interest?'

Tom hesitated. 'No, sir. I didn't have time.'

'Maybe Rafikov was telling the truth and a Stasi colonel

was on his way to kill you.' Fitz's brow furrowed. 'The question is, why would an old KGB hand like Rafikov bother to save you?'

'Repaying a debt. That's what he says.'

'That bloody mess in Moscow with Sir Edward Masterton's daughter . . .'

Tom wondered who'd told the old man about that. And realized, a second ahead of asking, that he had no idea who'd pulled Fitz out of retirement, and couldn't possibly ask without getting a lecture on need to know.

Fitz was right though. *That bloody mess* had seen a KGB general killed and Gorbachev nearly unseated by the Soviet old guard. Alex Masterton's kidnapping had been just one sticky thread in a much bigger and nastier web. It was undoubtedly why Rafikov was helping. Tom had begun to wonder if it was the only reason.

'Your father-in-law called the Foreign Minister to say your orders were to bring Cecil Blackburn home. He refused to believe you had anything to do with the murder.'

'And the Foreign Minister called you?'

'No, when the FO wasn't receptive, Masterton called the Blessed M direct. Don't scowl. I know you don't like the woman but she is Prime Minister. If not for her, you'd have been abandoned to your . . .'

FitzSymonds stopped.

'Ah,' he said. 'Time's up.'

Fitz's pimply shadow was back, looking nervous.

'I should go anyway,' Fitz said. 'I'm having lunch with the ambassador. And I'd like to drop in on the library at the Humboldt if there's time.' He hesitated. 'By the way . . . What are you reading at the moment?'

'Nothing, Fitz. I'm reading nothing.'

'The compound doesn't have a library?'

'If it does I don't have a library card.'

'And it's probably all depressingly Russian . . .' Fitz-Symonds dug into his briefcase. 'Here,' he said. 'Have this.' He held out a new le Carré. 'One of his better ones, in my opinion. Although, obviously, they're all good. Oh, and Tom . . .'

Tom knew they'd reached what mattered.

'You do have the memoirs, don't you? Stashed safely. Thing is, Sir Cecil said he gave them to you.'

'That's not true.'

'We intercepted a letter. And no, you can't ask to whom. Given the shit shambles you're in it's best you don't know.'

'Fitz. The fireplace was full of ash.'

'The thing is . . . My guess is Rafikov has a deal in mind and I might have trouble selling it to London. Not having the memoirs could be a deal-breaker.'

'For Moscow?' Tom asked, puzzled.

'Christ, Tom. For us.'

57

Nothing hidden between the pages.

Turning the novel spine up, Tom flicked through just to make sure. Then pulled off its jacket to find perfectly ordinary boards behind. Nothing hidden in the gap between spine and pages, nothing written on the jacket's shiny inside. Why would there be? Fitz hadn't even known Tom was coming.

He checked all the same.

'What's that?'

Looking up, Tom saw General Rafikov in his doorway.

Rafikov held out his hand and Tom passed the book across. *The Perfect Spy.* The Russian flicked through the pages as Tom had done.

'Nothing,' Tom said. 'I've checked.'

'What were you looking for?'

'A file,' Tom said. 'For the bars to the windows.'

'There are no bars on the windows.'

'A key then.'

'The door is unlocked. You're free to come and go. You can even take your chances with the East Germans if you'd rather.' Rafikov grinned wolfishly. 'I'll have to confiscate this, obviously. You realize that, don't you? Check London haven't replaced all the full stops with microdots, hidden a transmitter in the spine, that kind of thing. I can find you a copy of *Pravda* if you're bored.'

'You like le Carré?'

'Who doesn't?'

'I'm surprised,' Tom admitted.

'You mean . . . *When I hear the word culture I reach for my revolver?* Goering was an idiot as well as a fascist. One can have both. Bulgakov in one hand. A B-10 recoilless in the other. You've read Bulgakov, haven't you?'

'Who hasn't?'

The rezident smiled. 'I should go,' he said.

At the door, he turned back looking suddenly serious.

'I'm sorry, I forgot. Dr Wakefield hanged himself.' He shrugged. 'These things happen, unfortunately. I'll let you know if the novel is as good as your friend Fitz-Symonds says.'

58

'Humphrey-Baker, Sherwen, Wong, Michaelides, Bennett . . .' Mr James walked the length of the junior table handing out that morning's mail. 'Right,' he said. 'Remember to take your envelopes with you.'

He stopped behind Charlie, and the boy's heart sank at the sight of another parcel in Mr James' hands. 'Are you sure you haven't had a birthday?'

'Quite sure, sir,' Charlie said firmly.

He had no desire to be given the bumps. Although, if this went on much longer, they'd give him the bumps just to be sure. He took the parcel from Mr James and remembered to say, 'Thank you, sir.'

Charlie wished everyone would stop staring.

The boys wanted to know why he'd been sent another present. The masters . . . Charlie had seen how they watched him. There was something they weren't saying. Mummy too. Her Friday letters were full of Granny did this, Grandpa said that. She didn't mention Daddy. She never said anything about herself. Not even when he wrote to ask if she was all right. She'd stopped her Sunday afternoon telephone calls too.

'Aren't you going to open it then?'

Michaelides, obviously.

It was as neatly wrapped as the parcel before, the same crisp brown paper and tightly knotted string. As if hearing

Charlie's thoughts, Mr James dipped into his jacket and held out his pearl-handled penknife.

'This must be . . . ?'

'The third one, sir.'

Mr James watched as Charlie cut the string, put it to one side, removed the first layer of brown paper and folded it carefully. Charlie didn't want any more presents. The first one, the 007 car, had been nice. Mummy hated *nice*, but Charlie still used it when talking to Becca or himself. The second present less so. This one made him feel . . . Charlie wasn't good at feelings.

Not right, possibly.

Inside the second layer of paper was a hand-made cardboard box, and inside that, wrapped in tissue, a purple Rolls-Royce. It was long and low, with an open top, plastic jewels for headlights, doors that opened and front seats in which sat two people. Charlie peered at them carefully.

One of them seemed to be him.

59

Harry FitzSymonds was already outside East Berlin's famous televison tower, a *Reisebüro der DDR* guide in one hand. His other held a half-eaten frankfurter that had been drowned in bright-yellow mustard and pushed into a hollowed-out roll.

Ignoring him, Tom marched towards the *Fernsehturm*'s entrance.

At 365 metres high, the Toothpick was the tallest structure in Europe. Constructed in the 1960s, it had a metal sphere near its top containing a visitor platform and revolving restaurant. When struck by sunlight at a particular angle the sides of the sphere lit up with a glowing cross. The locals called this *the Pope's revenge*. That last bit was not in FitzSymonds's guidebook.

Tom bought his ticket, and pushed his way to the head of a queue for one of the two lifts, and felt rather than saw Fitz join a small group behind him. It was early and a weekday, there were no school parties and, as Tom had hoped, Fitz's shadow decided to wait below; safe in the knowledge his target was going nowhere except 200 metres straight up to an observation platform.

Berlin was laid out below and set in a green patchwork of lakes, forests and fields. The Wall made the West of the city brutally obvious. It was brighter, faster, more crowded. Tom wondered if the East Germans around him were envious. How did it feel to look down on that alien little enclave?

'Careful,' FitzSymonds said. 'Don't go native on me.'

He pushed his guidebook under Tom's nose and pointed randomly. Anyone looking would have assumed he was asking a question.

'You were scowling,' he added. 'Practically glaring like a good Communist Party member regarding Sodom. Or are we Babylon these days? I forget . . . How did you know I was here?'

'Rafikov suggested I visit the *Fernsehturm*.'

'Subtle,' Fitz said. 'He took the le Carré, I imagine. Did you get a look first?'

'Only to skim the jacket copy.'

'There was a letter written on the endpapers. Invisible ink.'

'How on earth was I . . . ?'

'Oh God, not for you.' Fitz turned over a couple of pages and pointed at something else. Tom pretended to read a line. 'It was for Rafikov. All very Moscow Rules. He's old school enough to appreciate the gesture.'

'You're negotiating my release?'

FitzSymonds hesitated.

'There's the possibility,' he said carefully, 'that Moscow might be willing to force Berlin to declare you innocent and return you.'

'Berlin thinks I'm dead.'

'Schneider doesn't.'

'What's the catch?'

'Moscow want us to release one of theirs. No one important, they say. Which suggests he is. At the moment, he's taking a nice little wander round the nature reserve near Wormwood Scrubs with someone from their embassy.'

Fitz looked around him, dismissed a local family as unimportant, scanned the observation platform and pushed his book at Tom again. In a way, Tom was impressed. Only a stupid foreigner would keep pushing a guidebook at a KGB colonel. Because only a stupid foreigner wouldn't know what the sky-blue band on his cap signified. 'Now,' Fitz said. 'You'd better tell me who gave the order.'

'What order?'

The old man's eyes tightened.

'Tom . . . There's a narrow window between that gymnast of Sir Cecil's going out and his daughter turning up. Ten minutes max. You were seen arriving. You were seen leaving. Who ordered you to kill him?'

'I wasn't acting on orders.'

'Christ, Tom . . .'

'*Fitz*. I didn't do it.'

'Charlie Eddington didn't . . . ?'

'No,' Tom said firmly. 'He didn't.'

'I have your word on that?' FitzSymonds said.

Tom nodded, and the old man stared at the aluminium façade of Centrum Warenhaus, East Germany's largest department store. 'Probably just as well . . . This place used to be beautiful,' he added sadly. 'Now it looks as if some spoilt brat kicked over a bucket of Lego.'

He hesitated. With FitzSymonds you could never tell if the hesitations were real or simply stage-setting. The older Fitz got, the more Tom suspected that he was simply playing himself. Maybe that happened to everybody.

'Look,' Fitz said suddenly. 'This is confidential. Three

years ago we nearly went to war. For real. Neither side came out well and it made the Cuban Missile Crisis look like a minor scare. War games got out of hand and neither NATO nor the Warsaw Pact had protocols in place for backing down. We scared each other. More importantly, we scared ourselves.'

'Glasnost was the result?'

'One of the results. The PM's started to wonder if Gorbachev's for real. Reagan too. There's a round of Arms Reduction Talks scheduled . . .'

He hesitated, and this time Tom had the feeling it was for real.

'Sir Cecil was about to name names. We thought he'd given them all up. Price for admission, etc. I imagine the Soviets thought they had them all too. Cecil always was a devious bastard. After his defection, their London attaché began to make approaches. Too fast and too clumsily. You can guess the rest.'

'Broken crockery?'

'One heart attack, one car crash, one skiing accident, one drowning, one unexpected fire at a very pretty thatched cottage near Exeter.' Fitz scowled. 'A black Labrador died. I've always felt sorry about that.'

'And more recently . . . ?' Tom asked.

'Rafikov's been talking?'

Tom thought of Sir Henry Petty's overdose. The cast list for that damn play. The alpha in the notebook against his name.

'Call it an educated guess.'

'Have you tried to contact Caro recently?'

Tom blinked at the change of subject. 'No,' he said

flatly. 'I was in a prison camp until a couple of days ago. And any call would have to go through Karlshorst. Doesn't mean I'm not desperate to.'

'Best not,' FitzSymonds said. 'One, the Russians will listen in. And two, she'll only tell her father, who'll tell his friends. Next thing you know, it will filter back to Schneider and we'll have to come up with another plan. At the moment, the Stasi think you're a KGB psychologist shipped in from Moscow to turn me.' FitzSymonds smiled. 'Let's keep things tight if we can.'

Tom hesitated. 'Do you think Charlie thinks I'm dead?'

'I do hope not,' FitzSymonds said.

60

The le Carré was back on Tom's desk, with a single tarot card marking a page where Rafikov had underlined a sentence.

The tarot card was Death. Of course it was.

The sentence read, 'Sometimes our actions are questions, not answers.'

Tucked into the title page was a note outlining what General Rafikov liked about the plotting, characters and depictions of tradecraft, and what he considered the book's errors. The novel's endpapers had been removed. So neatly that unless you looked it was hard to see that they'd been there at all.

The note ended, 'Don't trust FitzSymonds.'

Tom would have dismissed this as an attempt to unsettle him if not for the way Fitz had used Caro to turn the conversation away from what they'd been discussing. The old man hadn't admitted to a new round of *spring cleaning*, but he hadn't denied it either. And that mention of the arms talks . . . They fitted into this somehow. As it was, Rafikov's dig worked, and Tom was still worrying away at what Fitz had said long after he'd turned his bedside light off, the noise of the block had settled and he desperately needed sleep.

Tom ate breakfast alone in the Mess. He'd already acquired the reputation of a loner, and although a couple of junior officers nodded politely, no one tried to join his table. Tom made do with grunts when his coffee was brought. It was good coffee. Substantially better than he expected.

'Angola,' the man serving said, seeing his surprise.

Emptying his cup, Tom lifted it for a refill.

'We gave them guns, Comrade Colonel. They gave us beans.'

Tom smiled.

The man smiled back, waited to see if Tom wanted anything else and vanished when it became obvious he simply wanted to get back to his paper. A dissident released. A ballet unbanned. A poet so successful the queue for his new book stretched right around the block. The only obvious untruths were about Afghanistan and Chernobyl. Tom imagined few people had any real idea of what had happened with the nuclear power station in the Ukraine. And most of those who did were probably already dead. But he could recognize propaganda and knew damage limitation when he saw it.

Afghanistan was different. There the approach was simply to lie.

Pravda was full of Afghan towns taken and soldiers welcomed, hospitals opened and religious fanatics beaten back. There was nothing about ambushed convoys. Nothing about the number of helicopters that had begun to drop out of the sky. The Soviet Union was changing but not so fast that it could afford to tell the truth about things like that.

There were photographs of Gorbachev.

There were always photographs. But he was smiling, looking vaguely human; not stern-faced, or smiling in the way that Stalin used to be photographed smiling, as if wondering which bit to bite off small children first.

'Interesting?' Rafikov asked.

The general nodded to a free chair and Tom stood, indicating that Rafikov should take it. He remained standing until the general sat.

'Sit,' Rafikov said. 'Sit.'

Folding his paper away, Tom said, 'Never less than interesting.'

'You mean that, don't you?'

'Of course.' He paused so the waiter could pour Rafikov coffee. The general sipped, looked pleasantly surprised.

'Angolan,' said the waiter.

'We give them guns,' Tom said. 'They give us beans.'

The waiter had to stop himself from laughing.

'I used to read *The Times*,' Rafikov said, as soon as the man was gone. 'Back in the days when I was based in London. I'd have brought today's *Times* but our friends might find that strange.' His nod took in the other officers, all acutely aware that their rezident was talking to the psychologist from Moscow, but careful not to look as if they were paying too much attention.

'What does it say?'

'Your millionth council house has been sold.' Rafikov smiled. 'We spent decades turning our kulaks into workers. In seven years, with right to buy, you've turned your workers into kulaks. What else? The Japanese have opened a factory in the Midlands. Cars obviously. Your sculptor Henry Moore has died. Unemployment has reached three million . . .' He hesitated, and Tom knew they'd reached what mattered. 'And you're alive.'

'I'm . . . ?'

'It must be true. It says so in *The Times*.' His mouth twisted. 'It seems the reports of your death were incorrect. You're currently being held by the Kriminalpolizei. Under arrest, obviously.'

'Do the Kripo know that?'

'They do now. And this afternoon's paper will note that you've been released following the appearance of evidence that establishes your innocence.'

'How did you sell this to the Stasi?' Tom asked.

General Rafikov looked disappointed. 'My friend, really . . .'

'You've told them I've been turned?'

'Of course. You have been turned, most successfully. They understand that now. And so I must return you to the pond to swim happily with all the other fish. It's been interesting and I'll be sad to see you go but . . .' He shrugged. 'Needs must.'

'What about Sir Cecil?'

'A terrible man by all accounts. His killer has confessed.'

'He's confessed?'

'She. If she hasn't, she will have done by tomorrow. I wouldn't be surprised if she wasn't a drug addict. One of those *Instandbesetzer* who've been squatting old buildings. Her husband was a traitor. He died trying to betray his country.'

Tom remembered the grey-haired woman in the squat.

'General . . .'

Rafikov looked up and his eyes were suddenly hard. 'There's a saying,' he said. 'You might have heard it. About gift horses . . .'

61

Tom's room at the Palasthotel looked as if he'd left it that morning to have breakfast at the KGB rezidentura and returned an hour later: not taken a round trip to the Baltic, woken up in a morgue following a mock firing squad and spent two days as the guest of a Soviet general.

His dark glasses were on the desk, his wallet on a side table, his watch laid out neatly beside it.

The William Gibson novel he'd bought for the flight from the Bahamas was open at the page he'd reached, face down on the side of the bed he didn't use. Exactly as it had been when he abandoned his room.

The domesticity of it all unnerved him.

The last time he'd seen his wallet he'd been handing it over to a hard-eyed Grenztruppen guard at the Bösebrücke crossing. He couldn't tell you the last time he'd seen his Ray-Bans. The Gibson? Well, that had probably been here all along. Or wherever they took his possessions, because Tom doubted they'd simply left them here for the whole time he'd been gone. His room would have been photographed following his arrest; and they'd put everything back exactly as he'd left it.

The thought made him uneasy.

Stripping off the civvies that Rafikov gave him to replace his uniform, Tom climbed into his 501s, pulled on a check shirt and found the leather jacket he'd bought in Brunswick hanging in the cupboard. Last time he'd seen that the grey-haired woman at the squat had been wearing it.

He wondered how badly they'd hurt her. What else they'd made her confess to . . . A knock at the door dragged him away from those thoughts.

It took Tom a second to place his visitor, and it was clear that Henderson noticed that. 'Welcome back,' Henderson said.

'Glad to be here.'

'We thought you were dead.'

'So did I,' Tom said.

Henderson glanced across.

'They put me in front of a firing squad.'

'Dear God. Blanks . . . ?'

'Something like that.' Tom indicated a chair.

'I thought we might try the balcony bar.'

Tom glanced at his Omega. Eleven was early even for him.

'They do coffee,' Henderson said heavily.

Tom doubted it tasted much like the coffee he'd had for breakfast but he nodded, and took his leather jacket from the back of a chair, reaching for his wallet. The East German currency was there. His illegal US dollars were gone.

'You know they've arrested someone for the murders?' Henderson said.

Tom nodded. 'So I was told.'

The other man's eyes narrowed. 'Really? Who by?'

'Can't remember. It was said in passing.'

Henderson nodded doubtfully. 'We've been asked to expedite your return, which actually translates as leaving first thing tomorrow. They've really had you in a Kripo prison all this time?'

'They moved me around a bit.'

'But you weren't shipped back to Moscow?'

'Dear God no.' Tom hesitated. 'What made you ask?'

'Someone heard a rumour that the Soviets were holding you.'

Henderson's bonhomie was wearing. Wearing thin, and wearing both of them out. The man wanted something and seemed unwilling to come to the point. 'Come on,' Tom said. 'Let's go to that bar.'

And by the time they'd queued for the lifts – two of which were out of order, and one was staff only – beer looked more attractive than coffee, and so that was what Tom had, with a saucer of almonds on the side that Henderson snorted at and then began absent-mindedly demolishing.

'I need to make a call,' Tom said.

Henderson grinned. 'Of nature?'

'My wife.'

Caro needed to know that he was safe. Tom needed a way of telling her that he definitely hadn't killed Cecil Blackburn, without suggesting he imagined she might have thought he had . . . At reception, he asked for a call to be put through. He gave his name, room number, the telephone number he wanted and his wife as the person he wanted to talk to. When a bell rang in one of the booths, a receptionist indicated that he should take it.

The first voice he heard was Charlie's.

'Mummy, Daddy and Charlie aren't here right now. Leave a message after the beep and Mummy or Daddy will call you back. I'll probably be at school . . .'

'Caro,' he said, 'hi, it's me. Miss you. I'll try your parents.'

The receptionist was put out at being asked to fix

266

another foreign call but took the new details. This time the telephone was answered.

'Is Caro there?'

'Tom?'

Who else would he be?

'Yes,' he said. 'It's me. I'm in Berlin.'

'Yes,' Lady Eddington said. 'We heard.' Her voice was so brittle, Tom practically heard her force herself to be polite. 'Is everything all right?'

I've been accused of murder, arrested, released, and spent the last few days providing amusement to a Soviet general who runs the KGB rezidentura in Berlin, probably the biggest KGB outpost anywhere in the world.

Apart from that . . .

'I need to talk to Caro. Is she there?'

'No,' Lady Eddington said shortly, deciding he'd been rude in not answering her question. 'She's not.'

'Do you know where she is?'

There was a moment's hesitation. 'I'm afraid not. Have you tried the house?' She said this so brightly Tom knew it was a brush-off.

'Is your husband with you?'

'He's in London.'

'Ah. I'll try his office.'

'I don't think he's there.' She sounded momentarily flustered. 'In fact, I'm sure he's not. I think he said he had meetings.'

What the fuck was going on?

'If you talk to Caro could you let her know I called?'

'Of course. If I do.'

There was a click and Caro's mother killed the call.

62

Back at the balcony bar, Henderson was watching a group of Cuban students who'd been brought to admire the Palasthotel. They looked cold and tired and more than ready to go home. He had his gaze fixed on a girl with wild hair and an over-tight jersey. He started when he realized Tom was there.

'Everything all right?' he asked.

'Answerphone. Not at her parents' either.'

'Probably shopping,' Henderson said. 'That's what my wife's usually doing.'

'You're married?'

'For my sins. Now, Sir Cecil's memoirs.'

'Look. I've already told Harry FitzSymonds –'

Henderson's scowl killed what Tom was about to say. When Henderson reached for his coffee Tom knew it was to have something to do with his hands, and his knuckles were white. He sipped slowly, and seemed to be trying to calm himself. Quite possibly he was counting to ten.

'FitzSymonds is in Berlin?'

'Well, he was yesterday.'

'This side of the Wall?'

'Yes,' said Tom, wondering why he didn't just admit that Fitz had been here for a couple of days. But if Henderson didn't know that then Fitz must have his reasons. Fitz always had his reasons.

'You gave him the memoirs?'

Tom shook his head and he could have sworn that Henderson looked relieved. Then the man went back to staring at foreign students, and sipping his coffee in what he probably imagined was an enigmatic way. Tom waited.

'So you still have them?'

'I've never had them,' Tom said.

Henderson opened his mouth and Tom held up his hand. He didn't mean to be rude, he was simply thinking. Henderson flushed all the same, his face got a little harder and his voice a little more clipped.

'We are going to need them.'

'So everyone keeps saying.'

Apparently, that wasn't the right thing to say either.

FitzSymonds and Henderson were evidently terrified of them falling into the wrong hands. The question was, whose hands was that? The Stasi's? The CIA's? The hands of the UK press. Each other's?

'What's in them?' Tom asked.

'Fox. For God's sake . . .'

Now was when Tom should tell Henderson about Flo Wakefield's notebook; the one that Sir Cecil took. It wasn't the memoirs but it contained names. But something about the way Henderson had reacted to Fitz being here worried Tom. And Henderson's flicker of relief at discovering FitzSymonds didn't have the memoirs worried him even more.

This bloody city was getting to him. *Trust nobody* was a good maxim for someone in Tom's line of business. Somehow, though, since starting to look at Patroclus, trust nobody had turned into nobody could be trusted.

Even Caro's father was named in that bloody notebook.

'Do you know,' said Tom, 'if officers in Berlin after the war were given different security clearances? Say alpha, beta, gamma, delta . . . ?'

'This has to do with the memoirs?'

'No,' said Tom. 'My gut feeling is that Sir Cecil's memoir was burnt. I saw ash from burnt paper in the grate. And it was too hot a day to need a fire in the normal way of things.' *Fuck it, I burnt my hand pulling the last page of the appendices from the flames . . .*

'Sir Cecil said he gave them to you.'

'He lied,' Tom said. 'I don't have them. I've never had them.'

Henderson put down his cup and stared at Tom for a second. His face was unreadable. 'I'm not sure I believe you,' he said.

63

'Well,' said Colonel Schneider, approaching Tom's table on the balcony bar. 'That went well, didn't it?' He sat without being asked, pushed Henderson's cold coffee to one side and waved away the waitress who hurried over to see if he wanted to order anything.

It took Tom a moment to recognize the elegant Stasi officer who'd wanted him to sign a confession at Kripo head-quarters. This time round, Schneider was dressed in a light silk jacket, open-necked shirt and fawn slacks. He wore his Patriotic Order of Merit discreetly in his buttonhole.

'I believe you're leaving us soon?'

'Tomorrow.'

The colonel's mouth twisted. 'Ah well,' he said, sounding resigned. 'Needs must. Can't win them all, I suppose.'

'You still think I did it?'

'I know you did it.'

'I'm an army officer,' Tom said. 'Not a murderer.'

'Of course you are. And I'm a colonel in the Stasi. But that's not a proper answer, is it?' He looked to where an elegantly dressed woman was pushing a small girl on a swing in neat gardens below. She was smiling when she looked up.

'You know her?' Tom asked.

'My wife,' Schneider said. 'We're going to see a film in a minute.'

'With the child?'

'Of course. It's a cartoon.'

'And me?' Tom said.

'I'm afraid Natalia only bought three tickets.'

Tom laughed, picked up his beer and raised it in a toast.

Leaning across, Colonel Schneider touched Tom on the wrist and there was something almost proprietorial in the action. Tom forced himself not to react. He looked up to find Schneider staring at him.

'Heightened sense of responsibility, heightened aware- ness of touch, heightened sense of other people's emotions, heightened threshold for pain. A fear that his fury can't be held in check . . .'

Tom waited. There was something the colonel had left off his list. An ability to wait.

'You know who has all those traits?'

'Someone with too much training and not enough sleep?'

The colonel smiled. 'That's possible. I was thinking more of those who've been badly hurt. You know, abused children, women who've been raped, torture victims. Our psychologists tell me these things apply equally to all three. Were you happy to find Sir Cecil dead?'

'I didn't kill him.'

'Once again, that's not quite an answer. You have good friends in Moscow. Friends who insist that we be nice to you. Maybe that's why your side no longer trusts you. Maybe they know that you have good friends in Moscow.'

'You've talked to General Rafikov?'

'Oh yes. A most interesting conversation. We must look to the future, apparently. All of us. The general is either a very clever man or a lunatic. I hope the first.' The colonel shrugged. 'Of course,' he said, 'hope is overrated.' He picked up Tom's beer, sipped it and looked thoughtful.

'If I was your side,' he said, 'I'd kill you.'

64

Tom's mistake was going down to the bar.

If he'd stayed in his hotel room and read either of his books he'd have been fine. Although the utterly artificial normality of his room was surreal enough to make him want a drink. He was unnerved by his things being there.

All of them. Neatly laid out or put away.

The more he thought about it, the less he liked the idea that someone had taken photographs of his possessions before they were packed away as evidence, then used the same photographs to put everything back.

He couldn't stop thinking about it.

In part because if he did he'd start thinking about Caro instead. Tom was working hard not to think about Caro; where she was and why her mother had been so brittle on the telephone. Caro's words wouldn't leave him.

I'm having an affair. Long term and nobody you know. The stupid thing is that under other circumstances you'd really like him. I'll finish it the moment we get home . . . How long could an affair take to end? Even one that was long term, with someone he'd like *in other circumstances.*

Tom found himself heading to the bar without having made a conscious decision. Even then, he'd have been fine if he'd just chosen one of the dark wood armchairs at the back, as far from the modernist chandelier over the bar as possible, and stuck to Stolichnaya washed down with

Braugold. Several of those, and a headache later, he could have dragged himself upstairs and fallen into bed, drunk enough to pretend he'd stopped worrying about where Caro was and who she was with. Then he could have packed his bag and headed home with a light heart and a heavy head. But that wasn't the way it worked out. That wasn't the way it worked out at all.

A short-haired woman propping up the bar watched him enter, left him alone long enough for a waitress to take his order and then headed straight over. 'I'm really sorry,' she said.

Tom squinted into the light.

'Dr Blackburn,' she said. 'Amelia Blackburn.'

He knew who she was. The flowery boots were gone, her jeans had been replaced by black trousers. In place of a Gaia T-shirt she wore a shirt that looked sheer and was quite possibly silk. The only thing that remained was the slightly combative way she stared at him, and the nervous energy she wore like an aura. She'd had both in that bar behind Hackescher Markt when she'd brought the police with her. She grimaced. 'I thought . . .'

'That I killed your father?'

She hesitated, shrugged. 'I just wanted to . . .'

Tom picked up his vodka, killed it in one. 'Consider it said.'

The bar in the Palasthotel featured only shades of brown, had an appalling terracotta-coloured carpet and uneven lighting, but he still saw her flush. Looking cross with herself, Amelia turned away. When she turned back, Tom knew what she wanted to say. At least he thought he did.

'No,' he said. 'I don't think they have the right person.'

'I was going to ask if they treated you okay.'

'They half gassed me, stripped me, beat me and gave me a mock execution.' Tom wasn't sure why he said it. Actually, he was. He simply wanted her to go away and didn't care if the bar was wired for sound. He probably wasn't telling them anything they didn't already know.

And they'd be rid of him tomorrow.

'Christ,' she said. 'Sorry.'

She sat without being asked and Tom glared at her.

'What?' she asked.

'That was your cue to go away. Why are you even in Berlin anyway? I'd have thought they'd have sent you home.' Tom signalled for another vodka and the waitress brought it, collecting what remained of Amelia Blackburn's wine from the bar on her way over. Amelia killed it in one.

'I'll have the same again,' she said.

The waitress smiled.

By the time Amelia's wine arrived, with a fresh Braugold Pils that Tom hadn't asked for, but was quite prepared to drink, Amelia had just launched into a description of her work with wolf packs in the Ukraine.

'I thought you'd flown in from the UK.'

'I told you,' she said.

'Did you?' He shrugged. 'I was probably thinking about something else . . .'

She looked momentarily put out.

'I had stuff going on,' Tom reminded her.

She had the grace to look embarrassed in her turn.

All the same, the Ukraine? If he'd bothered to think of her at all, he'd have imagined her safe in a Chelsea flat, with Mummy living in a nice rectory in Cambridge, unless her link with Sir Cecil was too painful and she'd taken a little cottage in the Cotswolds.

His chip, Caro called it. Caro was right.

'You're a biologist?'

'An animal psychologist.' She smiled. 'I'm told you're a spy.'

'Who told you that?'

'I overheard one of the girls on the desk. I'm not sure she knew I speak German. She'd been up to your room.'

'Not while I was there.'

'I imagine not.'

'Tell me about wolves,' he said.

An Olympic athlete could manage 24 mph over a very short distance, and that fell fast at anything over a hundred yards. At full tilt, wolves could reach 40 mph and at over a hundred yards they'd barely got started.

'Don't try to outrun a wolf?'

'Only if you're feeling particularly stupid.'

They lived about six to eight years in the wild, could measure over sixty inches, with another twenty inches of tail, and weighed as much as 175 pounds. They mostly formed packs of under a dozen, and their howl could be a call or a warning. They travelled an average of twelve miles a day, gorged their food and could devour twenty pounds of meat in one sitting.

They would follow the scent of blood for miles, working as a team to corner their prey. The pack leader might lead the hunt, and be ferocious to other packs, but he was capable of letting the young feed first, happy to rough and tumble with his cubs and leave decisions to his mate.

'That's true,' Amelia said.

'I didn't say it wasn't.'

'No,' she said, 'you just looked disbelieving . . . I mean it when I say decisions are often made by the pack's matriarch.'

'This is your own research?'

'And others'.' Amelia leant closer, her face bleak. 'You know you said you didn't think they had the right person? I know they haven't. I studied under Claudia Strauss at the Humboldt. She's not violent. She's not an addict. There's no reason she'd go anywhere near that flat. But her husband died trying to cross the Wall and she's in disgrace.'

Tom remembered the grey-haired woman from the squat.

'They tortured her,' Amelia whispered. 'They must have. I know her. There's no way she'd confess to something she didn't do otherwise. You've been arrested by the Stasi. You know what they're like. You have to help me get her released.'

65

Tom slept better than he deserved and woke to a thumping headache, what remained of an insanely overpriced bottle of Sovetskoye Shampanskoye, and Amelia Blackburn half dressed, with one leg slipped off the bed, beside him. She was snoring gently, her face squashed into a pillow.

He was sitting on the edge of his bed, staring down at her and wondering what the hell, if anything, had happened, when his hotel telephone rang and Amelia opened her eyes. 'Better answer that,' she said.

'Fox,' Tom said.

He hoped it wasn't Caro. He wasn't sure he'd cope if it was.

'All packed, I hope?' Henderson was on the other end, sounding nauseatingly brisk. 'I'm in reception. See you in a minute.' He put the phone down without giving Tom time to reply and left him staring at the receiver.

'That's your car?' Amelia said.

Tom nodded.

'At least consider what I said.'

She wanted him to tell Fleet Street that the East Germans had arrested the wrong person. That Dr Claudia Strauss was no guiltier than he'd been. She wanted him to contact Amnesty International . . .

'Did we . . . ?'

279

She looked at him. 'Did we what?'

Tom looked at the state of the bed, her shoes kicked into one corner, his jacket simply dropped on the floor. His head hurt, his mouth tasted foul, and he couldn't work out if they'd taken off just enough clothes to have sex, or kept on just enough to ensure they couldn't.

'I don't sleep with people who are drunk,' Amelia said. She looked at him. 'At least not the first time . . . Could you do me a favour?'

'What?' Tom asked.

'Could you take something back for me?'

Tom felt suddenly sick. As if the hangover he deserved from the previous night had just caught up with him. 'You have the memoirs?'

'God. What is it with everyone? I didn't even know he was writing his bloody memoirs. I've never read them. I don't know what was in them. I have absolutely no interest in reading them –'

'You've been asked that before then?'

She glared at him.

Tom smiled. 'What do you want me to take back?'

'It's a letter to a friend at Imperial. About wolves. We used to work together. It looks like I'm going to be stuck here for a while. And I thought as you're going back you could post it when you arrive.'

'You don't trust the East German post?'

'Would you?'

66

'Took your time,' Henderson said.

Tom checked his Omega. 'Five minutes max.'

'More like ten.'

'We're running to a tight schedule?'

'Of course. Alex here will drive us to Checkpoint Charlie. You'll need to get out to cross on foot, as we're on embassy plates and the GDR resolutely refuse to give you diplomatic status. Don't worry though, your paperwork's in order. We've confirmed that. We'll pick you up the moment you're through.'

'And drive me to Tegel?'

'The airport? We need to go to the consulate first. London's idea. They've asked me to debrief you.'

About what? Tom wondered. *Being arrested, being interrogated, being held in an East German prison?*

'And then the airport?'

'Don't worry,' Henderson said heartily. 'We'll get you home.'

He nodded to his driver and the blue embassy Jaguar backed out of its slot, made an elegant three-point turn and slid itself into the traffic. Half a dozen East Berliners turned to watch it pass. Tom could see how the Jags had been chosen to give an ideal image of the UK, although he wasn't sure that he or Henderson really merited one. Maybe Henderson simply wanted to make an impression.

'Why are we crossing to West Berlin anyway?' Tom asked.

Henderson looked at him slightly strangely. 'To get you home.'

'Why not just fly me Interflug from Schönefeld?'

Henderson's driver glanced in his mirror and pushed a button that raised a glass screen. A red light that said a microphone was live clicked off.

'Makes sense for me to debrief you here. I fixed your original plans. London agrees I should do the debrief.'

'When do I leave Berlin?'

'Tomorrow. Just a couple of formalities first. Then we'll have you out of here and safely home. That's a promise.'

Henderson sat back, looked out of the window and fell silent. And Henderson was not the silent type. The pavements thronged with schoolchildren and East Berliners going to work. The sun was bright, the day colder than the brightness suggested. It was that time of year when summer ended without autumn having quite begun. 'Everything okay?' Tom asked.

'Sir Cecil really didn't pass you his memoir?'

'He didn't.'

'He very clearly said he did in a letter we intercepted. Strange thing for him to lie about.'

'Very,' Tom said firmly.

The car slowed a little. It shouldn't have slowed. The road was clear, the privacy screen was up and the listening light off. The rear of the Jaguar should have been cocooned, their words safely private. Tom glanced at the driver's mirror but the man was looking straight ahead. 'What I'm asking,' Henderson said, 'is what are the chances of the East Germans having it?'

'It was burnt,' Tom said. 'I saw the ashes.'

'There could be a carbon copy.'

He didn't . . . Tom almost said it. He was thinking of the typed cast list, the lack of carbon-paper smudging on the back. Watching Henderson squirm, Tom wondered if it was really the communists that Henderson was worrying about. He'd started to think Henderson's concerns were closer to home. That made Tom wonder what they'd actually had planned for Sir Cecil.

Whether he'd have got his day in court after all.

Henderson scowled so fiercely at the traffic building up that Tom wondered what his urgency was. And beyond the glass, the driver stared at the rear bumper of a Trabant. He stared so fixedly that Tom suspected it was the listening light and not the microphone that had been turned off.

'I'm still surprised he didn't try to take Frederika.'

'Oh, he did,' Henderson said. 'I told him he couldn't.'

'I bet she liked that.'

'She didn't know. At least, I don't imagine she did. I told him not to tell her. I mean, he could hardly expect to be welcomed back into the bosom of his family if he arrived arm in arm with a highly strung Ossi gymnast. He calmed down a bit after I showed him her file. Rather more lovers than he'd imagined.'

'The bodyguard? Evgeny?'

'Of course. Plus a couple of politicians. An actor. One of their dreadful rock stars. And she had a bit of a thing for a Stasi colonel. What really fixed it, though, was telling him why she was thrown off the team.'

'Hip injury, I heard.'

'While catching a child who fell from the wall bars . . .'

Henderson sneered. 'I'm surprised they didn't have her injuring herself saving a puppy from a swirling stream. I don't suppose you watched that saccharine little bio-pic DDR-FS produced when she retired? Fiction from start to finish. The little bitch tried to strangle a teammate. Almost killed her too.'

'*Christ . . .*' Tom thought of the ligature round Evgeny's neck. And then of Amelia's friend, the grey-haired woman from the squat, who'd had a breakdown trying to live out the lie that she'd hated her husband. A man who died trying to get through the wall he was about to cross.

No wonder the GDR needed a scapegoat. Tom didn't doubt that she'd been tortured into a confession.

Henderson's driver had cut west on Karl-Liebknecht-Strasse and crossed the Schlossbrücke on to Unter den Linden, before turning left into Friedrichstrasse. Main roads the whole way. There was now an MZ motorbike behind and a Wartburg ahead. Tom tried to remember when the filthy Trabant became an almost-new Wartburg. 'And Frederika's hip?' he asked.

'She threw herself out of a window.'

Henderson must have felt Tom's glance because he shook his head.

'For real,' he said. 'She wasn't tossed.'

Evgeny had been hit from behind, then strangled. The garrotting brutal enough to crush his windpipe. Tom's first thoughts had been wrong. He was sure of it. The person who killed Evgeny wasn't highly trained. Evgeny simply trusted her enough to let her close.

Amelia's friend from the squat was taking the fall for a

murder neither she nor Tom had committed. Rafikov would never know who'd killed his nephew. And the person who did it was going to get away. As for Tom, he wasn't sure what he was walking into . . . But he was pretty sure it wasn't a simple debriefing. Henderson was far too nervous, far too worked up.

The traffic was thickening on Friedrichstrasse.

Up ahead, lights were changing, green passing through amber to red. A signpost indicated that the checkpoint was a quarter of a mile away, and cars were edging into the right lanes. The thickness of the traffic said that the guards were being thorough today.

'Who did you see in Moscow?' Henderson asked.

Tom glanced across. A tic had started up in the corner of Henderson's eye. The glance he gave Tom was impassive though. Studiedly so.

'I didn't go to Moscow,' Tom said.

'Oh, must have got that wrong. I thought you did.'

'What's going on?' Tom demanded.

Henderson made himself sit back. Fold one knee over the other. It might have been more convincing if his fingers hadn't gripped the Jaguar's door handle so tightly. *Who did you see in Moscow?*

Tom wondered how much trouble he was in. What was waiting for him. How hard it was going to be to talk his way out of it . . .

Red, through amber to green.

When the Wartburg in front mistimed its gear change and stalled, Henderson swore viciously, the Jaguar shuddered to a halt and Tom made his decision. There were cars backed up in a side street wanting to push in, the

Jaguar was blocking their way and pedestrians had begun to squeeze through the static traffic.

Unclipping his seat belt, Tom reached for the handle. 'What the –?'

Henderson's driver should have reversed; used his rear door to trap Tom so Henderson could drag him back inside. Instead, the Jaguar lurched into the Wartburg. And Tom was out of his seat, slamming the door behind him. Cutting through the middle of a shocked family, he headed for the busiest side street to lose himself in the crowd. He stopped only once, glancing back, one of a dozen pedestrians wondering what the commotion was. The boy who'd been riding the two-stroke MZ was standing on a bollard, scanning the crowd.

Tom ducked into a doorway before he could be seen.

Now he had the Stasi to worry about again. The doorway led into communal flats, and Tom followed a long corridor, thinking he'd trapped himself, until it exited into a small park where bronze children played with bronze marbles. Patting one of the statues on the head, Tom looked for the *Fernsehturm* towering over the city.

He found it and headed towards it. This time he kept his head up and shoulders back and concentrated on looking as if he belonged. He already knew where he was going.

67

'Fox. Your Great-Uncle Max is here . . .'

The Soviet Union was red and spread halfway round the world from Leningrad to Vladivostok. In the atlas in Grandpa's house the British empire was red and spread from Canada to New Zealand. If one was red then and one was red now, perhaps they'd swapped places?

'Fox. I said your Great-Uncle Max is here.'

Charlie looked up to met Mr Marcher's gaze.

He didn't like Mr Marcher. This was a problem because Mr Marcher was his house tutor. He wasn't sure if he didn't like Mr Marcher because Mr Marcher didn't like him or if it was the other way around.

There were a number of things Charlie could say, but a brief look at Mr Marcher's scowl told Charlie that none would improve matters. So he nodded, which was politer than the shrug he wanted to give, although still not polite enough to judge from Mr Marcher's expression, shut the atlas and put it back.

Charlie liked the library. There were new books and old books, and books locked away behind leaded glass doors. The glass doors had little brass escutcheons around the keyholes. Escutcheon was a good word.

It sounded like it looked and most things didn't.

He still hadn't managed to pick any of the glass doors but he intended to before the term was out. He wanted to read *Anatomy of Melancholy*. He knew what *Anatomy* was. And he'd looked up *Melancholy* in the dictionary.

He was interested in how they'd fit together.

'Fox . . . Did you hear me?'

'Yes, sir. I'm on my way.'

Mr Marcher wanted to say, *No, you're not.*

But Charlie was already dodging round his house tutor, leaving the man scowling after him. Grandpa helped. Grandpa had been to school here. Daddy hadn't. Mr Marcher was always very polite to Grandpa.

'Fox . . .' Mr James was on the stairs.

'My Great-Uncle Max is waiting?'

Mr James flicked a lock of hair out of his eyes. 'Is he the one who sent you the Corgi toys?'

Charlie looked through the window to where a Rolls-Royce was parked at an angle in the forecourt. It was purple, with a canvas top folded back. It was the same car as his last model, just much larger. In the driver's seat, an old man puffed contentedly on a cigar and watched in amusement as a Volvo estate tried to fit into a space his arrival had made too narrow.

'1957 Silver Cloud Coupé.' Mr James sounded awed.

'You like cars, don't you, sir?'

'Cars like that.'

Charlie said, 'Better go down, I suppose.'

'Be back by three-thirty,' Mr James said. 'Make sure he remembers that.' Mr James looked at the man with the cigar thoughtfully. As if suspecting he was the kind of man who might ignore rules.

'I'll be back long before then,' Charlie said firmly.

*

288

'I'm Charlie Fox,' said Charlie, standing at the passenger's side.

The old man removed his cigar, blew smoke from the side of his mouth so that it didn't drift over Charlie, and smiled.

'Of course you are. You have your father's eyes.'

'And my mother's nose.'

The man peered closely. 'That's possible,' he said.

'Have we met?' Charlie asked. He hoped that was polite enough; sometimes it was hard to be sure.

'At your sister's funeral.'

'I don't remember,' Charlie said.

'Of course you don't.' The old man's voice was matter of fact. 'No one ever remembers who's at a funeral. Are you ready to roll?'

Charlie looked at him.

'I thought a pub. Or there's an old-fashioned hotel ten miles from here, with very uncomfortable chairs, where we'll have to sit quietly and they'll scowl if we ask for more jam to go with our scones . . .'

He smiled and Charlie smiled back.

'Or we could go to the house.'

'You live near here?'

'I live lots of places,' the man said. 'One of them is near here. It belonged to a friend but he doesn't need it any more. Red-brick thing. A Victorian copy of an Elizabethan country house. Built for a sugar baron.'

'Our Moscow embassy was built for a sugar baron.'

The old man with the cigar looked at him.

'Daddy told me,' Charlie said.

'Then I'm sure you're right. Scalextric or model trains?'

'Model trains,' Charlie replied firmly.

'How very traditional. That's a compliment, by the way. The house has an exceptionally large train set. Most of its engines are original.'

'You sent me the toy cars, didn't you?'

'Did you like them?'

'Very much,' Charlie said carefully. That wasn't true because the mechanism that drove the ejector seat of the first one was surprisingly clunky and the bullet screen could have fitted its slot better. And the second had made him feel uneasy. And the third one had that note about Daddy. A note saying Daddy was in big trouble. Saying thank you was the right response to most things, however. So that's what Charlie did.

'Daddy . . .'

'Needs your help.'

'You've seen him. Recently?'

'Oh yes,' the old man said. 'Very recently.'

'What was he doing?'

The old man looked amused. 'Wearing someone else's clothes.' Leaning over, he pulled a handle to open the door of the Rolls.

Charlie hesitated. Other boys were watching and even Michaelides looked impressed. His father had a big Rover. One of the old-fashioned ones with a Viking face on the bonnet. It was cream. Charlie knew. Michaelides was leaning against it.

'Who's that?' the old man said.

Mr Marcher was approaching.

'My housemaster.'

'You don't like him?'

Charlie shook his head.

'Didn't like my housemaster either.'

'Six for the bigger boys,' Mr Marcher said. 'Three-thirty for the littles. If you could have him back by then . . .'

'Of course.' The old man examined the end of his cigar. 'Should you talk to Charlie's father, could you remind him that he has a book of mine?'

'If I talk to –'

'Only if you do,' the old man said.

The car door closed behind Charlie with a satisfying thud, and the gap between door and frame was tight, as it should be.

The engine sounded nice too.

It purred into life and Charlie sat back and shut his eyes to feel the sun on his face as the car turned a surprisingly tight circle. When the sunlight dappled, Charlie knew they were passing under the oaks along the drive. He felt the Rolls-Royce turn on to the road and accelerate with a roar.

As ways to escape went, this was a good one. Charlie had spent the whole term not having the courage to run away. He wondered who the man was, how much trouble Daddy was in, and what would happen if he never went back.

68

Tom found the gym easily enough. The one where Frederika taught children who'd represent East Germany in the next Olympics or the Olympics after. He recognized it from the tendrils of ivy moulded into the brick either side of its windows. Germany had been an empire when the hall was built, then at war, a republic, a fascist state, at war again, conquered, occupied and split down the middle.

The more I see of people the more I like my dogs.

The French writer Madame de Staël had been exiled to Berlin for being too intelligent for Napoleon to stomach. Tom agreed with her, provided you swap buildings for dogs. So maybe Anglicanism was perfect after all. All those lovely churches, with no need to hammer on about faith and doubt.

He was with St Francis.

'Preach the gospel. If necessary, use words.'

Their approaches differed, however.

It was too early in the day for many students to be around and the doors at ground level were shut. The door at the top of the fire escape he'd used last time was slightly open though. Tom climbed its rusting steps quietly.

She was there all right, tongue-lashing a child who stood hands folded in front of her. Brutal as a punishment beating, the scolding lasted another minute. When the child raised one hand to wipe away tears, Frederika screamed at her to stand properly. Looking up, the child saw Tom on the fire escape and her eyes widened.

Tom put his finger to his lips.

She looked at him for a second, then nodded to Frederika and began backing towards the door. She kept her stare on Frederika, who answered with a glare, her shoulders rigid at what she saw as insolence. Reaching for the handle, the child dropped an almost mocking curtsy and slammed the door behind her. Frederika opened her mouth to shout.

'Hello, Frederika,' Tom said.

She spun round, eyes wide.

'Shout,' he said, 'and you'll get hurt.'

Walking to the inside door, he locked it, pocketed the key and returned to the fire escape, his eyes fixed on her the whole way. Locking that door, he dropped the blind. He pressed Play and Record on the tape recorder in the corner, set the spool running and fixed his glare on Frederika the way she'd fixed hers on the child. 'Murderer,' she said.

'Yes,' Tom said. 'You are.'

Her gaze met his and her jaw tightened.

'You killed Cecil,' she said. 'You killed my chance of escaping this.' Her face for a second looked hollow, her eyes dark, seeing nothing.

'You know I didn't kill him.'

'Liar.' She spat the word at him. 'You did. It's all your doing.'

She meant it too. Her face was white with anger. It was in her voice. She held Tom accountable for Sir Cecil's death.

'Frederika. I didn't kill him.'

293

'Yes, you did,' she said furiously. 'I hate you.'

'Frederika –'

'Your fault,' she said. 'It's your fault I'm trapped here. He was going to take me to London with him. I was going to be free.'

'He wasn't,' Tom said. 'He was leaving you behind.'

'That's a lie. He promised me.'

'His daughter was travelling with him, his wife was going to meet the plane. He was going back to his family, Frederika. He had no intention of taking you to London. In fact, he'd been told he couldn't.'

'That's not true.' Tears filled her eyes and she turned away. 'It was you,' Frederika muttered. 'You shot an old man and strangled his bodyguard. Now you're going to kill me.'

Shot? Tom froze.

He thought of Sir Cecil's battered body. Evgeny dead just inside the door, the back of his head bloodied, a cord around his neck.

'How do you know Evgeny was strangled?' Tom demanded.

She stared at him. Not yet understanding. 'I saw the body,' she said.

'No, you didn't. Both caskets were sealed.'

'Then I read the reports.'

'Those said both men were shot.'

Frederika shook her head crossly. 'What does it matter?'

'Because you're lying,' Tom said.

It was there, lightning fast. A flicker of doubt.

'You were lovers, weren't you?'

'You know we were. I adored Sir Cecil.'

'Did Evgeny tell you he was General Rafikov's nephew?'

Frederika looked slightly sick. 'I don't know why you're talking about Evgeny. I don't know what you're suggesting.'

'Was being lovers why he let you close?'

'Fascist,' she said. 'Sent here to shoot a sweet old man. That's what you are. A fascist. You're all fascists. You couldn't even let Cecil die in peace.'

'Did Evgeny shoot Sir Cecil?'

'Of course he bloody didn't . . .' Her voice trailed away. 'I don't know what you're talking about. You've got it all wrong. Fascist.'

'You've done that bit.'

She launched herself at him and Tom stepped aside.

Her fingers hooked for his face and he blocked them, knocking her hand away. He could feel blood on his cheek. She was breathing heavily, her mouth open and nostrils flared. Her face white with fury.

Maybe Rafikov would take insanity into account. Staring into the darkness of her eyes was looking into a void. Yet a soul stared out of them, damned and damaged, but a soul still. 'You need to tell me what happened,' Tom said.

She looked at him and her face was hollow.

'Me,' Tom said, 'General Rafikov, a Stasi colonel, the Kripo men on duty, a couple of paramedics. We're the only people who know Evgeny was strangled. It wasn't on the news. It wasn't in the papers. We know because we were there. How do you know, Frederika?'

'You can't blame Cecil's death on me.'

'Then who should I blame?' Tom asked.

Her shoulders slumped and half the fight went out of

her as fresh tears gathered in her eyes. She looked for a split second like the child she'd never been allowed to be. She'd reached the point he needed. Where the need to talk was stronger than the need to stay silent.

'Why?' he asked. 'What happened in Nikolaiviertel?'

She was crying too hard to answer.

The reel-to-reel recorder still turned, almost silently. Someone came to the door, rattled the handle and left again. Outside a crow cawed. And Frederika wrestled the dregs of her desire to say she had no idea what he was talking about. Her need to talk won.

'I was given no choice,' she said flatly.

To kill him? It hadn't occurred to Tom she'd been acting on orders.

Frederika shook her head. 'Cecil wanted a boy. They wouldn't give him that. I was young. Not properly developed, even then. I was to tell them everything he said. They lost interest when they realized he had nothing interesting to say. But they left me there, trapped, with a disgusting old man. I don't even know why they gave him asylum. He wasn't a communist.'

'He wasn't?'

'He'd read Marx. He could quote Lenin, badly. Mostly he liked Montesquieu and Voltaire. Marcus Aurelius too. He liked Marcus Aurelius. And de Sade . . .'

'He was a sadist?'

Frederika sneered. 'He didn't have the imagination.'

'I'm not sure you need imagination to be a sadist.'

'I disagree. He was a bully though. A know-all. He disliked women. I think he was scared of them. Being a bully isn't the same as being a sadist. Believe me, I know.'

'He disliked women?'

'Grown ones. Mostly, he liked teenage boys . . .'

'I thought you said he wasn't allowed that?'

'He wasn't allowed one at the flat. He'd find them though. Always the same type. Blue-eyed, blonde-haired, crew cut. In need of money. There are a lot of those in Berlin. He had a studio. He liked to photograph them.'

'Frederika. What happened?'

'Evgeny went to see a girlfriend. When he came back Cecil was on the floor in his study. He'd been shot once through the back of his head. Just here . . .' She tapped the base of her skull.

'No one heard the break-in?'

'There was no break in. I had to use my keys and that's when I saw Evgeny kneeling by Cecil's body, looking shocked. He told me to call the police. He was meant to keep Cecil alive.'

'Frederika . . .'

'How could I get to London if Cecil was dead?'

'You killed Evgeny?'

'I hit him with the Chinese vase. Then . . .' She hesitated. 'I wrapped the rope round his neck. He was meant to keep Cecil alive.'

'You made it look like a break-in?'

Frederika nodded.

'Why attack Sir Cecil's body?'

'I was angry. Evgeny said he loved me. Sir Cecil said he'd take me to England. Everybody lies. Everybody always lies.' She blinked at Tom, looking like someone who'd woken to find her bad dreams still there.

'You burnt the manuscript, didn't you?'

She nodded.

'Did he mention Patroclus?'

'That's what he was writing about. So he said.'

'He talked about the London club?'

She stared at Tom. 'Berlin,' she said. 'He said it was in Berlin.'

Christ, Tom thought. How could he be so stupid? Of course it was. At least at the beginning.

Wakefield's words came into his head. 'The ruins turned us all into rats . . . The self can be pretty vile if let off the leash.' All those feral children. All that hunger and starvation. It must have been a feeding frenzy for someone like Blackburn. He wouldn't have been alone either. Men like that recognized each other, hunted in packs, and protected each other. Maybe they were still protecting each other; or maybe the hunters were now hunted.

69

Just a couple of meetings first. Then we'll have you out of here and safely home. That's a promise. Henderson's words.

It was the safely home bit Tom hadn't believed.

Up ahead he could see the Volkspolizei HQ on Keibelstrasse, a stark building with red-brick pillars like prison bars. Should he walk past or turn back? Tom was trying to hold the reel of tape unobtrusively, when he noticed the playground. It had a seesaw, a slide, climbing bars and swings. And beyond the swings, just outside the fence, telephone boxes.

Volkspolizei 110.

Feuerwehr 112.

Rotes Kreuz 115.

Emergency numbers circled the dial. A slot in the top took coins. A chute at the bottom returned change. Everything the same and different. Looking into a metal mirror, Tom winced at the bleakness of his face.

He was a fool, of course. Too tired, too hung-over, too stupid to think straight. He should have kept walking. He should have headed for KGB Karlshorst. Instead here he was, trying to get through on the phone.

'Comrade General Rafikov, please.'

'Can I ask who's calling?'

Tom hesitated. 'Could I have your name first, please?'

It was the right answer. The receptionist's response was

to put him through without reply. A second woman picked up and Tom asked again.

'*Yes. Who is this?*'

Who is this? Her careful politeness said she was unsure of his rank but knew he spoke Russian and had asked for Rafikov. He'd heard the same caution from secretaries in Whitehall.

'It's Major Tom Fox,' Tom said.

There was a stunned silence from the other end.

Then Tom heard the scrape of a chair, a question asked sotto voce and a different woman answer. 'If you'd just hold . . .'

'I'm in a phone box.'

'Where?'

Tom hesitated.

'I'll call you right back.'

'It doesn't matter . . .' It did though. They both knew that.

'Please,' she said. She said it in English, adding, 'He'll be cross if I don't.'

He gave her the number, heard urgent pips demanding he put in a second coin and seconds later the line went dead. He was still holding the receiver in his hand when the phone rang, its tone loud and ugly.

'We're trying to find him, Comrade Major.'

God. It hadn't occurred to Tom that the general wouldn't be at the compound. 'Look,' he said. 'Do you have a tape recorder?'

'A tape recorder?'

'I want you to tape this conversation.'

The woman hesitated. She seemed to be considering saying something. When she spoke it was kindly, as if speaking to a child. 'Comrade Major. All telephone calls to and from this office are recorded.'

Of course they were. 'But you do have a recorder?'

'You wish this to be recorded twice?'

'Yes,' Tom said. 'If possible.'

'Of course, Comrade Major.'

He could almost hear the amusement in her voice.

If they could delete one recording they could delete two. All the same, she was ready to humour him and that told Tom she not only knew who he was but regarded him as worth humouring. He wondered what General Rafikov had said about him or if his disappearance was simply local news.

'If you'd like to speak now,' she said.

'Right, this is a message for Comrade General Rafikov. Sir Cecil was shot. A single shot to the back of his skull. The other wounds were post mortem, delivered later. There was no break-in. Something I imagine the East Germans already know. Your nephew Evgeny was absent when the killing happened. He was clubbed from behind with a Chinese vase as he knelt beside Sir Cecil's body, then strangled.'

The woman on the other end of the phone said something. When Tom didn't reply she repeated it, louder.

'Comrade Major, how do you know this?'

'I have Frau Schmitt's confession on tape.' Tom was about to say more when he heard a police siren. As he listened he realized it was getting closer. 'Did you send for the Volkspolizei?'

'What?'

'Are these cars coming for me?'

'Of course not.' The woman sounded flustered. 'Major Fox. You need to stay on the line.' But Tom was already gone.

70

Finding vodka was what told Tom that Sir Cecil's photographic studio hadn't yet been searched. If it had, the Volkspolizei would have stolen the Stolichnaya.

Reluctantly returning the bottle to its shelf, Tom went back to combing the little attic of a run-down house in Hackescher Markt. He worked methodically. What he wanted, besides the obvious, the memoirs, was to discover why Sir Cecil had decided to return to London, and who had changed his mind.

The area was ordinary, the studio run down.

Safely anonymous might be one way to describe it.

A single bed, metal-framed. 'He liked to *photograph* them . . .'

A kitchen alcove with a gas ring. A tiny bathroom, lavatory cracked. A chintz chair with broken springs. Tom had put the tape containing Frederika's confession beside the telephone on a table by the door.

> *Water, water everywhere . . .*
> *Nor any drop to drink.*

Another telephone he couldn't use.

Another operator who wouldn't put him through. The East Germans would find him eventually. Tom's time was running out and only a fool would think it wasn't. He wanted to call Caro. He knew he should have found a way to get a message to Eddington.

In a drawer he found a Praktica SLR camera, a handful of Zeiss lenses, a rangefinder Zorki, which was an obvious copy of a Leica II. In a tiny darkroom, he found an enlarger, developing baths, developing chemicals, and strip after strip of already developed film.

Holding a strip up to the light, Tom saw naked boys and knew he'd never expected anything else. Some were in their early teens, a few older than that, and a handful younger. All lay on the bed or stood against a wall in this room.

Tom had Frederika to thank for the address.

He'd asked if she'd read Sir Cecil's manuscript, and she said that until she saw the pile of paper on his desk she hadn't even believed there was a manuscript. She'd thought he was boasting, showing off. And no, she hadn't read it before she burnt it and she doubted he'd made a copy. But that if he had, it would be at the studio. She seemed surprised Tom didn't know that there *was* a studio.

Tom didn't find a copy but he found something almost as interesting.

An East German-made 9mm Makarov.

Double-action/single-action semi-automatic with a magazine capacity of . . . Tom dropped out the magazine and checked the load. Eight rounds of 9mm, all present and correct. Sir Cecil hadn't struck him as the pistol-carrying kind. Had Tom been wrong about that? Or had the old man acquired it when the threats started? That was possible.

The barrel was clean.

Slowly, methodically, Tom took the Makarov apart, laid the pieces out, admired them and put them back together.

There was a friendly familiarity to the handle's feel in his fingers. Tom made himself put the weapon down.

He got to thinking about how few videos Sir Cecil had to justify owning a high-quality Lowe VCR machine. *The Jungle Book, The Aristocats, Robin Hood, The Rescuers.* Plus *Raiders of the Lost Ark, ET, Ghostbusters, Back to the Future* . . .

Bait for the boys, probably.

There were no tapes hidden in the studio. Tom was on the right track, though. Sir Cecil's other videos lived in an in-tray that hooked to the underside of the bench in the darkroom. A simple and surprisingly effective hiding place if you knew nothing about effective and simple hiding places.

They were sleazy but no more.

Small boys skinny-dipping in a lake.

A group of youths in pants performing stretches.

A boy of about ten, on his back, with another boy holding his leg flat to the ground, while Frederika lifted the other leg towards his chest until he performed the perfect splits. It was obvious that the child was in pain. A wooden sign behind Frederika read . . . Winding the tape back, Tom stopped it when 'Reinickendorf-Tegelerforst' came in view. That had been the heading in the notebook.

The one with all the names.

When someone knocked at the studio door, Tom ignored them. Next time they knocked he swore so fluently in Russian he could hear shocked silence on the other side. It worked though. They went away.

He went back to looking at the sign.

Wondering what it meant.

71

The third time someone knocked on the studio door they shouted something. They shouted it three times. *Polizei. Polizei. Polizei.*

In case he hadn't heard the first few times, the officer shouted again and Tom heard a solid tap in the silence that followed. A hydraulic ram being positioned below a handle. For an absurd second, he considered hiding in Sir Cecil's darkroom; but it was small, boxed off from the studio with chipboard, and not remotely bulletproof. He doubted they'd pay attention to Sir Cecil's hand-scrawled note: *No Entry Under Any Circumstances When The Red Light Is On.*

Looking round, Tom discovered he was already standing beside the studio door. The Makarov in his hand. Eight rounds. One in the breech. He was impressed to find himself there without having to think about it.

Outside, they'd be doing that silent sign thing. *You there, me there, you first, me second . . .* Tom counted down in his head, wondering how many officers there were. Whether he should start firing.

The door blew. Flipping back, it hit the wall.

Now was when he'd throw a flash bang. Maybe tear gas, if he could grab the door and trap whomever was inside. Instead a Volkspolizei officer sidled in. Only to drop her pistol the moment Tom elbowed her throat.

'Fuck,' he said.

He had to fight the urge to apologize.

Instead he swung her round to use as a shield and put his Makarov to her head. Seeing two pairs of eyes stare from the doorway.

'In,' he barked. He barked it in Russian.

When those outside glanced at each other, Tom tightened his finger on the trigger and that was enough. They shuffled through the studio door.

'Take out your side arms,' he ordered. 'Put them on the floor and kick them across. I'll shoot the first of you to disobey.'

Since he didn't have anywhere to store their weapons, he put them in the darkroom, intending to lock it. A decent kick would break the lock, but, then again, he could shoot faster than they could kick.

It was as he was deciding this that Tom wondered why Sir Cecil had needed such a grand enlarger. There were no massive photographs pinned to the walls, the chemicals were in modest-sized bottles and Sir Cecil owned no developing baths larger than A4.

Why then?

'*Oh fuck*,' Tom said.

Tumblers fell into place.

'You're not Russian,' a sergeant said.

To live without hope is to cease to live. Dostoevsky had nailed it. Tom glanced beyond the Volkspolizei to the telephone, the seeds of a plan forming.

'Some days,' Tom said. 'I think I should be.'

Sir Cecil had had Third Reich Intelligence files put on microfilm and flown back to London for decryption and archiving. Thousands of them, tens of thousands. He'd made bonfires of the originals.

That's what Henderson had said.

If there was a copy of Sir Cecil's memoirs it was on microfiche; carbon paper didn't come into it. Tom looked at the man behind the sergeant. He was in civvies. 'You're Stasi,' Tom said accusingly.

'I'm a detective.'

'Are you drunk?'

The man shook his head.

Breaking the seal on the Stolichnaya bottle, Tom held it out.

72

'I want a number in England.'

'Impossible.' The detective stared at Tom in shock.

'Do it,' Tom said.

'They won't give it to you.'

'They're not giving it to me. They're giving it to you. You think the operator knows I'm here? Tell her whatever you need. Say it's official. Say it's state business. Tell her the KGB rezidcnt will be very cross if she doesn't give you the number. Tell her he'll be very cross with you. Tell her that if she tries to record it she will be jailed.'

The man went from looking drunk to looking drunk and sick.

Picking up the receiver, he began a conversation that grew increasingly heated until he tossed the word KGB into the mix and the operator began backing down. 'Here,' he said.

Tom took the receiver.

The dial tone changed and Tom heard the familiar, but very distant, sound of a telephone ringing in the UK. It rang seven times and then someone picked up, recited the school's number and waited.

'This is Major Fox. I'd like to speak to my son.'

'Major Fox . . .'

It would be. The master who'd taken the call that time

he telephoned from Moscow. 'I believe it's still before lights out?' Tom said.

'You're in Moscow?'

'Berlin this time. If I could speak to my son?'

'Oh,' Mr Marcher said. 'It's exeat. Your son's not here.'

Tom groaned. He needed his son to be there. Today was Saturday; the smallest boys were allowed phone calls on Sunday. It helped with homesickness. How could Charlie pass a message for his mother to pass to her father if he wasn't there? It wasn't even a complicated message. *Can you ask Mummy to tell Grandpa I'm in Berlin and might be able to find that book he wanted . . .*

'My wife collected him?'

The silence was stricter this time. It suggested that Tom should know these things. In it was everything Tom hated about Charlie's prep school, and why he hadn't wanted Caro to send him there. 'Who then? His grandfather?'

'Not Lord Eddington,' said Mr Marcher, taking obvious pleasure in the title. 'I must say his Great-Uncle Max drives a magnificent car.'

'*What?*'

'That purple Rolls-Royce.'

This wasn't the question Tom was asking. He wasn't actually asking a question. His *what* was instead of a swear word.

'My son was collected by his great-uncle?'

'Yes,' said Mr Marcher, not liking Tom's tone. 'Who said that, should I talk to you, please tell you that you have something of his. A book. He'd like it back.'

Oh Christ . . . Tom's guts felt hollow. 'Mr Marcher. My son doesn't have a great-uncle.'

'He must have.'

'Believe me, I'd know. There are no great-uncles on either side of the family. When was my son taken?'

'Taken?'

'Mr Marcher. When did Charlie leave?'

'This morning, obviously. Exeat starts at ten.'

'And ends when?'

'Three-thirty for the smalls.'

'And what's the time at your end?'

'It's almost four.'

'Is my son back?'

'Major Fox,' Mr Marcher said. 'Parents are sometimes late.'

'He's not with his parents,' Tom said flatly. 'He's with a stranger. Call the police. Do it now.'

'I think we should wait. It might be a family friend. A friend of his grandfather's. The car might simply have become stuck in traffic.'

Tom's fingers tightened on the receiver.

'Call the police,' he ordered.

'I'm going to call Charlie's grandfather,' Mr Marcher said suddenly, sounding stubborn. 'He'll know what to do. Is his number still –'

'Describe the man.'

'Major Fox –'

'Tall, short, fair, dark?'

'Old. Swept-back hair. Patrician.'

'You saw Charlie leave?'

'Yes,' Mr Marcher said, defensively. 'He climbed into the car willingly enough.'

'He probably liked its colour, its shape or the sound of

its engine. You were there, Marcher. You let this happen. I hold you responsible.'

'Really, Major Fox —'

'If anything happens to my son, I will have you killed. I won't even bother to do it myself. I'll just look at the photographs.'

73

The Kripo detective's hand hovered over the telephone.

'What should I say?'

'Whatever you need to say to get through.'

Tom's Makarov wasn't pointed at his head. It wasn't pointed at him at all. But it hung loose and Tom was the only person in that room with a sidearm. Cold fury had burnt the alcohol from Tom's system. He imagined this showed in his face. That the detective realized he was wound tight enough to use it.

He'd like his book back.

'Do it,' Tom ordered.

Picking up the receiver, the detective demanded something of the operator. A few seconds of silence followed and then he came to attention.

'Yes, Comrade General,' he said.

He offered Tom the receiver.

'It's me,' Tom said, not bothering to introduce himself. 'We need to meet . . . Yes,' he said. 'Now.'

74

The courtyard that Sir Cecil's studio overlooked was cluttered with rubbish, cracked and peeling. Its art deco buildings had been beautiful once, quite possibly elegant. These days . . . They looked as ruined as Tom felt.

Tom was heading for the road, the Makarov held loosely at his side, when he realized the rezident was already on his way in.

'I brought your post,' Rafikov said.

A card, bought for Anna, the American girl that Charlie met at Guantánamo, but never sent. On one side was a sunset, on the other Charlie's neatest writing. He asked if Daddy was sending him toy cars.

'Here,' Tom said, handing over his pistol.

'Major, what's wrong?' The levity was gone from the rezident's voice.

'My son's been kidnapped.'

'By whom?'

'I don't know.'

'Your government?'

'They're not like that.'

'All governments are like that.' Pulling a packet of Belomor Kanal from his pocket, General Rafikov lit two and passed one to Tom, who took it without thinking. 'Perhaps you've been told this to unsettle you?'

'I called his school. They said he was with his

great-uncle. He doesn't have a great-uncle . . .' Tom's voice was matter-of-fact. When this was done, he'd rage. Until then, he needed his anger in tight control.

The monsters had finally crawled from the walls. It was no longer Tom's dreams they haunted, he no longer simply had to keep his nightmares at bay. Unable to reach him, they'd gone after his boy.

He'd like his book back.

The original was gone, burnt to ash by Frederika. What if Tom was wrong and Sir Cecil hadn't transferred the manuscript to microfiche? What if he had and Tom couldn't find it? He couldn't swap his son for something he didn't have. The blackness threatened to destroy him.

'I need to get home.'

'That will help how?'

'I'm going to find my son.'

'You're going to get yourself arrested. London believes you killed Sir Cecil, you know that, don't you? They're already worried you're working for me. What would you think if you were them? What would you do?'

'I have to help Charlie.'

'How will getting arrested help him?'

It wouldn't. In fact it might get him killed.

Tom reran that thought, feeling it settle in his guts with the certainty of stone. He couldn't risk a false move. The toy cars had been a warning of what would happen if he got his next move wrong. His silence, the elusive memoirs, Flo Wakefield's HMSO notebook. He needed to work out which of those would be enough to save Charlie. Perhaps all three . . .

In which case, he'd need to get the notebook.

His duty was to get it to Lord Eddington. But this was Charlie. How could he be expected to put duty above that? How could anyone? He would demand proof that his son was alive. As long as Tom was in East Berlin they would have to keep Charlie alive. And if they hurt the boy in *any* way, then he would hunt them down, kill them. He needed them left in no doubt of that.

'You were told to help me, weren't you?' Tom said.

'And I did.' Rafikov's voice was smooth. 'You're still alive. You owe me that. Besides,' he shrugged, 'who says I was told to help you?'

'It was the commissar's idea to send me to that camp.'

'Marshal Milov's plan to send you. My idea to extract you. Strange as it sounds, I have an interest in keeping you alive. Quite possibly, at this moment, I'm the only person in East or West Berlin who can say that.'

Tom believed him. 'What do you know about Reinicken-dorf-Tegelerforst?'

'Absolutely nothing.' Rafikov's eyes became hard.

Tom took a gamble, although probably less of one than it felt. 'There are Russians mentioned in Sir Cecil's mem-oirs. East Germans too.'

'There are no memoirs, remember?'

Tom kept his face impassive.

'They were burnt,' Rafikov said. 'You told Henderson that they were burnt. You told FitzSymonds that too. You said there were no copies.'

'What if I was wrong?'

'You know where a copy is?'

Trust no one. It was Fitz that taught him that. Trust no one, not even yourself. Tom hesitated . . . 'In a message

315

FitzSymonds intercepted, Sir Cecil said he'd given me the memoirs. He hadn't. But he must have given me a clue.'

'Which was what?'

'If I knew that I'd have the memoirs.'

'One day,' said General Rafikov, 'we must play cards for real. If you live that long.' He smiled. 'What do you consider the chances of my glorious allies finding this copy before you do?'

'The GDR? Unlikely, but not impossible.'

'And what do you think London would do with this copy should they get their hands on it?'

'Suppress it.' That was the only answer that made sense. For all the fuss about whether *Spycatcher* should be published, there was no way they'd let Sir Cecil's memoirs be released.

'Having read them first?'

'Of course,' Tom said. 'I'm told you debriefed Sir Cecil. So I doubt there's much in there you don't know. My guess is that you didn't share everything Sir Cecil told you with your East German allies . . .'

Rafikov smiled thinly. 'So many layers to an onion,' he said.

Tom remembered Amelia's comment about wolf packs. How similar they were to humans in their social structures. How their leaders could be ferocious, territorial and protective. Fitz hunted alone. Rafikov looked out for himself but also looked after his own.

What was the USSR's interest in this?

This was bigger than naming names. Although that was the place to start because that was what everything kept coming back to. Their names, our names. Anyone named would be vulnerable, blackmailable, at the very least an embarrassment. *Glasnost. Perestroika. The arms talks . . .*

'That's it,' Tom said. 'You don't want anything to derail the arms talks.'

General Rafikov smiled.

'Your East German allies, however . . .'

'I have to ask,' Rafikov said. 'It would be best if you weren't offended. You're a smart man. A good officer. You understand things. Why don't you come over to Moscow's side?'

'Why the fuck would I do that?'

'Your government doesn't trust you. Your friends think you're a murderer. Your woman is having an affair. Your child is probably dead.'

'He's alive,' Tom said fiercely.

'Kidnappers tend to kill their victims.'

'I'd know if he was dead.'

'You'd know?'

'Of course I would.'

'All the same. You should consider my offer.'

'And embrace a world where clothes don't fit, you can't buy the books you want, vodka's the only thing that will keep you warm, and you have to wait fifteen years for a washing machine only to discover that it doesn't work?'

Rafikov smiled sadly.

'See,' he said. 'You're half Russian already.'

75

Four decanters stood on a walnut Welsh dresser in Great-Uncle Max's house. It was the kind of dresser that was too large and too well made to have lived in a Welsh cottage. Around the neck of each decanter was a silver label on a finely wrought chain. Two of the labels were Georgian, perhaps Edwardian copies, one was art deco, the last high Victorian. Granny would know.

It was shaped like a vine leaf and full of very swirly holes that made it look like lace. In order, the labels read port, brandy, brandy and Madeira. All of the decanters were crystal, two were hand-cut, one machine-cut, one wide-bottomed and smooth. That one was a ship's decanter, because the wide bottom stopped it sliding off the table in a storm.

As all of the decanters were a third full, Charlie decided that must be the polite level for decanters to be filled. He sniffed the stoppers of them all, tasted the brandy and decided he didn't like it. And then he tried the Madeira and decided that he liked it enough to take another sip.

Great-Uncle Max's house was seemingly empty.

It was also, Charlie had decided, huge, as big as his school, perhaps bigger. So far the only people that he'd seen were gardeners who walked the grounds in pairs at intervals so regular that Charlie could time them on his Seiko. Most of the boys at school wore Timex and they liked his Seiko. Even Michaelides.

Charlie liked it too.

A pair of gardeners passed the terrace every twenty minutes.

That meant it took an hour to walk right round Great-Uncle Max's garden since he had three pairs of gardeners. Unless only two pairs walked, of course, while one rested. In which case the time fell to forty minutes. The circumference of the grounds was four miles if everyone walked at 4 mph, which was how fast books said humans walked. If only two of the three pairs walked at any one time then the circumference fell to 2.7 miles. This only held true if no one stopped to talk or have a cup of tea.

Charlie didn't think they did.

They seemed very intent on their walking.

Checking his watch, he decided that Great-Uncle Max must have forgotten the time. It had been a strange day, which didn't mean it had been a bad one. A race through country lanes in a Rolls-Royce that purred and roared and bucked on the corners had been especially exciting, if only because Great-Uncle Max used his gears to break and insisted on accelerating out of corners early.

Since then, Charlie had eaten lunch in the kitchens, served by an old man who'd looked at him so strangely that he'd excused himself to check his reflection in a looking glass in a downstairs loo. His hair was neat, his top button fastened and his tie straight.

These were the usual things that worried grown-ups.

Charlie had buttoned his jacket in case it wasn't meant to be undone. Only the sixth form were allowed to walk around at school with their jackets unbuttoned. They could put their hands in their pockets too.

It didn't make any difference.

The old man still looked at him strangely.

Lunch was cheese ploughman's. Charlie knew what a cheese ploughman's was because this was what Grandpa ordered in the Bugle, if they went there at the weekend. After lunch, the old man showed him to the billiard room, which held a table like a pool table but bigger, with fat legs carved from dark wood.

Apparently the table was so heavy the roof had to be taken off and a crane used to lower it into place. That was how Charlie knew the man was really very old. The man had been there. The table was old, so if he'd been there when it was new he must be older.

When Charlie had suggested Great-Uncle Max might like a game the old man had looked worried. He'd gone to London, he told Charlie.

'But I have to be back at school by three-thirty.'

'I'm sure he'll be back before then.'

It was business, you see.

'Is he a friend of my grandpa's?'

The old man said that he was sure they knew each other. Great-Uncle Max knew everybody. And Charlie said, in that case, they definitely knew each other because Grandpa knew everybody too. The man smiled a little at that and asked if Charlie would like anything else to eat. But the ploughman's had been large and Charlie had only eaten the last of it to be polite.

'I'm fine, thank you,' Charlie said.

The old man had nodded, slightly doubtfully, and suggested that Charlie play billiards against himself. Charlie didn't want to admit that he didn't know the rules; so he nodded and waited until the man left, before putting down the cue he'd picked to pretend to play the game.

The old man had locked the door behind him, which seemed strange.

Walking across to check, Charlie realized the doorknob had a face. It didn't look like Great-Uncle Max. Not even a much younger Great-Uncle Max. He wondered if Great-Uncle Max was on the other side. Although he knew the door was locked, he tried it anyway.

Human nature.

That was what Grandpa blamed for most things people did that didn't make sense. Charlie had applied this maxim to school, and realized quite quickly that tradition also played its part. Things that didn't make sense tended to involve human nature, tradition or both . . .

Charlie wondered where people with animal legs fitted in.

There were two of them, carved in marble and standing either side of an empty fireplace. The woman had no clothes and a twist of ivy across her tummy. The man had horns and legs so hairy he might have been wearing shaggy plus fours. He was carrying panpipes. The woman was holding a large curling shell.

Charlie tried every door in the billiard room in turn.

One opened on a shallow cupboard lined with billiard cues. Another let through to a shabby utility room with a glass door to the gardens. The final door revealed a lavatory with a cast-iron cistern set high on the wall. Charlie set its chain swinging and watched it for a while.

The glass door to the garden was unlocked, so Charlie sat on the brick steps and watched the sky fade through colours so muted he couldn't quite say when one became another. As he sat, he tried to work out why the old man would lock the billiard room but leave the glassdoor open.

His original thought was that the man had wanted to keep him in.

That would have been odd. Now he wondered if it was to keep him out of the rest of the house, which would be odder. Not least because Charlie could walk round to the side and simply let himself in by another door.

Instead he went to look at the box hedges.

If you pretended a line ran from each that couldn't be crossed you could make a maze in your head. After a while Charlie gave up that game and headed down narrow stone steps and between trees to a little graveyard.

He liked it.

Most of all he liked the stone angel.

She was wearing a nightie and the rain had worn her nose smooth. It was possible her stone was cheap because bits of her cheek came away on his fingers when he stroked it. In the distance one of the gardeners glanced over.

So Charlie waved. After a moment the man waved back.

He said something to his companion, who pulled out a radio and began talking. He didn't stop though, or come over to say Charlie shouldn't be touching the angel. They just kept walking. Charlie watched until they were out of sight.

'*Master Fox . . . Master Fox . . .*'

The old man sounded so worried that Charlie felt guilty.

'Out here,' he shouted, then remembered shouting was rude and scrambled to his feet as the old man hurried down from the terrace.

The man breathed a sigh of relief at the sight of him.

'I'm sorry,' Charlie said.

'It's all right,' the old man said.

He looked back at the house and seemed puzzled. 'The door to the garden was open,' Charlie explained. 'I didn't think you'd mind.'

'Don't get old,' the man said. 'Now. Time for bed.'

'But I have to be back at school.' Charlie checked his Seiko and it was worse than he'd imagined. Much worse. 'They're going to be cross.'

'It's all right,' the old man promised. 'Great-Uncle Max called them. Said that his meeting had run late. The head-master said it would be fine to bring you back tomorrow.'

'But I don't have pyjamas. And where will I sleep?'

'We've prepared you a bedroom.'

'We?' Charlie asked.

'I mean me. Let me make you some cocoa first.'

'Thank you,' Charlie said. He didn't like cocoa, not really; but it was the right thing to say, and he followed the old man up to the terrace and into the house. The kitchen where he'd had his lunch was huge, with three sinks, which was one more than Granny had. He sat where he'd sat for lunch and waited while the old man heated a saucepan of milk and fussed around in the pantry.

'Where's the man who collected me from school?'

'He'll be back later.'

'And then?'

'He'll return you.' Putting a plate of biscuits on the table, the old man fetched a big mug and filled it with cocoa. 'Drink up before it gets cold.'

The biscuits were foil wrapped with *Viscount* written on

them and tasted of orange, as you might think orange would taste, if you'd only ever heard it described. Charlie loved them. He ate the first carefully, nibbling round the edges. When the man didn't scowl, he took another and ate that faster.

'Your cocoa's going cold,' the man reminded him.

Reaching for the cup, Charlie took a mouthful. The chocolate taste was disappointingly thin after the biscuits. The old man was right though. His cocoa was lukewarm and not really that nice. Charlie drank it quickly.

He started to feel strange a few minutes later.

'Another biscuit?' the old man asked.

Charlie shook his head, and heard as much as felt the thud as he fell forward and hit the table. It wasn't enough to keep him awake.

76

It was early in the morning, too early for regular visitors, and East Berlin was only just stirring, when a Red Army guard at the entrance to the Soviet embassy on Unter den Linden stepped forward to deal with a taxi that had stopped unexpectedly, right outside the gates.

His determination to make the driver's life hell wilted the moment General Rafikov wound down a rear window.

'Get that barrier up now.'

The guard wondered if he should apologize, took one look at Rafikov's scowl and decided silence was safer. He'd done what he should do. Stopped an unexpected car. Inside that car, Tom Fox was shocked to realize just how much he was counting on help from the man they'd come to meet. How much less certain he was these days that he could.

Marshal Milov, *the commissar.*

The lieutenant at the front desk was expecting them. He recognized Rafikov. And the officer at Rafikov's side, a grim-faced KGB colonel, didn't look like someone who'd appreciate being asked his name.

'The old man's here?' Rafikov demanded.

'He landed an hour ago, Comrade General.'

'Is he alone?'

The lieutenant hesitated. 'I'm not sure, sir.'

That would be a no. Rafikov sighed. 'We'll show ourselves up.'

As they walked towards the lifts, Rafikov turned to Tom and said, 'I should tell you that Frederika Schmitt is dead. She threw herself from the fire escape at the gym rather than face arrest.'

'It wasn't that high,' Tom said.

Rafikov shrugged. 'She died in the ambulance.'

'I'm sorry,' Tom said. He meant it too.

'I'd have thought you'd be delighted.'

'And the woman they arrested at the squat?'

Rafikov sucked his teeth. 'You should be less of a romantic,' he said. 'It's not a good quality in a man like you. Now, FitzSymonds ... You wouldn't find him making that mistake. He and I, we're cut from the same cloth.'

'All the same . . .'

'The Kripo have a copy of that tape you recorded and the case is closed. They've decided that Frederika killed both men. So, yes, I'm sure they've kicked your *Instandbesetzer* back on to the streets.'

'And me?' Tom asked. 'Am I likely to be arrested?'

'Of course not. I'm sure there's a room for you at the Palasthotel if you want it. Although you might need to buy clothes.' General Rafikov looked amused. 'I'm told your luggage went to West Berlin, even if you didn't. I believe Colonel Schneider has invited the British consulate in West Berlin to make arrangements for your return. He's waiting to hear back . . .'

The lift let them out on a landing painted in improbable blues. A huge oil of the Russian steppes filled a spot where Stalin's portrait once hung. A marble bust of Lenin stood on a plinth in one corner. A door stood open and in the doorway stood a white-bearded man with hair to his shoulders. Marshal Milov appeared to be wearing a yellow silk smoking jacket.

'That uniform suits you,' he said.

'That's exactly what General Rafikov said.'

'No doubt he tried to turn you. I told him you wouldn't.'

The marshal's hair was thinner than the last time he and Tom had met; but his beard was combed through and his eyes as fierce as ever. He'd reached an age where his face was so lined it was hard to tell what were scars and what were creases. 'Still,' Milov said. 'Suppose I'd better ask too. Do you wish to defect?'

'No, sir.' Tom shook his head.

'We'd promise to appreciate you.'

'I don't believe in what the Soviet Union stands for.'

'You don't believe in what the United Kingdom stands for either.'

'I was born there . . .'

'No,' the commissar said. 'You were born on some shitty little military base in Cyprus. I checked. Born dead, brought back to life, given to nuns for the first week in case you died again.'

He looked at Tom's face.

'You realize there's more at stake here than your son's life?'

Not for me, Tom thought. *Not for me.*

77

Charlie woke and wondered why he wasn't wearing any clothes. He also wondered where he was and why there was no furniture in the room, not even curtains to stop the light from waking him.

Finally, he wondered how scared he should be.

'You shouldn't be.'

'Be what?'

'Scared. It won't help.'

'How do you . . . ?'

'Know what you're thinking?' The girl in a nightie sitting on the bare boards by his feet smiled. 'How do you think I know?'

Charlie rubbed his eyes and she laughed.

'Hello,' Becca said.

'I thought you only came at night. When everyone was asleep. That's what you said. Were you telling lies?'

'This is an emergency.'

He felt too sleepy for it to be a real emergency; but under the sleepiness his tummy was tying itself into knots and his heart was beating too fast. Charlie wasn't good at recognizing feelings. That was always one of the problems. But he thought he must be quite frightened for Becca to come in daylight.

'Is that door locked?'

'What do you think?' she asked.

He thought she should have answered properly.

Sulkily, he climbed to his feet and almost fell over. His knees were rubbery and his legs weren't working very well. His fingers didn't feel properly connected to everything else. Catching sight of himself in a window, Charlie decided he looked very small. And decided that might be because the room was very big and the ceiling very high. Becca didn't look anything because she didn't have a reflection.

One door, locked. Three windows, painted shut.

He was still in Great-Uncle Max's house, though. He recognized the terrace and the gardens. A fireplace on the longest wall was covered with plywood. The plywood was screwed tight at the corners. Charlie tried pulling at the edge and broke a nail. 'Don't cry,' Becca said.

'It hurts.'

'You can't start crying yet. You shouldn't cry at all.'

'What should I be doing?'

'Looking for something useful.'

'Like what?' Charlie asked crossly.

Becca looked worried. 'I don't know.'

'You're the oldest. You're meant to know.'

'It's all right. No need to get upset.' She brushed her fingers across his bare shoulder. It felt somewhere between a shadow and a breeze.

'I'm not normal,' he said. 'That's what they say at school.'

Becca laughed. 'No one is. But you have to discover that for yourself.' She looked sad. 'By then the damage is usually done.'

'Can I ask what happened?'

'Best not,' she said, sounding scarily like Dad. 'You'd

only tell them. And it's not like I really know. It was lots of little things.'

'Mummy's straw that broke the camel's back?'

'It was an accident, you know. You can tell Daddy that. He pretends he believes it, but he doesn't really.'

'Was it?' Charlie asked. 'You promise?'

'If I promise, does that mean you'll tell Daddy?'

Charlie nodded. 'I promise.'

'And so do I,' Becca said. 'We should have been better friends. I'm sorry.'

'The gap was too big.'

'Who said that?'

'Mummy, when she was talking to Daddy. She thought I couldn't hear.'

'They always think you can't hear.'

'I know,' Charlie said. 'Did you know I was an accident?'

The girl came to kneel in front of him and she put up her hand to hold his face, although Charlie couldn't quite feel her fingers. 'That was me,' she said. 'I'm the reason they got married. Mummy wanted you . . .'

'I'm sorry,' Charlie said. 'I'm sorry.'

He was crying and looking round for his sister but she was gone. The room was empty, the windows painted shut, the plywood still firmly fixed over the fireplace. There was no way out.

'Keep looking,' she said. Her voice was in his head, not outside like last time.

'I've looked,' Charlie protested.

'Look again . . .'

78

It was only when Marshal Milov shut the door behind them that Tom realized General Rafikov was not included in their conversation.

The office that Milov had commandeered was panelled in dark wood and smelt and felt like the inside of a cigar box. Opening a window, the commissar reached for a humidor and hesitated. 'Want one?' he asked.

Tom shook his head.

'I'm meant to be giving up too.'

With a sigh, Commissar Milov, Marshal of the Soviet Union, settled himself behind a desk and indicated that Tom should pour him a glass of water, and then take a chair. 'In your own words,' he said.

'My son's been taken and my wife is having an affair.'

'Are the two related?'

'No,' Tom said. 'They're not.'

'That's good,' the commissar said. 'In situations like this, simple is best.' He reached for the humidor he'd resisted, bit the end off a Cohiba and spat towards the waste basket.

'Here,' Tom said, flicking a heavy gold desk lighter.

'This is when you tell me who took him.'

'I don't know,' he said.

'Of course you do. There's no point taking him otherwise.'

Marshal Milov sat back and blew smoke at the ceiling. Then he drew deep on the cigar and shut his eyes, keeping his thoughts and the smoke inside. 'Such things are done to frighten,' he said finally. 'To bend the victim to the shape required. These people will not kill him. Not yet. Not until they're certain you cannot be bent to shape.'

Reaching into his pocket, Tom put Charlie's postcard on the desk. 'Being killed isn't the worst thing that can happen to a child.'

'You speak from experience?'

'Yes,' Tom said.

'Do they know that?'

'I would imagine so . . .'

'Then they found the right lever.' The commissar drew on his cigar and held the smoke before letting it rise in a trickle. Standing up, he opened the window a little wider.

'Maya will complain,' he said. 'She always does.'

'She's here?'

Wax Angel had been a sniper in Stalingrad in her teens, a ballerina in her twenties, a prisoner of the gulags shortly after. When Tom first met her six months before, she'd been a beggar, sitting on church steps in Moscow, carving winged figures from stolen candles. It was the candles that gave Maya her nickname.

Wax Angel.

'You think she'd let me come alone?'

Marshal Milov looked at the Cohiba sadly, stubbed it out on the inside of a drawer and pushed it into his pocket. 'Now all I need to do is remember it's there . . . Don't get old,' he added. 'Not if you can avoid it.'

'Sir?'

'I fought at Stalingrad. I led tanks across the Vistula into Germany. I was there when Berlin fell. I stood up to the Boss in the worst of the bad days and lived. Now I worry about being discovered smoking.'

'You control the destiny of millions.'

'It's not as much fun as it should be. That's the truth of it, Tom. I'm old. I'm tired. I'm glad the woman I love is with me. I'm glad my granddaughter's found a man she loves enough to give him a child. I'm glad Gorbachev's in the Kremlin scaring the shit out of old men like me. But I've had enough of it. Even giants should be allowed to sleep.'

The marshal said it without irony, and Tom realized he was speaking for his entire generation: those who'd turned back the Nazi invasion at a cost of dead brothers, fathers and sons; who fought beside their sisters, mothers and daughters. Men for whom the ghosts of those dead were more important than the lives of the living, because it was only a matter of time before they joined them. The commissar hated Moscow and barely left his dacha. For Tom, his son's abduction was everything. But Tom was not a fool, he knew something bigger was needed to bring a man like Milov to Berlin.

'What is this really about?' Tom asked.

'You expect me to tell you?'

'A man can hope.'

'Hope gets you killed, Tom.'

'*Luck is good. Skill is better.* Something my son said.'

'A wise child.'

Looking up, Tom met the old man's eyes.

'Sir Cecil Blackburn was a paedophile. In Berlin after the war he ran a club of some sort. It was used by British,

American and Soviet officers . . .' Tom stared at the old man. 'I'm not telling you anything you don't know, am I?'

The commissar smiled.

'He was blackmailing London,' Tom said, 'into letting him return. And I was the officer sent to . . .'

'Kill him?'

'Bring him back. I don't believe we intended to let Sir Cecil publish his memoirs. I doubt we even intended to let him appear in court. I think we simply felt it would be safer if he was in our hands.'

'Any idea why?'

Tom thought of Flo's missing name; Lord Brannon, the Queen's cousin, blown up to order on a Westmorland lake. London would do anything to stop that getting out. Including taking Sir Cecil back.

He shook his head.

Reaching for the humidor, Milov took another cigar, lit it and closed his eyes. There was a moment of silence. When he opened them again, Tom could tell he'd made a decision.

'I will need the memoirs.'

Tom opened his mouth to object and the commissar held up his hand. For a second he said nothing, and simply seemed to be thinking, unless he was collecting his thoughts. 'When you find them, when that time comes,' he said, 'I will need the memoirs. That is my price for helping save your son.'

'You'll get me to London?'

'So you can be arrested? Of course he won't . . .'

The voice came from a different doorway, and Tom stood to greet the elderly woman who'd slipped into the room. She sniffed the air, looked at the open window and glanced reproachfully at her husband. She smiled at Tom, though.

They hugged, and Wax Angel stepped back to examine his face, one hand coming up to touch it. Her own face was high-cheeked and lined, weathered from work camps and a life lived outdoors.

'What are you doing here?' Tom asked.

'You think I'd let him out alone?'

Despite himself, Tom laughed.

'That's better,' Maya said. 'Now, tell me all about it. Begin with your boy being abducted. How did your enemies do this?' She listened carefully, stopping Tom only once to check a detail. 'A Rolls-Royce Silver Cloud Coupé? Right. Now him' – she glanced at her husband – 'what price has he asked?'

'Sir Cecil Blackburn's memoirs.'

'If he finds them,' Marshal Milov added.

'When he finds them,' Maya said. 'When he finds them it might be best if he loses them again, permanently. Isn't that right?'

'Maya.' Marshal Milov's voice was sharp.

'The world is changing,' she said. 'We should let it change. Gorbachev would like to abolish nuclear weapons. This the West has refused. So he will accept a reduction instead. There are to be talks. It's possible that people in the negotiations are named in the memoirs. Not kindly.'

'*Maya . . .*'

'He should destroy them. The world cannot afford these talks to be derailed.' Wax Angel glared at her husband. 'The commissar knows this. He knows, too, that there are people on your side and ours who would like nothing more.'

Marshal Milov sighed.

Walking to the humidor, he took a cigar and shrugged. 'You're cross anyway. What difference will it make?'

'It will make me crosser.' She took the cigar from his fingers and returned it to the box, letting her hand brush against his.

'Tell Tom the rest,' she ordered.

The commissar sighed. 'We have someone in the GDR Politburo.'

'With respect,' Tom said, 'they're your puppets.'

'Less so, year on year. So it still pays to have someone inside. Now would be a bad time for that to be revealed. So, you can see, for a while at least, London and Moscow's interests align.'

'Your man might be on Sir Cecil's list?'

'We can't take that risk.'

'Who will you send to London?' Tom asked.

Maya came to stand in front of him. Her face was stern and her gaze steady. For all her age, her determination was steely.

'Who do you think?' she demanded.

79

There was a story about a spider Mummy used to tell Charlie before he learnt to tie his shoes properly. He had to be able to tie his shoes to go to school. He only discovered that later.

If he'd known, he'd never have learnt to tie them at all.

The spider kept making a bad web, which kept breaking. The king, who was hiding from his enemies, watched the spider endlessly making bad webs and decided to have another go at getting his kingdom back. This time he managed it, just as the spider eventually managed to make a web. It couldn't have been very good at being a spider though. None of the spiders Charlie had seen had ever had trouble making webs.

Charlie shivered. He wasn't cold exactly, but he felt very naked, and there was nowhere to go to the loo. He didn't need to go but was worried about when he did need to. He also wanted to know why they had taken his clothes. He knew he was definitely still at Great-Uncle Max's because the gardeners passed by the window regular as clockwork. Hammering on the glass didn't help.

None of them even glanced at the house.

Not only was the sash window on which he hammered painted shut but it also had a bolt sunk into its crossbar. The bolt needed a hexagonal key to remove it and there were identical bolts on the other windows. Trying not to be dispirited, Charlie turned his attention to the door. He began by listing everything about it that was strange.

For a start, it had locks, plural.

Secondly, the newer of the locks was fixed the wrong way round.

A shiny Yale had its slot facing into the room. The only reason you would do that was . . . This bit wasn't really part of the list.

It was more of a conclusion.

The only reason you'd do that was so people inside would need a key to let themselves out; while those outside would only need to turn a latch to let themselves in. That thought didn't make Charlie feel any better.

The bottom lock was Victorian, very simple, and the deadbolt hadn't been engaged. Its black metal cover looked flimsy. Perhaps they didn't think it worth locking. Either that, or it was so old that they'd long since lost the key.

What Charlie needed was his picks.

Except those were at school, where he should have been. The school would have noticed that he hadn't returned. Matron always came round to check everyone was in bed before the bell rang for lights out. Daylight outside said that now was tomorrow. He should definitely have been back at school by now.

Yale locks were easier to pick than mortise locks. So Felix, the man in Cuba, had said. But to pick the Yale he'd need . . .

Charlie wished Becca would come back.

He missed her in real life and he missed her here; and he knew Mummy said life wasn't fair, every time he said something was unfair; but Becca dying really wasn't. It wasn't fair to anyone. He couldn't even remember the last thing that Becca had said to him before she got in her Mini that morning.

Don't touch my things, probably.

It was possible she was telling the truth about not driving into the tree on purpose. She'd looked normal when she said goodbye, and hadn't sounded strange. Charlie was much better at sensing what other people were feeling than he was at working out what he felt himself. Becca must have looked and behaved normally when she got into the car or he'd have noticed.

Keep looking, she said.

I've looked.

Well. Look again . . .

If she told him to look then there must be something in this room that he needed to find. It would be cruel otherwise. He could waste a whole day, if he had a day, looking for something that wasn't there.

Remember the spider, Mummy would have said.

He began searching the floorboards for a nail that he could prise up or work loose; but all of the nails were hammered flat and so firmly sunk into the boards that, even if he didn't have bitten fingernails, he'd never be able to get them up.

Maybe there was something else?

Something trapped in the filthy cracks between the boards.

Charlie skimmed the room, walking too fast and looking left and right without really seeing anything. He hated himself in the window. It wasn't simply that he looked afraid. He was much too little for his age.

He decided it would be best if he stopped looking at his reflection and started looking at the floorboards instead, properly this time. Walking up one edge of the room, he looked only at the gap between boards one and two. Then he walked back, looking at the gap between boards two and three. He made the turns at each end without letting himself stop or look away from the floor.

Charlie had searched almost all the room before he started to panic. It was hard not to be worried when you'd looked at eighteen gaps and there were only two to go. *Missed it.*

That sounded like Becca.

But the voice had been his own.

Charlie walked back over the bit he'd just covered.

Kneeling, he peered at the dust and grit trapped between the boards. There, half buried, was a hairgrip. One of those pieces of bent metal covered with tortoiseshell plastic that small girls and women wear. Becca used to hate them.

He couldn't get it with his fingers and had no nails to reach into the gap. So he needed to think. That was fine. Thinking was about the one thing he could do. He found a floorboard splintered enough at the edge to let him break free a needle of wood and he used that to coax the hairgrip from the gap.

As he reached for the hairgrip, he heard tyres on gravel and the rumble of an engine he recognized. The Rolls-Royce was back.

80

Sun glinted off the Moskva River on to the Vodovzvod-
naya Tower.

The roof of the British embassy could be seen across
the river from the Kremlin office that Sir Edward Masterton was about to visit. Her Majesty's ambassador to the
USSR had been here before.

Not often, but once or twice.

Then, as now, he'd entered through the Borovistky
Gate, the Spasskaya Tower entrance being reserved for
heads of state. As Sir Edward's car passed into the Kremlin, he remembered a joke Premier Khrushchev had told
years before.

A farmer from the Urals drives into Red Square and
parks in front of the Spasskaya Tower. A guard rushes
over. 'Don't park there. The Politburo use this entrance.'
The peasant looks at the gate, considers his rusting lorry
and shrugs. 'It's okay,' he says. 'I've locked it.'

Smiling, Sir Edward climbed languidly from his Jaguar.

The ambassador worked hard to be never less than elegant. He was English, it was expected. He'd be happier,
however, if he knew why he'd been summoned.

London had been no help. Chernobyl, the coming arms
summit, Baltic autumn exercises ... Nothing had happened or not happened as far as they were aware. His call
had worried them though. The Foreign Office had ended

the call from Sir Edward dreading whatever bombshell Gorbachev intended to drop now. The grandson of peasants, the son of a tractor driver wounded killing Nazis, he was a hard man to read.

Sir Edward put the man's unusual approach down to his having been a child when his grandfather was arrested. Although not shot, his grandfather had been tortured for months as a Trotskyite and the effect on Gorbachev's family had been devastating. Gorbachev said he wanted to see those days gone for ever and Sir Edward was inclined to believe him.

Chernobyl seemed the most likely reason.

Reports of emergency field hospitals set up to treat those irradiated while trying to cap the reactor were still coming in. It was fairly obvious that news from the area was being heavily censored. And given what *Pravda* was saying, God only knows what was being kept back. Sir Edward looked at the woman who'd climbed from the Jaguar's other side. She was black, immaculately dressed and ferociously bright. Mary Batten ran the embassy's Intelligence.

'Ready when you are, sir.'

The doors into the Kremlin offices opened and Sir Edward allowed himself to be shown to the lifts. If lifts anywhere in the USSR could be expected to work then those in the Politburo's inner sanctum had to head that list.

They rose smoothly to an upper floor.

The last tsar had kept an office here. Lenin had slept for a while on a camp bed in one of the dressing rooms, with teenage Bolsheviks guarding his door. Stalin had so disliked the sight of the Union Flag flying from the British embassy that he'd demanded that London sell him the building.

When they refused he had curtains fitted instead.

'We're here,' Sir Edward said.

Their guard had stopped by a gilded doorway.

Stepping forward, he knocked smartly. When there was no reply he opened the door anyway and indicated that they should enter. A coffee pot stood on a desk beside a dish piled high with biscuits. What Sir Edward really noticed though was a red telephone. The guard indicated the telephone, the coffee and biscuits, nodded politely and withdrew. A few seconds later, the telephone rang.

'I think you should answer it, sir.'

The ambassador hesitated for only a second. 'Masterton,' he said.

Tom sat back in his seat, watched the door close behind Marshal Milov, and wondered if he was telling the truth when he promised not a single word of this call would be recorded. It seemed unlikely.

But with the commissar you could never tell.

'Sir Edward,' Tom said. 'It's Tom Fox.'

'*What?*'

'I'm telephoning from Berlin. I'm assured by Marshal Milov, who is here in person, that this line is entirely secure.'

'Milov is with you?'

'He's no longer in the room.'

'I don't imagine he needs to be.'

'He gave me his word,' Tom said.

Sir Edward considered that. 'Thought this was about

Chernobyl,' he said crossly. 'I've been preparing myself the whole bloody way.'

'The place is going to be radioactive for a thousand years.'

'Milov told you that?' Sir Edward sounded shocked.

'I had it from someone in the area.'

'Was he dying?'

'She,' Tom said. 'And I hope not.' He tried to brush away the guilt of getting drunk with Amelia and failed.

'Then she can't have been that close.'

'Footage from an over-flight shows birds sickening on the wing and plummeting into the broken reactor. The cinematographer died within a day and his camera was so radioactive they buried it. I had that from my friend. It was her friend who died.'

'Christ,' Sir Edward said.

'Indeed.' Tom steeled himself. 'I have a question . . .'

'So do I,' Sir Edward said.

'I didn't kill Sir Cecil.'

'That wasn't my question. And I've never believed you did. Cold-blooded murder of a man you've never met? Not your style, Fox.'

'What's the question, sir?'

'Have you defected? Are you thinking of defecting? Are you a double agent?'

The strangeness of his situation hit Tom. He was in Berlin searching for the truth, while relying on a Russian ballerina to rescue his son, and he was on the telephone to an Englishman in Moscow who doubted his loyalty.

'No,' Tom said firmly. 'I'm none of those things.'

'Are you prepared to swear it?'

'Yes,' Tom said.

'What matters to you?'

'My son,' Tom said it without hesitation.

'Right then. Are you prepared to swear it on his life?'

Tom was silent.

'Don't expect me to play nice,' Sir Edward said. 'In my job I can't afford to be. Are you prepared to swear on your son's life that you haven't defected, you don't intend to defect and you're not working against the state?'

'I swear. On my hopes of getting him back alive.'

'Getting him back?'

'He's been taken, sir.'

'Why?' Sir Edward's question was abrupt.

'That's what I'm trying to work out. What does Reinickendorf-Tegelerforst mean to you, sir?'

'Nothing.' Sir Edward's reply was instant. 'Never heard of it.' He seemed to think for a second. 'Wait. Isn't it a district in Berlin?'

'It relates to why my son's been taken. Quite possibly to why Sir Cecil was killed. And why I'm here,' Tom added, 'when I should be back home finding him.'

He felt close to fury.

'Sir,' he heard himself say. 'I think you should answer.'

81

The bellboy who carried Maya Milova's Harrods bags into her room was sweet. Young enough, really, to be a boy. Thin as a dancer and with cheekbones to make Nureyev jealous. 'Are you all right, madam?'

'Yes.' Her voice was abrupt.

She wasn't, of course. The stop-off in Paris had been a mistake.

Given what Rudolph Nureyev's defection did to Maya's world she should have hated him. But he was dying, damn him. Down to skin and bones. His flesh ravaged, his hair falling out. Hidden behind shutters in that Parisian apartment of his. No sign left of the glorious god who'd commanded every stage on which he ever danced. No one was meant to know he had the American disease.

Word had got out just the same. Rudi was denying it, of course.

You would. Wouldn't you?

He'd been spoilt and self-obsessed, a nightmare to work with. His defection had destroyed the tour, thrown the Kirov Ballet under suspicion and seen some of them jailed. But she'd been wrong to doubt his abilities. He really was the greatest male dancer in the world.

The videos showed him as better than she remembered.

'Put those down here,' Maya ordered.

The bellboy nodded, putting her Harrods bags on a

346

fold-out table designed to take luggage, and bowed slightly. He looked shocked when Maya put out her hand for him to shake and slipped him a folded £5 note with the casual finesse of a businessman asking a maître d' for a better table.

She could do this stuff without thinking.

When he looked at her he saw an elderly and, she hoped, elegant Russian woman dressed in a Soviet copy of a Chanel black dress. A bad copy, she had to admit, and she'd be doing something about that.

When she looked at herself she saw the prima ballerina. The woman who'd travelled from New York to Paris to London representing the Soviet state.

Unless she looked closely, of course.

Then she saw what the boy saw. A Muscovite trying hard not to look too obviously at the luxury around her. The commissar had given her English currency, enough of it for her to check that he realized how much he'd given.

He had, of course.

She was in London as a tourist. A pilgrim, really.

Maya thought of the interview she'd just done with the *Guardian*.

Their journalist had obviously looked her up. The *Guardian* was not like *Pravda*. None of their newspapers were.

She'd said she'd lived through the Great Patriotic War, Stalin's terror, the Khrushchev thaw. That she'd danced for kings and been imprisoned in the Lubyanka. That she'd never felt as proud of the Soviet Union or as hopeful about the possibilities for peace as she did today.

347

'Was that what your Soviet handlers told you to say?' the journalist had asked.

'It's what I'd have said anyway. You'll find I speak my mind, whatever the consequences.'

The girl had been friendlier after that.

To the English she was a dissident . . .

Arrest, trial, public confession. Time in the gulags. That practically made her a saint for them. It helped that she'd been famous; that she'd been imprisoned; that she'd been a sniper at Stalingrad. It also helped that she was old, able to speak English, could be charming and understated, and just a little bit sharp with the young if necessary.

More than anything it helped that she'd danced with Nureyev.

Of course, she'd danced at the Coliseum long before the Tartar was old enough to perform in public. The Kirov Ballet took its foreign trips seriously. They were government-funded, government-promoted, government-ordered. They showed the world that the USSR was a civilized, cultured place. Every aficionado of ballet who walked away from seeing her dance couldn't help but think differently about a country that could inculcate that level of perfection.

It was propaganda. Of course it was.

The Politburo would never have let them out of the country if it was simply about art. The other side did the same. Everyone knew that. From Jackson Pollock to Beat poetry, most modern Western work was CIA-inspired.

The English had given her a tourist visa.

That was important to remember. Her being in London was not official.

She'd be making a pilgrimage to Marx's grave in Highgate. And visiting his rooms in Soho's Dean Street, where he and his wife, Jenny von Westphalen, lived in such poverty that three of their children died. She would walk, if her legs allowed, from Camden, where he later had a house, to the British Museum, where he wrote *Das Kapital*. If they followed her at all, Maya doubted it would be for long. At least, she hoped not.

On her way to the lifts, Maya stopped in front of a huge gold mirror to admire the Chanel dress she'd bought in Harrods that morning. It was beautifully made, exactly the right depth of black and stupidly expensive.

Maya liked her new life, with its cars, warm clothes and shopping, for all her granddaughter disapproved of the last. But she hadn't changed. She'd simply folded herself inside a brighter, more impressive layer of rags.

Inside she was the same.

She was the person who'd unfolded herself from the snow, on the steps of a church in Moscow, where she used to steal candles to carve angels, and found herself staring into the face of a man whose eyes held an even greater wilderness than her own. Tom Fox was the one she'd been waiting for.

She was not sure he knew it, even now.

God help the world if that child of his was killed. Because what he kept in that locked room inside his head would break free.

And who would cage it then?

No one would, because if he couldn't, nobody could.

Who knew these things better than her? She'd taken her

madness out to Moscow's street corners, huddled with it in church doorways, sharpened it with shards of glass, pissed it in narrow alleys for people to walk through. Its final manifestation was the little wax figures tourists used to buy without knowing what they bought. Maya was proof that, if God was kind, no matter how far madness took you, you could find your way back to food, warmth, even your family. Tom had played his part in that.

It was her turn to help him.

In reception, a smart young man rushed to get the hotel door. While another, already standing outside, hailed a taxi.

'Fortnum's,' Maya told the driver. 'I'm meeting a friend for tea.'

82

The man Maya was meeting on the fourth floor of Fortnum & Mason in Piccadilly had never met her. But Tom's
father-in-law would recognize her all the same. Her hair,
her clothes, her manner. How many other elderly Soviet
ballerinas would be taking tea?

She liked the Fortnum tearooms. Always had. She
hoped that they were still the strange, almost turquoise,
duck-egg blue she remembered. Did they know how Russian a colour that was, how imperial? Although perhaps
this could be forgiven in a country still primitive enough
to have a queen.

She had a request for Lord Eddington when they met.

A request that was simple, if slightly odd. In the very
early sixties, she would tell him, Cecil Beaton had taken
her photograph in Trafalgar Square, while police kept the
crowds away. He'd photographed her in a huge hat, leaning on the bonnet of a purple Rolls-Royce. It was a lie that
the car had been purple. It had, in fact, been a very ordinary blue. And afterwards she'd been driven round
Trafalgar Square in it. A journalist from *The Times* had
asked what she thought of the vehicle and she'd said it was
wonderful. That too had been a lie.

It was less impressive than a Zil.

All the same, for the purposes of telling Lord Eddington, the Rolls would become purple. A purple Silver Cloud

Coupé. She would explain that she wanted to have her photograph taken in such a car again. For old times' sake. In memory of a world that had vanished. She was a friend of his son-in-law. An admirer of his country. She wondered if he or any of his government colleagues knew who owned such a vehicle . . .

'Do try one of the biscuits . . .'

The man opposite lifted a bone china plate and waited expectantly. He was younger than Maya had expected, with that pink English look and swept-back, slightly greying hair. He'd been handsome once. If you liked the type.

She could tell that he'd fallen back on good manners as a way of keeping his distress under control. His grandson had been abducted, his son-in-law was suspected of being a traitor, his daughter . . .

Who knew what was going on there? The man had closed up like a shell when Maya asked after Tom's wife.

'You were in the war?' she asked.

'Just missed it,' he said. 'I believe you served?'

He'd done his research, like that girl at the *Guardian*. Although he'd probably been examining more interesting files. Maya bit into the biscuit she'd dutifully taken. It was good, depressingly so. Lemon zest, fresh butter, good sugar. Quite possibly made that morning.

'Stalingrad,' she said. 'We ate rats.'

Lord Eddington looked shocked.

'When those were gone we ate our leather boots.'

He changed the subject slightly, probably because he

couldn't tell whether or not she was joking. 'You were a soldier?'

'I was a sniper.'

'And you're here with?'

'Nobody,' she said. 'You know this. I'm alone.'

He nodded unhappily to himself. 'My son-in-law . . .'

'Trusts me,' Maya said. 'You should do the same.'

It was hard to have a conversation when neither side was allowed to say what they were actually thinking; when talking about one thing was really talking about something else. But, by the end of tea, she'd acquired a handful of facts. He would ask around about Rolls-Royces. The only purple one that sprung to mind belonged to a famous actor. It was unlikely to be available, however. Because he'd very sadly, and very recently, died of an overdose.

The man's voice trembled as he said this and Maya realized Lord Eddington was afraid. For his grandson, she imagined.

'One final thing,' he said. 'My daughter doesn't know.'

Maya stared at him. 'That I'm here?'

'About anything. Nor do the police. I had to make a call. I ordered the school not to tell her. Not to tell the police.' He looked at Maya, face hollow. 'Most kidnapped children die at the point the authorities become involved.'

Maya waited.

'The other boys have been told he's ill.' Eddington hesitated. 'I have friends who might help. But whoever has done this obviously has friends too. I've stopped knowing who to trust.'

Maya could remember how that felt.

'Caro will hate me when she finds out,' Eddington said. 'But she's been having a hard time of it.' He looked haunted. 'A private matter . . . I hope to see Tom soon, but if you see him first, perhaps you could tell him? Until this is resolved, it's best Caro doesn't know.'

83

The two boys had met three weeks earlier in the ruins of the Reich Chancellery, cameras in hand. Strangely, perhaps not so strangely, they were back there a week later. And the week after that. They were the same age but the English boy looked older, his face unshaven and shadowy, while the Russian was unshaven and smooth. It was September 1945, a week before the Victory Parade.

They wore uniforms and had chosen to walk the last of the way.

This was uphill and in darkness, with roots and dried dirt underfoot, rustling trees around them and stars in the sky above.

The Russian boy felt the Englishman's knuckles brush his and looked across to see the Englishman's silhouette look away. It might have been an accident but they both knew it wasn't. Next time, the Russian let his knuckles brush the back of the Englishman's hand and fingers found each other.

They walked up the path together.

The wind was warm and the breeze scented, and they were both soothed by the stillness of the night, and shocked to find themselves holding hands. For all they'd both been in uniform a year, they were very young and this was not what they'd expected to happen. At least, not consciously.

There might have been a hope, a whisper, a rustle of

thought and desire as quiet as that night's breeze; but that was all it was, and it was not a whisper they were used to hearing.

If they'd been less taken up with the strangeness of their fingers entwined they might have heard the ragged boys before they got close. The first either of them knew about it was the glare of a torch in their eyes and mocking laughter. The boy holding the torch held a knife in his other hand.

It was sharp and narrow.

The pommel and cross guard were brass, the handle black, the blade was shaped like an elongated leaf and glinted in the moonlight. The original owner of the Hitler Youth presentation dagger was probably dead; unless he'd had the sense to run away when his city was overrun, unless he was the one who jabbed it towards them. That seemed unlikely.

Most of that kind died like rats in the ruins.

Although the ragged boys circled, there was no need, because their prey was surrounded. All of the boys had knives, and one held both a knife and a flare gun. They were jeering, not loudly but with feeling.

Eddie Masterton, newly arrived in the city, felt the Russian boy beside him grip his hand tightly for a second and then let go. Reaching for the revolver in his belt, Nicolai drew it faster than Eddie would have thought possible and shot the boy with the torch through the head.

Brightness split the night.

The boy with the knife and flare gun went down next.

The killing was so swift and brutal that Eddie realized this wasn't, this couldn't have been, the first action his friend had seen. The others were running now but Nicolai kept firing. A boy he hit in the shoulder lurched forward and staggered on. Another took a bullet to his leg and fell, lying in a sobbing heap, wailing for his friends to come back for him.

None of them did.

'Let him live,' Eddie said.

'Nyet.' Nicolai shook his head.

Walking over as casually as if going to post a letter, Nicolai glanced down, shrugged and shot the boy through the head. His pleas for mercy ending mid-word. The aftermath was silence. A silence stripped of the birdsong that had filled the night before their attackers arrived. If the leaves rustled, Eddie Masterton no longer heard them.

'It's okay,' Nicolai said. 'It's okay.'

Eddie was hugging himself, he realized. His arms wrapped tight around his own shoulders. The next thing he knew, he was against a tree and Nicolai was kissing him. After a startled second, without even really thinking about it, Eddie began kissing back. That was all he did, that was all they did, but they did it for a long time, and with an intensity that put the stars back in the sky.

'Now,' Nicolai said, 'let's find this club.'

Eddie hadn't been but he'd heard rumours.

The club had gambling, drinking, food and working girls; the staples of every cellar bar in Berlin, a city where families sold daughters for food. Only this wasn't in a cellar, it operated from a hunting lodge.

A place called Reinickendorf-Tegelerforst.

84

Inside the lodge, a small man looked up from behind a leather-topped desk that had once been luxurious but now looked merely ruined. Much like the city really, Eddie decided. The man looked French. At least, he did to Eddie. Brylcreemed hair, a narrow moustache, olive-skinned, bags under his eyes . . .

'We haven't been before.'

'No,' said the man, 'you haven't.'

English, Eddie realized. He had an accent. Eddie wasn't good on accents. He thought Manchester, maybe. The man looked them over slowly.

'I'd remember if you had. Who told you about the club?'

Eddie racked his brains, wondering if it mattered. It would be embarrassing to bring Nicolai here only to discover they couldn't get in. 'I can't remember,' he said miserably. 'I was drunk at the time.'

The man smiled. 'Good answer,' he said.

Before he could say anything else, a French major stumbled through a pair of velvet curtains and stood there blinking at them. His flies were open and his jacket done up with the wrong buttons. A second later, a blonde woman bustled through. She was bare-chested, the top half of her dress flapping like a skirt around her hips. She grabbed the major and tried to drag him back.

'If you'd excuse me.'

Whatever the man at the desk said worked; because the French officer settled and the blonde woman stopped wrestling him and they both let themselves be shooed towards the curtains.

Eddie felt Nicolai's fingers reach for his.

The man was back, his eyes not missing the moment the young men in front of him let go of each other's hands. He nodded, mostly it seemed to himself. Then he pulled open a drawer, extracted a tiny HMSO notebook and opened it towards the front. 'It's five shillings and I'll need names.'

He looked momentarily apologetic.

'We take sterling, francs and dollars. We don't usually take roubles and we definitely don't take reichsmarks.'

'I'll pay for both,' Eddie said hastily.

'No need. This time your friend comes in free.'

'I'm Eddie Masterton,' Eddie said. He offered his hand and after a moment the man shook it. He looked more amused than ever.

'Why do you need our names?'

The man's gaze hardened a little as he turned to Nicolai. 'Everything that happens here stays here. Your names are our security.'

'Do you tell us your name?'

'Tony Wakefield.'

'You're Intelligence?'

The man laughed. 'I'm a medical officer. Now . . .' In tiny writing he noted down Eddie's and Nicolai's names, took the money that Eddie offered and nodded towards the velvet curtain where a door had once been. 'Will you find your own way or would you like the tour?'

'We'll find our own way,' Nicolai said.

'Right you are. Third star to the right and straight on until morning.'

The club had been built as a hunting lodge and replaced a concrete and glass monstrosity designed by a degenerate from the Bauhaus School of Art. Major Kraus, the site's new owner, had taken great pleasure in having that ripped down and a good, solid German building put in its place.

A Soviet colonel, named Milov, later shot Major Kraus through the head, while Kraus was trying to negotiate free passage for women from a U-bahn station, which he intended to defend to the death with a small group of SS, and a Volkssturm battalion formed from children pulled out of school and old men too sick to have been drafted before. The women, children and old men lived.

Kraus, his ADC and immediate staff didn't.

None of this was known to the Allied officers who stumbled on the empty building a week or two after the French took Reinickendorf as part of their section of Berlin. At that point, there was free movement between sectors, with Americans visiting the Soviet section, Soviet officers dining with British officers, French officers taking American stenographers as lovers.

The lodge was empty only in the sense that no one official had claimed it. And since this was France's sector, and the French were embarrassed by the lateness of their arrival in Berlin, they moved quickly to clear the lodge of children who'd found refuge there after the city fell.

There were 53,000 homeless children in Berlin that summer. Most were orphans. Many had seen their mothers, sisters and grandmothers raped in front of them, many had been raped themselves. They survived on scraps, roots grubbed from the dirt and anything they could steal. The French cleared a dozen of them from the lodge with such brutality that, even in the first weeks, when it was still left empty at night, none of the lost children tried to return.

Later still, they learnt to keep well away.

Never having had the honour of visiting Hitler's house in the Bavarian Alps, Major Kraus had made do with lovingly collected postcards of the Berghof, the holiday home Hitler bought with his royalties from *Mein Kampf.* He also took inspiration from *Homes & Gardens*, an English magazine that had several interesting things to say about the aesthetic underlying the Führer's taste.

The major had insisted on cembra pine for the panelling, since this was what the Führer had. He'd installed a red marble fireplace in the hall, and a collection of majolica cacti pots in the lobby for similar reasons. There was even a sliding window opening on to wooded slopes. Although the trees at Tegelerforst could not compete with the splendour of the Bavarian Alps.

When the Allied officers found the lodge, the marble bust of Minerva just inside the front door was missing a breast, the painting of Frederick the Great in the hall had been slashed from shoulder to hip, and the bearskin rug in the drawing room had a hole from where someone had lit a fire on its back.

By that September, when Lieutenant Masterton introduced Nicolai to the club, Frederick had been crudely repaired, Minerva had acquired a sheet to hide her damage and the rug was long gone.

There were two main rooms to the club.

The great hall was for gambling; this being mostly cards. Although a roulette wheel stood in one corner, it was crooked and favoured *Voisins du Zero*, the numbers nearest the nought. The house soon stopped taking bets once they realized that. As for the drawing room, this had leather chairs, a chaise longue, and a bar staffed by a Moroccan sergeant who served brandy, whisky or vodka from behind his low counter. The working girls, most of them German, with a few Poles, sat on stools along one wall. The Moroccan took the money, keeping careful records of the sums taken.

'Nothing beyond this,' an English captain said.

'We're just taking a look,' Eddie replied. 'Finding our feet.'

'Suit yourselves.' The man grabbed a girl half his age and pulled her on to his lap, his hand sliding under her shirt before she was even seated. Her smile was in place by the time she turned her head to his.

'Are you lost?'

Eddie turned to find a US major behind him. He was dashingly dressed, with a narrow moustache like a film star, his hair just a tiny bit too long. He looked like an American David Niven. 'No, sir. Just wandering.'

'Lonely as a cloud, eh?'

Eddie smiled at the joke and the major looked gratified. 'Talk to Tony, did you?' he said.

'Sir?'

'At the door. Tony Wakefield.'

'Yes, sir. He took our money and our names.'

'*Our money and our names . . .*' The man repeated Eddie's

words in a way that suggested he thought they were particularly clever. And Eddie wondered how drunk the major really was. Drunker than he looked from the sound of it. He pointed to a heavy door in the far wall.

'The room you want is through there.'

'I thought there was nothing beyond this room.'

The man clapped Eddie on the shoulder. 'There isn't,' he said. 'Believe me, there isn't.' He smiled to himself and headed the way Nicolai and Eddie had just come, without bothering to say goodbye.

A dozen men fixed their gaze on the pair in the doorway, expressions softening when the Russian boy gave them a winning smile. Ushering Eddie in, Nicolai shut the door firmly behind them. This room was smaller than the others, more intimate. Its lights were low, and while the two were looking round, someone turned them lower, had second thoughts and turned them off altogether.

The noises began slowly at first, becoming urgent later. And the darkness ... That was warm and welcoming. Warm, welcoming, dark and safely anonymous.

'I like this,' Nicolai said.

85

'It was a gay club?' Tom asked.

On the other end of the line, Sir Edward Masterton hesitated.

'Sir . . . ?'

Silence said Sir Edward was battling with himself. 'Not just a gay club,' he said finally. 'It was something for everyone. For most officers it was a brothel and somewhere to get drunk. You have to understand how things were then. I'm not saying that makes it right. It's just how things were. And you don't tell Anna. My wife must never know any of this.'

'Of course not, sir.'

'Berlin was in ruins. Most of its men were dead. Its children ran wild to be picked off like vermin, at least in the early days. Any girl older than ten had been raped already. They dressed in rags, didn't wipe themselves, never bathed, smeared their faces with ash. It made no damn difference. In the two months between the city's surrender and the rest of us arriving, the Soviets did to Berlin what they'd already done to its women.

'Bank vaults were looted, factories cleared of machinery, art galleries emptied of paintings. If a museum still stood, chances were its collection had been loaded on to a truck and shipped east. The streets were pitted, the metro wrecked. There was no food in the city and precious little left in the countryside beyond.'

Sir Edward fell silent. 'The Russians had their reasons,' he said finally. 'God knows, they had their reasons. But, you have to understand ... Most of the Berliners were starving. In a city like that a packet of cigarettes will buy you anything or anyone. I was shocked, Tom. It was like stepping into hell. The problem is, some men like hell. They feel at home there.'

'Nicolai, sir?'

When he spoke, Sir Edward sounded sad. 'No, he had his dark side. We all did. Some more than others. Nicolai ...' His voice faltered and the sentence drifted into silence.

'Sir?' Tom said.

'I'm getting there. The girls changed every few weeks. Some were in their twenties, others younger. Fourteen, fifteen. I don't know where the Moroccan found them. I don't know where they went afterwards.'

'And in the other room?'

'I'm assuming you don't mean the games room?'

Tom didn't bother to answer.

'Gambling was why most officers came, you know. That and those poor women and the drink. We were bored. Absurd as that sounds. Our days were full of admin. Our nights ... What do you do at night in a city that's largely ruins?'

Tom waited to be told.

'The room Nicolai and I found was private. Entry by invitation only. We should never have been there. But we were, and we came back the next week, and the week after and the week after that. We kept coming back until the day Nicolai didn't appear when he was meant to ...'

The ambassador's voice faltered.

'I went to the Hauptbahnhof, which was where we usually met. I waited until dark and then – because I still couldn't believe he'd stood me up – I waited some more, in a grubby little bar we sometimes used, in a cellar below a clothes shop. Perhaps, because I was more than a little infatuated, I decided I had to find him. I was drunk by the time I left. I had to be to walk through Tegelerforst alone on the wrong side of midnight.

'It's a wilderness. Well, it was then. Hills, rivers and even a small lake inside the city boundary. No one troubled me. Maybe no one was there. Maybe they had more sense. I was drunk, I had my revolver drawn, I was perhaps already a little not right in the head. Although I'd considered myself relatively undamaged by war until that night.'

86

Somewhere on his journey between the Hauptbahnhof and Tegelerforst, Eddie convinced himself that Nicolai would be at the lodge. There had obviously been a misunderstanding. Nicolai must have thought Tegelerforst not the Hauptbahnhof was where they were due to meet. The hope that this was true carried Eddie up the hillside and through rustling trees.

The lodge was on a ridge, with hillside rising behind and forest filling the slope below. The curtains were always drawn at night, as if the city was still in blackout against bombing raids. Perhaps it still was inside everybody's head. Everyone had become so used to navigating darkness.

And yet, and yet . . .

The curtains at the lodge were never so well drawn that they wouldn't anger an air raid warden for showing light had that rule still applied. A compromise, maybe, between the habits of war and the prospect of peace.

Wait, Eddie told himself. *Not yet.*

He wasn't sure when he'd decided that it might be best if he circled the lodge first. What he was looking for he wasn't sure. Maybe simply to settle himself, to summon his courage to go inside. Perhaps he could peer through the gaps in the curtains to check if Nicolai was there. As if he'd always known this was where he'd find him.

That was what he needed to do.

At a side window he watched a German girl straddle a pot-bellied man, reach down to position him and lower herself. He just grinned while she rode him and Eddie moved on. It wasn't that the sight didn't interest him. It wasn't that he hadn't had women. There'd been prostitutes in France. He hadn't enjoyed it though.

He'd hated the little towns through which they'd had to pass. All those shifty-eyed men and pinch-faced women proving their patriotism by stripping teenage girls and shaving their heads.

In the games room, officers sat in a circle round a table, a bottle of Martell in the middle, cigars in their mouths and cards tight to their chests. American uniforms, British uniforms, French uniforms. A Soviet major sat clutching the ace of spades and a handful of minor cards. They were waiting for him to play. There was even a man in a suit. From the anxious way that he glanced around, Eddie realized he must be German.

As for the room beyond, it was in darkness.

Eddie could sense rather than see movement. His fingers to the glass sensed a room that was full and trembling. He wondered what those clutching cards or being straddled by prostitutes thought happened in there. Whether they knew the room even existed. It was possible Nicolai was in there.

He realized he rather hoped not.

Taking his fingers from the window as if saying good-bye, Eddie kept going because he'd already decided to walk right round the lodge. And that was how he found himself peering between curtains into a kitchen block at the back.

A boy was being held down.

A man stood at one end of a pine table gripping his wrists, while at the other end . . . The boy's ragged shorts were round his ankles and his top bare. There were other officers in there, and other children. A girl barely old enough to have the shadow of breasts was being pushed towards a fat man. He snapped something at her and her struggling stopped.

Eddie looked at the revolver in his hand.

He looked back through the window and the boy was crying. The girl was crying too. There were . . . He tried to count. Half a dozen children and twice as many adults? He was at the door before he realized it. Already reaching for the handle when it was opened from inside.

'What are you doing here, Lieutenant?'

'Looking for someone.'

The major blocking the doorway scowled. A colonel came to stand behind him. 'Looking for someone, sir,' the colonel said heavily. 'Understood?'

'Yes, sir,' Eddie said. 'Sorry, sir.'

'This is a private party. You won't find them here.'

'No, sir. I'd better get back.'

'Yes, you had,' he said. 'Now, put that damn sidearm away before you hurt yourself. And don't let me see you here again.'

Lowering the hammer on his revolver, Eddie turned away.

87

'I should have killed them,' Sir Edward said. 'My shame is that I didn't. I never went back to the lodge. That night, I never even went inside. I simply walked back through that forest to my quarters, sat on my bed and cried. I should have reported them. I know that.'

'They were ours, sir?'

'The major was. James Foley. Funnily enough, he killed himself the other day. I did wonder if guilt had anything to do with it.'

'Was there anyone else you recognized?'

Sir Edward hesitated. 'It was dark.'

'All the same, sir . . .'

Tom heard the ambassador shift in his seat, sensed rather than heard him open his mouth to say something, then shut it again. He waited, giving Sir Edward time to find the words.

'There was a terrorist outrage in the Lake District about ten years ago. I don't know if you remember it?'

Lord Brannon. Tom remembered.

'Who else, sir?'

Sir Edward fell silent and Tom wondered if that was it. If the conversation was over. He'd just decided it was when Sir Edward spoke again.

'How secure is this line?'

'I have Marshal Milov's promise that it's totally secure. It's the one General Rafikov, the rezident, uses to report to the Kremlin. That's why things have been set up like this.'

'Well,' Sir Edward said heavily, 'I don't imagine even Milov would want what I'm about to say recorded. There were a dozen men in that disgusting little room. Ours, French, American, Soviet . . .'

Here it comes, Tom thought.

Dmitri Luzhin. A name he didn't recognize.

'Soviet negotiator,' Sir Edward said.

Oh sweet God. Tom sat back. He could see how Moscow wouldn't want that known. 'The arms talks?'

'One of their best.'

'Anyone looking to derail the treaty?'

'Would do well to start there,' Sir Edward agreed. 'I'm not sure I'd have told anyone else this, Tom. And I'm not sure I'd have told you if not for your boy.'

'You didn't think of . . . ?'

'Gods, Tom.' Sir Edward sounded exasperated. 'Of course I thought of reporting it. But I was a lieutenant and they were senior officers. I never went back. I might not have told anyone. But I never went back. You think it's easy living with the shame of not reporting it?'

'One last question.'

'Ask away.'

'Did you ever see Caro's father in there?'

'In that room? Christ, Tom. Don't even think it. Eddington came to the lodge, right enough . . .' The ambassador stopped. Realization striking. 'You have the membership list? Dear God. Of course you do. You must.' He sounded slightly sick. 'No wonder everyone wants your head on a plate. You ever played cards with Eddington?'

371

'No, sir. I haven't.'

'Can't hold a poker face to save his life. It wasn't boys or cards Eddington came for. It certainly wasn't that obscene little room at the back. This isn't something to tell your wife, Tom, but he couldn't get enough of the women.'

Tom let out a deep breath.

'Thank you, sir,' he said, meaning it.

88

The Rolls had swept up the drive and scattered gravel in front of Great-Uncle Max's house, its door slamming with a satisfying thunk. Its engine had ticked like an erratic clock as it cooled. In other circumstances Charlie would have enjoyed that.

He'd seen the driver get out, come towards the house and vanish inside. But the man still hadn't come upstairs. After a while, Charlie decided that the man was obviously doing something else and he should go back to escaping.

Everything turned on the hairgrip.

It was a very ordinary hairgrip; a thin length of wire bent back on itself, with fat blobs at the end so girls didn't scratch their scalps on sharp metal.

There was a single strand of hair hooked through the bend like thread through a needle. Charlie wondered whose it was and wished he hadn't. It was blonde, like Becca's. He imagined the owner had this room before him. Perhaps she'd tried to escape and someone had grabbed her hair. That would pull a grip out. If you were a girl and someone grabbed you by the hair.

Charlie's brain wasn't really built to panic. At school, one of his biggest problems was that he wasn't good at fear. Sometimes he'd get hit and it was always a surprise. Other boys seemed to be able to work out when they were about to be bullied and see it coming. He never could. And the things that really upset him, like noise and untidiness, barely seemed to touch others at all.

But he thought he was probably afraid now.

'Charlie,' a voice said.

What if they'd killed her? What if she was buried under a flowerbed? Those gardeners probably knew where she was buried.

'Charles . . . Stop it.'

Becca didn't call him Charles. Not even when she was angry. Granny did, sometimes. Towards the end, Becca hadn't really seemed to notice he existed at all. And now she didn't, and he was the one remembering her.

You mustn't cry, he told himself crossly.

He tried to tell himself it was Becca who had said that but she was gone.

She was fading no matter how hard he tried to keep her there. No matter how hard he tried to call her back. He woke up looking for her, and sometimes she was there, and sometimes she wasn't. And he was finding it harder and harder to remember her face. He had a photograph. He wasn't meant to because Mummy had hidden the photographs because they made everyone sad.

But Charlie had one at the bottom of his sliding pencil case, under his six-inch ruler, his dividers and protractor. The only time he ever hit someone at school was when they tried to steal his pencil case.

It was her photograph he was protecting.

You can do this, he told himself.

It was something that Becca would say when she was helping him with something. Like learning to tie his

374

shoelaces. There had seemed to be so many better ways than the way Mummy wanted. It was Becca who explained that it wasn't about the quickest, prettiest or even most efficient way of tying laces. It was all about being able to tie a bow.

Was he really telling her he couldn't manage a bow?

Glancing at his reflection in the window, Charlie gave himself a Paddington stare. Was he really telling himself he couldn't pick that lock?

89

Tom ran through what he'd learnt from Sir Edward.

Flo Wakefield had definitely been the man on the door. Sir Edward, little more than a boy himself, had taken his Russian there. And Caro's father had spent his evenings getting drunk with German girls for whom servicing their conquerors was marginally better than being dead.

That this was a *Thank God* moment was horrific. But Tom would have been lying to pretend it was anything else. The idea of Lord Eddington being involved in Patroclus was more than he could bear. If the post-war city could be distilled into one place, it was that lodge in Tegelerforst; and its darkest manifestation was the room at the back.

It was Brannon and Foley who interested Tom, because both had alpha next to their names in Flo Wakefield's notebook. And both were dead, Tom reminded himself. As was Cecil Blackburn, also marked alpha. Edward Masterton had been beta. Tom would put money on his Russian friend being beta too.

Charles Eddington was gamma.

Was it that simple? Everyone marked alpha came for the room at the back. Those marked beta came for the room that Edward Masterton and Nicolai found. The gammas, the Eddingtons of the world, came for the women, alcohol and gambling. Maybe Wakefield had read Huxley's *Brave New World* with society divided into alphas, betas, gammas and deltas.

Maybe that was how those in that room thought of themselves. Men who stood above the herd. A group to whom lesser laws didn't apply. If that was true, then every person marked alpha was at risk from Sir Cecil's memoirs. No wonder Sir Cecil thought he was in a position of power. No wonder he was dead.

At risk from Sir Cecil's memoirs . . .

But not necessarily, Tom imagined, in the way they thought.

Funnily enough, he killed himself the other day. I did wonder if guilt had anything to do with it. As well as Colonel Foley, found alone at his cottage, there was Sir Henry, killed by an overdose. Robby Croft, Master of Hounds and roué about town, fatally thrown at a fence. Tom wondered if the notebook wasn't more dangerous than the memoirs.

He needed to reclaim it, and soon.

Without being spotted, without being followed, without being seen.

General Rafikov could organize their return. He'd probably be delighted to organize their return. Tom just didn't rate his own chances of getting them back unexamined, un-photographed and on time . . .

He'd trust Wax Angel with it.

But he'd trusted her with finding Charlie, saving him.

What Tom really wanted to do was drop everything, return to England and find Charlie. Killing his kidnappers could come later. Only, returning would be the quickest way to get Charlie killed. He thanked God for

Wax Angel. She'd stepped in at the very point that contradiction had threatened to tear him apart.

He couldn't risk using Rafikov to reclaim the notebook in case he decided to keep it; because, if the notebook would do in place of the memoirs, Tom needed it at hand, so that he could give it to Charlie's kidnappers. And he would give it to them. He had no doubt about that.

He needed them to make contact.

That was the one thing that really worried him. Why no one had made contact. Why no one would tell him the price he was expected to pay.

90

The secret was in how you broke the hairgrip.

You needed it in two parts and they had to be slightly different.

Charlie snapped it on the bend, working it backwards and forwards until the metal grew hot and sheared where he wanted. One side of the hairgrip kept most of the bend, which made it his torsion bar. The other side had just enough bend left to use as a pick. Pushing the torsion bar into the Yale's slot, Charlie turned it to set the tension and began to work at the pins. He did it first by feel, and by trying to listen for clicks as they rose, while the tension on the cylinder kept them from falling. After a while, he gave that up and simply shut his eyes.

If you emptied your head, the bit of you that wasn't paying attention could work out which pins you'd managed to raise and how many you had to go. It was the last of them that gave Charlie trouble.

Realizing that brought him back to himself.

The half-hairgrip putting tension on the cylinder kept getting in the way and stopping his pick from reading the first pin. What he didn't want, what would really make him cry, was if the torsion bar slipped free and all the pins dropped back into place. Because then he'd have to start again.

And starting again would make him tense. And most

things in life were much harder to do when you were tense. Scottish kings and spiders aside, Charlie wasn't sure that he could face it. He was finding it really hard to do once.

He'd almost given up, and knew it was only a matter of time before the bar slipped and the pins betrayed him, when the pin rose and the cylinder turned slightly. Charlie didn't dare believe he'd done it. He put a little more pressure on the bar, expecting it to slip free and everything to lock solid. Instead the cylinder turned inside the lock and the catch came free.

Very slowly. Very slowly indeed, Charlie hooked his little finger into the keyhole of the useless Victorian lock below and pulled the door towards him.

It was gloomy on the landing because the curtains were closed.

Opening them slightly, he squinted at the purple Rolls-Royce, but it was too far away to see if Great-Uncle Max had removed the keys. It was too nice a car to be owned by the man who owned it. It deserved someone better. Someone who didn't make you late back and lock you in a room without clothes.

Charlie sucked his teeth.

He needed to remember how to make a car start if the keys weren't there. Except remembering wasn't the right word because he'd never known. Also, what if Great-Uncle Max came to investigate?

Investigate was a word used lots at school.

Lots of things were investigated. They usually ended badly for the boy concerned. *The boy concerned* was used almost as much. Charlie wondered for a moment why Great-Uncle Max hadn't come to see where he was.

The answer was obvious, though. He didn't need to, because he already knew. Charlie was locked in a room until needed.

Only, he wasn't locked in any more, was he?

Time to go, Charlie decided.

Shutting the door to the room he'd been in, so that everyone would think he was still in there, he turned for the stairs. He was halfway down the first flight when he met a white-haired man coming up.

'Hello, Charlie,' the man said.

Charlie looked at him. 'Who are you?'

The man scowled. Probably because that was a rude thing to say. He made a shooing gesture to say that Charlie should back up. And since it was rude to cross on the stairs, Charlie did.

'I'm Great-Uncle Max,' the man said.

'No, you're not. You can't be.' This man was small with wispy white hair and wore a red velvet jacket. He looked nothing like Great-Uncle Max.

'We're all Great-Uncle Max.'

The man held a tray with a bowl of shredded wheat on it. The blue jug next to it probably held milk. Charlie wasn't tall enough to tell.

'Now. What are you doing out here?'

'I woke up. I wanted to find someone.'

'And the door just opened?' this new Great-Uncle Max asked.

'It wasn't properly shut,' Charlie said. He needed to stop the man thinking too hard about that. So he looked at the bowl, and said, 'If I eat that is it going to make me go to sleep again?'

'You are clever, aren't you?' the man said. 'They told me you were. Very clever, they said. A little strange but very clever. No, it won't make you go to sleep. But it will stop you being hungry. You are hungry, aren't you?'

Charlie was. Very.

'Back we go then. We have to keep you safe. I'll have to make sure the door's shut properly this time.' The man smiled, slightly sadly. 'Don't worry. This will all be over soon.'

91

'What do you want?' Amelia demanded.

'Your help.' Tom put the wine he'd just bought in front of her, slid himself on to the velvet banquette and scanned the Palasthotel's darkened bar.

'The boy behind the counter is new,' Amelia said. 'And there's a young woman in the corner with a paperback who's doing a bad job of not staring.'

'Have you heard from your friend?'

Amelia paused with her glass halfway to her mouth.

'If she hasn't been freed yet,' Tom said, 'she will be. The case is now closed.'

'You're certain?'

'Yes,' Tom said. 'I'm certain.'

'I thought you were meant to be in West Berlin.'

'I am meant to be in West Berlin. A few things happened.'

'To do with Claudia Strauss?'

'Your friend? In part . . .'

'Thank you,' Amelia said. She leant forward and kissed his cheek. 'You should understand,' she said, 'that I don't usually make a habit of this. Making up to strange men in bars.'

'No. Of course not.'

'That was your cue to say you don't either.'

'I don't –' Tom didn't finish that sentence and felt rather

than saw Amelia turn to look at him. The lighting inside the Palasthotel's bar was dim but it was good enough for him to read the sudden sharpness in her eyes.

'I used to,' he admitted. 'And take them to bed.'

'Christ,' she said. 'That's –'

'Honest.'

'Are we being tapped?' Amelia asked, suddenly worried.

'It's possible. Are you planning to say anything you shouldn't?'

Her mouth quirked. 'It's probably too late in my life to start worrying about that. All the same, do you think we are?'

'It's possible,' Tom said. 'Also cameras.'

'Cameras?'

'Most rooms here are wired for sound. Some of the suites, though, have cameras in the light fittings above the beds and behind the vanity mirrors in the bathrooms.'

'Great,' Amelia said. 'I'll never pee again. You said you needed help . . .'

Tom hesitated.

'Major Fox. What do you actually want?'

'My son's been kidnapped from his school in Kent.' Tom muted his voice to a whisper. 'I need your help retrieving something that I believe might save his life. I'd like to do it now.'

Amelia's face froze at the first statement. Tom watched her wrestle with the second. When she spoke her voice was as sombre as his had been.

'This has to do with my father . . .'

He thought it a question and then realized it wasn't. It was a simple statement. She glanced towards the exit and he gave a slight nod. Finishing her glass in a single gulp, she said, 'I'm going to powder my nose.'

'I'll buy you another.'

Having ordered drinks for both, Tom headed for the men's lavatories, seeing Amelia standing beyond. They took the stairs to the ground level and left through doors beyond the auditorium. As they passed, the last speech of the day ended and dutiful clapping began. A few moments later, doors opened, and delegates for whatever conference it was began streaming out.

'Lucky timing,' Amelia said.

In the car park, Tom glanced back but saw no shadow. When he looked again thirty seconds later the result was the same. Cutting between parked cars, he headed for Spandauer Strasse, away from the area he wanted. Tom intended to work his way back to the iron bridge when he was certain they hadn't drawn attention. It was twilight, with couples walking arm in arm, and families going home.

Tom and Amelia looked less out of place than they might.

'And you really didn't kill my father?'

'I really didn't kill him.'

'But you have killed?'

When Tom stopped, Amelia nudged his arm to keep him walking. 'That's a question you don't ask,' Tom said.

'There are too many bloody questions *you don't ask*.' Amelia scowled. 'Do you enjoy it?'

'Amelia . . .'

'It's a fair question.'

'No,' Tom said, 'it isn't, and I don't.'

'Not even a little bit? I'm told most men dream of it.'

'My dreams . . .' Tom decided that was a conversation too far. 'Killing eats a little bit of your soul. Every fucking time.'

'But you do it anyway? If that's really true, and you really don't enjoy it, and killing doesn't make you feel special, and you don't get off on having done your *duty*' – in Amelia's mouth that last word sounded obscene – 'you're more dangerous than you know. Because you still –'

'Can we stop now?'

There must have been something in his voice because she let him take her hand and lock his fingers around hers, holding tight. They walked like that for a while. Tom imagined she knew she was a lifebelt.

That without her he'd drown.

92

'The strangest thing,' Tom told Amelia, 'is the feeling of gratitude you get when you realize you're still alive and that you aren't going to die.'

They were crossing the Spree for the third time, the dark water sliding silently by below their bridge. They were talking about Tom's childhood. The bits of it he didn't talk about. To anyone watching – and Tom increasingly felt confident that no one was – they must look like any other couple deep in conversation. He'd wanted to make straight for the iron bridge to reclaim the notebook. Of course he had. But he'd resisted the urge; the apparent aimlessness of their wandering was what would keep them safe.

The conversation had begun with Charlie. All recent conversations, particularly those that Tom had with himself, began and ended with Charlie. From there, he'd been shocked by how many places it touched on the way.

'Have you told your wife this?' Amelia asked.

'She knows none of it.'

'Will you?'

Tom shook his head. 'There's nothing she needs to know.'

'Do you want to tell her?'

It was a surprisingly astute question, although why should he have been surprised, unless it was at realizing the answer.

'Yes,' he said. 'I do.'

'But you won't.' Amelia smiled. 'It really is love, isn't it?'

'Sometimes I surprise myself.'

'When the police came,' Amelia said, 'I thought it was because he'd run away. Defected was the word we learnt to use. That wasn't it . . .'

'They searched the house?'

'How do you know about that?'

'It was a guess,' said Tom, thinking about the package stuffed behind a greasy girder on the bridge they were approaching.

'I'm not sure they really knew what they wanted. Maybe one of them did. They found photographs, though. Under a drawer in Daddy's desk.'

It was the first time she'd called Blackburn that. Amelia was deep in her childhood, Tom realized. Probably far deeper than she wanted to go.

'My mother said they exaggerated. The detectives blew it out of proportion. My father taught at a university. Young boys fresh out of school. He'd always been good with a camera. He liked messing around in his darkroom. Of course he was going to ask some of them to model . . .'

She fell silent. 'Why am I telling you this?'

'Because you have nobody else to tell. Because I've told you things I've never told anybody.'

'Was that all true about your son?'

'Dear God. Who'd lie about something like that?'

'At the embassy they said you were a bad one. Those were the words they used. I went, you know. To see if they'd get me home. They said I came here at the GDR's invitation. No doubt my hosts would return me eventually.'

388

'Who told you that?'

'A man called Henderson.'

'Henderson doesn't work at the embassy. He's based at the consulate-general in West Berlin.'

'What does it matter?'

Tom wasn't sure. He just felt it did.

'We're here?' Amelia asked, looking at the steps down to the water's edge. A river path led under the bridge. She went first; and they stopped at the bottom to watch black water swirl below their feet. It was dark now, a city of street lighting and headlights.

'Where's the package?'

'I'll go,' Tom said.

Amelia shook her head. 'I'm going to have a pee.'

Tom looked at her and she sighed.

'We've been to a bar, had too much to drink, now you're a man keeping watch while his companion has a quick pee. Where under there did you hide this package of yours?'

Tom told her.

'What are you going to do with it?'

'I'm going to give it to them in return for Charlie. If it's what they want —'

'They'll kill you,' Amelia said. 'The moment they have it. You know that, don't you?'

93

Berlin 1945. Summer was giving way to autumn and Moscow's allies, having finally arrived, had begun talking about how cold the captured city would be come winter. As if anything in Western Europe merited that word.

The Soviets were half a week into a tidying-up operation. There were rats in the ruins, human and otherwise; feral children running in gangs, and recidivist Nazis, who traded on the fear they'd spent a lifetime sowing to keep themselves hidden. Maya had been at work for a week.

Monday was meant to be her day off.

It began with a message to call Milov, newly promoted and decorated for his part in the fall of Berlin. They were lovers by then, not yet married. He'd won the trust of those whose distrust saw you disappear.

Maya went to see him instead.

'Look what I found,' she announced. 'Brandy. The real stuff.'

She'd found it in the cellar of a ruined restaurant near the Reichstag. She expected him to smile but his face was sombre and her own fell. When the commissar indicated a chair, she knew this was official.

Unslinging her rifle, Maya took the chair.

He sat in silence and she waited him out. She was good at that. Waiting people out. 'I have a job for you,' he said finally.

The file he pushed over had a KGB crest.

Inside, a photograph showed an NKVD general, said to have the ear of Lavrentiy Beria himself, scowling into a camera. A second photograph showed his ADC, a young man known to be ambitious.

'May I ask a question?'

'If you must,' Milov said.

'If they're traitors, then . . . Why not just arrest them?'

The commissar came from behind his desk and dropped to a crouch beside her. 'Maya,' he said. 'These are not people you'd want to let live. And I was told to give you this.' He handed her a heavy roll of canvas.

The clue was in his words.

You would want . . . I was told.

This order came from above. The men to be killed were not traitors, they were dirty. Given that the Red Army had raped its way through Greater Germany, without Stavka, the high command, objecting . . . Maya wondered what you had to do for them to regard you as dirty.

Inside the canvas roll was a German WG sniper rifle, self-loading, semi-automatic. With it came two rounds. Maya would have put money on 7.92 $\times$ 57mm Mauser, full metal jacketed, with precisely measured propellant that let it retain supersonic velocity for 1,000+ metres. But these had unlacquered steel cases.

'*Anschusspatrone*,' the commissar said. 'Sighting-in bullets, machined to a brutally tight tolerance. Better than their standard sniper round.' He hesitated. 'Better than anything we can offer you.'

'It's to be done when?' she asked.

'Today. Without fail.'

'Where do I find them?'

'Reinickendorf-Tegelerforst. In a hunting lodge. There's a footpath, with open ground before the forest begins. Catch them on their way home, do it there.'

Always shoot the officer first. That rule had been drummed into her at Stalingrad, and she'd carried it all the way to Berlin. *If there are two officers, shoot the senior one . . .* Sighting her rifle, Maya breathed in and let out half her breath, tightening her finger as they came into view.

Two thousand seven hundred feet a second.

Her round took the general between the eyes, cut his brain stem and sucked out enough bone, blood and jelly to splatter a tree behind. The bullet itself drilled through the tree and buried itself in a trunk beyond.

Maya noticed none of that. Her attention was locked on the ADC, who'd dived for a ditch and was fumbling at his holster. She had him almost square in her crosshairs, when light glittered behind him and training rolled her sideways, as she hunted for the source. Same rifle as hers, same scope, same uniform.

Her mirror image was dug in under a fallen tree.

The telescopic sight of his rifle stilled as he found her.

They aimed at each other in the same second and she fired first, her shot taking him through the eye, glass from his scope following her bullet through his brain. Swivelling back to her target, Maya saw him run for the trees and fired from habit, hearing a dry click.

She crawled across to where the dead sniper lay and jacked the unfired bullet from his rifle, sliding it into her own. He, too, had been given only the number of rounds he'd need. In his case one. He was in uniform but without papers. The back of his head was missing and so were his dogtags. She waited patiently, through nightfall, night itself and into the dawn, but no one came. So she abandoned her rifle, kicked the dead sniper once to relieve her frustration, and headed home.

The next night fifteen officers simply disappeared.

Dmitri Luzhin, the ADC she'd been meant to kill, wasn't one of them.

94

In the door of an administrative office near the zoo turn-stile a middle-aged woman was shouting at a young driver, whose refrigerated lorry was parked by the entrance, smoke billowing from its badly fitted exhaust.

When the woman finished, the young man shrugged, shrugged again and climbed into his vehicle, leaving her glaring after him.

'He's only brought half the required meat,' Amelia explained.

Hearing Tom laugh, the woman glared at him instead.

'Outrageous,' Tom said hurriedly.

Amelia folded her arm through his.

When Tom looked at her, she shrugged. 'Your German is dreadful,' she muttered. 'And speaking Russian only draws attention to yourself. There's no point using me as cover if you're going to get yourself arrested.'

Amelia's logic was impeccable. He needed her if he was to pass unremarked in Tierpark, the 400-acre zoo built by East Berliners in the gardens of an old palace. The deal was she'd leave when the public did, and he'd remain. Pointing to a hoarding of a howling wolf against trees wild enough to be deep forest, she said, 'That I have to see.'

'Not sure the run's open yet,' Tom muttered.

'You've been here before?'

'Yes,' he said, thinking of Fitz.

Amelia folded her arm through his when someone looked over.

She was right. They blended in better as a couple. In her jeans, white shirt and black jacket she looked like a waitress. At least Tom thought she did, but it was still smarter than anything else he'd seen her wear. She even had a bag. Although it was more a cross between a rucksack and a satchel.

'Two, please,' Amelia said.

The woman said something and Amelia nodded.

'It shuts at sunset,' Amelia muttered. 'We'll have less than an hour.' Beyond the stile, she stopped at a rack of animal postcards. 'Mate for life,' she said, holding up swans. 'And these? Fuck like rabbits. Although that should probably be rabbits fuck like bonobos.'

When Tom blinked, she smiled.

'Academics can be quite blunt about –' Amelia switched suddenly to German and fired off a machine-gun fast sentence that ended with a laugh. Tom nodded to the woman approaching, which made her smile.

'Where are you meeting him?' Amelia asked.

'The petting zoo.'

Her eyes widened. 'That's sick.'

I have news of your son. Meet me after dusk at the petting zoo.

Knowing Henderson, it was probably his idea of a joke.

The children's area was beyond a wooden café with metal seats set outside, and a small orchestra on a dais, coming to the end of its performance. Half the chairs were occupied and a crowd had gathered behind those seated, unwilling to commit to being a proper audience but listening just the same. Couples held hands. An old man had fallen asleep in the front row. Everything felt so normal.

Tom wondered why he thought it wouldn't be.

A small lake to one side. Open space to the other, with trees beyond. The lavatories straight ahead. The children's zoo directly behind. It was well chosen. A man could easily spot another man coming.

Toddlers fed corn to chickens, a girl of about five stroked a lamb grown big after spring, and a boy laughed as he fed an apple to a billy goat with balls the size of pomegranates. 'Seen all you need?' Amelia asked.

Tom jerked his chin towards the block. 'I'm just going to . . .'

The cubicle doors locked and the windows above the basins opened, although Tom doubted an adult could climb through. By unspoken agreement they let the time creep to the point where Amelia should leave, and then slide beyond. The rest of the public left, animals settled, trucks trundled down narrow roads delivering food, while gangs of workers cleaned out cages, repaired fences and retired. Amelia and Tom watched and listened to all this from the trees.

'What if it isn't Henderson?' she asked. 'What if it's someone else?'

Tom shrugged. 'I'd still have come.'

95

'Your son's going to be all right,' Amelia said.

Tom wanted to believe her. After a while, he felt Amelia's hand brush his and reached for her fingers. They held hands like teenagers, letting the sky darken and the horizon change colour, the fierceness of their grip entirely innocent. After darkness came quiet as the animals stilled. Soon the only sound came from whispering trees, wind in the wire of the fences and shuffling creatures settling for sleep. Only when they were certain of the silence did they head back to the petting zoo, slipping inside the lavatory block to keep watch through a slightly open window.

'Over there,' Amelia said.

'Yeah,' Tom muttered. 'Seen him.'

Henderson disengaged from the trees opposite, half an hour earlier than the time agreed. Stopping to stare at the building they were in, he crouched low and headed across the play area.

A few seconds later he reappeared.

'Hang on. That's not him,' Amelia said.

She was right, it wasn't.

Colonel Schneider had edged into the moonlight.

He still wore his metal-rimmed glasses; and if the glint on his lapel meant anything, he was wearing his Order of Patriotic Merit pin too. In his hand was a Makarov *Pistolet*

Besshumnyy. Integral silencer, which meant a short slide, with the spring in the handle. Still took eight rounds though.

The colonel's eyes were shadowed beneath a hat but the rest of his face showed white in the darkness. As Tom watched, Schneider headed after Henderson. A moment later he was hidden by trees.

'Who's that?' Amelia asked.

'A Stasi officer.'

'You think he's brought reinforcements?'

'I'd better find out.'

Using the door at the front was too big a risk, so Tom opened a window at the back, and proved himself wrong by scraping through a gap he'd thought too narrow. 'Don't get yourself killed,' Amelia said.

Backing towards a wooden shed, Tom froze as a twig cracked away to one side. He slid behind the shed and watched the block he'd just left to check that no one else was approaching it. He stayed utterly still until he was as certain as he could be that no one was there.

It was always movement that gave you away.

Readying himself to follow Schneider, Tom dropped to a crouch at the sharp cough of a suppressed pistol and pressed himself tight to his tree. No bullet whistled past his head or hummed away behind.

He wasn't the target. Not this time.

Creeping forward, using scrub for cover, Tom skirted the playground as he headed for where the shot had been fired. He moved slowly, placing his feet with care and pausing between steps. On the edge of a crazy golf course, he stopped at a crouch and looked around.

Henderson lay face down in a sandpit, quite obviously dead. Whatever news he'd had of Charlie, he wouldn't be passing it on.

A small, very neat and barely bloody hole at the base of his skull indicated how he'd died. Someone had trickled sand over his body.

96

Tom approached the block as carefully as he'd left it, stopping in the shadows to check that no one was following, no one was watching and his way was clear. He saw no movement and the play area itself was silent.

'Amelia?' he whispered.

'She's with me.' Schneider's voice was cold. 'Now, come join us.'

Tightening his grip on the pistol he'd lifted from Henderson, Tom debated his next move.

There was a gasp from Amelia.

'Fox,' said Schneider. 'You don't want me to hurt her, do you?'

'She's a British citizen.'

'She's a friend of *Instandbesetzer*, troublemakers. And she's been on your own government's watch list for years. Greenham Common. Protests at power stations. A fire at Porton Down . . . Now. In you come.'

Tom did as ordered.

'And turn on the lights.'

He did that too.

'Off we go,' Schneider said.

Amelia shuffled from a cubicle for nursing mothers, with the Stasi officer behind her, gripping her by her upper arm, a Makarov to her head.

'Does she know you killed her father?' he asked.

'I didn't,' Tom said.

'A single shot to the back of the head,' Schneider said. 'Clear evidence of execution. It would have been so much easier if Frederika hadn't . . .' He hesitated '. . . become upset.'

'What do you want?' Tom demanded.

'What does anybody want? The memoirs.'

'You were at Tegelerforst?'

Colonel Schneider pushed his pistol against Amelia's skull, and, when she tried to duck away, ground it harder. 'I was a child in those days,' he said flatly. 'I'm simply here to do a job . . . Now.' He indicated Tom's weapon.

Crouching, Tom put it on the floor.

'Anything else?'

Taking an expandable cosh he'd also lifted from Henderson, Tom put that on the tiles beside the pistol.

'Willing to bet her life on my not finding anything else?'

'There's this,' Tom said.

He pulled a lock knife from his jacket.

'Anything else you'd like to confess? Quite sure?'

Dragging Amelia with him, Schneider let go of her long enough to pat Tom down, keeping his pistol pointed at her the entire time. Stepping back, he gripped her upper arm and dug his thumb into flesh.

'You followed Henderson here?' Tom asked.

'Obviously.'

Schneider kicked Tom's pistol, cosh and knife under the door of a stall, a slight side-swipe with his foot proving sufficient for each.

'The memoirs,' he ordered.

'Does Marshal Milov know you're here?'

'Moscow and Berlin's interests have diverged.'

'The arms talks?'

'Give me the memoirs.'

'This has to do with the talks?'

'Of course it does. The American military hate the idea of arms reduction. American Intelligence dislike it too. We need to give them a reason to dig their heels in. Imagine how their press will react on discovering that an esteemed Soviet negotiator used to molest children. And that's before they're told one of their own senators backing this deal did the same.'

The colonel stared at Tom, who stared back.

'It will be enough,' Schneider said. 'We'll make sure it's enough.'

He held out his hand.

'I don't have the memoirs,' Tom said.

Sighing, Schneider let go of Amelia's arm, stepped back and aimed his automatic at her knee.

'Frederika burnt them,' Tom said. 'You know that.'

'Sir Cecil told a friend you had a copy.'

'He lied. But I have a notebook. Names and dates from the lodge at Reinickendorf-Tegelerforst. French, English, German, American, Russian.'

'Without his memoir they're just names.'

'That's not true,' Tom insisted.

'You're right. It's not. They're suspects. Sir Cecil's memoirs would give us . . . Certainty. We like certainty.'

'At least look . . .'

Schneider skimmed the notebook, stopping a couple of times, then turned it over. Having examined the ink drawings in the back, he slipped the notebook into his pocket.

'Someone you know?' Tom asked.

The man's gaze hardened. 'Give me the memoirs.'

'I don't have the memoirs,' Tom said.

'Then I have no use for you, do I?' This time, when Schneider raised his pistol, Tom knew he intended to fire.

97

It had been a bad year for butterflies in Kent. A new kind of pesticide was slowing their breeding, an unexplained fire on the Downs had destroyed much of their habitat and the weather had been erratic. The butterfly that landed on drying bracken at twilight stayed only briefly to rest, then rose and flew in search of fresh flowers, better pastures.

The fronds of the bracken grew still as two men passed, talking intently to each other. Twenty minutes it took between patrols. The bracken knew this because it had been timing them. The next pair to come into sight found an olive-skinned beggar woman sitting by a freshly made fire. She looked at them, and saw how the next few seconds would unfold. To them, entirely unexpected.

To her, entirely predictable.

Her hair was filthy and her face unwashed. She did a good job of seeming shocked to see them. Maya hated to say it but she felt almost happy to be back in her rags.

'Bloody gypsies,' said one.

'You,' the other one said. 'Get up.'

The old woman stayed seated. She had a metal bowl on her lap and a filthy horse blanket over her legs, which were folded under her.

'I said get up.'

Either the woman was deaf or didn't understand English, because she stayed where she was, although she put

404

down her bowl and planted her hands flat to the earth, as if feeling its power. Even when one of them unhooked a long metal flashlight of the kind usually carried by people who really wanted a club, she remained seated, her dark eyes watching his advance.

It should have been obvious, even to someone deaf or stupid, what was about to happen. And the beggar woman seemed to realize it at the last second, cowering back as the man reached for her.

His grip never closed.

Kicking out, Maya caught his ankle.

As the ex-squaddie went down, she slammed the edge of her bowl into his mouth, forcing open his jaw and breaking it at the hinge. The man's mouth was too full of blood for him to scream.

The second man should have run.

Instead, he gaped in horror as Maya rolled the first man into the flames. Her attacker had just enough time to realize his head was on fire, before she clubbed him with his flashlight. Scooping embers into her bowl, she flung them into the second man's face. Stumbling back, he turned to run and died with a Sykes-Fairburn in his back. She was proud of that touch.

If anyone bothered to do a proper autopsy, and personally she doubted it, they'd discover that one of the security detail was killed with a classic English commando dagger. That should give them . . . *Pause for thought* was a fine phrase.

One Lord Eddington used.

The poor man had been told his grandson would die horribly if he made any sort of fuss. A call to the house, late at night. Very well spoken, quietly confident. One of us. It had taken Eddington a while to admit those facts. Maya had rather thought it was something like that.

Rolling the body over, she took back her knife.

Ex British Army to judge from his wrist tattoo. So obviously he carried an American-designed gun, built by Belgians. As did the Germans and pretty much every other US ally. It felt better in her hand than either a Makarov or a Tokarev. Not that she'd have dreamt of admitting that.

Grinning, she checked the magazine. The full thirteen rounds. Nine millimetre Parabellum. She'd have preferred .45 but . . .

Maya was shocked to discover she was enjoying herself.

She was on the side of the angels, and you only had to read the Bible to know that nowhere in there did it say that the angels had to play clean. In fact, if you read the book carefully, you'd discover that they generally played very dirty indeed.

98

At the exact point the lights in the Tierpark lavatory block went out, Tom dragged Amelia to the tiled floor and Schneider's gun blazed. He felt a bullet scrape his skull and saw a man materialize in the doorway, backlit by moonlight. The newcomer lifted his hand, almost in greeting, and threw . . .

His blade cut the air and Schneider grunted. Tumbling back, he hit the wall, hand to his chest. Stepping into the room, the newcomer closed the gap and slammed his palm against the hilt, driving the dagger home.

'Sorry I'm late,' FitzSymonds said.

99

Shooting the pencil beam towards Tom, FitzSymonds flicked past Amelia and settled it on his victim. Schneider sat bolt upright against the wall, but was quite obviously dead. A puddle of black spread out around him. As Tom watched, the dead man's shoes twitched and his nervous system began shutting down. 'Found Henderson,' FitzSymonds said.

'Dead,' Tom said.

'Very,' FitzSymonds agreed.

'Fitz, Charlie's been taken.'

'So I've just heard. It doesn't look good, Tom. These aren't nice people. None of us were in those days. So many of the old guard gone. We'll work something out, though. Trust me.'

It doesn't look good . . .

It was all Tom could do not to vomit. He swayed for a second, fighting the shock, and Amelia took his arm, steadying him.

Fitz did a double-take, appearing to notice Tom wasn't alone for the first time. 'We haven't met,' he said, putting out his hand.

Amelia stepped forward and shook.

'Harry FitzSymonds,' Fitz said. 'You'd better call me Fitz. Everyone else does.' He ran the torch across her face. 'Friend of Tom's?'

'I'm Sir Cecil's daughter.'

Fitz sucked his teeth. 'Are you now.'

His pencil torch, for all its smallness, had been taped either side of the lens to narrow its beam still further. He took a look at Tom's skull and sucked his teeth again dismissively. 'Barely scratched.'

'Let me.' Amelia cut a strip from a dark-blue roller towel and bound it tight around Tom's head, putting the nail scissors back in her bag.

FitzSymonds looked impressed.

'If you wouldn't mind, Tom,' he said.

Tom trained the torch on Schneider as FitzSymonds dipped, slightly gingerly, and removed his blade with a grunt. Taking the torch back, he ran the beam across Schneider's body and let it settle on the Makarov. That was when Tom noticed that his old boss was wearing black leather gloves. With Fitz, that always meant business.

'I really am sorry,' FitzSymonds said. 'About Charlie.'

Tom's mouth set into a line of misery.

'Did you ever hear back from your Russian?'

'General Rafikov?'

'No. The one in London. Last thing I heard she was trying to track down a Silver Cloud Coupé. Purple no less. Not having much luck from what I heard.'

'It was used to take Charlie . . .'

'Think she ran into a couple of dead ends . . .' Fitz-Symonds shrugged. 'Now's not the time. We can talk about this when we're alone.'

Looking across, Amelia said, 'He's lying.'

'*Amelia*,' Tom said.

'Trust me. I don't care if he's an old friend. He's lying. He's lying about the Rolls-Royce. He's lying about helping.'

'Really,' FitzSymonds said.

'What *are* you doing here?' Tom said to him.

'Saving your life, since you ask. Hers too. Suppose you'd better take Schneider's Makarov.'

'Fitz . . .'

'Yes, I know. Piece of shit. Nearly got killed in Korea when one jammed on me. All the same, take it.'

Reaching for the weapon, Tom hesitated.

He wanted the notebook from Schneider's pocket. Only that would tell Fitz he had it. *Tell Fitz?* When the hell had Tom started to wonder whether or not his old boss could be trusted?

'Wait,' Amelia said.

'He can't wait,' FitzSymonds said. 'This has gone too far. I need to get Tom to the embassy, now. He can't be found here.'

'I'll catch you up then.'

'You'll . . . ?' Tom said.

Amelia shot him a look. 'Girl stuff,' she said. 'I need to use the loo.'

Wild goats shifted uneasily on the concrete slopes of a toy mountain as Tom and Fitz put distance between themselves and the petting zoo. Amelia caught up with them outside an aviary a few minutes later. A poster showed a vulture in a tree staring down at bleached bones.

'You're going in the wrong direction,' she said.

Stopping, FitzSymonds said, 'Feel free to go in any direction you like.' Tom watched his face harden. 'Actually, don't. You'll come with us. I've no intention of letting Tom be caught because the Stasi take you and you can't keep your mouth shut under questioning.' Turning back, he said to Tom, 'That was good, you know. Back there. It took real guts to bluff with Schneider's pistol in your face.'

'It was my face,' Amelia said.

FitzSymonds ignored her. 'We need everyone to believe the memoir was burnt.'

'It *was* burnt, Fitz.'

FitzSymonds sighed. 'Tom, this is me. I know Sir Cecil gave them to you. It's on record. You don't have to worry about your friend here. She won't be saying anything.' There was an edge to his words.

'*Fitz. Listen —*'

'No, you listen. What were your orders?'

'To bring Sir Cecil back.'

'Not kill him and take his memoirs?'

Behind him, Tom felt Amelia go very still.

'Definitely not,' he said firmly. 'I was to bring him back to stand trial.'

'Then you didn't do a very good job of it, did you?' FitzSymonds's voice was suddenly less chummy. 'Friendship only counts for so much, Tom. I have a job, as you had a job. The difference is I will do mine.'

'And what is your job?' Tom asked.

'This,' FitzSymonds said.

When he moved it was brutally fast. One second he was glaring at Tom, the next he'd grabbed his wrist and twisted Schneider's *Pistolet Besshumnyy* from his grip. When Fitz-Symonds stepped back, it was to point the Makarov at Tom. There was a moment of shock so absolute Tom could hear his own heart beat.

'Now. Where have you hidden the memoirs?'

'Fitz . . . For God's sake.'

FitzSymonds swept one hand through his hair, looking old and tired and disappointed. 'Christ, Tom. Who do you think took your brat? Who do you think set this whole thing up? You give me the memoirs. I return the child. It's that simple. Otherwise . . .'

Tom stepped forward.

'Don't think I won't shoot.'

Amelia's voice was hard. 'You'll die if you do.'

In her hand was the Makarov that Tom had last seen kicked under a cubicle in the petting zoo. She held it in two hands, the muzzle pointed straight at FitzSymonds's head. When the old man began to shift, she grunted.

'Try me,' she said.

100

Tom looked in shock from Amelia to the man who'd over-seen his training. The man to whom he'd reported for more than a decade; sometimes at Whitehall, at other times in anonymous safe houses in grim suburbs of London or Birmingham, once on the thirty-second floor of a Glasgow tower block.

'You took Charlie?'

'I did my duty.'

There was something unexpectedly dark in Fitz-Symonds's eyes. A malevolence found behind the eyes of murderers, rapists and fanatics. Something ancient and evil. Pieces began falling into place. 'All those dead national treasures,' Tom said. 'Colonel Foley, Robby Croft, Sir Henry . . . You organized that. Didn't you?'

'At least one of us is still capable of doing his job.'

'Saving the government embarrassment?'

'Sir Cecil's memoirs are only as potent as the number of people in them left alive. Someone had to tidy up.'

'This is about the arms talks?'

'Christ, Tom . . . It's about Brannon. Why would it be about anything else? Foley taught the man who killed him how to make bombs. Our pet thespian helped perfect his Irish accent. Not only did Cecil Blackburn own the cot-tage overlooking Windermere, he issued the invitation that got Brannon up there.'

'And Robby Croft?'

'The man was a banker, for God's sake. The operation was far too sensitive to go through our accounts. He funded the entire thing. They were Patroclus, the lot of them. Their cooperation was the price they paid for their lives.'

'You ordered their deaths.'

'Situations change.'

'And the man who killed Brannon?'

FitzSymonds shrugged. 'Never met him. Never needed to. Brannon's proclivities were going to get out, you know. A journalist had photographs. We needed to act. It would have been irresponsible not to.'

'And my father?' Amelia asked.

FitzSymonds turned his gaze on her. He seemed amused. 'You killed him, didn't you?'

'He shouldn't have changed his mind.'

The gun in Amelia's hand was trembling. She still held it with both hands, her arms outstretched. 'Tom,' she said. 'We need to go.'

'I'm sure he'd rather stay,' FitzSymonds said. 'He'll want to know how his son died.' He glanced at Tom. 'Yes, I'm afraid I killed him too.'

'He's lying,' Amelia said.

'Fox knows I never lie to my friends.'

'Tom,' Amelia said, 'back towards that sign.'

Bialoweiża – Lowland European Bison. Tom glanced behind him and saw that the path split, with one section vanishing into trees. Amelia followed, her aim never faltering.

'He bled out. I'm sure you know where.'

Tom froze.

'Don't rise to it,' Amelia ordered. 'Keep moving.'

They reached the trees before FitzSymonds fired. Silenced or not, the pistol sounded loud. The bison stampeded, and wolves began howling to the north of them. 'Run,' Amelia said.

The path forked again and Tom chose the least used, hearing Amelia crashing behind him, her breathing jagged. When he slowed to see what was wrong, she pushed past him. Hesitating for a second at a zookeeper's hut, she stumbled down the side and halted behind it, one hand against the back wall.

'You okay?' Tom asked.

She thrust the pistol at him.

Blood stained her side and Amelia touched the patch and winced. 'It's not serious,' she snapped when Tom stepped forward. Twisting away, she reached into her bag for a long cotton scarf.

'Wait.' Tom took Amelia's bag. 'What else is in there?'

Riffling through it, he found four straws of sugar of the kind that come with coffee in cafés.

'These'll do.'

Ripping the top from the first sachet, he patted sugar on the wound, hearing Amelia gasp. He did the same with the next three sachets, handing her the scarf so that she could bind her ribs.

'In a moment,' Amelia said. Pulling out a T-shirt Tom hadn't known she was carrying, she stripped off her blood-stained shirt, rolled it up and stuffed it into her bag. 'I've no intention of walking round a zoo smelling like food.'

Dipping into the bag again, she added, 'And you'll want this.'

Tom looked at a clip of 9mm Makarov.

'Where did you get that?'

'Where do you think?'

From Schneider's pocket.

'I don't suppose . . . ?' he asked.

She handed him the notebook.

There was something unnerving about this woman.

A path behind the hut led through to sheds in a clearing, with spades, brooms and wheelbarrows leant against them. Between the sheds were low-level brambles that could be trusted to tumble back into place. Indicating them, Tom lifted one aside and stepped through, holding it back for Amelia.

Across the clearing, he heard a twig snap, followed by the faintest hint of a curse. After which, only silence.

'Bugger,' he muttered.

Fitz in tracker mode was dangerous. Amelia shook her head when Tom asked if she'd mind if he kept the Makarov. 'I'm a pacifist,' she whispered.

'You helped burn down Porton Down.'

'That's different.'

'Tom,' a voice called. 'For God's sake be reasonable.'

'Ignore him,' Amelia hissed.

FitzSymonds's answer splintered the shed they'd just abandoned. The dull crack of his *Pistolet Besshumnyy* arrived a split-second later. Birds screamed and the wolves howled louder. 'Tom!' FitzSymonds shouted.

Turning, Tom fired once, his pistol far louder. For a second, he was blinded by his own muzzle flare but training made him step sideways, an instant before a round hissed through where he'd been.

Amelia ran for the trees, Tom following.

101

With the dead guards a quarter of a mile behind her, Maya stopped in the shadow of a fat oak. One of those very English, very traditional oaks clipped flat below its canopy. She'd been cross about messing up her shot, all those years before. She'd been cross with the commissar, who'd had to work hard to convince her he hadn't knowingly sent her to her death.

She knew he hadn't, and those days were so black that she wouldn't have really blamed him if he had, but she made him work to get her back into bed.

If she'd had her way, they'd have burnt the lodge at Reinickendorf-Tegelerforst to the ground, with all of its inhabitants in it. She wasn't minded to make nice distinctions about the kind of men who went there. The men who made those kind of decisions had disagreed. Of course they had.

She saw the purple Rolls-Royce in the drive.

Patting it as she passed, Maya hammered on the front door. The watery-eyed old man who answered opened his mouth to ask who she was, and shut it again. He recognized death when she came calling. Maya walked him back from the steps, along a dank corridor with cracked tiles, through a box room filled with cardboard boxes, into a tiny lavatory with no windows. He already knew what was about to happen.

'Where's the boy?' Maya demanded.

He nodded upwards.

'Where upstairs?'

'The white door at the top. There's a lock outside.'

'Is he hurt?'

The old man shook his head.

'Are you quite sure?'

He nodded fiercely.

'How many guards?'

'Three pairs. In the gardens.'

Two pairs, Maya thought.

She couldn't shake the feeling, looking into his faded eyes, that he'd been expecting something like this to happen. Perhaps for a while.

Shutting the lavatory door muffled her shot.

It didn't muffle it enough, though. Two crop-haired men raced across the lawn towards a French window, and Maya killed them both as they rushed inside. She shot them twice. *Double tap*, a great British special-forces tradition.

She hoped the coroner liked that touch too.

In the drawing room she found a small man in a red jacket, telephone gripped in one hand, desperately dialling a number with his other. She shot him before he could do more than say, *hello, hello* . . .

Picking up the receiver, Maya listened, while an English voice demanded to know what was happening. 'Your man is dead,' she said. She left the receiver hanging.

The last pair of guards split up and entered through separate doors. For a while they were hunting each other, freezing with each creek of floorboards or squeak of a door. She watched them from above, hidden in a minstrel's gallery that looked down on the entrance hall.

It looked for a bit as if they might kill each other but one of them realized just in time what was happening and called out, both of them coming into the hall from different directions.

That was when Maya shot them.

Head and heart. It wasn't that she was better trained, had seen more action, or was even necessarily more prepared to kill. She simply knew what was going on and they didn't. The seconds it took them to work that out gave her the edge.

At the top of the stairs was the white door that the old man had told Maya to expect. A Yale fitted to the outside.

Maya knocked.

'Charlie,' she said, stepping to the side. She stepped to the side in case somebody she'd missed was in there and shot her through the door.

No one fired and no one answered.

She'd hoped that knowing Charlie's name would reassure the boy. Maybe not though. The man who took him would have known it too. Maya wondered, and didn't want to wonder, what state she'd find Tom's son in. Whether the dead man downstairs had lied. When calling produced no answer, she turned the knob and eased open the door.

The room was empty. Charlie was gone.

102

Crouching, Tom removed the magazine, reached for the spare and thumbed out a round to give his pistol a full clip. As an afterthought, he jacked a round into the breech, removed the magazine again, pressing in another.

FitzSymonds knew how many rounds a Makarov took. He'd have to guess, though, if Tom had chambered one extra.

'You're good at this,' Amelia said.

There was enough anger in her voice to make Tom look across to where she crouched, hand to her ribs. He listened for a moment to see if he could hear FitzSymonds and went back to the thought.

'It's about the one thing I know how to do.'

He weighed the pistol in his hand, folding his fingers round its familiar grip. Nine rounds of 9mm Makarov. You could do a lot of damage with that.

'Tom,' a voice called. 'You need to listen to me.'

Tom didn't reply.

'Caro doesn't know about Charlie. She's ill. Seriously so. Eddington hasn't dared tell her. She's going to need you, Tom. She's just started chemo. I don't think the prognosis is good.'

Standing, Tom fired a shot and heard wild horses stampede, their hooves hammering dry earth.

'You're wasting ammunition, Tom.'

'You wish.' Tom stepped away from where Amelia crouched, feeling rather than hearing a round that cut through the leaves above him. Away to one side, parakeets added to the noise.

'Two clips,' he shouted at FitzSymonds. 'One more than you.'

'I have a spare.'

'Of course you do . . .'

Five shots from FitzSymonds, possibly six.

How many rounds did the old man have left? Tom thought three, and wondered if he'd be willing to bet his life on it. 'Here.' Digging into his pocket, he found the notebook. 'You have to give this to Charles Eddington, Lord Eddington. Tell him I gave it to you. Tell him it used to belong to Flo Wakefield. Tell him everything you heard FitzSymonds say.'

Amelia grabbed him as he stood.

'What are you doing?'

'Finishing this . . .'

'That's what he wants.'

'Tom.' The voice came from somewhere slightly different. FitzSymonds had worked his way round to the left. 'At least talk to me.'

'About what?' Tom called.

Instead of an answering shot, Fitz said, 'Listen.'

The sirens were here at last. Several minutes after Tom expected them. Two cars in the distance. Approaching from different directions.

Maybe another car, maybe an echo.

The other car was more than an echo now.

'Give me the memoirs,' FitzSymonds called. 'I'll pull

every string I can to get London to help you. We'll offer a trade. Two of theirs for one of ours. Three of theirs . . .'

Sirens howled as police vehicles cut up from Karlshorst and down from Lichtenberg. How many had been despatched? Gunshots in the night in a city where public order was mandatory and infringement savagely punished . . . Tom doubted they contained Volkspolizei.

At the very least, VPB. Riot police. Quite possibly *spetsnaz*. Even FitzSymonds would baulk at fighting them.

'Tom,' FitzSymonds said.

But Amelia was shaking his shoulder. 'Up there.'

The chop of a helicopter, slow and steady as it approached the zoo. As it reached Tierpark's edge, a searchlight snapped on and Tom saw the beam hit trees away to his left. They'd just become someone else's target as well.

'That's an Mi-2 Hoplite,' he said.

Amelia scowled at him.

'Saw one in Cuba.'

'It makes a difference?'

Tom shrugged. 'Know your enemy.'

'Your enemy is over there,' Amelia said.

The wind was rising, clouds shifting direction overhead.

The parakeets that had started screaming fell silent. And, as Tom listened for police sirens, he discovered they'd fallen silent too. All he could hear was the creak of trees, rustling leaves, wild sheep shuffling down to a fence to see who they were, and the heartbeat of the helicopter overhead.

No Entry Without Authorization.

Tom imagined that was what the sheep-pen gate said. Yanking back its bolt, he dragged it open, leaving it wide. When the sheep just looked at him, he said, 'Help me drive them out of there.'

'Why?' Amelia demanded.

'We need to increase the number of targets.'

She stared at him.

'They'll have night scopes. A dozen warm dots getting lost in the trees will mix things up nicely. If nothing else, we'll know in advance if they're operating shoot to kill . . .'

In the skies above, the Mi-2 Hoplite made a sloping turn and began another sweep, its light picking out animal pens below. An elephant harrumphed, and the parakeets went back to shrieking.

'Where are you going?' Tom asked.

'Somewhere you're not,' Amelia replied.

He caught up with her beside an ice cream kiosk next to the reptile house. A strange world, with sullen lights above the doors of an otherwise dark concrete block that held whole continents: tropical forests, South American swamps and Egyptian desert. Posters promised them spiders and snakes.

Glancing back, Amelia said, 'He's still following.'

'Of course he is.'

Men like FitzSymonds always followed.

This didn't end at the edge of the park. Tom knew that now.

It didn't end with a flight to London, a train to Brunswick. Tom's choices were end this or exile in Moscow. Fitz would follow, and he would keep following. It didn't matter that Frederika had burnt the original. Fitz would take this to the wire. And even if Tom had had the memoirs, Fitz was responsible for what had happened to Charlie.

Tom couldn't have given them up.

Not now.

103

'I know why I was chosen for this.'

Amelia stopped, steadying Tom with a hand to his shoulder.

His father-in-law hadn't lied, Tom realized, he simply didn't know the whole truth. Eddington's given reason – Tom's Russian connections – mattered. And they'd paid off, just not in the way those who sent Tom imagined. But there was more. 'And, I've just realized why Fitz-Symonds was.'

'He was your old boss. You said.'

'I was one of the boys.'

'And Fitz . . . ?'

'Patroclus. He must have been.'

'The people who sent him. You're saying they knew?'

'Some of them,' Tom said. 'Some of them must.' He didn't believe Caro's father was among them. But there would be others . . .

Old men with convenient memories.

There'd been a point at school, usually late afternoon, when the lambs knew what awaited and the wolves had yet to descend. Those hours were the worst. Tom remembered them better than what came after.

He should probably be grateful for that.

'Why does he believe you have the memoirs?'

'An intercepted letter from your father said I had them.'

'And he gave you nothing?'

'Not a bloody –' Tom stopped.

'What?' Amelia demanded.

Digging into his pocket, Tom's fingers closed on metal and for a second he felt afraid to remove it, as if the tiny metal Trabant might have become something else. It looked so ordinary in the moonlight.

It was ordinary. Entirely so. He'd kept it because . . .

Tom knew why he'd kept it, because once upon a time he'd never have dared throw a car like this away. Shaking the toy Trabant produced no rattle.

He opened the metal doors and there was nothing inside.

It was entirely ordinary. Cream body, pale-blue roof, doors that opened, jewelled headlights, slightly tinted . . .

Tom became still.

How many diecast cars came with tinted windows? No one was likely to know the answer to that except someone who had seen too many. Tom thought of the little darkroom in Hackescher Markt with its over-elaborate enlarger. The bottles of developer. The developing trays.

'Tell me,' Amelia demanded.

'After the war your father had charge of miniaturizing Nazi Intelligence archives. They were put on to microfiche and flown to London. The originals were burnt . . .'

'Burnt?'

There was no manuscript. What there was, Tom was willing to bet, was a key to Flo Wakefield's notebook, quite possibly shrunken pages of the notebook itself, perhaps an unexpurgated section of memoir dealing directly with Reinickendorf-Tegelerforst. He'd had it all along.

426

'We need to move,' Amelia said.

She was right and Tom knew where he was going.

Looking back, he saw FitzSymonds break cover and glance around. Amelia shifted, and FitzSymonds spotted her movement.

Raising his pistol, the old man hesitated.

'Weave,' Tom shouted.

Amelia did without looking back or asking why. Simply hunched her shoulders, and jinked from side to side as she ran towards trees.

FitzSymonds's mistake was to shoot anyway.

A silenced Makarov is effective to fifty yards. Amelia was beyond that and he should have factored in the fact that his muzzle flash would attract the helo. The old man flinched as its searchlight swept towards him.

Tom and Amelia ran, not looking back, trying not to think of the helicopter. When they reached the safety of an open-sided shelter, the helo was hovering and its beam stabbed the ground where Fitz had been.

'He's gone,' Amelia said. Her words ragged.

'That's what he does,' Tom replied.

It was too. He turned up, things happened, he vanished. Very little of the blame, if blame there was, ever stuck to him. Most of the politicians who breathed a sigh of relief when what they wanted to happen unexpectedly happened never stopped to wonder how or why, or even knew of his existence.

Turning, Tom headed north.

Looking back, he said, 'You might want to strike out on your own.'

'Abandoning me?' Amelia demanded.

'Trying to save you from what comes next.'

Amelia stopped, slid the latch on a gate into a compound and dragged it open, freeing wild horses. '*Equus ferus prze-walskii*,' she said. 'This is my world. Not yours. We stick together . . .'

104

Just inside the door was a broken hairgrip. A breakfast tray rested on the floor in the far corner. It contained a bowl of dry cereal and a small jug of milk, both untouched. Nothing else to suggest the room had been used.

It shouldn't have been empty.

The white door on the third floor at the top of the stairs. That was what the old man had said and he'd spoken the truth. She'd seen it in his face. Maya was sure this was the room and yet Charlie wasn't here.

Who had just moved him?

Not the old man who answered the door. Not the guards, dead on the floor, their pistols beside their fallen bodies. Nor the small man in the red jacket, who lay dead on a Bokhara rug in the drawing room, telephone call unfinished, a hole where his heart should be. He was going nowhere. Although the Rolls-Royce he arrived in would be: its keys were in Maya's pocket.

No longer caring about noise, she raced up narrow stairs to the attics and shot the door open, splintering its lock. The space she stood in was small, its door to bigger rooms beyond padlocked and the padlock rusty. No one had passed this way in years.

She went down the stairs fast, checked off the guest-rooms, seeing herself – small and intense, and older than she remembered – in endless dark mirrors as she threw open wardrobes and dressing rooms, and gutted an airing cupboard stacked to head-height with yellowing sheets.

All the places a frightened child might hide.

She searched the ground floor. Stepping over bodies. She didn't remember that many bodies. And then, feeling sick to her guts, her body exhausted, her legs tired from all those stairs, she returned to where Charlie should have been. As she reached the top, she heard scrabbling.

It came from behind the door of a bathroom she'd already checked and found empty. Opening the door slowly, she slid herself into the room, with her pistol held tight to her chest. In the far corner, below a window, was a bath with taps the size of statuettes, and lion's claws for feet. Stepping forward for a closer look, Maya found herself staring down at a naked child, lying there, clutching a Browning he'd obviously taken from one of the dead.

'Hello Charlie,' she said.

105

It wasn't revenge for Charlie's death that Tom wanted. The word was too small, too personal. He wanted fire in the skies, winds that ripped apart trees and blood like rain. He wanted vengeance.

FitzSymonds was somewhere out in the darkness. Like Tom, he'd be aware of the hovering Mi-2 Hoplite, the approaching daylight, the elite soldiers spreading out through the 400 acres of Tierpark zoo. He'd know that the sound of gunfire would draw them; that muzzle flash in the night was as good as saying, *I'm here* . . .

He'd still have to make his move soon.

The wire fence to the wolf run was high.

Eight feet tall, with eighteen inches of barbed-wire-topped mesh angled inwards to make the jump harder. In case FitzSymonds needed tempting, Tom left the gates slightly open. The wolves were waiting to welcome him. Tom could hear them. They'd been howling on and off for the best part of an hour; drawing Tom closer, waiting for the idea to form in his mind.

The new run was long and narrow, cut out of the northern edge of the park, heavily wooded and obviously only just finished. He found the wolves several hundred yards beyond the gate, out of sight behind a strand of beech trees. Four cages raised on breeze blocks. Three large cages, and a smaller one. A smoky shadow in the small cage bared its teeth as Tom drew near. Its growl low and intense, far more threatening than any howl.

He bent to take a closer look.

Amelia yanked him back.

She looked horrified at Tom's stupidity. Unless she was just appalled by his ignorance. 'That's a she-wolf. She has pups. Threaten her litter and she'll take whatever bit of you she can reach.' Amelia's face twisted as she stared at the bars. 'I hate to see her in a cage that small.'

'Don't worry,' Tom said. 'She won't be there for long.'

The she-wolf stood over her litter, ready to hurl herself at the bars if Tom came any closer. He approached slowly, halting when she growled. He was shocked by how big she was. How hot her gaze.

'Don't stare her out,' Amelia warned. 'You'll look like a threat.'

Tom looked away, heard the growling lessen and slowly reached for the lever that controlled the door. Pulling it back, he felt the catch come free.

'Wait,' Amelia said.

Too late, the door was already swinging open.

Amelia was holding her breath, Tom realized. He stepped backwards, very carefully, wincing as a twig cracked under-foot. For a moment, nothing happened. And then the wolf turned a full circle, looking at her tiny cage, looking beyond the bars at the two of them. Nudging her pups to their feet, she streaked like smoke from the cage, her litter following behind.

'She's hungry,' said Amelia.

Those still caged watched her go. They were wide-eyed and febrile, with greyish-silver ruffs, raised silver fur along

432

their spines. Tom could almost feel their seething anger. They wanted their freedom too.

'Tom . . .'

'Seen him.'

FitzSymonds was silhouetted on the path. A blink later and he was gone. He appeared, shadow-like, for a second between trees, disappearing just as quickly. 'Remind me why you don't just shoot him?' Amelia asked.

'You're a pacifist, remember?'

'Apart from that?' she whispered back.

Because muzzle flare showed at night. Because the noise of a shot would call troops to the area. Because the wolves were wound tight enough already. It was nerves that had Amelia talking, nerves that made Tom reply. He felt hollowed out and empty. Until Berlin he'd have said Fitz was the closest thing he'd had to a father. How warped was that?

The helo swept along the park's northern edge and set the wolves howling. Then it began a looping turn to take it back over the petting zoo, lake and cafés towards the turnstiles that let the public in. The howling lessened and the wolves went back to being twisting shadows and furious darkness.

'Wolves,' Tom said. 'What should I know?'

Amelia laughed. It was bleak, half despairing.

'Please,' Tom said.

'Not a word you use often, I imagine.'

She looked at him, shook herself, and said, 'Attacks are rarer than you'd think. They usually start with a feint designed to test your defences. Attacks can be broken into rabid, non-rabid, provoked and predatory.'

'Which means what?'

'Don't poke them. Avoid the hungry ones. Don't let them get behind you. Don't trip and start crawling around or you'll look like prey. Wolves hunt in packs and kill their food on the run. So don't try to outrun them. They're twice as fast as humans and can go ten times the distance. Oh, and they can scent wounded prey from afar ...' Putting her hand to her ribs, she examined her fingers.

Tom couldn't see if there was fresh blood or not.

'What did you do with your old shirt?' he asked.

'Still in here.' Amelia lifted her tote bag.

Tom held out his hand.

'They're not beagles. If you're planning a drag hunt.' Her words were harsh; her smile in the moonlight kinder.

'I don't approve of hunting.'

'Join the club.'

'What else should I know?' Tom asked.

'From instinct, they kill the young, the old and the injured in that order. It's said no healthy wolf attacks a human. That depends how you define healthy. Soldiers at Stalingrad savaged by animals more starving than they might disagree.'

'That's it?'

'Stand tall. Make yourself scary.'

'And if that doesn't work?'

'Try climbing a tree. That said, I've seen photographs of wolves in trees.'

Tom looked at her.

'If things get really bad,' she said, 'curl into a ball and protect your face.'

106

Three wolf cages unopened. Two with half a dozen animals in each. One with a single, mangy-looking male who limped and snarled and twitched with fury at the bars around him. Tom wondered where the beasts came from. Whether they'd been born wild. Whether they'd grown used to humans. Wolves that had grown used to humans were more likely to attack.

The beasts were watching him.

They glared from between their bars, hard-eyed and wide-mouthed.

Amelia had insisted that their lolling tongues simply reflected how they breathed but it was still the stuff of nightmares. *You could die here*, he told himself. But then you could die anywhere. 'I still think you should leave,' he said.

'I don't,' Amelia replied firmly.

She took the pistol though, agreed to stay close to the cages, and promised to shoot back if FitzSymonds shot at her.

Tom regarded that as a victory of sorts.

'Ready?' he asked.

Amelia nodded.

Tom tugged at the lever of the next cage, its clang loud enough to ring across the clearing. A huge wolf padded forward, hesitated for a second in the doorway and then flowed into the darkness. There was no other way to describe it. The animal shimmered like tarnished quicksilver. The rest of them followed him, the last one glancing sideways, and apparently deciding that Tom and Amelia belonged there.

In the cage beyond that, half a dozen wolves jostled, their jaws open and their tongues lolling. They tensed as Tom approached, stilling entirely when he reached for the handle. This time there was no hesitation. They knew exactly what was going to happen. Sweeping through the open doorway, they crossed the clearing and vanished into the trees. In the last cage the old wolf turned to face them.

'What about him?' Amelia asked.

'I'm saving him for later.'

Tom's plan was to lead FitzSymonds and the wolves away from Amelia and towards the gates. Well, that was the first part; the second part involved killing Fitz, and releasing the wolves into the park to keep the *spetsnaz* busy.

The wolves had other ideas.

Tom was a quarter of the way to the gate when he saw the first shadow, half hidden behind trees. When he looked again it was gone. Turning, he discovered there was one on the other side, half a dozen paces away.

He had outriders.

When he slowed, they slowed, silent and waiting.

When he started again, he found three where previously there had been two and they were closer than before. He increased his speed and immediately one of them howled, an answering howl coming from the trees.

Tom stopped dead, raising his arms to make himself look bigger.

He wanted his pistol back. At the very least, his knife.

Shouting helped, Amelia had said, but Tom couldn't afford to shout at the wolves. Not if it brought Fitz-Symonds. He would shout though, and throw stones, if that's what it came to. He had more chance of outwitting FitzSymonds than surviving an attack by a pack of hungry wolves.

There was a growling, and Tom spun to find a huge wolf almost right behind him. Its mouth was open and its tongue lolling. There was a fierce intensity to its gaze. *Run*, its stare said. *You know you want to.*

It was all Tom could do not to obey.

He backed away, while trying to keep the others in sight. He could sense, rather than see, others joining the pack. It wasn't quite a hunt, not yet. Keeping his eyes on the biggest, Tom stepped back again, and then again.

He must be halfway to the gate.

FitzSymonds could be right behind him.

Tom turned to check no one was there and immediately the wolf crept closer. When he turned to face it, it slunk away. When he took a step backwards, the wolves began following again.

His was a slow, agonizing retreat.

Every so often the wind would shift and he'd catch the stink of them. The smell was musty, stronger than he'd expected. Around him, eyes flared in the half-dark and shadows swirled. They slunk in and out of the trees, sometimes there, sometimes vanishing. Always he could feel their presence.

The wolves wanted him to run.

They were frustrated by his refusal.

How could they be certain he was prey if he wouldn't run?

And then, with a moon half behind cloud, and the helo beginning another sweep over the northern edge of the park, the rules changed. Far behind them all, the old wolf still in its cage howled, and the pack stilled, listening intently.

The largest called in reply, and the pack raced ahead, leaving Tom behind them. It was only when Tom reached open ground at the run's end that he realized they hadn't escaped into the park as he'd hoped.

They were blocking his way to the gate.

Wolves and human faced each other and for a moment nobody moved.

Away to one side, the helicopter was hovering, its searchlight stabbing the ground at every movement. Wild sheep, most probably. Tom tried to remember what else he and Amelia had released on their way through. Didn't matter really. As long as the freed animals kept the helicopter and the *spetsnaz* busy.

When Tom stepped forward, the largest wolf bared its teeth.

When he took another step, it growled. That was the signal for the rest to do the same. Between them, lips curled and growling, they began driving Tom back towards the trees he'd just left.

At first, he tried to stand his ground, but fell back when they began to encircle him. *Don't let them get behind you.* Hanging Amelia's bloody shirt on a nearby bush as a diversion, Tom put his back to the oak a few yards behind it, grabbed a broken branch to use as a club and waited.

Although the largest of them wrinkled its nose at the shirt, it kept coming.

If it had been a guard dog, Tom would have stared it out and done his best to break its neck on the spring. But guard dogs usually came in pairs, not packs. Even if he killed this one he'd have to face the others.

Sweat beaded the back of his neck, and trickled down his sides.

Don't show fear, Amelia had said.

Tom's body wasn't listening.

He forced himself to relax. It was in the breathing. It was in the way he released the tension in his shoulders. In the way he emptied himself of everything but now. *Fear me*, the creature said. This time Tom refused.

He sensed rather than saw the wolf begin a slow circle of his tree, hackles bristling and rough hair half standing on its spine. Remembering what Amelia had said, Tom stood taller and the creature swung away, quicksilver through undergrowth as it disappeared.

Tom's relief was short-lived.

When it returned it was with two others.

To Tom's horror, they flanked it like an honour guard.

This time when they bared their teeth it was to growl low in their throats. They had their ears back and their hackles stood. Away behind Tom, the only wolf still in its cage howled in despair. And the wolf in front of Tom answered.

Tom accepted the inevitable.

Slipping round the tree, he began backing towards the distant cage, returning the way he'd come. He couldn't always see those herding him, but he could hear their claws on the dry dirt, their breath rasping in their throats as they edged him away from the gates. They came together

439

and split apart a dozen times. A semicircle of writhing grey that spread before him, weaving between trees as they drove him back. He was just one of a dozen warm dots, seemingly moving in sequence, to anyone using a night scope from the helicopter.

That was his sole consolation.

Don't stumble, Amelia had warned.

He stumbled anyway, taken down by a root he'd been too busy watching the wolves to notice. Hot eyes pinned him. Climbing purposefully to his feet, Tom made himself stand tall and froze. FitzSymonds was thirty paces away, knife in hand, his entire attention on something out of sight. As Tom watched, a wolf broke from the undergrowth and Fitz switched the knife to his other hand. The old man had found spoor and smeared himself in shit.

Tom could smell him when the wind rose.

The bastard was good at this.

He glanced once in Tom's direction, his gaze almost reaching where Tom stood; but the wolf crept in and FitzSymonds retreated through the trees. And all the while, the wolves edged both men towards the cages. Tom worried about what would happen when they arrived.

107

'Remember me?' Amelia said.

FitzSymonds turned in surprise to find her sitting in the open doorway of an empty cage. Her pistol was pointed firmly at him.

'I'd face the wolves if I were you,' she said.

FitzSymonds turned back and realized that Tom now stood a dozen paces away, watching wolves gather in the gaps between trees.

Judges? A jury? Tom wasn't sure.

'I've been tracking you,' Tom said.

'That's not true.' There was enough doubt in Fitz-Symonds's eyes to put a quaver in his voice. Tom was glad of that.

'You still do that little juggling thing with your knife, I see.'

The knife was still in the old man's hand, which meant the pistol was probably pushed into his belt. There wasn't enough moonlight to let Tom confirm that. He watched the old man glance from his knife to the silent wolves, then to the pistol Amelia held in her unwavering hands.

'I lied,' he said. 'Charlie's safe.'

'Don't trust him,' Amelia said.

'He's being held at Henry Petty's old place. I left Henry's dresser and an old friend of mine looking after him. He'll be fine.'

'And Caro?' Tom asked. 'You going to tell me that's a lie too?'

The old man hesitated. 'No,' he said. 'That's the truth. I'm sorry, Tom. We can still make good on this, though. But I'm going to need the memoirs, and you have to help me find them.'

Tom wasn't listening. He was thinking of Caro, of her having to begin chemo with him not there to help her. When he looked up, the wolves had edged closer and FitzSymonds was staring at them. They stood in a half-circle at the edge of the clearing that held the cages. Their silence was more unnerving than their howls.

'What do they want?' FitzSymonds demanded.

Tom looked to Amelia.

'They want Tom to do the right thing,' she said.

She nodded to where the caged male growled to itself, turning frustrated circles behind its rusting bars. It was moth-eaten and limping, one-eyed. As furious as the rest at not having been fed, but foul-tempered from being kept caged when the others were free.

'Don't,' FitzSymonds protested. 'It's probably rabid.'

'No,' said Amelia. 'It's not.' Her voice was firm.

Walking to the cage, Tom reached for the latch.

'Don't,' FitzSymonds warned.

When Tom ignored him, the old man switched his blade to his other hand and reached for his pistol, freeing it just as the door swung back.

For a second the wolf stood in the doorway.

Then FitzSymonds raised the pistol and aimed at the wolf, his finger already closing on the trigger. The wolf's head jerked at the click, its gaze locking on the old man.

'You're out of bullets,' Tom told him.

'Can't be. It carries eight.'

'That's what you've fired, Fitz.'

The old man looked almost lost. He stiffened slightly as the wolf loped towards him, and stepped back. Dipping his hand into his pocket, Tom found the Trabant and tossed it into the cage. Both the wolf and FitzSymonds turning at the unexpected noise.

'You wanted the memoirs, didn't you?' Tom nodded to the toy lying on the filthy floor. 'There you go. He reduced them to microfiche.'

'You've had them all along?'

'Yes,' Tom said. 'I've had it all along.'

'Well, fuck you.' When the old man moved it was fast. He held his knife with both hands, low, groin level. Ready to stab.

All his effort went into one swift strike.

As Tom blocked, Amelia fired and FitzSymonds shrieked.

He dropped the knife and clamped his hand to his leg, his stumble triggering deep instincts in the old wolf. Its nostrils wrinkled at the smell of fresh blood, its lips curled and FitzSymonds became the only thing in its world. As for the other wolves, they simply watched. Silent. Static.

Don't turn your back, Amelia had said.

FitzSymonds limped towards the cage.

If the animal hadn't been old, half blind and lame itself, the matter would have been settled. Instead, FitzSymonds just made it. Dragging himself through the door, the old man pulled it shut as the wolf slammed into it. The beast lunged for his fingers, its teeth scraping metal. And

FitzSymonds jerked his hand away, grabbing for the little car and holding it tight.

In reaching for the car, he let go of the door.

The wolf nosed at the gap and snarled as FitzSymonds yanked it shut. The old man tried to reach the bolt but the wolf reared, yellow teeth snapping. They closed on air as Fitz stumbled back.

The door began to swing open again.

'Shoot it,' he told Amelia.

'I like wolves,' she said.

'Tom . . . for fuck's sake. Kill the thing.'

Reaching for his spare magazine, Tom thumbed free all rounds but one and held it up. 'Still want the memoirs?'

'What?'

'You wanted the memoirs. Remember? If you've changed your mind, you could swap them for this.'

Fitz clutched the car tighter.

As he did, the door to his cage swung further open and the old wolf turned at the creak of its hinges. It stalked towards the widening gap and FitzSymonds grabbed for the door, dragging it shut.

The wolf lunged for his hand.

Letting go again, FitzSymonds tumbled backwards, swearing as he landed on his wounded leg. The door began to swing open.

'Here,' FitzSymonds said. 'Here.'

He hurled the car at Tom.

Scooping it up, Tom tossed FitzSymonds the clip and turned away as the wolf pushed its way into the cage.

'*Shit*,' FitzSymonds said. '*Shit* . . .'

Slamming the clip into his pistol, he jacked the slide just

as the wolf sunk on to its haunches. There were eyes watching Tom as he walked to the cage where Amelia waited to bolt its door behind them. There had always been eyes watching him. He heard a shot and Fitz began screaming. He'd fired at the wolf. Quite possibly he'd hit the animal. It was a mistake.

He should have shot himself.

108

The death of Harry FitzSymonds from a heart attack in Berlin was respectfully reported in *The Times*, the *Telegraph* and the *Daily Mail*. The *Guardian* was altogether less respectful but still managed to avoid suggesting that he was anything more than a man lost in a world that had moved on when he had not.

No mention was made of Amelia Blackburn or Tom Fox.

The arms talks were postponed to take account of both the death of Dmitri Luzhin, one of the Soviet negotiators, and the unexpected resignation of an American senator, who wanted to spend more time with his family. There were, however, firm plans for later meetings to go ahead.

A photograph of Maya Milova, one of the world's most famous dancers, was runner-up in the British National Photographic Awards. It showed her leaning against the bonnet of a Rolls-Royce Silver Cloud Coupé. The caption referred to beauty being timeless. A piece in *Spare Rib*, from a well-known feminist activist, lambasted the exhibition for reducing the life of a Red Army sniper, gulag survivor and prima ballerina to a matter of looks.

Maya Milova agreed.

Epilogue

There were people in Heathrow Arrivals hall watching and Tom didn't care. Scooping up the boy who came running, he hugged Charlie so tightly that Charlie looked momentarily worried, then grinned and hugged him back. As Tom gripped his son, he thought of a lake in Cumbria, and a young girl who'd popped up beside him wanting to borrow binoculars. He could still remember the scream that the sight of her grandfather's exploding boat had dragged from her body.

He hugged his son tighter.

'I thought you were in Berlin,' Charlie said.

'I was,' Tom told him.

'Then why did we meet a Moscow plane?'

'It's complicated.'

'That's what Mummy said.'

'How is she?'

'Tired . . .' Charlie hesitated, the first part of his conversation not yet finished. Charlie liked maps. He particularly liked that the world was a spherical jigsaw made of countries. He consulted his mental map and looked puzzled. 'Isn't it longer to fly from Berlin via Moscow?'

'Yes,' said Tom. 'But sometimes simpler.'

'Who was the lady?' asked Charlie.

'Woman,' Charlie's grandfather corrected. 'Unless she has a title.' He caught Tom's stare and shrugged, looking almost apologetic. 'Caro would have corrected him,' he offered as a defence.

'A friend of mine. Amelia. She studies wolves.'

Charlie's eyes widened. 'Does she keep them as pets?'

'I'm not sure wolves would make good pets.'

'Is she Russian?'

'Scottish,' Tom said.

Charlie looked disappointed. Then he brightened. 'Wax Angel says I must stay with her in Moscow. Next holiday. If that's all right with you. She says I'm very good at picking locks. Many of her friends are good at picking locks too.'

Lord Eddington gave Tom a pointed stare.

'I brought you a present,' Tom said, ignoring his father-in-law. He held out a toy car bought in Moscow airport, and watched Charlie's face light up.

'It's a jeep,' Charlie said.

'It's a Soviet UAZ-3151.'

'It looks like a jeep.'

'Better not tell the Russians that. And I brought Grandpa this.'

Lord Eddington took the toy Trabant and examined it quizzically.

Around them, passengers flowed into the Arrivals hall and shook the hands of their drivers or fell into the arms of their families. And Tom stood in his little huddle, away to one side, with the son he wasn't sure he still had until Maya Milova, whom he still thought of as Wax Angel, telephoned to tell him that Charlie was safe.

'Its windows are missing.'

'They weren't very well fixed.'

The microfiche had burnt nicely on the floor of the cage he'd shared with Amelia, while the old wolf was finishing its meal. Duty to Eddington, and promises to Marshal Milov apart, Tom owed Wax Angel that.

'A souvenir from Berlin?'

'A memento.'

'Thank you, Tom.' Eddington glanced to where Charlie raced his Soviet jeep along the back of a bench, which was thankfully unoccupied. 'I realize there should be a proper inquest into Patroclus,' he said. 'I accept that. And I'd like to be able to tell you that there will be, but . . .'

'But what?' Tom said.

'The main players are dead. And the Prime Minister is keen to avoid any suggestion of scandal. Its files are now classified.'

'Under the thirty-year rule?'

'Sevent—' Eddington stopped.

That was how Tom knew that Charlie was back. So Tom asked Caro's father the only question that really mattered anyway. 'How is she?'

'Caro? As well as can be expected,' Eddington said carefully.

'What about . . . C. H. E. M. O?'

'They can't do that again yet,' Charlie said. 'Can they, Grandpa?'

His grandfather smiled sadly. Gesturing towards the exit, he said, 'In a few weeks perhaps. We should go. Mummy's expecting us.'

Amelia Blackburn was standing beside Lord Eddington's Range Rover, her expression unreadable. That was her

449

default, Tom realized. Some people smiled, some frowned, others scowled. Her face revealed nothing.

'I thought that this might be yours,' she said.

Lord Eddington looked at her. 'What made you think that?'

'I guessed.'

'You're the wolf woman,' Charlie said.

Amelia's eyes widened.

'I told him you liked wolves,' Tom said hastily.

'I watch them,' Amelia said. 'Study how they behave. Did your dad tell you we saw some?'

'Really?' Charlie sounded excited.

'Can I help you?' Lord Eddington asked.

Digging into her pocket, Amelia produced the envelope she'd wanted Tom to post and that he'd later returned to her. 'You may want to give this to the Chief Scientific Officer,' she said. 'It's a copy of a first-hand report from Chernobyl. Don't worry, it's not radioactive. But you can tell him the person who wrote it died within a day. It has details, data. Your government has no idea what happened there. It's probably best you do. That way you can stop it happening here.'

'You sound like one of those women from Greenham Common.'

'I *am* one of those women from Greenham Common.'

'If you'd excuse me, sir?' Tom said.

He led Amelia to one side, aware that his father-in-law and his son were watching, and that Amelia wasn't the sort of person you lead.

'For all you know he'll simply sit on it.'

'No,' she said. 'He'll show it to the CSO, then sit on it.'

'And that doesn't worry you?'

'It's one copy,' she said. 'I've made others.'

A tug disturbed Tom's sleeve. And he wrapped his arm round Charlie's shoulders and felt the small boy lean into him. 'Grandpa says that we should probably go now.'

'I hope your mum feels better,' Amelia said.

'I do too.' He looked at her, wide-eyed. 'You really saw wolves?'

'Lots of wolves.' She dropped to his level, grunted slightly.

'Are you all right?' Charlie sounded worried.

'A bad man shot me.'

'What happened to him?'

'The wolves ate him for me.'

Charlie's eyes widened. 'They ate him?'

'He was a very bad man,' Amelia said. 'Very bad indeed.'

Charlie thought about it. 'I like wolves,' he said. And Tom knew he meant it. His son's mind had been made up on the subject of wolves. He would like them for life. 'I need to go now though,' Charlie said.

He put his hand out.

'I'm Charlie Fox,' he said politely. 'Bye bye.'

Acknowledgements

Nightfall Berlin is a work of fiction. Names, places and incidents are the products of my imagination or used fictitiously. Any resemblance to actual events, etc . . .

That said, this is a hard subject to write about, and I'm grateful to those who have talked on and off the record. As I'm also grateful to those who shared their experiences of working behind the Iron Curtain.

My thanks to Jonny Geller, my agent at Curtis Brown, who fixed the deal; and Rowland White, my editor at Penguin Random House, for believing in the book. Thanks to Sarah Gabriel for her edit, Mark Handsley for his copy-edit and Nick Lowndes for not minding that I was never in the right place to receive the proofs!

As ever, gratitude to my partner, Sam Baker, who put up with me vanishing off to Berlin and Paris while she was stuck in London working like a lunatic on *The Pool*.

Thank you.

And finally, no thanks at all to easyJet, who hooked everyone off a flight from Berlin, provided zero information, took off insanely late, landed at Gatwick just in time for the last Express into London but not to make any onward connections, and then refused to accept any responsibility – because it was God's decision to throw a crow at the front of their plane.

Having said that, walking across Westminster Bridge at four in the morning, in ice cold, utterly clear weather, with a pitch-black sky and lights on the river, was an unexpected joy. (And will undoubtedly turn up in a novel somewhere . . .)

Edinburgh
December 2017